*I dedicate this book to Seth Glidewell. I hope
you realize one day how strong you are.*

Penultimate Citizen
Michael Williams

CHAPTER 1:

6,450,739 circled Simon's mind as he made his breakfast. The early morning monsters had already been dealt with, and the ticking had just stopped.

Hardboiling eggs was the first comfortable moment of the day. Simon ate them, his purple pill and nutrient bar with careful efficiency. Dressing came next. He changed into the standard B-class gray buttoned suit and tie with nervous obsession, although the only real cause for worry was the additional 5.5 seconds it took to tie his Windsor knot and adjust the ever-present headband symmetrically along his hairline, feeling hundreds of tiny pricks as various sensors retreated and re-injected into his epidermis. Simon looked in the mirror to make certain his hair was fully black. It naturally was strikingly silver, a trait that, in addition to its rarity among adults in their late twenties, was also illegal. His friend Charlie suffered similar genetics and the excuse of being ten years older. They both dyed monthly, although today it wouldn't be necessary.

With the most stressful morning duties fulfilled, Simon stepped outside. He was careful not to feel his natural release of tension too suddenly. Outside was more pleasant than the unit, and the sun he hadn't looked up at in years pleased his skin, but he didn't want his headband to pick up too strongly on the serotonin differential.

His first cause for alarm came as he caught himself mumbling while walking through his neighborhood. This was almost inevitably where his focus wavered, amidst the endless transposition of identically dull houses and smooth, featureless roadways. His mumbling was, as always, about work, the source of interest in his life. He knew he wasn't supposed to mumble. A proper punishment had thus far been withheld because it had been known for years that he had always wanted to become either a poet or a clinical psychologist. A modicum of strangeness was to be expected from people with that particular pair of fantasies.

He hastily guided his attention from the illicit thought, allowing his heart rate to perk up briefly due to stress before returning to its usual walking rhythm, in calculated panic. That way, at least the survey would know that he recognized his mistake and that the error repulsed him. He glued his mind onto the paved walkway, a meditation both encouraged and necessary. The surface was smoothed at almost the molecular level, uncontoured to the point of threatening the very concept of friction. The whole structure was one immense mirror, latticed throughout the residential zone, its expansion halted only by streets built for vehicles. It was all too easy to trip on its unnatural smoothness. Tripping was an expensive microliberty. If he tried, he might even have been able to slide himself multiple feet across the synthetic surface, but such a playful action was out of the question. Having just been allowed to relocate to an upper B-class neighborhood, he could afford to do nothing short of maintaining his good vigilance as he placed one foot in front of the other.

He found his stride, and cautiously began to think about work again.

His mumbling had been about Vernon, one of his eighteen subjects. At the start, he'd had as many as thirty-four, but that number had steadily trimmed over the past two years. This was highly encouraging. Being assigned fewer subjects generally meant the subjects kept under his watchful eye were selected to be more challenging. Their disobediences were delightfully subtle.

Vernon was a B-class, 48 year old married food worker in california. Simon's favorite subject, though, was Sarah, a C-class, fifty two year old trucker who lacked a stationary home, sleeping exclusively in streetside motels, a true continental tenant. She was his only remaining C-class subject. She also had the same job as his father, last he checked.

Casper, Jaquel, Gable, Seth, Sophia, Sofia (completely different person), Killion, Jonas, Blake, Jasmine, Colette, Nicolette, Jillian, Burton, and Micah. He knew them each better than their families did. Colette was particularly noteworthy to Simon, because she shared his profession. For all he knew, he was one of her subjects in return. Perhaps they rated each other.

One symptom, or perhaps it was the cause, of wanting to be a poet and psychologist, was an inbuilt desire to understand humanity. To immerse himself into people's lives and personalities, to perceive every microscopic decision that they made, to study them so intently that versions of them began to live inside his mind, whispering in his ear what their real counterparts were thinking. His parents would be appalled at the ethics of his job, but he perceived it as the noble work it was. And he obsessed over his work, even while resting. Perhaps that was why his survey granted him some clemency when he mumbled about it.

There were unspoken rules for what thoughts were safe, and how long they could last before headbands noticed. Simon learned these rules on his own through trial and error over the years, even before becoming an overseer. Although discussing them openly with someone would have been inconceivably naive, he was certain the rules were common knowledge among all A and B-class citizens. The one minute rule posited that he could think about something innocent but off-task for up to a minute before it became a concern. The twenty second rule applied if his off-task thought was more effortful or critical in some way. The five second rule applied to instances where he thought of something improper, such as the contour of his coworker Penelope's breasts, or wondering why Citizenship walkways were designed to discomfort pedestrians. His instinctual defense mechanism in all cases was to return to thinking about his subjects.

The B-permit bus reached the stop as he did. He gladly walked on, grateful for the friction. The 19 minute bus ride contained no more mumbling, but anxiety, as usual, remained his companion as he wondered how his subjects' rankings would change today. Half the excitement of his job came in seeing how those seven and eight figure numbers rose and fell as the days passed.

The bus arrived, and Simon disembarked with exactly one other person, the usual other person. He knew her name was Lucy. Beyond that, she was an enigma, one of hundreds who passed him by each day, walking with less space between them than between two bedmates, yet as unknowable as the Europeans or the Chinese, or Martians if they were real. Beyond his subjects, there was nobody who he could say he knew intimately. Even his assigned friends, Charlie and Beckett, kept everything important behind a mask.

His morning routine was nearly complete, a rather subpar but passable performance of well-executed motion and modulated thought, diligently tracked by his headband, waiting to be judged by the survey, which was likely to declare no major shortcomings. He had even managed to keep his wandering syndrome mostly under check today. He had only faltered twice so far.

Walking to his desk, he nodded his ritual greetings to Penelope, John, Casper, and Dustin. He knew each of them precisely as well as the survey meant him to, and was proud to say that beyond their names and appearances, he couldn't have confessed a single noteworthy fact about any of them.

Simon finished by waving to the side of the floor

opposite his desk, where his boss Jules sat. The short yet fit, ever stern, bespectacled man occupied a desk over twice the size of his own. The two of them had never spoken.

He reached his desk. Its surface activated as he applied headgear, displaying a matrix of the faces of his subjects. He considered which face he should press first; which of his subjects he should prioritize immersion into. He loved this moment of the day, of choosing whose life to enter. Choice was rare in Simon's life.

Studying Sarah was Simon's preferred start. She whistled and belted as she trekked across the Citizenship with whatever large cargo she was steering. Her musical efforts were always well confined to the realm of encouraged songs and were hardly excellent. Nonetheless, there was a certain beauty in listening to the woman's most intimate efforts at self-expression, efforts he could never mirror.

Today, however, he saw a notice on his desk surface right as his hand reached over Sarah's face

Start with Vernon, Colette, and Micah. Sarah after.

There would be no choice today. Without hesitation, his hand pivoted and he clicked on Vernon. Immersion began.

Kitchens were one of the workplaces worthy of cameras, allowing food workers to be scrutinized visually so that culinary malpractice could be effectively recorded and appropriate punishments decided. Over eight hours of kitchen footage involving Vernon was accessible from the previous day, but thankfully Simon only had to view snippets. Most of the footage was selected for him, using some nuanced algorithm he had no hope of understanding.

The first scene showed Vernon standing at his assigned stall, preparing a hamburger. Simon pulled up accompanying sound and blood pressure data from the man's headband, which was displayed in a complex ecosystem of graphs interacting in front of his eyes. This overwhelming information forest represented a small segment of the dataset that would be used by surveys to automatically classify all thoughts he was having second to second. People like Simon were necessary mostly as a means to seek out those thoughts that were nonobvious, or unintentional. The smallest of missteps, the minute subconscious errors that even the most loyal citizens sometimes committed. His eyes blinked rapidly between the multiple information streams for the next minute, carefully absorbing data and feeling the rhythm of a dozen interralated patterns.

The burger was clearly being prepared for A-class customers; this was too decadent a meal to be eaten by B-classers. Vernon moved around the burger with his usual care as he worked. Simon had been selected to take a rudimentary culinary course to qualify him for food work oversight. Almost half of his subjects worked with food. With his years of experience observing the rhythms of this particular profession, it was clear Vernon was doing an exceptional job. The reason Simon was told to focus on Vernon, most likely, was due to a theory he had recently logged, stemming from a hard-earned professional intuition built from years of collating millions of pieces of human data. He had theorized that Vernon was subconsciously diverging ever slightly from the correct preparation procedure out of artistic boredom.

There was ample reason to believe this. Vernon was diagnosed with wandering syndrome, same as Simon. The syndrome was hardly lethal, although it made certain aspects of life challenging. Repetitive tasks became more difficult to perform well. An urge to create variation, to experiment, to seek expressive outlet, was the leading symptom and usual precursor to diagnosis. People with wandering syndrome were usually competent enough to avoid obvious mistakes, but of course, all behaviors were seen by the surveys eventually, even the unspeakably subtle ones. Simon's own indulgences had been noticed ages ago. It was human nature, he figured, for one to want to find the biggest possible way in which they could be expressive without risking backlash.

Simon was now fully certain that Vernon had deviated

from the perfection of burger construction. The placement of every ingredient was predetermined to within a tenth of an inch with distribution models that human chefs spent months studying and learning how to implement. In Vernon's defense, the level of exactness was pointless practically, although there was no point in questioning it. Simon gathered clues across the terabytes of Vernon's blood data.

These clues came from patterns. Human details that in a past era were unassailably private, but could now be expertly scrutinized, collated with thousands of other data points, and interpreted. The nuanced patterns of artists, performers, thinkers, laborers, caregivers, could be used to make hundreds of meaningful deductions about them, how they conducted their work, how they saw the world. Those slightest of changes in the flow of blood, the once unstudied rises and drops in fluid and hormonal activity through the body, the way muscles tensed, twitched, relaxed, and competed with one another for activation during even the most thoughtless tasks...This information could be gathered, and from it, higher levels of truth could be distilled.

Simon's eyes continued to shift between video and datastream as Vernon moved onto his second, third, fourth burger. Eventually, he noticed something. a micropascal vs millisecond graph implied a particularly steep mapping between activity in Vernon's fingers and the radial placement of lettuce on the paddy. This relationship could normally be discarded as unconnected, but Simon pulled up footage from the corresponding timestamps, and saw that the pattern held. The variance from the graphical norm peaked while Vernon was positioning the upper bun, but was caused, Simon intuited, by his placement of the third and fourth leaves of lettuce on his product 4.6 seconds earlier. He requested a few nonstandard detection programs be run on these particular scenes, and flagged them, but already understood the truth. This was that final level of analysis that surveys had yet to master on their own. While algorithms often noticed these disparate correlations, they couldn't yet discern their relevance, or their deeper causes.

Simon closed his eyes and became Vernon. Some configurations of placing leaves onto paddies were indeed more symmetric than others. A useless aesthetic, which he nonetheless intimately appreciated because he'd done this countless times. He couldn't help himself when he thought of how much more pleasant some configurations of lettuce looked compared to others. It seemed insignificant. This small extra care he put into his product was, if anything, a good thing. In his mind's eye, sometimes, the leaves looked just a little nicer when they were placed in a flower configuration instead of standard side-by-side with 0.4 inch overlap. Or even if one extra leaf was placed on the burger than was meant to be.

These minutiae I fix for the good of the Citizenship he thought with pride.

Simon returned to his own thoughts. It wasn't his place to decide a reprimand. He merely spotted the behavior and reported the perceived cause. He pulled up the appropriate template and wrote his report, linking it to the specialized module he had requested be run on the corresponding timestamps. He worried for Vernon, who should have known better than to toy with the aesthetics of lettuce arrangement, of all things. His current rank was 12,341,150. It would probably be in the twenty millions by tomorrow.

He moved onto Micah. Writers were always interesting to study. Simon, for his part, always loved the idea of writing concise informative articles about the wider world. That dream was unattainable. However, his desire was well documented, which was why, even ahead of food workers, wordsmiths made up the largest portion of his subjects.

Micah specialized in writing wilderness awareness columns sent out to certain A and B-classers in Quebec. His articles, like the one about the gradual recovery of caribou populations in northern latitudes, were meant to point out the successful recovery initiatives successfully conducted in wilderness sectors of that province following the midcentury horror. Simon became Micah and read through the draft. The text was entirely supportive of Citizenship values, and word choice was pristine. Micah wrote with an intelligent fear of flaw, and was rewarded with the impressive rank of 4,220,589. Simon saw that Micah's next assignment would be on beavers, although Micah himself didn't know this. A vague suspicion tugged in the back of his mind that the upcoming article might yield a problem. Years of studying vast quantities of human data gave him a nearly unmatched intuition for this sort of thing, one exceeded only by a few of his colleagues, and in certain respects by the survey algorithm.

He moved on. Colette was about Simon's age, in her mid-twenties, had the same job as him, and seemed to perform it in much a similar manner. They had nearly identical IQs and social habits, and succumbed similarly to wandering syndrome, although Colette admittedly did a better job of hiding it. Her angular face and black hair even made her look like a more feminine Simon. Inhabiting her mind was easy.

He watched her through a camera embedded in her desk in the same way there was certainly one embedded in his. He was viewing her real-time footage, seeing her stone face and intelligent grey eyes darting around her desk. She was studying one of her subjects, a professional bowler who was refining his technique for an event. Most of the next twenty minutes was spent analyzing her heart rate patterns from the latter half of the previous day. He'd become intimately familiar with the times of day when she was most likely to think divergent thoughts, and submitted a few reports regarding specific moments where he was quite certain she had pondered what book she would read later, or whether her husband still loved her.

After working an hour, he exercised a microliberty to look up from his desk and glance around. He was allowed one such motion every fifteen minutes, but had missed the last opportunity, so he took about two and a half seconds longer than he knew he should have. He looked back down and went to his favorite subject.

Sarah was also his lowest ranked subject, today being 71,498,832. She was feeling quite musical today. The second his headgear integrated with her sound data, he heard her whistling a lively tune to a backdrop of her behemoth vehicle thrumming symphonically along a vast highway somewhere down south. He checked her location. She was transporting a 120 ton fruit cargo from Mexico to Louisiana.

As a C-class citizen, Sarah was easy. She never said or did anything truly problematic, although the way she moved held a certain freedom. She smiled, laughed, and raged in a way people Simon's age never did. Sarah was born in the forties and acted like it.

Eventually, he had to move through the rest of his subjects, but not before writing a memo he hoped might bump up her rank by at least fifty thousand. He spent the next few hours collecting timestamps of those unavoidable brief moments when people likely had held a subversive, or an extraneous thought for longer than they had to, as well as their moments of unintentional arousal, lowered or heightened productivity, and any other "strange seconds", as overseers called those unexplained moments when the mind did things that couldn't quite be predicted or explained, even under close observation. Simon's subjects were all adults who had practiced self-control for years. None of them intentionally behaved outlandishly, exempting Sarah of course, but someone her age had to be held to a looser standard.

Simon's second and final meal began five hours in. Reaching the cafeteria, he immediately saw Charlie and Beckett. His headband buzzed into his skull, a pattern indicating he should go talk to them. He wasn't sure why it always gave him this command; it was what he was planning to do anyway.

"Hey guys," he said neutrally after joining them in their spot at the back of the line for what looked like chicken noodle soup, a salad, and a compound drink.

"Hey. We're at a standstill, help us." Beckett said.

"What he means," said Charlie, his quiet and smooth voice by far the more massaged of the two, "is that I'm not convinced the First-Citizen is going to do his flying high Citizenship act this year."

"He absolutely is going to sing and soar again," Beckett responded with as much passion as he was allowed. "Why wouldn't he repeat? Unless of course he has something better planned."

"Or has a good reason to do nothing," Simon said. Personally, he thought the production two years ago was rather ridiculous, an unfortunate opinion he wished he could have hidden. The First-Citizen had broken in the twenty-acre olympic field in a surprise appearance, singing beautifully just before the first event. As the song reached its climax, he was made to look like he was levitating ten feet in the air, his arms raised dramatically in a messianic pose. It was visually effective propaganda. Simon appreciated the staging, but he'd long since lost the capacity to rave over those sorts of performances the way Beckett could.

They reached the front of the line and paused for a moment to gather their food neatly onto their trays. They could not talk while receiving it. It was important to analyse it quietly and to meditate on their privilege while receiving. A minute later, conversation resumed where it had stopped.

"It's simply because the man has a beautiful voice, and his performance was such a hit two years ago in Tijuana. I mean, it's one of the few events worthy of our leader's onscreen appearance." Beckett said.

"That's precisely why he isn't doing it," Charlie replied. "He's disappointed in Australia. Their governor, I mean Warden, Mallory, has overseen a failure. Australia was supposed to have lithium. Would have meant more material to build more cameras, gather more in-house data, bring proper surveillance to poorer quarters, all that. From what I hear, she managed to collect less than a sixth of the projection. And most of those materials probably need to be kept in Australia for their new headbands, so it can't be brought here. I don't envision him rewarding her administration with an anthem."

"Apples and oranges, Charlie." Beckett countered. "Either of you know the Warden's rank, anyway?"

"She got to three hundred last week, but it's definitely gone down. She might even be out of the thankful thousand." Charlie said.

Charlie sensed the real question in the room. He always seemed to know things before others, to everyone's bewilderment, particularly with Australia. "All I know is, they've got about twenty million citizens, so if they give 'em to us all at once, we'll be in for some serious overtime. Not that I mind the work."

Simon was pleased to hear he knew as much as Charlie. That was ideal; it meant he'd learned as much as he was meant to. They found their usual table and talked more about Australia, mostly wondering whether the new citizens there would be much different from North Americans.

Charlie and Beckett were as different as any two B-class citizens were allowed to be. Beckett was younger, and compared to most was an overtly amicable and outgoing person; an extrovert constantly applying effort to stifle an even more extroverted personality. His flamboyance cost him nearly all of his allowed microliberties. He protected his survey score by flawlessly aligning himself with all recommended behaviors, interests, and opinions. Charlie on the other hand maintained an exquisite neutral facade, wasting no energy on unnecessary words or expressions. His microliberties were carefully reserved for an occasional remark, or minor opinion, that stood just at the edge of what his survey would tolerate. Simon found either one of them by themselves to be a little boring, but together they discharged off each other in interesting ways.

Work the rest of the day was entirely regular. Sarah

reached a truck stop and flirted with a station clerk. Micah received his beaver assignment. Colette entered deeper into her flow state, her wandering syndrome and marital insecurities momentarily held at bay. Killion, one of his more bland subjects, was removed from his list. Simon's adrenaline spiked when he saw the alert. Seventeen subjects, two months after being at twenty, was cause for celebration. Equally exciting, all but two of his subjects went up in ranking by the end of the day.

He met Charlie and Beckett again at the building bus stop. There was one final obligation before he could return home and find calm in his dreams.

Simon might have eventually introduced himself to Charlie and Beckett without being told to, but he certainly wouldn't have made a habit out of bowling with them if his survey hadn't adamantly suggested it. The alley was conveniently near their bus route, and all three of their homes, so mathematically it was the optimal activity to encourage. It was pleasantly furnished to the point where an A-class father would occasionally be seen taking his children there to hone their skill before they could be shown off somewhere more exclusive.

Bowling was a sport of perfection, in the enlightened estimation of the First-Citizen. To become a virtuoso at it, one simply had to repeat an exact motion over, and over, and over again, without faltering. Simon wasn't good at it, but Beckett was, and he usually won. Tonight was no exception.

They talked numbers as their game wrapped up. Memorizing bowling statistics guaranteed endless conversation with most Citizenship citizens, so Simon always researched the top players and their contest stats. He didn't particularly love doing it, except that it turned out he was quite good at it and the habit made bonding with his friends infinitely easier.

Beckett had to go relieve himself, and Charlie, noticing Simon's exhaustion, subtly gestured to the building clock, indicating that the next bus was about to leave. Simon left his friends to board.

CHAPTER 2

Simon disembarked and walked along a memorized route of reflective sidewalks to his unit. He caught the sun setting in his peripheral, and neighborhood lights were dimly lit to compensate for the absence. The dim town lights also served to overpower the light of the stars on the mirror-like surface he walked on. The stars would have looked beautiful reflected on the sidewalks at night, Simon suspected, although they would have usurped the minimalist aesthetic.

Simon carted in the 24 eggs the drone had dropped. The home's open floor plan was the standard for one or two adult B-class Citizenship citizens, an identical copy to over thirty million such structures across the continent. The walls were all covered with some synthetic substance that highlighted their light blue surface (or maybe it was green). Whatever the color, it was nearly as smooth and dulcetly reflective as the roads outside.

In his old unit, which had little more than a bedroom and bathroom, a small kitchen, and a TV stall, he had tried to cultivate a quality of uniqueness. There had been four dark blue paintings hanging in the three rooms of his old home, but, like a drug addicted capitalist from the past century being weaned, he was gradually relieved of their complicating presence. One by one, he sent his four paintings off on a drone, being commended each time for his sacrifice. The only remaining artwork in the house was a hyper-realistic life-size poster of the First-Citizen, about a meter wide and twice as tall, hanging directly above his television in the living room, displaying his more or less handsome face sitting atop a powerful body, at least three inches taller than Simon, who was himself rather tall. While putting away his eggs, he wondered if he'd messed up his utensil stacking again. He hoped his survey wouldn't know, given that he didn't.

<<*Welcome home Simon.*>>

His survey said, its evenly feminine voice emulating a flute's timbre from at least three, possibly four point sources in the house. Hearing the refined, inhuman voice perfectly converge onto his ears from many directions created an impression of gentle omniscience.

<<*Are you ready for question 1?*>>

"No, sorry, I just need to use the bathroom first." *Damnit* he thought. He was distracted, and made the decision without thinking. His score would suffer.

He went hurriedly and returned, hands undried. "I'm ready now."

<<*Good. Question 1: Do you consider your comfort to take precedence over the recommended time to this survey?*>>

"No, not at all. I just really needed to relieve myself, but I still had every intention to complete this survey. You know that's the truth."

<<*CORRECTION: do not use second person in reference to your survey.*>>

"Yes, sorry. My bad." He pinched himself for faltering a second time.

<<*Question 2: You have engaged in this behavior five times in the past year. Do you intend for there to be future occurrences?*>>

"No, of course not. It was an oversight on my part. I'll be better." A small pause.

<<*Question 3: Why did you not relieve yourself while with Beckett, miss your bus, and utilize the added time to talk with him about timely Citizenship affairs?*>>

This survey was not going well, but at least his headband would detect how his failures sat with him. His internal disappointment tended to go a long way in protecting his score.

"I guess I was tired and didn't want to wait longer than I had to. Also, Charlie encouraged me."

A longer pause, likely meant as an opportunity for self-reflection, gave Simon a chance to breathe and focus. The increased blood flowing to his brain would look favorable.

<<Question 4: You mumbled 12 words on your way to work today, down from yesterday's value of 26 by over 50%. How was this improvement achieved?>>

The questions were thankfully becoming more typical, and Simon allowed himself to drift into autopilot as he perfunctorily replied to the remaining queries. After 19 questions were asked and answered, the survey gave Simon a decent aggregate score of 171. So long as it didn't dip below 160, he had no reason to panic. His rank went down by about a hundred thousand, to 6,560,421. A new number to bounce around his head.

A ringtone sounded everywhere in the house to indicate survey completion. It was an hour from midnight, and the day's duties had depleted him. He changed clothes and spent his remaining waking minutes responsibly watching an encouraged television broadcast about the rich natural history of the recently occupied Australian continent, enjoying the desert imagery and noting that the lithium shortage was no better than thought yesterday. After he figured he'd watched enough, he changed the channel for a few minutes to some reality show about feuding A-classers, which he found himself nodding off to. He idly wondered if the suits A-classers wore to signal their elite status were comfortable, and performed his sleep ritual.

Sleep brought Simon his freedom. Although he kept his headband on, gauging his every twitch as well as the intensity and general emotions of his dreams, he had a little more leeway in what he could imagine. That was why, over the past decade, he'd studiously developed and refined his ability to lucid dream.

The coloristic stupor of preconsciousness gradually intensified into a proper dream scene, which Simon had learned to morph into whatever setting suited him. He created a forest. He'd loved seeing forests as a child, and this was now the only way he could see so many trees in one place. He didn't do much in this dream, beyond walking amongst the evergreens pulled from an old memory. Having come to a similar place many times over many years, his fictional forest had turned into something of a highly realized and detailed project. Certain recurring dream characters had become, in a way, his friends. Many types of flora and fauna, both real and imaginary, had crossed paths with him and interacted with each other in surprisingly complex ways that he still couldn't govern. Certain dream plots involving a wise blue snake, warring forest tribes, and intricate treetop battles offered him an excitement that the waking world lacked. His characters invigorated him with their independence, complexity, and unpredictability. Tonight, however, would be simpler. He brushed his head, feeling the headband gone. He felt a jolting thrill at not feeling it on him that almost woke him up.

What an adventure. He thought.

"Bring me an extinct animal!" he shouted into his dreamscape. It of course obliged him; even his subconscious had long forgotten how to refuse an order. A distant thumping sound came from behind. He turned and saw three gray giants he recognized from a documentary his mother had made him watch when he was seven or so. The tusked creatures approached, towering over him. He couldn't remember what they were called. He thought maybe they were el-phishes. The el-phishes rumbled along, and he decided to walk with the creatures. The experience was almost spiritual. He knew that el-phishes no longer roamed any physical forests. He felt honored to host them in his dream.

6,560,421 was plastered on Simon's mind as his headband told him to wake.

The calibrated pulsing into his skull dispatched the fleeting freedom that sleep had brought. Within seconds, his dream was forgotten, shudderingly replaced with the daily imperative to defeat the morning monsters. His headband began harshly ticking seconds into his head from four directions, ensuring everything would be timed to clockwork accuracy.

The first monster was to open his eyes and lift his bedsheet. There was no margin for error in either of these actions, and to indulge in the natural tendency to rub his eyes or blink was to fail. Simon made quick, groggy calculations and performed a dozen small actions precisely as they were meant to be done, culminating in his lifting of the blanket in front of him into the prescribed triangle fold. It looked more creased than he would have liked, and his fold was off by an inch. He very nearly blinked one more time than he was supposed to. He used exactly 18 seconds, as he should have.

His march out of bed required more fearful calculations. Mornings were sacred. When the waking mind was the most susceptible to dream-state reflections was the most important time to display loyalty and patriotism. The first two minutes of consciousness had to go more or less perfectly, or his entire day's performance would be beyond saving. Simon stood correctly, defeating the second monster.

The third monster was the hallwalk. It was to take thirty seconds to walk the hallway from bedroom to kitchen, in a procession during which he was required to speak his resolutions of the day. He had to quasi-improvise these, and they had to correspond to the previous night's survey. And he had to count to thirty in his mind while saying them.

"I will not mumble. I will not have sexual thoughts about Penelope. I will prioritize my survey over my physical comfort. I will respect my time with Charlie and Beckett…" He reached the hallway.

I was too vague this time. My heart wasn't in the words. My tempo was off near the end. Did I miss a tick and take 31 seconds?

The final early morning monster before the reprieve of breakfast was adoration. Simon stood in front of the painting of the First-Citizen that hung in his living room next to his kitchen.

"Thank you, First-Citizen" He said to the painting. He couldn't say how much he still felt the words. There were days that they seemed meaningful, that having such a powerfully benevolent leader seemed a privilege meant to be cherished. Then there were times when the entire ritual seemed vain and absurd. Today was regrettably one of the latter, and Simon struggled to make himself feel the warming positive emotion he'd accessed easily as a child. The ticking stopped.

He made his way to work by the usual means, taking exquisite care to not mumble a single word or glance in a useless direction, in hopes of making up ground from his aggressive dream and half-hearted adoration.

Following his hunch the previous day, Simon initiated his work the next morning with an especially careful reading of Micah's work on his beaver article. The first few paragraphs were as free of flaws as any he had written, but a passage near the end caught his attention.

The recovery of the beaver populations in the southern half of this beautiful province is hardly a surprise. Beavers are exceptionally intelligent mammals, and incredibly, they are known to form tight family bonds, from which they build an unbreakable community of dam-builders. There is no denying that this social fabric is the central reason that this creature has survived and adapted so effectively in spite of the unsustainable hunting industrial complex maintained by our misguided capitalist forebears.

Micah slipped. This whole article would be unpublishable until he fixed it. *Tight family bonds* was a tough mistake to forgive. The implication that family loyalty was a chief cause of the animal's success could not be tolerated. Families had been split apart for various highly justified reasons since before the ascendancy of the First-

Citizen. Simon knew better than most. Children who grew up in Academy tended to mature into more effective patriots than those raised by their parents, many of whom lacked the committed loyalty necessary to impart to the next generation. Simon had many fond memories from Academy.

He made a note of the flawed wording, describing it in his memo as "poetically compelling in an outdated sense, a philosophically incorrect synthesis of correct facts." He could have simply stated "beaver family fact bad", but he enjoyed pushing language just a little.

Micah's career, which had been advancing so well, was endangered. Normally Simon would be glad to have one less subject, but this once he hoped to see the same row of faces on his desk tomorrow. If not, it would mean Micah was no longer a B-class citizen.

The day slowed. Sarah was a little more silent, resting in a motel on a rare break day. Colette was productive, but boring As he wrapped up his final report on Vernon, he received a message displayed on his desk surface.

Do not go bowling with Charlie and Beckett. Go straight home.

This command was irregular. Simon had an idea of what it might mean and silently begged the First-Citizen to let his intuition be wrong.

He rode the bus, keeping his mind trained on work as alternating views of streets, neighborhoods, and the new megafacilities passed through his eyes with forgettable familiarity. He reached his stop and walked the rest of the way.

The reason for his recall became clear when he turned onto the street that his unit was on. The man stood leaning against his door, a provocative posture meant to achieve comfort, although he didn't look quite comfortable. He gave that effortless smile that Simon could recognize anywhere.

"Hey, Simon. Your new place doesn't have a fu... sorry, a chair. There's nowhere out here to sit. You might as well not have a lawn at this point."

"Hey Alex."

"No more 'hey dad' I suppose?"

"Well, Alex is your legal name. Thanks for not swearing."

"Yeah yeah, of course."

Simon approached his father. The blue C-class uniform looked wrong on him. He made to embrace, and Simon awkwardly mirrored the gesture. Touching someone felt weird.

"I happened to be trucking through Portland today, so the management let me have a day off. Mighty nice of them."

"Yeah. Nice."

The two of them stood facing each other. Hours ago he traversed a fictional forest with El-phishes, yet this felt more absurd.

"You hungry? We should go out. They haven't phased all the breweries out of Portland yet, right I've heard rumors that a couple here are still around."

"A couple are. But you shouldn't have alcohol, or you'll trip on the walkways. Citizenship Coffee is closer anyways."

"Yeah, alright, Coffee works. You don't drink at all anymore?"

"I stopped a couple years ago. Wasn't worth the cost."

"Well, that's fair. It's a nasty habit when It gets out of hand. Not that you'd let it." Alex looked down the neighborhood street as though he was cataloging an alien world.

"Lead the way, my boy. It's been too long and I want to hear everything."

Simon walked back the way he came. His father elected to use the time to describe the continent, repeatedly emphasizing the beauty of its vistas of forest, farmland, mountain, and desert which he had the privilege to drive through, trying regularly to prompt his son to contribute to the conversation. Simon appreciated the obvious effort being made; it was one he had observed several of his older subjects make towards their children. Their generation, when it was patriotic, expressed such patriotism bombastically, and if they had their way they would express disdain for the country that nourished them with equal bombast. Fortunately, Alex wasn't a fool and kept his comments positive. He tripped on the road twice and impressively refrained from swearing both times.

"Truckers don't get put on surfaces like this" was his only reply each time.

Citizenship Coffee had a location across from the bus stop. The shops' interior looked as austere as the exterior, the universal refrain of every building built for B-classers.

Alex tried to order a frappuccino and was politely declined. They both ordered small decafs.

"Do you even know what a frappuccino is?" Alex asked.

"Yes. I've heard of it." He'd had several of them with Sybil, back when real coffee shops were more accessible. He'd loved them.

"You're missing out, my son. It's a beautiful drink. They're a rare treat that you stumble across if you're lucky. You know, there's still a scattering of select spots around the continent where you can find them. The lake has dried, but puddles remain. Wherever I'm in a shop, I always ask. I think it's been eight months since my last success."

"Portland has no puddles." Simon replied. This wasn't strictly true, there were a few shops down the far side of the river that still sold frappuccinos. But there was no reason to say that.

Alex finally pressed his lips together and stopped speaking. The silence was no better, because he elected instead to silently stare at Simon with an inscrutable lack of expression. Simon realized he still couldn't intuit the man's thoughts so well as he could those of even his most evasive subject. Their coffee was served.

"Thanks miss," Alex said. He continued staring with easy composure. He was probably considered charismatic in his day, back when people could be charismatic.

"Simon, tell me about your job. Your, er, clients?" He said

after around two hundred seconds.

"Subjects. They're only clients when they're A-class."

"Oh right, of course." The man made his first grimace of the evening, a familiar expression, but corrected it instantly.

"Work is well. I'm down to seventeen subjects, which means they might start shifting me to higher B-class citizens. Which means more interesting work. I actually have another trucker right now." He added that last bit in hopes of an actual conversation happening between them.

"Oh, what's her name? Sliver of a chance I know her."

"Sarah."

Alex shook his head. "Nope. I guess they wouldn't have assigned her to you if we knew each other. They're too smart for that."

Simon didn't reply. Alex started to frown.

"Oh, damn all this to hell. Simon, I'll just say what I'm here to say, since I don't have long. I've been wanting to ask you for a while. I just, well, asking in person seemed the only way to do it. That's why I haven't reached out."

"What are you talking about?"

"Leave with me. Get yourself set up as a trucker. There are all sorts of openings now. You're a quick study, you'd be able to ship out within weeks. See the continent. Maybe even see a little more of me."

"We don't need to see more of each other, Alex. I'm not becoming a trucker."

Simon immediately regretted what he said. But he couldn't show it. Family meetings were never not tests. It seemed more than likely that this particular test, if he passed, was precedent to a substantial career leap. There was no other explanation for his father being given work driving through Portland, granted a rare day off, and told precisely where his son lived.

Alex lost that faint easy smile that always held up the creases of his face. When Simon was younger, he'd always say "Happiness is a lake when you have it, but puddles should stay with you even when it dries. That's how you know it's real." Lakes to puddles was his favorite metaphor. There were puddles in his frown.

"Son...."

He paused and shifted weight uncertainly.

"I just... I don't want you to waste your life. The Citizenship, it, well...you know what my opinions have been. And you were right to do what you did to your mother and me." Saying this was obviously difficult for him. Men of his generation were prone to showing when they were close to tears. Simon had received an excellent education and was masking his own emotions beautifully.

"I know you have a successful career, a lucrative one even. I get that. But they still allow B-classers to step into C-class roles. I think you're unhappy here, and you've been calibrated to be incapable of realizing it. Leave this city. Soar around the continent. Stop living every day as a carbon copy of the previous one. I know that's how it is for you. You're a theme with no variations. It's hard to recognize when it's all you know."

Simon carefully checked in with his body to attend to the common physical tells of emotional compromise. His heart rate had begun to climb, and he knew hormones were entering his bloodstream that would affect the purity of his thoughts. He said a stupid thing.

"If I did what you suggested, would I be able to see mom?"

Alex brought his hand to his chin.

"I don't know."

Not knowing what else to do, Simon drank a large sip of his still hot decaf, burning his throat. It was the greatest sensation the flavorless drink would ever give him.

That was a stupid question. I should have just said no.

"Simon, I can't make you do anything. But please think about it. They might not let B-classers become truckers down the line. These...options... They've had this way of slowly falling out of everyone's reach for a long time, even from when I was a kid. I know I'm not supposed to say it out loud, but I'm getting old, and I don't care much anymore. Except about you."

"And mom."

"Yes, and your mother. But there's nothing I can do for her right now."

"So here you are, recruiting me."

"Well, yeah. I'm just doing what I can. I know it's not much. I just want a good life for you."

"I do live a good life. But you raised me in an obsolete way. My job, it's respectable and stimulating. And it's moving us all into the future, don't you see? Driving from Portland to Quebec to Chicago to Tijuana isn't going to give me more purpose than oversight does. Please, don't say something you'll regret. Just stop." Simon sensed his father was about to say something dangerous even by his own standards.

"Alright. Fine. I won't try recruiting you again. Think about it on your own time. Let's enjoy our shitty coffee together. And really, I forgive you. I forgave you years ago. You need to hear that, I think."

They drank quickly.

"Alright then, what are the sights of Portland? When I was young this city was completely different. You simply wouldn't believe me if I described it to you."

"There are no sights in Portland. It's just a city. People live and work here."

"Yeah, well, most cities are like that now. But I always hope, you know?"

"I know."

"Well. It sounds like you want this to be it."

Alex forced a smile, a lake without the puddles. He'd smiled like that a lot during the months before he went away.

"I think so."

"Well, alright. At least walk me to the bus stop. I won't bug you anymore."

"That term is discouraged now. 'Bug' is too nonliteral.

And you really shouldn't have sworn about the coffee."

"Oh, Simon. You could have been such a poet once."

They left the Citizenship Coffee and walked across the street. Simon offered a handshake to prevent a hug which would have been too compromising for either of them, and they parted wordlessly at the bus stop.

CHAPTER 3

I'm livin' the life...
The Citizenship life...
I'm glidin' in a dream...scape of happiness with you,
You're livin' the life...
The Citizenship life...
We share a dream turned to re-al-i-ty....

Sarah sang joyfully today, the lead song of the new continental Top Fifty album, released yesterday on all stations. Notably, her truck had driven near what must have been one of the few remaining local radio stations in all of North America, so she had heard the song only once. Her memory was impressive, the music's simplicity considered.

Simon was trying to focus, and failing. The previous night, he had tossed in his bed three more times than he was supposed to. His mind pulled him in a thousand directions. He'd done everything right yesterday. He certainly didn't enjoy the encounter, but whatever type of test it was meant to be, he was quite sure he passed.

And yet, he felt how he felt.

He glanced up towards Jule's office for the second time that day, hoping that the adrenaline rush of taking such a large microliberty might jolt his attention. To his horror, the office overseer glanced up towards him in return.

Shit. He must be studying me right now.

Simon looked down quickly and put his mind to work analyzing his next subject. A message dominated his screen.

You are encouraged to take day leave for recuperation. Use this free time to restore emotional stability and be ready to resume work tomorrow.

Simon subdued what would have been an impressive sigh of relief, got up from his chair, and walked to the elevator, allowing himself one sweeping glance at all of his coworkers and noting that none of them had chosen to look up as he passed.

As he commuted home on a bus just for him, he tried to allow the notion of relaxation to enter his mind. He hadn't expected such a generous accommodation. Jules, and anyone else assigned to oversee him, must have filed a report, knowing full well what he had done yesterday, and determined that a day of contemplation might help him process his actions. Perhaps it was an act of pity. While it was a mercy, it was a practical one, which came with an expectation of quickly getting over any feeling of sentimentality towards his father. A day off was just as much a warning as a courtesy.

As relaxation finally spread from mind to body, Simon slumped into his bus seat slightly, and tilted his head toward the window, a more comfortable posture, which he usually avoided due to the microliberty cost. He could spend more today.

He decided to use his relaxation time to wander mentally, and idly think about things he normally wouldn't. He could only do so much of this, before needing to worry about being discovered. It was fortunate that headbands couldn't read actual thoughts, or know with complete precision what he was considering at every given moment, but even so, the subtle changes in blood flow, the way his skin twitched, his patterns of limb movement, all correlated in intricately unseen ways to the types of thoughts he was allowing into his head. So, he picked his contemplations with some care, and didn't allow himself to stay on any one thought for too long.

For the past couple years he had wondered about the police. When he was younger he saw them everywhere, mostly in their slick black-coated vehicles called cars, but also in person and in their distinctive all-body bullet-resistant uniforms. They had been rather terrifying, their helmet-covered faces birthing a single monolithic identity that they all shared. He'd witnessed several arrests, which seemed to happen all the time back in the day, and on the news the heroic police were featured quite prominently, actively competing even with the First-Citizen for screentime. No officer was ever named, and their faces were never shown, but their praises were sung nonetheless as the nation's great unidentified heroes. Any cop that anyone saw anywhere, might well have been the hero who made headlines the previous week. There was no way of knowing.

In the past couple years their visibility had lessened significantly. However, right whenever he would start to doubt whether they even still existed, he would always see one or more of their cars riding along next to his bus, or pass near him while he was walking on a sidewalk, as though they plotted their motions according to the tides of his disbelief. He was confused why they would no longer be as numerous as they once had been. Had dissidents stopped being dissentious? Or were most of them needed in another part of the country? Or in Australia? Having no desire to test how his survey score would be affected if he externally asked any of these questions, it seemed likely he would never know. He decided he'd already thought about this for too long and moved onto something tamer.

Coffee shops. His father, for all his flaws, was right: there were far fewer of them now. There were only two local places left in the region that offered precious variety in their menus, and he no longer dared visit either. He killed the thought before it could become critical of the Citizenship. He looked out the window and enjoyed the repetitive lul of the buildings.

Feeling just a little dangerous, Simon's thoughts grazed the ultimate question, the one everybody wished to talk about but was too terrified to: How was the First-Citizen so damn young?

It should have been an easy question, but Simon, and everyone his age, almost certainly remembered the glorious leader from their childhoods two decades ago. He knew from distant memories of his parents that the First-Citizen had been in power for quite some time before then, although he seemed to also recall being told that his power was once less absolute. What Simon knew with complete certainty was that the First-Citizen of his childhood looked ancient and the First-Citizen of today didn't.

There were numerous explanations to be offered, each treasonous to propose out loud. Perhaps he had a son, who secretly inherited his fathers mantle, and the Citizenship had silently morphed into a monarchy. Or he may have been cloned. Or he hasn't made a real public appearance in years, and plucked an attractive lookalike from among his citizenry to maintain his image of virility. Simon leaned slightly towards the third option, but didn't know enough to say. He supposed it didn't really matter.

While walking again through his homogeneous suburbia, he elected to cease all abstract thought, and focused on the clouds wispy reflections in front of him. Reflective streets in the Citizenship, though frustrating, really were beautiful some days. He saw C-classers sweeping the road, a rare sight since he was hardly here in the middle of the day like this.

Simon's first undertaking in his unit was to nap. He sank into a deep comatose slumber that transitioned into the rich internal world of dreamhood. He always relished the temporary illusion of freedom.

This dream brought him to an endless savannah. Simon had never seen a place like this in person, but had watched it in that same documentary with the el-phishes. He looked around but saw none of the comforting giants. C-classers pointlessly swept at the tall grasses around him.

He saw a grid in the sky. Black dots high in the air delineated rows and columns of identical diamonds. The grid translated slowly across the sky like a scrolling map. It took him a moment to realize that he was staring at a fleet of aircraft. A booming voice echoed from all directions while the planes seemed to sink closer to the ground, towards him.

Order confirmed. Drop the payload. Drop everything. Make me the devil.

The famous command issued by the General George Lackley preceding the bombing of Mexico City, words that had been quoted innumerable times in Simon's waking world, and the only legally quotable phrase in the English language to make religious mention. The poet in him grown to like the quote. A thousand bombs dropped from the planes and began plummeting.

The drumming vibrations of a city-leveling explosion struck him at the same time as the glowing image of a rapidly growing bubble spread across half the skyline. All other objects and characters of the dream disintegrated into insignificant wisps, as the hemispherical explosion expanded into the entirety of the experience. It was as though the explosion *was* him, for a fleetingly intense moment. The overwhelming sensation of it woke him.

Simon slowly moved his naked form off his bed and stretched. He did his best to luxuriate in the lack of the usual panic that accompanied his wakeups, but found that the habit was too ingrained, and he still got up with quite some care. Despite the potent dream, he felt more rested than he had in the past two days. He decided to shower. Actually, he decided to use this time first to re-dye his hair.

Before he entered his bathroom to mix his dye and developer, He removed his headband. Normally citizens couldn't remove their headbands except in emergencies or to charge it, and even kept them on while showering. The requirement that Simon's hair be periodically recolored gave him a rare one hour pass every two months. Once his headband was placed on its charging pad, Simon allowed himself the faintest feeling of lightness. He had spent less than a percent of his adult life not wearing his headband, and when it was off he felt at once free and ashamedly naked. Simon went through the dying procedure. He separated his hair into four sections, put on gloves, mixed his developer with his pitch black dye, and began application. Even with his body unmonitored, he habitually tried to work as efficiently as possible.

Soon enough, he had finished, and placed a shower cap around his hair to allow the new dye to percolate. He had about fifty minutes before he could put his headband back on; the Citizenship was stingy about staining them even slightly. Simon decided, in a flight of fancy, to walk aimlessly around the unit for a few minutes. His route took him from his living room across the open floor through his kitchen, then back. He didn't know exactly how far he was allowed to push absurdity on an off day like this, but he figured a little exercise around his home fell within reason. He'd been told to spend the day in mental recuperation, which walking helped with.

His little bout of insanity escalated, and, seeking further stimulation, he started singing and snapping as he traced an infinity around his couch and kitchen island, that song he'd heard Sarah singing to herself earlier. Not completely oblivious to what his house sensors were picking up, his throaty singing quickly lowered to a subdued hum.

"I'm livin the life, that Citizenship life. I'm gliding in a dreamscape of happiness, with you." He couldn't remember the rest of the words, something sappy about everyone else joining the singer's dream, maybe. He awkwardly shifted focus to his snapping. Not remembering the actual words, he sang "snap" every other beat when he snapped rhythm. He hadn't done something like this since before Academy.

Right when he would have started to become cognizant of the absurdity of the whole activity and stop, he made a simple observation. He was snapping very, very loudly. Of course, he hadn't heard someone snap since his early days at Academy, but it seemed doubtful that it would be at all easy to achieve the powerful decibel he was now while fake-singing the old propagandic hit song.

He brought his fingers to eye level and snapped experimentally. Each of these snaps were the weak sparks of sound he had come to expect from the motion.

Weird.

He went back to singing, and immediately, the more powerful snaps returned. "What the..." he mumbled louder, standing in confused posture while considering his fingers. His snapping technique was utterly consistent, and yet, some of these snaps were discernibly louder than the rest, to the point where he almost worried that a neighbor might hear. He had an absurd hypothesis, and tested it, by singing a different, much older song while he snapped. "Oh say can you seeeee (snap) by the dawn's ear-ly liiight (snap)." Those snaps were no louder than usual.

Simon tried to let the mystery rest. He noticed that he got a drop of black dye on his left hand, and went to his kitchen sink to try and scrub it out. As the water ran in the faucet, Simon mused philosophically that the sound of running water sounded kind of like a rapid succession of many quiet snaps, melding their discrete pricks of sound into one another and creating a new, continuous eruption. This was the kind of abstract thought he would normally need to kill after five seconds, but this once he savored it. The dye dropped into his finger was annoyingly persistent.

In a flash, insight struck.

It isn't the singing! it's the word!

He thought loudly. He lifted his fingers and said "snap" while actually snapping. A powerful sound sparked from his fingers, one so strong that it almost sounded like a clap. In a moment of panic, knowing that his house heard everything, he clapped a few times with his hands and tried to replicate the sound, knowing that, while clapping was still strange, it was better than his survey thinking that sound came from snapping. He focused his mind, and, knowing that he would soon have to redress his headband, decided to experiment with his discovery quickly and concisely. Today would definitely be a weak survey day, but he would likely only be demerited for "solitary playfulness", which was at most a mid tier sin so long as it happened infrequently.

He finished trying to scrub the permanent dye out of his wrist, and sang the word "snap" all the while. Within a minute, he felt, and heard, a snapping sound emanate from somewhere near his wrist every time he said the word, his fingers unmoving. The sound seemed to come from some aether, a place he thought maybe he could vaguely sense near him, but couldn't reach out towards. The experience was becoming absurd, and he briefly considered if he was dreaming. He knew he was being listened to, so he put his effort into crafting in his voice a vibe of playful absurdity. He mixed in utterances of words in a comically simple song to make his actions seem undirected and playful. "I love the Citizenship (snap) oh yes I do (snap) I serve the Citizenship (snap) it's what I live to do".

Once he reached the end of his improvised musical number, each utterance of snap was creating a sound pushing the threshold of natural human ability, while his fingers remained still. He played around with singing "snap" in another song, and determined that, not only could he will the snapping sound to be as quiet as he wanted, but, after a number of tries, he learned how to create two snapping sounds at once, and make each one sound distinct, as thought coming from two different people. He wanted nothing more than to study how far he could extend this ability, to play around with what other sounds he could create merely by speaking a word, but knew that he needed caution.

"Humm" he hummed, inspired to achieve something similar with a different type of sound. His hum sounded entirely ordinary. *Maybe I need to speak the word several times before I can notice anything. It's a learned process.* In his mind he held his goal, which was to replicate the sound of a hum without needing to actually hum himself. His heart galloped with undetected excitement.

"Hum, hum, hum..." he hummed to himself, resuming his circular walk. After around a dozen utterances, he stopped humming, and, to his amazement, he continued to hear his voice faintly holding pitch, coming from that same untouchable aether as his snapping. Maintaining within his voice a charade of indifference was difficult. He continued to utter "hum" until he could replicate his own hum at a full volume with his breath held.

The sound reverberated modestly around him. Although his body wasn't producing it, as far as he could tell, he found he was faintly able to feel it, as though it still originated from some part of him. He felt compelled to keep pushing boundaries. He wanted to attempt to sustain multiple hums, and form chords, or to mimic the voices of different people. Such actions were out of the question.

What else can I try? He wanted to explore something separate from sound, to see how versatile his mysterious talent was. His options were limited, given that the nature of what he was doing needed to remain unguessed by anyone assigned to interpreting his home's sound, chemical, and temperature sensors.

Simon realized there was an existing problem he might try solving. "Dye" he uttered to himself with convincing lightheartedness. "Dye, dye..." He imagined the splotch on his finger coalescing back into a singular drop that could bleed off his hand into the sink. It took time, and saying the word in repetition felt less natural than the previous time had, but something happened. The area the dye on his finger covered was cut in two as the material contracted and thickened towards the middle. The act of physically washing it into the sink felt satisfying, and made the odd behavior more explainable to his survey. *So, my ability applies to at least one thing beyond sound.* He pinched himself for a fourth time to make certain he wasn't dreaming.

He decided to embark on a final brave exploration,

before completely abandoning the enterprise out of fear of safety. Since he was only going to allow himself one additional word, he knew what he wanted to try. He hoped, illogically, that the risk wouldn't immediately get him arrested, and began.

He needed to go and sit in front of his television. Although it was hardly ever talked about, it was generally accepted that only A-class citizens were worth home cameras in the midst of the raw material shortage. If this happened to be untrue, he figured he was already doomed anyway. He turned the TV on, and did not have to scroll far through his recommendeds to find a channel talking about a recent forest fire sweeping British Columbia. He first used this opportunity to try and see if he needed to speak a word out loud. If he could utter it in his mind's ear only, it would be much easier to experiment.

Fire. He thought as loudly and intently as he could. *Fire, fire, fire...* he chanted and visualized with all the mental power he had. A few minutes went by. He thought maybe he felt the subtlest of changes, but the flame he visualized didn't manifest. *Fuck.*

"Fire" he finally spoke aloud, with quiet intimacy. The word would be picked up regardless of volume, so he tried to sell it off as interest in the program. "Fire" he said again casually, holding his palm in front of him with an expression of sheer focus. "Fire, fire, fire..". Fear began catching up to him, and he nearly gave up the endeavor, but on his sixth utterance of "fire", a spark shimmered for the slightest moment above the largest crease of his palm. "Fire" he uttered again, and another spark, enduring perhaps a half second longer, pinged into and out of existence. He watched the program, becoming more careful to utter "fire" only when clips of a physical fire were shown to him, which happened every ten to twenty seconds. The news was conveniently formulaic in the images it cycled through displaying.

Around five minutes later, he accumulated enough

utterances from the viewing that he was now sustaining a baby orange flame in his right palm. He kept the fire going, and each new utterance of the word "fire" now made it slightly less diminutive. He focused his mind on cultivating the fire and tending the heat it generated to carefully avoid any contact with his skin, and so far had succeeded in feeling no more than a faint tinge of warmth bristling his palm. The modest flame actually felt almost like a part of his body, like he was slowly growing a new finger.

He spent a final minute constructing an ability to hold an orb of flame in each of his palms at once, and, for a tantalizing second, considered if he could make them larger. He then remembered from his education that fire required a fuel to burn. Whatever fuel source he was mystically summoning from his aether to supply his flame was likely to soon be detected by house chemical sensors, if it wasn't already. This epiphany made him promptly cease the effort. The fires in his hands fizzled out.

The full realization of his idiocy finally broke Simon's reverie, and he sank too quickly into the tight seat of his channel-back couch, watching the forest fire coverage with faked interest. *Thank fortune I'm not wearing my headband.*

The previous half hour of his life must have expended more microliberty than the entire preceding decade. It was an utter breakdown of living technique. Even during a day of recuperation, B-class citizens were not, ever, supposed to express themselves in such a stupid manner as singing and snapping! Even that was assuming that the nature of whatever it was he had done wasn't somehow gleaned by his overseers or the brilliant algorithms that extrapolated the happenings of his home with well-honed efficiency. Every aspect of his behavior from that second onwards needed to be within a single meandering thought's distance of technical perfection.

It was a reasonable guess that he might be deported that night. They would of course use the word "relocate"-a more innocent descriptor of the same fate. His career would for all intents and purposes be reset. It would be years before he'd again be entrusted with his current job. He'd likely be sent to a part of the country deemed to have fewer "negative environmental factors" inhibiting his ability to function properly as a citizen. If nothing else, it would give him an exciting new monotony to acclimate to. He decided to spend the next few hours watching quality Citizenship content, and, once work hours ended, he would socialize.

<<Please retrieve your headband.>> His house informed him, in a dispassionate male voice that was only slightly less intimidating than the more feminine vocalization of his surveys.

"House, please tell Charlie and Beckett I'll still be joining them today." He said as he got up from his couch and went to recover his headband.

<<Done.>> It was fortunate the house approved his decision. Simon sat back down and spent the next two and a half hours watching national bowling competitions. He needed to catch up on matches anyways.

"Hey hey, he's arrived!" Beckett loudly announced as Simon found him and Charlie waiting in front of the bowling center. "I hope I didn't keep you." Simon said.

"We've been here barely a minute," said Charlie. "Have you been watching the Baja strip matchup?" Beckett asked. "Yeah, I just saw." Simon said. "It's been surprising."

"I'll say. I've never seen such a tight bowling match in my life. They might even do well against Texas."

"It's actually not that surprising, given the recent lineup changes." Charlie pointed out. The two of them began arguing the finer points of team selection as they entered the facility, picked a lane, and scanned in for three appropriately-sized bowling balls to slide into their slot. Simon turned to his lane, and grabbed his designated ball in a fluid motion molded by repetition. He had a risky idea that, he hoped, could be used to make his earlier behavior make more sense in the eyes of his overseers. "Strike!" he half shouted as he rolled.

"What's that now?" Beckett said.

"You don't say strike until after you successfully pull one off, which, I'm sorry, my friend, you clearly have not done." Beckett was of course correct, as nine out of the ten initial pins remained standing.

"I'm trying something new. Positive reinforcement, all that.." Simon offered, surprised at how confident he sounded in his lie. He almost convinced himself.

"Alrighty then " Beckett said, understandably hesitant to vocalize approval at the surprise behavior. He rolled next. The pattern persisted, with Simon uttering the word "strike" every time he rolled, all the while intently imagining the ball reorienting itself onto an optimal central trajectory. It took five more rounds, but on his sixth role of the night, as he was beginning to feel a certain guiding power marshaling itself behind the word every time he said it, he spoke, rolled, and could just barely sense the essence of the bowling ball making minute directional adjustments towards the center of the lane. It didn't quite make it that time, but did manage to knock six over, which was his best that night.

"Not bad, maybe your little trick works, " Charlie said.

From then on, Charlie and Beckett joined in the verbalizing act, figuring they wouldn't be punished for doing something that Simon came up with, and in so doing consummated it as tradition. By Simon's next turn, all three of them were shouting "strike!" in conjunction with each roll, and as Simon had more repetitions, the effects became obvious. For the last six rounds of the game, every single one of his roles struck.

CHAPTER 4

Simon walked from the bus through a minimally pierced veil of darkness, the lampposts in front of him lighting dimly as a vanguard for his route, the ones behind him already returned to inactivity to conserve electricity. The stars would be clearly visible if Simon looked up, if only he could afford to. He wondered if the stars were still being studied, by anyone. If the Citizenship cared about the universe beyond their planet. Such a profound thought was a welcome distraction from his impending survey.

When Simon entered home, the monotone yet utterly distinctive female voice responded. <<*Are you ready for your survey?*>> It asked politely. Having no desire to irritate it, Simon held his aching bowels and curtly replied "Yes".

<<*Good*>> The word almost seemed to hold the subtlest quantity of contempt, but Simon decided he was likely projecting a biased characteristic onto the algorithmically perfected mouthpiece of his government.

<<*"Question 1: You enacted a list of several worrisome behaviors earlier today, to the extent that a human overseer has flagged a possible issue. How would you characterize the nature of the behavior being referred to?*>>

Simon gulped, palpably nervous. He wasn't so sure that the emotion was helping him this time. "Well, um, earlier today I, uh, I just felt very burdened. After my nap, I might have overindulged in my relaxation and took to some unusual wordplay. I would repeat words and enjoy hearing the sound of them." This wasn't entirely a lie, as Simon knew fully unbelieved lies were detectable with complete accuracy. This was instead a true statement; the way he spent that part of his day was most certainly a direct result of uncommon stress and relaxation tilting his behavior in an unanticipated way. He was highly adept at masking partial deceptions behind his belief of the true aspects of statements he uttered. Or at least he hoped he was.

<<*Your "wordplay" as you describe it was highly unusual and possibly indicative of a worrisome relapse of neurodivergence. This is an unanticipated event and may be prompted by an undiagnosed deformity. Have you noticed yourself having unusual thoughts recently, possibly during your heightened level of cranial bloodflow on the bus returning from work?*>>

This was by every stretch of the imagination going horribly, yet it gave Simon a degree of comfort to know that the apparent violation of universal laws did not appear to be on the survey's radar. He suppressed his relief, out of worry that any comfort during that moment would prompt its own question.

"I don't believe I've had any unusual experiences, er, neurologically. I do suffer from wandering syndrome, obviously, and still suffer thoughts on matters beyond my relevance or sanctioned interest, but personally, I guess the greatest issue today was that I am not used to feeling so relaxed. I've been careful to avoid needing to be issued medical relaxants since I don't want them to interfere with my work, and as a result I feel I've become stressed."

<<*Your statement has been noted for possible reference by a psychologist. If any further divergent behaviors of this sort are observed, you will be referred to said psychologist for further diagnosis and possible medication. Until then, you will take no medication and will remain under standard B-class oversight. Is this understood?*>>

"Yes." He'd always dreaded the dangerous intimacy of meeting a psychologist. They did what he did, but with a more penetrating gaze.

<<*Good.*>>

Again, that subtlest emotion seemed to gleam through. At this point though Simon no longer knew whether he was inventing it.

<<*Question 3: The words you most repeated during your episode were "snap" accompanied by you snapping, "hum" accompanied by you humming, and "fire" without accompaniment. How did you select these words? Your behavior around the word "fire" is of particular interest.*>>

Simon thought for a second but decided overthinking could be fatal. The delicate art of surviving a poorly progressing survey was defined by an impossible balance between thinking through how one wanted to give their answer, and not taking too long to fabricate a response. Taking too long always, without fail, lowered scores.

"I started snapping when I said the word snap, and the same when I hummed, so those went hand in hand. I was excited to find that I was able to snap quite loudly, which I hadn't realized I was capable of before. That heightened my excitement. Me feeling musical prompted the humming. It is known that I've always wanted to make my own music. Fire was less direct. Watching the forest fire drone footage earlier, I started wondering about how fire and sound are related. They must have some similarities, no? They both travel through air and have many different shades and intensities. They are also both very useful to humans, so I indulged in some playful philosophizing about their sameness, and wanted to express that."

The survey actually paused for a second. Usually, it knew exactly what to ask as its next question and didn't hesitate unless it had asked a question meant to chastise him. Perhaps Simon's answer was genuinely a rare one, something it wasn't yet efficient at responding to.

<<*Your response indicates worrisome behavior typically correlated with individuals of significantly lower intellectual maturity than you possess. This worrisome playfulness, as well as the mental energy you chose to divert into useless considerations*

about fire, which are of no relevance to your specific life mission, are behaviors that you must immediately purge. How will you work to prevent another episode?>>

Simon listed at least ten ideas for how he might never repeat the act. In a desperate moment, he added, "...Also, I might consider dating and finding a partner to be helpful to me."

<<All are reasonable precautions, and it is highly encouraged that you take them.>> No pause.

<<Question 4: when you went bowling with colleagues Charlie Buchannan and Beckett Litman, you initiated a practice of loudly saying "strike" whenever you threw your ball into your lane. This appears to have aided your success but draws parallels to your behavior earlier in the day. Do you believe that these two events are similar by coincidence, or causality?>>

The question was clearly rhetorical, yet another sign that his earlier explorations probably weren't worth this inevitable outcome and that this survey had become tragic.

"Yes, I believe they are causally linked. I found that expressing myself with simpler words helped keep me more grounded, and gave me clarity. I believe this shows itself well in the fact that my performance in the match clearly improved the more I employed the tactic. Of course, if you wish for me to stop looking for clarity in such a manner, then I can stop."

<<Reminder: A citizen's usage of the personal pronoun "you" in surveys is highly discouraged. Better phrasing would be: 'If it would be preferable for me to stop looking for mental clarity via this method, then I will stop.'>>

"Understood," Simon said, cursing his semantic lapse.

<<Question 5: Regarding your work, you achieved a level of heightened cortisol production that exceeded your workplace daily production record by 14%. Do you continue to feel burdened by how you behaved with your father yesterday?>>

Simon shrugged meekly. He knew what came next.

"I feel fine. I'd request a relaxant but I'd worry about it getting in the way of my work."

<<*Your concern for your work is admirable. However, a limited dose will be added to your pill for the next two weeks experimentally.*

Question 6: What was the cause of the spike in blood flow to your brain 32 minutes ago while on the bus?

It sounded like the survey's most important questions had been asked. Having five "important" questions was highly unusual. Ideally, all questions would be matters of refinement. Asking whether a head tilt at work around 10:00 in the morning was done for comfort or to glance at Penelope, who was recorded to have incidentally aroused him fifteen times in the past year. Wondering at the differences in his gait walking to work, compared to walking from it, compared to walking to the bowling alley. Inquiring about his thoughts while eating soup at work for the eight seconds he was sitting alone. Asking what he lucid dreamed about. He greatly enjoyed answering his dream questions. It was his one chance each day to properly tell a story. As he recounted, he hoped the survey might tell him what the extinct giants were called. The survey offered no such clarification.

<<*Survey completed. Score: 142 Rank: 9,147, 353.*>>.

Simon paled. He anticipated doing poorly, but the grade struck a blow. Scoring 142 two days in a row could ruin his life. Relocation at a bare minimum. For all he knew, scoring so low three days in a row could get him incarcerated. He was fairly sure he'd never met anyone who had done it, at least not a B-classer. Such people were kept from him. And to have dropped in rank by over three million... It was distinctly possible that he would be moved tomorrow.

There would be no warning. He would be told during work to go to a different address at the end of the day, to a smaller apartment farther away from the city. Or maybe even to one of the commune facilities, the elderly and single workers who weren't allowed to date and have families lived. If he was lucky, his few personal belongings would be waiting there. Equally likely, they would be kept from him, and his material comforts would need to be re-earned.

Simon went to bed that night but remained far removed from any pleasant dreams he might have had. He lay, turning and twisting in his bed as he contemplated what he would have to do to keep 142 from overturning the life he had built.

CHAPTER 5

From the perspective of the analytics the Citizenship government ran on all citizens, Simon had the best two weeks of his life following the incident. His thoughts were pure. His actions were reasonable and logical. He never tilted his head further than he had to. He never faltered from focus during work. He defeated his morning monsters flawlessly.

This transformation was distinguished by two notable changes. He began regularly exercising with Beckett. The two of them would go on runs together every day before work. This required Simon to appear before his bus stop 45 minutes earlier than he typically did, making waking up even more effortful, but this personal sacrifice soon proved to be entirely worth it, as his survey average increased by 5 points from this choice alone. He soon recovered his former rank record of about six million.

His second change was he stopped mumbling. It surprised him how thoroughly he was able to kill the habit once the desperate urge for perfection was awoken. He always knew mumbling dragged his scores by some amount, but was shocked to find that the first day he went without ended in a whopping 188, 7 points higher than the previous day and the highest he'd ever received. Down to five million.

A plethora of additional refinements to his living strategy emerged over these few days in his attempt to perfect the quality of his citizenship. He adopted Beckett's practice of eating no pleasure food. Curating a diet entirely for function was far more difficult than he thought it would be; he'd grown accustomed to a single piece of chocolate at the end of every workday as a small comfort. The sacrifice was noticed and propped him up by about a point each Saturday. Shortening the length of his showers to three minutes (five was the standard, eight the cutoff) challenged him further, but, within a week of the change, he had completely acclimated to a more frantic self-washing.

One day in particular, about a week and a half after his incident, the very first question his survey asked him was about why he allowed himself to shower for three minutes and nineteen seconds that day. He had felt such pride to be asked that. Surveys only focused on small questions in the absence of large ones. He slid down further, to four and a half million. His overseers were probably proud of him.

Of all the changes he was enacting, Simon was most proud of the improvement to his workflow. The exercise, dieting, and obsessive focus that dictated his lifestyle naturally phased him into a state of frenzied productivity. He would arrive at the office with Beckett, sit in front of his desk, pull up his first subject, and analyze. His mind now effortlessly connected to the elusive flow state that had struck him all too inconsistently in the past; the cobwebs of his wandering syndrome strung into alignment. He joyfully studied the thousands of human data points displayed before him for hours on end in search of deeper insights.

It truly was a blessed occupation, in a way that his obsolete father never understood. Simon could live the lives of his subjects. He heard the constant humming of Sarah's truck giving her a reference pitch to try singing to. He could feel Vernon's careful craftsmanship as he assembled his burgers, trying to do so as plainly as his innately creative mind would allow. He could peer at the cautious writing of Micah as he ponderously evaluated each word before he wrote it, knowing that, even if he edited later, his mistakes could only be truly hidden from those monitoring him if he never typed them in the first place. Knowing that even then, he might not be able to hide all the mistaken notions he had been trying so hard to bury. The highs and the lows of all of their lives, and their rankings, could be vicariously felt by Simon when he was in his flow state, sustained through the constant absorption of rich streams of data that allowed his understanding of his subjects, in some ways, to surpass even their understanding of themselves.

Three weeks into this inspired surge in conformity, a single problem remained that, despite his wishes, Simon couldn't dispel. Once or twice each day, his mind, which was otherwise a paragon of focus, would be derailed, for many precious seconds, by thoughts of the unexplored and entirely absurd ability that he apparently possessed. Merely thinking about it became dangerous in a way it wasn't before, because they were now the only unregulated thoughts left to dispel. All it would take was a single survey question about a spike in brain activity at the wrong minute, and a single slipup on his end, and he could be led down an unwinnable sequence of questions that would inevitably force him to confess to a power that he didn't understand and wanted nothing to do with. *It doesn't matter. It wasn't real. Think about work.* Became a recurring mantra whenever he was alone.

He couldn't always put his heart behind those words, and the thoughts continued. One particular day, three Tuesdays following the incident, he caught himself musing about it, as he had each of the past twenty days. His abilities had seemed to grow with repeated use and indicated considerable versatility, so perhaps he could do more with it than simply holding filaments of fire. What other words could he...*It doesn't matter! It wasn't real. Think about work.* He repeated the mantra a few times as calmly as he could, but the mantra could only be repeated so many times before it risked prompting its own question. He couldn't kill his innate curiosity. *If only I could have a single day where I was unobserved. One day of true privacy like my great-grandparents had. That might be enough time to satisfy my questions.* A dangerous thought to be sure, one he committed to never repeat.

His risky contemplation was blessedly cut short as his bus arrived. He got off, being the only person at this early hour arriving at his place of work. Surprisingly, he missed getting off with Lucia, the woman he'd never spoken to. He always liked to imagine what he would have said to her if he'd ever found the courage. Beckett was waiting.

"I'm feeling ambitious, I think we can run it in under 40 minutes today."

Simon nodded. "Yeah, we can try. I think if we can do it in 45 we're doing fine though."

"Oh come on, have some ambition."

"Alright, 43 minutes." They began to run.

Their route, prescribed to them as an optimal one, started at a horseshoe plaza a couple blocks from the only tree in portland, and took them through a jumbled grid of lots and office spaces to the nearest public lockers, where they could shower, change, and hop a bus to their building. It was a difficult habit to maintain, but virtually guaranteed a decent survey score barring other accidents. Today, they managed the route in 42 minutes and 46 seconds. Beckett was proud, despite not making 40.

"You just gotta aim high, that's what my survey tells me. Half-achieving an ambitious benchmark is almost always still quite impressive."

"Uh huh" Simon nodded, still recovering his breath.

"That's why, tomorrow, we really need to beat 35."

"Funny guy," Simon said between still-labored breaths.

Simon and Beckett spent their bus ride discussing matters of work, pausing only when they reached Simon's floor on the elevator. He performed his perfunctory sequence of morning greetings, reached his desk, and pulled up the subject list. His heart began to race.

Where yesterday he had fourteen subjects, today, he had two.

Phineas Burgh. Age: 41. Class: A. Role: Author. Rank:

268,209.

Gina Harshaw. Age: 36. Class: A. Rank: 311,520.

Simon breathed in deeply. *Two A-class subjects...no, not subjects. Clients. I have clients now.* It took a moment to allow the transition to wash over him. Work began the moment after.

He shifted his attention to Phineas first. Upon entering the recently archived data that Phineas possessed, he quickly found that there was far, far more to look over than there had been for any of his subjects. There was at least one camera in each room of the man's house from which Simon could draw footage.

Blood pressure fluctuation data was more precise. Muscular twitching and sweat production were similarly recorded and displayed with more than an order of magnitude greater scope and precision than any B-class interface had ever displayed. The sheer quantity of information Simon had access to began to overwhelm him.

He decided, for the time being, to ignore the physiological information, most of which would be analyzed algorithmically anyway, and looked into the man's recent authorial output. Upon pressing the panel that contained the man's recent writings, a prominently bolded memo blocked him.

This is not to be spoken of.

A space was provided below the text for Simon to write his signature.

He was instantly taken to the real-time draft of the novel Phineas was working on. The first page displayed the title: "The Life and Times of George Lackley."

The General. Simon felt his body shake with visceral excitement, and cursed his reaction as being too B-class of him. A few moments were all he needed to return his mind to a calm state, and he began to consider how he should best approach this elite new client.

George Lackey was a giant. The heroic winner of war had entered his thoughts, and his dreams, many times when he was younger. To be connected to him, even indirectly, was by far the greatest honor of his life.

Around the time of Simon's birth, there was to the south of the Citizenship a country called Mexico. It was a powerful nation, as far as nations back then went, and yet was conquered quickly when the time came. Although the Citizenship did have the more powerful military, the real reason for the expedient absorption of Mexico could be most attributed to two factors: the quasimatter bomb which vaporized all life in and around the capital city on the second day of the war, and, following that decisive blow and leading into the garrison efforts, the inspired leadership of the general George Lackley, who had so famously facilitated the decimation of Mexico City at the behest of the First-Citizen.

The general's Victories in the short war were assured from the beginning, but it had been remarked in Academy that a lesser general would not have been nearly so efficient in the consolidation of power, territory, and loyalty that this newly conquered country had to offer. His tactics were brutal, and yet, following the quasimatter decimation, which wiped over a tenth of the great nation's population in a single minute, he had to take an exceedingly small number of lives.

The lives he did take were tortured, strategically advertized, and above all, were taken with purpose. Mexico had since become the largest and most economically influential single province in the Citizenship, surpassing California, Texas, the plains, and Quebec. The general was offered a hero's retirement but had purportedly elected to continue serving and aiding the cultural integration of Mexico into the Citizenship for many years.

Simon considered this, and other details he'd learned of the general during his schooling. He realized he couldn't tell a single interesting story about any other military figure.

Moving on to the draft, he began reading what was written, hoping to discern any flaws in depiction or tone that might indicate the standard lapses in judgment or patriotism. He did not expect to find anything, and to his lack of surprise the prose was flawless. A-class citizens never attained their status easily. They were the lot of them masters of discipline and self-regulation. Their every breath was conducted inerrantly, stripped of hungry indulgence. Rumor had it that A-class citizens were such masters of their bodies that they were immune to both hiccups and sneezes. If this was at all an exaggeration, it was a slim one.

Phineas had completed four chapters, all about the general's childhood and years at the Westpoint school. Nothing had yet been written regarding the event that cemented his fame.

After over an hour of screening the man's text, Simon grew frustrated at the lack of even a possibility of a mistake and wrote a memo diplomatically expressing as much. If he didn't find at least one flaw in the entirety of the man's past daily conduct, he might not keep him as a client, so he spent the next hour combing the man's physiological data. His muscular, circulatory, and respiratory systems were a clockwork symphony. A masterpiece of anatomical usage more flawlessly conducted than anything Simon had ever studied. The ups and downs of activity matched with the man's physical actions on his keyboard exactly as they were meant to. To someone who had spent thousands of hours staring at real-time human physiological data, Phineas's display looked gorgeous.

He eventually found the smallest of incongruencies, an almost-laugh made while writing a sentence about the general's early friendship with the First-Citizen that itself might need to be rephrased, but most likely was fine. He contented himself with the useless observation and moved onto Gina.

He wondered who she was observing. Dealing with such

high-profile citizenry as psychologists tended to, the overseer-to-client ratio tended to become increasingly 1:1, so she might well have only one, or possibly two clients. Just like he now had.

Gina was slightly less flawless than her counterpart, but that she performed her job unquestionably better than Simon performed his similar one was immediately clear. Her motions bespoke effortless competence and unbroken immersion in whoever her subject was. His intuition watching her work was that she only had one client, although he wasn't shown who for some reason. Her heart rate fluctuated fractions of a BPM at select moments during her observation. Despite her best efforts at composure, Simon gleaned that something Gina was seeing was upsetting to her, something which might overtly disgust a lesser overseer. He wrote a short memo positing his theory and continued observing her for the rest of the day, occasionally switching over to Phineas to make interpretive notes about his workflow and slight changes in energy and circulation. He became increasingly obsessed wondering who the unknown client was.

The workday passed by in moments; the adrenaline accompanying the shift from B-class subjects to his first A-class clientele had quickened his perception of time. The task of finding flaws in infamously flawless people was exhausting, and he nearly collapsed into his desk when he was told to finish.

Soon he was bowling again. The activity had for a short time become the most electrifying experience of every day, as Simon first explored his ability and harbored the fantasy of using it to go pro, to bring Portland back to the forefront of the Citizenship Bowling League. The CBL required absolute silence during rolls, however, so the dream quickly faded, and Simon soon found himself saying "strike" and willing nothing to change, only allowing himself success every two or three rolls to avoid attention.

"So friends, I have news." Beckett said after striking. He'd broken a rather long companionable silence between them.

"Yeah?" Simon said.

"I'm going on a first date tomorrow."

"Nice. Wait, but you and Lydia…when did you separate?"

"Oh, a couple days ago. I was considering marrying her actually, but my survey decided we weren't ultimately compatible. Apparently she frequently fantasized about other men while we were together."

"I'm sorry. She seemed perfect for you."

"Yeah I know. Shows that what we think we know about people is all useless, I suppose." Beckett became contemplatively sad for a moment, then quickly displayed his usual radiant smile.

"But I'm excited to meet Chloe! I'm gonna take her to the activity center."

"Have fun," Charlie said, patting him on the back with surprising affection.

"That I promise. So Simon, when are you gonna date?"

Both friends faced him, just as he was about to roll.

"By year's end, probably." He said. It would probably be sooner.

"Well, once you do, we gotta go on a double date. Charlie over here has a new partner each month who we never see. You know you're my last chance." *Your survey encouraged you to suggest that, didn't it?*

"I promise, I'll take you on a double date. The four of us can play drone tag or something."

You're a romantic." Beckett said, entirely seriously. The trio resumed their round.

Truthfully, Simon knew he would be dating within the fortnight. Yesterday, upon returning home, he was promptly asked what he would consider to be an optimal venue for a first date, were he to theoretically go on one. The day prior, he'd been asked to painstakingly describe every feature he could think of that attracted him to women. The message was becoming clear: an official and irrefusable encouragement to date was imminent.

"Storm warning," Charlie spoke while reading a surface that usually displayed their game scores. Simon checked, and sure enough the display read *Storm Alert: greater Portland region at high risk. Be sheltered within 25 minutes.*

"Only for a decade or two more; by then I'm sure CERE will have it fixed," Simon replied tactfully. He had noticed that verbalizing every time he had a genuine positive feeling towards his government he could improve his score sporadically by a point or two, fortifying his ranking.

The Citizenship Environmental Recovery Effort had made the bold claim that it would "solve all storms" well over a decade ago, but, while emergencies were certainly less frequent and beginning to falter in their devastation, the problem would likely persist well into Simon's middle age. He figured if he had grandchildren they might grow up free of biweekly torrents of treefalling wind and rainfall, and trees might be brought back to the city.

"Either way, safety first. I guess I'll see you in two days." With that Beckett walked into the quickly forming crowd towards the buses, and his friends followed. Simon and Charlie had a genuinely interesting conversation about weather and how badly their parents and grandparents must have had it during the midcentury horror until the buses came and they parted ways.

A rain-drenched Simon was relieved to hear his first survey question of the night be about Beckett and any impressions he had regarding how his friend was handling his separation. The second question was why he'd scratched his feet 7 times today while at work. He'd felt that he had a slightly slow workday, and had feared being chided for having fewer insights. Fortunately, this survey continued to be merciful.

<<*Simon, why have you not been active on the national love registry?*>>

Caught by surprise at what was seemingly the most

important question coming at the end, Simon was kicked out of the passive autopilot he had shifted into.

"Well, I suppose I have been busy with work, which has taken up significant time and energy. I've been working to better myself and my first goal has been to do that through my work and lifestyle."

<<*A Valid answer. However, from a holistic analytical perspective, you have reached an optimal state to begin searching for sexual and romantic partners. Your singular most worrisome statistic at the moment is the duration of time that has transpired since your last sexual encounter, which is 6 years, 8 months, 11 days, 23 hours, and 2 minutes. Do you know the statistical average duration between sexual engagements for a Citizenship male of your age?*>>

"No"

<<*2 days 14 hours and 16 minutes. You are encouraged to achieve a similar average yourself. Goodnight.*>>

Simon received his score, 182, and his updated ranking, 3,878,365. He just needed to get to a million. Then he'd be A-class eligible.

With the survey's new ultimatum on his mind, Simon went to bed, and when he woke, unusually, he couldn't remember what he'd dreamt about, although he knew at least part of it involved women. That morning, he couldn't help but think about his ability, and whether he would ever understand it. He decided on his walk to the bus that if he avoided thinking about it for long enough it might fade into memory, and no longer feel like something that actually happened. *It doesn't matter. It wasn't real. Think about work.*

CHAPTER 6

"In your own words, please, tell me why this appointment was made." The psychologist asked. She sat across from Simon, wearing the obsessively neutral facial expression that was the trademark of most A-class citizens. Every word she spoke carried a highly curated emotion behind it, not a monotone, but not quite organic either. Her extensive wooden desk possessed a classical grandeur blatantly exceeding anything in Simon's department. The only other entity of note, and the desk's sole tenant, was a mysterious multi-colored cubic toy off to the side that triggered a blurred memory. Simon caught himself staring at it a moment too long.

"...That shouldn't be difficult to answer, even with wandering syndrome," the psychologist said when Simon failed to respond immediately.

"Of course, sorry, I was just thinking. I apologize."

"By all means. Some thought is encouraged here."

"Well, I'm sure you are aware, but yesterday I uttered the word 'fire' in my residence, alone, repeating a behavior I first indulged about three weeks ago. It felt like an innocent act of playfulness to me, although I recognize that this behavior was unjustified since the word wasn't spoken for a productive purpose."

"Well spoken." the psychologist said. Simon was annoyed that she had never offered her name, as though it would be wasted effort to do so. Of course, he knew it was Evelyn, but it still struck him as odd that he somehow wasn't worthy of the timeless act of name exchange.

"...I do however want to point out that this is, by definition, a recurring behavior now that it's happened twice. Any future occurrence, no matter how innocent, could be a sign of growing imperfection if you don't remain diligent."

Simon nodded in agreement, careful to make each nod seem entirely respectful.

"Of course, you are generally in excellent mental health, which is why this behavior is so abnormal. Otherwise there'd be no reason for a face-to-face. I have a few questions for you, that might help me clarify your condition such as it is. I'm sure that as an overseer yourself you'd agree with me that there's always a more fundamental cause to these things." She looked down to a wristband she wore and typed into it.

Simon glanced at the cube again. He couldn't hold his curiosity.

"I'm sorry, but can I ask what that is?"

"Oh, that." Evelyn didn't move her head.

"That's a rubik's cube. It's a one-player puzzle toy that I and some of my patients play with. I tend to specialize in wandering syndrome, and many so afflicted tend to be quite gifted at puzzles. I keep this one on my desk to see how long it takes for someone to ask about it, if they do at all."

"Was I not supposed to ask about it?"

"Ask, or don't. Either is acceptable. Asking about it reveals yourself. For most people who truly have wandering syndrome, it's the most interesting object in the room. A completely neurotypical male would focus his interest in me because, frankly, I'm attractive, and also hold a position of authority over you. Your interest in me feels like an act."

Simon saw that the elite form of overseer in front of him had the syndrome herself. She grasped the nature of a mind that struggled with indulging its ideas and curiosities, and understood how such minds craved a partner to dance with. She was, he suspected, about as intelligent as a person could be in the Citizenship without it becoming their greatest source of suffering.

"First off, before I ask my questions, I'd like to commend you on your recent efforts to further refine your life over the past few weeks, using even fewer microliberties than you are granted. Rest assured that your sacrifice hasn't gone unnoticed, and as of today there is no indication that you will be penalized in any serious way for your lapse, so long as it remains contained."

So long as I don't too seriously ponder what I know.

"Relating to this improvement though, why are you only now putting such a vigorous effort into molding your lifestyle to best suit the Citizenship? From what I've gathered, you've been capable of this level of commitment your entire adult life, yet haven't exercised it until now. Do you feel something was holding you back?"

Simon prepared to answer, using his detectable worry as a move in a game, hoping that it conveyed uncertainty at the answer without implying fear.

"I've thought considerably about this over the past weeks. I believe it took me having a day in my life where I truly faltered in my path of service to realize how unfocused I have been. I know there's no excuse for not doing all I can to serve my community and the Citizenship every waking second, but a month ago I was shown that there was more that I could offer, and I have been trying to do that every day since. I don't quite understand what prompted me to misbehave that day. I'll be grateful for any insight you have."

Evelyn seemed to appreciate the deference Simon offered her in his answer. He realized that, as an interactive psychologist, she represented the lowest tier of all A-class citizens, stuck precariously at the bottom rung of the highest level in an endlessly brutal social contest. Her rank was probably mid to upper 900 thousands, a dangerous place for an A-classer to sit. Meetings with B-class subjects like him were probably the only instances where she could extract deference from another person. He felt a tinge of sympathy for her, but still thought they should have exchanged names.

"An excellent answer. Precisely crafted, and exactly what your survey would have wanted to hear. You've swallowed your ego, and are willing to do whatever it takes to improve, the whole script. Quite excellent. However, I'm not the survey. I can't detect lies and deceit quite as well as it can, but I can guess when an answer is incomplete. You ask me to give your answers for you. Are you quite sure you don't already know why you spoke those seemingly absurd mantras three weeks ago, and again yesterday?"

Shit. Can I lie? Maybe one well-selected lie, followed by many half-truths.

"I really can't explain it. To me it was just playful and, as you said, absurd. A moment of weakness. It excited me. That's what it was."

"And that's all?"

"As far as I know."

This was pushing limits. He had all but lied directly to a psychologist. It took a new kind of virtuosity of self-regulation to keep his expression, posture, and hormonal balance inconspicuous. Even if he managed it here, he knew it wouldn't be a replicable success. The survey would learn what he was doing to mask his deceit, it would be documented, and his overseers would learn to recognize his faked nonchalance.

"As I said, excellent. How do you feel about your father? It seems pretty clear that his visit less than a month ago rattled you. I'm surprised you haven't mentioned him yet."

"I don't know how I feel about him now, after everything. He wanted me to leave my job to become a trucker."

"And you were tempted?"

"Yes. Well, for a moment I was." He could afford no more lies, even small ones.

"Why?"

"I thought maybe I'd be able to see my mother if I said yes. A silly fantasy."

"But also a valid one. Thank you for your honesty. Do

you think your relationship with your father, a man who, much like yourself, has been tasked with suppressing a degree of natural linguistic talent, helped fuel that first outburst?"

Simon realized he wouldn't have to lie. His meeting with his father probably was the actual unintentional catalyst that prompted his odd behavior and led to discovering his ability. That part of the truth was safe.

"Yes, I believe that he was the cause, subconsciously."

Evelyn elegantly nodded her head. She placed her hands on the desk, for the first time adopting an asymmetrical posture.

"Feel free to grab the cube. It's a delightful tease."

Simon couldn't tell if this was a test, but decided not to disobey. He leaned forward to grab the object, which held most of the room's color. He quickly found after picking it up that he could rotate the cube's sides with a satisfying *click*. He did so eleven times and saw how it would be difficult to restore if he didn't know the steps to backtrack. It took him over a minute to remember the eleven moves he improvised, and to restore the cube to its default arrangement.

"Well, that was easy," Evelyn said.

"What was?" Simon looked up and saw she was smiling. It was the same cerebral smile he made every time he discovered a new hidden tick of one of his subjects.

"The way you obeyed that suggestion. Once I told you that you could touch the toy, you saw an opportunity to explore an intellectually novel experience. And you did it with such little hesitation, despite years of cultural conditioning against such curiosity. Over ninety percent of my clients either don't want to pick up the cube, or they do but only rotate a single side once, then rotate it back. Forget what the half a terabyte of data collected on you says. This is the thesis of who you are. An explorer. A wanderer."

"I'm trying not to be."

"I know. But it's in your nature. Your curiosity will be something you will need to fight vigilantly for the rest of your life. Maintain your good vigilance, and bright things are in your future. Coming from a fellow professional, I promise your career is moving in a very promising direction." Evelyn smiled in a different way this time. The gesture seemed surprisingly genuine. He smiled back.

"You see? We psychologists aren't so terrible. So, why do you think you've been sexually inactive these past few years?"

Thought you'd never ask.

"Well, I have been very focused on my work, and maintaining a relationship has seemed like something that would take too much time and devotion. Also, you must know how my last one ended. Despite that, I've recently begun rethinking my stance."

Evelyn paused considerately. "That's good. You've remained celibate for, well, quite a long time," she said with unnecessary seasoning on "quite", an almost flirtatious tone she could never use on another A-classer. "Psychological effects of prolonged celibacy vary, but I'm quite certain that your episodic, too-playful, solitary verbalizations will cease once you have a partner. As such, my professional advice to you, and I'm quite confident other parties would agree," she said, tapping her headband pointedly, "is that you get yourself laid."

"That's your prescription? Some pills, and sex?"

"From what I can tell talking to you, that seems like all you need. If problems persist we might need brain scans, but I doubt that will be necessary. I know your last arrangement ended unfortunately, but I promise the survey will match you favorably this time."

The psychologist paused for a moment, seemingly deciding if she should say something else. *I think she's lonely too. She wants to comfort me, but can't.*

"You are free to go."

"Thank you, Evelyn" Simon said, with his own slight over-emphasis being placed on her name, not entirely unintentionally.

His headband buzzed its distinctive exit-approval pattern as he left. Returning to the elevators, he tried to spot other patients travelling the horizon-stretching hallways. He sensed he wasn't alone. Whatever was in the rooms just beyond sight, whose doors blended perfectly into the surrounding walls, he could only guess. The sparseness of the facility began to feel oppressing. Simon confirmed he had company when he reached the elevator.

A man, clearly a regular patient, wearing blue C-class coveralls, stood in front of the gleaming doors. He stood still, his face holding an absent, statuelike expression. That his eyes were open at all seemed entirely incidental, like he'd long stopped using them, but kept them exposed to air solely from the inertia of habit. A spider could have spun a web between his depressed eye sockets, and the man seemed like he wouldn't notice.

Simon recognized what medication this person was on. He'd seen its work in two others as a teenager, in this same building, the day he was given his wandering syndrome diagnosis. The man in front of him must have been hopelessly brilliant to require such a debilitating dosage.

The elevator chirped, and the two of them entered, the other man more slowly, seeming to find placid struggle in every act of motion. What terrified Simon was that he actually had no idea what the name of that medication was. For all he knew, the stuff he had just been prescribed was a smaller dosage of the same venom.

CHAPTER 7

Simon awoke to his alarm the next day feeling calm, and after he vanquished the morning monsters, he found the sensation worrying. He was unused to calm, especially during mornings, and reminded himself that he hadn't taken the medication yet. He continued to feel reservations about relaxants. Lucidly hyperawareness was necessary if he was to have any chance of finding the tiniest of cracks in his two perfect clients. He knew Charlie and Beckett had been placed on something last year, and it had seemed to enhance their focus. The distinctive purple cylinders they were contained in were becoming as ubiquitous to his culture as surveys and headbands had become a decade ago. He took his dosage; nothing changed. Perhaps it took an hour to dissolve.

With some practiced skill, he tore his mind from his anxiety and committed to seizing the day as a medicated citizen. He calculated he could deviate from his expertly-honed morning routine just the once, to take care of a particular piece of business he knew not to put off.

"House, pull up the registry of love submission form."

The house complied, and his kitchen island surface instantly lit up with the required page, evidently eager to be invoked for this specific purpose.

Simon went through the short form and filled it out. There wasn't much for him to add himself, since everything he could possibly write about himself and much more was accessible information to the love registry algorithms. He mostly had to sign consent forms and confirm he had a preference for a relationship with a stronger chance of high duration as opposed to low duration which would have been his preference if he were trying to maximize sexual activity. *As though these choices are mine to make.*

A minute later, Simon Pontius was activated in the registry and would be alerted upon the selection of a match.

Scrolling through his descriptors, Simon was mildly amused to note that the registry knew the exact size and shape of his sexual organ, despite him having never measured it. This stumped him momentarily, since there were no cameras in his house and doctors didn't look at such things without cause. He concluded that his headband had likely used bloodflow rates during periods of his arousal to somehow calculate the volume and shape of the appendage. He couldn't help but wonder how this particular piece of information might affect his success.

With the deviation from his routine completed, Simon dressed and spent his walk to the bus wondering who he would be assigned first. Partners, at least at the beginning, tended to be assigned and reassigned quickly, to efficiently gather data on what mutual characteristics would best optimize couples' productivity and happiness. After a few test relationships, one or two longer ones would be observed, followed by a childbearing match intended to be lifelong. Rarely, a perfect match was found the first or second try, although Simon doubted it would happen with him. Wanderers were statistically much tougher to match.

His thoughts drifted to work. After his psychologists appointment the previous day, he'd taken the rest of his day off and split his time between catching up on Citizenship news and starting a recent bestselling novel about a fictional invasion of Brazil. The book was actually quite suspenseful, despite the preordained ending.

He wondered if Charlie and Beckett thought that he had been relocated, and that they would be given a new bowling buddy. It wouldn't be the first time a friend was suddenly replaced, for any of them. Such substitutions were part of life. Walking into the dead air of the building lobby, Simon for the first time appreciated its familiarity.

He'd hoped to run into Beckett bussing in after his run, which he did meticulously at 8:55 each morning, but he appeared to be two minutes late. Simon decided he would message later to confirm bowling, and, returning to his office, ignored the surprised stares Penelope and Dustin gave him.

Simon settled back into his routine with Phineas and Gina. A welcome mistake was finally made by Phineas in the first hour of work, when he used a strange adjective in his chapter about the general's marriage which was technically correct, but unstraightforward. Infuriatingly, Phineas corrected the word choice before Simon could report it. He instead wrote a memo that he hoped would move the author's rank up by at least four hundred for efficient self-editing.

A new client notification surfaced on the desk. Simon hesitated before pulling up the file. His performance on his two A-class clients had clearly shown that he wasn't qualified to oversee elites. Perhaps he was being assigned back to Sarah. Overseeing her had always been easy and pleasant.

He clicked on the notification.

George Lackley. Age: 82. Occupation: retired general. Class: S. Rank: 4.

Simon's heart nearly palpitated. Sweat saturated him.

He made himself open the client dataset before he had a chance to think. This was a job. The identity or rank of the client didn't change anything.

The first image of George Lackley, the Citizenship's greatest military leader, that Simon received on his desk was of the man vomiting into a toilet.

He practiced keeping his good vigilance, ignoring the itching discomfort slithering under his skin at the visual. Not knowing what else to do, he wrote a short memo mentioning that the general might have made one or more poor dietary choices in the past 48 hours.

He exited the disturbing real-time footage and began

delving into the past couple days. Nothing got better. He found himself compiling and evaluating a list of six separate instances of the general barfing into one of the eight toilets in his home. Why a home would need multiple toilets was beyond his understanding. It also held six bedrooms, a palatial kitchen, and an extensive walled garden, all despite the general appearing to be living alone.

It soon became clear that the general never left his mansion. His time was spent sitting in one of the multiple fine couches his home possessed, consuming copious quantities of alcohol, and reading. Thanks to the three hundred chameleon cameras lining the walls of his house, Simon discovered he could see clearly both the front cover and text of everything the general read. His preferred literature was of the most horrid sort: pre-Citizenship.

The book the general revisited most often was called *The Things They Carried*. Simon scrolled through the footage of a camera situated high on a wall behind the general's favorite reading chair, and isolated images that he then zoomed in on. He did not know if he was meant to do this, to know what horrid words the man was reading, but he figured it was his job to try until told to stop. He had to admit to himself that the idea of pre-Citizenship literature fascinated him, even if it was repulsive.

Magnifying the camera image into the open book, he found the words on the page slightly pixelated, but readable. In fact, with enough effort, he realized he could probably go back and read every page using this method.

The book was worn to the point of damage and had visibly already been read through many times. The general kept no bookmark, but, according to footage, would turn to a seemingly random chapter, or even a specific passage, each time he opened it, and would reread, as though he knew the mantra he wished to extract from it at any given moment. When he wasn't reading this book, it occupied an exclusive perch next to an opened bourbon bottle on the floor directly in front of his favorite chair. No other book, Simon determined, was ever placed in this coveted spot.

Earlier today, he had turned to a particular page and held his finger under a passage he appeared to be reading again and again, the mantra to which he drank his bourbon. Simon read the passage along with him.

It was my view then, and still is, that you don't make war without knowing why. Knowledge of course, is always imperfect, but it seemed to me that when a nation goes to war it must have reasonable confidence in the justice and imperative of its cause. You can't fix your mistakes. Once people are dead, you can't make them undead.

Never before had Simon read such an insidious piece of text. This book was obviously written a long time ago, in a different world. The word choice, the implied opinions...the *audacity* to challenge the principle of top-down warmongering. It was all wrong. If Simon were the one reading this book, even this paragraph, he would lose his B-class status in a heartbeat. In a fearful moment of self-awareness, he realized he *was* reading this passage, and should stop immediately. As he thought this, he received a notification on his desk.

The books are not to be read.

This came from Jules, his boss. He abandoned all plans to investigate further. He instead explored the rest of the general's room, which held many other books with various titles. *Dresden. Animal Farm. Jack and the Beanstalk. Gallipoli. Oppenheimer. Napoleon. Apollo 13. One hundred years of Solitude. 1984. I have no mouth and I must scream.* Exotic titles stood out to him in droves on the general's bookshelf. The vast majority of the books the man had were about people and events predating the Citizenship. Most book titles alluded to events that Simon had no notion of; they took place either decades or perhaps even centuries ago.

It was clear that this man had committed many sins of knowledge in the reading of his books, books that were challenging, pointless, meandering, and whose final chapters failed to describe an unequivocal Citizenship victory He hated to admit it, but he had a hunger to read those forbidden texts, to learn what thoughts and emotions could be felt in times before the one he knew.

He killed this thought with another startling observation: the general did not look like he was in his eighties. He looked sixty, at most, even as he stumbled from room to room looking for unfinished bottles of vodka. Simon knew better than to bring this fact up in any report. That felt more off-limits than reading the books.

There ultimately wasn't much to say about the general. He had broken down, plain and simple. Simon couldn't possibly imagine what reason there was for inviting an unimpressively ranked overseer to witness the national hero's collapsed state.

After multiple hours of searching for redeeming qualities in the man, piling over oceans of data, there was little that Simon could find impressive, beyond his inexplicably healthy body and his literary repertoire. The memos he normally wrote recommending an increase or decrease in rank didn't seem applicable to the fourth-highest-ranked individual on two continents, so he bypassed that too. He reluctantly moved onto Gina.

A notification appeared on his desk surface, and things made a little more sense.

Gina also evaluates the general. Evaluate her accordingly.

So it was Both of Simon's new clients whose job centered around his third client. He sensed a web of complexity beyond his paygrade. The general likely had several overseers, for no other reason than his status as an S-class citizen merited the attention. Each of them, Gina included, likely had several B-class overseers like Simon to evaluate them, to ensure that their evaluations were objective. Whether all of those B-class overseers were also assigned to the general, Simon had no notion.

PENULTIMATE CITIZEN | 73

There might well have been hundreds, perhaps even thousands, of individuals, all watching the man through the same cameras, reporting their insights. That way, every single detail of the famed general's behavior would be guaranteed to be noticed and studied scrupulously from every perspective. The general, miserably alone in the confines of his huge home with his books and alcohol, was potentially the least private person in history.

He decided not to theorize any further, not wanting to feel the buzz pattern his headband usually gave after more than thirty seconds of distraction. He focused his mind on the task of studying Gina. She performed her job admirably that day, displaying less of the feeling of disillusionment that Simon now understood her to have had previously.

Perhaps she too had read a passage from *the things they carried* or one of the other awful books, and it had distressed her. Or she had seen the general crying, another activity he practiced daily. Phineas continued working on his biography, blissfully unaware that its subject had devolved into an unhappy free-thinking drunkard who for some reason was still being propped up by the state.

Simon finished his workday with bowling, intentionally striking every third or so roll, then went home. Since he was not exhausted just yet, he did not need to complete his survey, and so he commenced his relaxation by pulling up his kitchen surface to read about the news of the world.

He was reading an article about a particularly powerful hurricane striking the coast of Georgia when the distinctive ping of a high-importance notification made him stop. Surprised to see a message coming from the registry of love, Simon clicked on the symbol in front of him. The notification was what he thought it was.

Assignment name: Louisa. Gender: female. Age: 28 years. Height: 5'8". Education: University of Alabama, computational microbiology, graduate with distinction. Occupation: advertiser.

Rank: 77,421,876.

A photo came with it. She was attractive, beautiful even, in a slightly unconventional way. Her hair was curled and as dark as Simon's when dyed. Her skin was darker still, and even more stunningly, she had piercing eyes that seemed to dig into his soul. He found himself instantly fascinated with the image displayed in front of him. Simon was partially colorblind, and wished he knew for sure what color her eyes were, but he was certain that they were distinctive regardless shade. It shocked him that a seemingly desirable person could have such a dismal ranking.

Information shown about her was fleeting, leading Simon to begin wondering about her education, and how she ended up in a role most B-class citizens could easily learn in a few months of training. It must not have been an important role, given her unimpressive rank. Perhaps she did work in one of the labs and couldn't talk about it.

<<*Would you like to send a greeting?*>> The house asked.

"Sure."

<<*Excellent. Speak when ready.*>>

Simon paused and pondered. He decided he didn't really have much to go on, so he asked his question straightforwardly.

"Hello. Want to meet up somewhere?"

He cringed at his unoriginality, but more interesting words evaded him.

<<*Do you want to send 'Hello. Want to meet up somewhere?' to Louisa?*>>

"Yeah, send it." He could hear the bemusement in the computer's voice.

The message sent.

Seeking something to do while waiting for a reply, Simon returned to his book about the Brazil invasion. Before he could even get through a page, the reply came.

"Yes. Tomorrow?" popped up.

Well, At least she's as talkative as I am.

<<Would you like to reply? >> The house asked.

Want to meet tomorrow at 7:00?

A reply came less than a minute later.

Ok. You can pick the venue, I'm new here.

Alright. Coffee sound good?

Yeah.

Great! I'll think of a spot and let you know tomorrow. So, you're new to Portland?

Yeah. See you then!

Simon could think of nothing to resuscitate the conversation and hoped she hadn't expected him to. She might well already hate him, for being the puppet she was ordered to date when she might not have even wanted to. He hoped that wasn't true, but wasn't sure how prepared he would be for the opposite scenario; that she was a woman with her eyes set on courtship.

After his survey, which was uncharacteristically kind to him, Simon drifted off to an early sleep. As he lucid dreamed, he lazily created as dream characters at least a dozen different potential versions of Louisa, and interacted with her. None of her avatars seemed right.

CHAPTER 8

The cafe was the nearest one to Simon's work, and he walked there in under twenty minutes. He sat on a bench by the front entrance, his headband buzzing patterns into his head giving streamlined packets of news of the brave C-classers digging through feet of rubble in Georgia to rescue a team of B-classers, as the province's recovery from the latest hurricane was already underway. There were certainly more comprehensive sources of information, but there was merit to being forced to pay attention to every minute blip into his forehead to follow along. At first he didn't notice her arrival. She alerted him to her presence by standing two feet in front of him.

Louisa really was beautiful. But it wasn't quite the classical beauty that was so universally propped up on television. Her slightly neutral features created warm symmetries throughout her body, a kind of form that, while not overtly masculine, made her seem nearly as physically strong as Simon. Her eyes betrayed complexity, as though they were meant to be stared into, not at. He could only say that they were either green or blue, and assumed green.

"Hey Simon" she said softly and confidently. She spoke too softly. And too firmly. That should have been trained out of her at Academy. They stared at one another for an awkward second. Awkward for him at least. She seemed perfectly comfortable. Simon felt that he was being sized up, which made him even more awkward as he stood to his full height. Louisa smiled warmly and he instantly felt less nervous, but still confused.

"Hello." He managed, with miscalculated tracheal strain.

"Want some coffee?"

"Sure." She was confident.

Words which he normally felt to be always under his command had abandoned him, and he cursed his verbal slump while they entered. An employee led them to a square table near a window facing the plaza. Louisa stared at him with a bemused expression. In fact, she'd been distinctly facially expressive for the entire eighty seconds he had known her. Perhaps that was the source of her dismal ranking.

"So, Citizenship Coffee. Is this oversized box usually your first choice for a date?" She asked bluntly.

"Um, I guess. I haven't dated in a long time, so coffee seemed reasonable. I'm sorry, is this a bad choice?"

"Oh no, I'm not actually offended." She laughed.

"It's just not the usual choice is all."

"Hmm. Well In my defense, I haven't done this in awhile."

She laughed again. Her laugh was illegally expressive, which he hated to admit made it particularly attractive.

"Well, at least you didn't take me to the activity center." She continued.

"You know, that was actually suggested by my survey but... wait, do you visit the center often?"

Louisa rolled her eyes, another heretical enough act to distract Simon from her body. "It's the first place men usually take me. Their surveys always suggest it. It's safe for them, but one gets tired of it after the first couple first dates."

Simon felt revulsion. This woman just directly insulted an iconic Citizenship social establishment! She was unbelievable. She'd probably both of them relocated. He considered standing and leaving without a second thought, but found he couldn't take his eyes off hers.

"I've enjoyed it the few times I've been." he added hastily, hoping he would be spared later that night so long as he defended his country. Louisa held his gaze, her perceptive eyes displaying an apology, and put her hands up placatingly.

"Oh, the facility's great. It does what it's supposed to, with a surprising amount of panache, given who built it. I've just been there so many times, you know? I'm glad you're trying something old school."

Simon glanced behind them and saw the couple eating at the next table looking visibly uncomfortable. They were obviously listening. They got up and left a few seconds later, their meals unfinished. Louisa might have noticed, but she didn't seem to care.

"I thought going on a date that forced us to talk might be good." Simon said. "If this goes horribly, we know faster that we're not compatible and we can move on."

Louisa smirked. "A sliver of honesty. I knew there was some bravery in you. You're very considerate, but I think I'll stick around a little. I'm curious if you're hiding any other characteristics I'd like."

"There's really not much, I promise. You see everything you get."

"I very much doubt that. You have nice eyes by the way. They're shy, but they shine."

The same worker who showed them their table brought them two coffees, aligned to their registered custom ratio of milk to sugar. This drink held nothing to what his dad grew up with, but Sybil might have liked it. She'd have described it as "a pinch of cinnamon short of decadence." A minute later, they glanced up at each other. The unexpected eye contact electrified him.

"So what do you do Simon?"

Simon sipped his coffee again while attempting to ignore hormones stirring awake from a long hibernation, and considered what he could disclose.

"I'm an overseer. A few B and C-class subjects. Nothing special."

Louisa nodded. "Yeah, that's a lie. Fine, don't talk about it. I guess it doesn't really matter anyways."

"Do you usually accuse first dates of deception, or are you specifically targeting me?" He didn't mean to sound angry. Even his dad couldn't affect him like this.

"No, I'm sorry. I shouldn't have said that. I think I see why we were matched."

"Why?" Years of practice finally kicked back in, and allowed Simon to return control to his voice.

"Well, I'm supposed to tell you that I work in advertising. I have a specific role, entertaining work stories, absolutely real coworkers, the whole deal. Fun little creative exercise, writing it all out. I could publish a book about it."

"I see. Maybe we don't need to talk about work, then."

"Maybe not. Although, I have some fun stories that I legally have to say are true, about ads I've purportedly had to censor, should we return to the topic."

"Intriguing." Simon tried thinking of a creative diverting question. "So, what do you do outside of work?"

How are all of my questions so dull?

"Hmm. I guess it depends on my mood. I eat, sleep, fuck, exercise, so all the usual stuff. I read old novels on occasion. Oh, and I enjoy origami."

"That word sounds foreign."

"All words are foreign. But you're not wrong. It's an old Japanese tradition of folding paper in intricate ways to create all sorts of beautiful shapes. Have you ever folded a paper airplane?"

"Yeah actually. I think my parents taught me not long after I learned to walk. Aren't they illegal now?"

"Well then, you and origami have already met. And it's entirely legal, and a great hobby to have. It annoys my sister. Annoyed my parents. Let's just say, if my family ran the Citizenship, origami would be a capital crime."

"Annoyed?"

"Oh, nothing like that, they're still alive. We're just living apart right now. They distracted me from my work even more than folding orchids did, if you can believe it."

"I'm sorry." He was surprised to find he really did feel sorry for her.

"Eh" she shrugged. "We can still call. It could be worse."

"Yes, it could." Simon agreed. Louisa wavered a little. She looked like she wanted to ask. He hoped she wouldn't.

"So, origami. Is it difficult to learn?"

"Not really. But near impossible to master. Or so I'm finding. When I have paper I can show you some easy folds that you could learn in a single session."

"That sounds like a second date."

"Yeah, I suppose it does."

"So, what kind of origami does an experienced folder go for? I imagine there are many possibilities."

"Oh, you have no idea. The viable permutations of folds are practically infinite."

Louisa began to talk enthusiastically about the plethora of different shapes that could be arrived at, from simple boats, planes, and hats up to more complex flowers, insects, and animals, to the geometric modular folds both stunningly intricate yet also minimalist in their profound symmetries. An entire artistic world opened up in Simon's mind as the woman across the table continued talking. He asked questions, his fascination deepening for an artform he had never seen.

"Make me something." Simon said, and passed her his untouched paper napkin.

"Here in public? Huh, you're braver than I'd have guessed."

She playfully took the napkin from him, her finger brushing his for a half a second, and he watched her work with rare focus. *Does this really make me brave?*

"Et voila" Louisa revealed her finished product.

"It's a plane?"

'Yeah. Go on, test it."

"Here?" Simon asked. Louisa nodded giddily. He took the flimsy plane and gently tossed it off the table. It traveled six feet.

"Not bad, right?"

Simon nodded. He grabbed it before someone saw.

His headband buzzed the curfew alert. Looking outside, he noticed that it was already getting dark.

"Wow, we've been here awhile. Crazy." Louisa remarked.

"Yeah, crazy. We should go."

The only other customers had left ten minutes ago, and Simon suspected that the poor server was ordered to stay for the two of them.

"You know, my place is actually walking distance from here. I mean, if you don't want to go all the way back to yours." Louisa said.

Simon gulped. His blood began warming again.

"I appreciate the offer. But I should really be heading home. I need to be at work early tomorrow, for something, and I don't know how rested I'll be at someone else's place."

"I get it. No pressure. Until next time, then." Louisa looked up at him, and leaned in. They kissed.

Simon made it to the bus in something of a daze. Louisa's existence seemed impossible. Every sentence that exited her mouth was treasonous in one way or another. Insulting the Citizenship. Rolling her eyes. Saying illegal words like "Damn" and "Voila". Talking openly about an unencouraged artform.

Although she didn't explicitly say it, she'd clearly been forcibly relocated. And yet, she acted as though she were immune to punishment. It made no sense. She should be dead, or incarcerated. The only explanation he could think of was that she had some irreplaceable talent making her so uniquely indispensable. He felt guilty joy knowing that someone like her might exist, uncommon as she was.

Inevitably he again thought about his unexplainable abilities.

He was on the shore of an ocean, and couldn't bring himself to sail. His headband was a prison. For the hundredth time, he cursed his father for having filled his young head with metaphors, analogies, and all the other snares of language. He wished he hadn't internalized them so well.

All the same, he couldn't deny the aptness of the metaphor. The situation was tantalizingly unsolvable. It seemed that all he needed to do was imagine a worldly process, be it a snap, hum, or burning flame, then encapsulate the process in a word, uttering it many times, and his capacity to execute said process would develop, extending with each attentive utterance. He knew he could create sounds, crack porcelain, sustain an orb of subdued, embered flame, like some wizard from the censored tales of a long dead generation. He wondered if perhaps he had hundreds of microscopic abilities; if every word he'd ever spoken had granted him some vanishingly insignificant capability too minute to ever notice.

He realized that, in the hormonal storm Louisa had prompted, his mind was put into a relatively unmapped state, leaving the relationship between his blood flow rate and his thoughtpatterns less than perfectly predictable. He had an opportunity of perhaps a couple minutes to more properly think about his abilities where his thoughts probably wouldn't be recognized as the treasonous wanderings they were.

As the bus came nearer to Simon's stop, his two streams of thoughts organically converged onto a single interesting question: How would the unexplainable Louisa behave, if she'd discovered the unexplainable ability in herself? Would she have reacted to it differently? How would she have discovered it? Once she did, what would she try that he hadn't considered?

Where Simon was drawn to sound initially, he suspected that an origami master might be more pulled by images, folds, three dimensional structures in space. Perhaps she would have tried uttering "light" or "beam", in an attempt to pull light patterns out of the air, or craft intricately unique holographic forms that could mold into rich varieties of appearances. Was he even capable of influencing light like that? Perhaps the better question was, what could he *not* learn to do, given enough time? Certainly there had to be limits.

The bus reached its destination, and as Simon walked

on the mirror-way towards his house, the neighborhood lamps lending just enough of their luminosity to guide him, Simon shifted his mind fully into survey mode. Following his recent high score streak, he braced himself. New life experiences always led to unpredictable surveys.

Simon initiated the survey within five seconds of entering his home.

<<*Hello Simon*>>

Simon took his seat.

<<*Question 1: How do you feel about your date tonight? Give adjectives.*>>

Simon paused briefly but quickly discerned that he wasn't meant to think long for this question. "Electrifying, engaging, unexpected, intriguing, informative, effervescent." His father had taught him that last word when he was six. It was one of those words that stuck in his mind, and seemed to surface at the oddest moments. Words always held a strange wonder to Simon's father, even the useless ones.

<<*Interesting set of words; atypical, but to be expected from you. Let's focus on 'unexpected'. Question 2: what about your date was unexpected?*>>

"Louisa herself. I've never met any woman like her. The way she spoke, what she spoke about, it was…contrary."

<<*An agreeable answer. Question 3: You displayed significantly heightened testosterone and cortisol levels, as well as a notably accelerated heart rate tonight, reaching numerous relative maximums during moments of direct physical contact with Louisa. Why did you not pursue intercourse with this woman?*>>

"Well, I had just met her, and haven't intercoursed in six years, not since Sybil. So there was fear. Louisa herself was off-putting, and I wasn't sure if a sexual relationship with her was wise. I was obviously attracted to her; my hesitation had nothing to do with that ."

<<*A Logical answer. However, a sexual relationship is at this time encouraged. Question 4: What is your impression of*

Louisa, based on all knowledge of her? List adjectives. >>

Simon sensed a difficult question approaching, an intuition which was usually not wrong. "Expressive, Funny, inquisitive, intelligent, playful, educated, attractive, I think sensual, I think extroverted but I'm not really sure yet."

<<*Confirmation: Louisa possesses a libido one standard deviation above the norm and could thus be characterized as "sensual". Correction: Gathered data shows Louisa to be an introvert. Her engagement with you conversationally is a statistical anomaly.*

Question 5: You characterized Louisa as being an 'expressive' individual just now. Could you elaborate? >>

Simon's intuition tugged harder. This wasn't the tough question, but there was certainly a way to answer it incorrectly that could hurt him. Some vast intelligence lurking behind the survey seemed to be baiting him, to see if he would admit the obvious fact both parties knew to be true.

"Well, she is very curious about things, and doesn't seem to mind asking people questions about subjects that don't directly pertain to her. She also has many opinions, which she shares generously."

<<*Louisa is a high-value individual within the Citizenship, and as such has certain immunities that are allotted to a highly select few. However, these immunities have limits in their scope, limits which Louisa often pushes, to her detriment. It is highly discouraged that someone with her privileges abuse them as she has. Question 6: What can you do, as her current partner, to mitigate Louisa's flawed speech patterns?* >>

Here it was. Simon shuddered ever slightly but kept his composure, hoping that the survey would respond well to him feeling a degree of anxiety and subsequently demonstrating control over it.

"I honestly am not sure how I can help her. I'd appreciate any insight you have, but…I suppose I could point out positive aspects of the Citizenship to her, such as the meteoric increase in our living standards coming out of the midcentury horror, and how we're sharing this elevated standard with Australia. And the work being done to restore ecosystems that were once thought irreparable. Maybe if I bring these facts up organically, I can help her be reasonable."

An unprompted mental image of Louisa playfully creating twin orbs of flame atop her breasts appeared in his mind's eye which he regrettably had to discard.

<<*An agreeable answer, albeit an optimistic one. You are nonetheless encouraged to try this tactic on your next date, and any that follow. Further suggestions will be given in due time. Question 7: How is your oversight of George Lackley progressing?*>>

"It's challenging, but it has become easier. Getting used to observing his lifestyle has been uncomfortable for me, since this man is, justly, idolized by the nation for his actions. But I have a job to do and I am determined to do it as well as I can."

<<*Nearly an agreeable answer. A point remains unaddressed, however. Question 8: Do you believe that the general's lifestyle is a wrong one?*>>

It dawned on Simon that the era of easy survey questions was coming to a close. He had A-class clients. He was no longer so far distant from consideration for entry into A-class himself. His answer to any one question could halt the advancement of his career.

"I think that his behavior shouldn't be emulated. However, he is an S class citizen, so perhaps his actions have a purpose beyond my understanding." His heart beat percussively against his ribcage.

<<*An agreeable answer.*>>

The survey fortunately became less tense after this point, with Simon drifting closer to his autopilot flow state that he much preferred to be in while answering questions. Six additional questions on more specific matters were asked, and once he was given his score of 189 and his new rank of 2,924,512, his fatigue caught up to him in a single slumping wave.

The next day, Simon tried to submerge himself in his work as he had done feverishly over the past few weeks, but found that some ineffable cognitive gear had shifted, his usual insights evading him. He wished instead to sit lazily and think about Louisa, and fantasize about what they might do together when they next met. For once he found it easy not to think about his ability.

CHAPTER 9

The following Saturday, a dangerously tempting thought occurred to Simon that he couldn't get out of his head. It occurred to him while running with Beckett, which continued to be the second most unpleasant event of every day, just behind the morning monsters. It was a ritual he wished he could have some agency against, but, just as it had been with bowling, once he started, it became impossible to stop without wrecking his survey score. If he missed even a single miserable morning sludging through three miles of cold wind, his career windfall could reverse in an instant.

His idea involved his ability. He frequently wondered if it did more than create sounds, cracks and flames. Maybe it was far more generalized, and could be used to somehow enhance biology. Specifically, his own ability to run without discomfort. The more he thought about it, the more far-fetched the notion seemed, but after a while the fantasy of a painless run became impossible to ignore.

"Careful!" Beckett shouted, a second and a half before a distracted Simon's left flank nearly collided with a light post.

"Are you ok?" Beckett asked.

"Yeah, just a little distracted."

"Oh, well. That wandering syndrome will really get ya, won't it?"

Simon nodded and smiled, suppressing his growing disdain for the term. He tried spending the rest of the run thinking pure thoughts, but found that the notion of trying to augment his stamina to lessen his screaming discomfort was too tantalizing. It worried him that this thought was exerting such a visceral pull on his body, as though it was convincing not only his mind, but every fiber of his skin, muscle, and bone to want to act on the impulse.

"38 minutes, not half bad!" Beckett expressed through his fatigue after they stopped. It was a minute better than yesterday.

"You know," Beckett said, "I was wondering if maybe you want to try doing the hill route where we turn right at the intersection?"

Simon died a little on the inside at the suggestion of a kilometer increase, but, in an instinct that stemmed more from trained loyalty than any desire for self-improvement, "yeah, that's a great idea." came out of his mouth.

He immediately regretted this choice, despite it being the only one.

In the public locker they had run to, and on the bus back to their building, Beckett was quite talkative, mentioning, more than once, his interest in meeting Louisa. Simon decided to withhold most of what he knew of her, which inevitably made his friend more curious.

Work was pleasant that morning. The general was actually almost sober today and, to Simon's amusement, began emotionally singing a song he recognized as the national anthem of the Citizenship's predecessor, and one of the songs he had sung when discovering his ability. *I have to stop thinking about this.*

A crew of nine workers had been at the building since dawn working to install the next generation of solar panels on the roof, as part of a continent-wide effort to decentralize the physical sources of power away from the small number of fusion and quasimatter centers that had kept basic infrastructure running since the midcentury horror.

The motivation was of course to protect the nation's energy supply from a concerted invasion attempt, which seemed a little unnecessary to Simon seeing as there hadn't been a single successful affront of any sort on the Citizenship in the past two decades. He hoped their modest cafeteria wouldn't overflow from the extra humanity.

Simon and Beckett were lucky that Charlie had come in just late enough that morning to notice the truck, and know that they would have to hurry to get good seats the moment lunch break began. C-class citizens, unlike their B-class counterparts, didn't have to worry about where they sat. Simon hurriedly got in line to grab soup, his thoughts returning to deciding which word could theoretically be used to help his running, when someone tapped his shoulder.

Turning around, he saw his childhood friend Frank Robbins, sporting blue coveralls the same as the rest of the installers. Save his face, the man was scarcely recognisable from their old schoolyard days, nearly twice as tall and half as wide as Simon remembered him. Frank, he recalled, had been a particularly valued lazer tag partner of his. They both smiled.

"Simon?" Frank said with surprise the moment they locked eyes. "Remember me? It's been an age!"

"Frank! How's it been?"

"Great, really great. Our crew's been busy, but I can't complain. It's great work!" Simon nodded in assent, slightly jealous at how enthusiastically Frank could execute his fed lines.

"That's wonderful. What you're doing is important, and we're all grateful."

Frank looked around the room, its seats now three-quarters full. "So what do you even do here? Something to do with writing or editing or some sort? You were gonna be a writer, right?" Simon told him they were overseers, hoping he wouldn't ask too many further questions. "Oh, interesting" Frank said, sounding politely unwilling to talk of it further. They collected their soup.

"Hey, Frank, you're welcome to sit with us. We have that corner over there staked out." Simon said, not knowing if it would help or hurt his score.

"Well that's very kind. Are you sure it's ok?" Frank asked, unsubtly referencing what they were both thinking. Simon suspected that sitting with a C-classer might be taken as a particularly large microliberty, but would be condoned as an isolated event. "Yeah, come, sit with us." Simon guided his old friend to Beckett and Charlie, and introduced everyone.

"Man, it's really been ages! I wasn't sure you'd even recognize me, what with the weight."

It was true; Frank was definitely much thinner than Simon remembered. In fact, he was respectably muscular.

"You see, they finally released a purple pill to solve weight. I bet you already knew that, it made the news and all. Oh how our society has improved, even since we were kids. It's unbelievable."

Frank was perceptibly nervous, having barely even glanced at Charlie or Beckett. He was probably close to B-class eligibility. People in that position tended to give too many compliments.

"So you and Simon were at Academy together?" Charlie asked.

"Oh yeah, we were mates for like three years. I swear, he was the most talkative kid I ever did meet. We went to a rally together this one time, and this legendary child would shout the First-Citizens praises at the top of his lungs for minutes at a time without stopping. I must say that's not a passion I was able to learn for my great country and the First-Citizen until later in life. This guy really helped inspire me."

"Is that so?" Beckett said incredulously.

"I'm learning all sorts about my friend today. So Frank, tell us more about this person I thought I knew." Frank turned to Simon, who reluctantly nodded approval. He then regaled the group with more stories from Academy.

"He's always been a model patriot. You couldn't say a damn thing against the Citizenship without him screaming disloyalty."

"Nowadays it's tough getting one sentence out of him."

Beckett said.

"That right?" Frank mirrored Becket's earlier disbelief.

"Well, we all mature in different ways. Those reserved types are usually the most loyal anyways. Maybe I should try talking a bit less, see if that puts my rank up a bit." Frank chuckled and the others joined in for his sake.

The awkward silence following this was punctuated by Charlie. "Simon, I hear you're with a woman now."

Beckett perked up like a gunshot before Simon could parse together a reply. "He most certainly is, and I'm quite certain he's hopeless for her. So when do we meet your match?"

Simon blushed, and realized that a blush had been what gave him away to Beckett in the first place. The downside of having an inexpressive face, it seemed, was that even the slightest slip was assumed to betray cataclysmic emotion.

"I'm meeting her again tomorrow, and after that, who knows? If we keep dating, Beckett, we can arrange that double date you're after." He admitted he enjoyed dangling Louisa in front of them, as the mysterious siren who had managed to awaken their dormant colleague. Mostly he just appreciated the excuse to think about her.

As he returned to his desk, he seriously debated whether he should tell Charlie and Beckett he had A-class clients. It was the steepest career jump of his life, and he hadn't told a single living person. He wanted his friends to express pride.

But, if he shared with them, they would assume that their time with him was coming to an end. That their friend, who was being ushered to a new level of success, was marked for relocation to a new building meant for people who oversaw at such a level, where he would be introduced to two new people to go bowling with each evening. That was how friendship worked. If Simon told them, they would distance themselves from him preemptively. And they would be right to.

Later that afternoon, the Australians were introduced

to the system. An alert went to each of the roughly three million overseers across the country, indicating that sufficient preliminary data had been collected on about a quarter of the new population to justify their integration. All overseers, regardless of their clientele, were to assist with the sudden influx. Simon spent the rest of the day looking at snippets of footage and headband data of Australians in a city called Melbourne. The idea of working with Australians was exciting, but the only interesting thing about it was the strange accent people spoke with, and the fact that they all were blatantly uncomfortable wearing headbands.

During the last hour, things escalated when one younger man assigned to him tore off his headband after getting home and started screaming at it. *"This is bullshit! You're a band of wanking scum who shoulda stayed in your hell! My grandparents used to fucking think that..."* Simon stopped listening and marked the man for arrest, then wrote a memo recommending him a temporary rank of about a hundred and five million, the lowest he ever suggested. He wondered if Australia had been a democratic country prior to the invasion. He cut the wandering thought short and moved onto sorting more people, giving all but one of them rankings lower than Sarah's.

It was on his walk home that Simon decided on what word he would utilize if, and only if, he were to try and use his ability to make jogging easier. He doubted it would have the effect he hoped it would, but even so, having the word jostling around in his head only worsened the temptation to try.

CHAPTER 10

His second date with Louisa was also at a coffee shop, despite the survey's unsubtle mentioning of the activity center as a wise option. Louisa had sounded like she didn't much enjoy the activity center, and he figured he could take her there later if the survey kept insisting. He instead decided to take a slight risk, and have her meet him at Tony's. The venue was ninety minutes out from the downtown, but it offered something that could not be found nearly anywhere. It still used archaic paper menus. Food was baked in-house, and, while it adhered to Citizenship standards, it was actually flavorful.

Entering through the door, the first thing Simon noticed was the scribbled and torn wood tables that, in their imperfections, gave a homey vibe that had been sterilized almost everywhere else. This was where he would have wanted to take his father, if his visit a month ago had not been so obviously a loyalty test. The waiter showed them to a table outside, granting them a lovely view of the garden that Tony's cafe agreed to maintain as part of its contract. Simon ordered a frappuccino, while Louisa went with a Cappuccino. His mouth watered in anticipation.

"It's nice here." Louisa said.

"Yeah."

A comfortable silence ensued.

"So, how's work?" Simon asked. He still wasn't sure how to talk to her.

"I love how brave you are. Nobody asks me that, especially on date two. Technically I'm not supposed to talk about it."

"And in practice? You can't even tell me if it's going well?"

"Due to the nature of my job, it's going well whenever I don't have to do it."

A pleasurable breeze swept over the two of them. Simon broke eye contact with her to stare off into the garden. She hadn't sounded defensive, but didn't seem interested in giving details. The plants were beautiful, to someone who hadn't seen them since last spring. He turned back to her and tried frantically to think of something different to talk about, that wasn't plants.

"You're kind of intense," she said.

"I am? I thought you didn't want to talk about work."

"I don't. But the few people brave enough to ask at least have somewhere to pivot. You just stopped talking and stared at the garden like some stoic philosopher."

"I don't know what that is."

"That's because you've probably never read anything pre-Citizenship before."

Simon's horror was covered by the waiter arriving with their drinks. Once they were reasonably alone again, he looked at her.

"You've read pre-Citizenship literature?" He whispered. "How?"

She laughed. "You're so cute when you're terrified. But don't be. I'm not about to be arrested, and neither are you."

"How do you know? Have you done this before?"

"Yeah." she said. "Although, second dates are rare for me. I scare people off."

"I can't imagine why."

"Sarcasm? Stop being so brave, you might excite me."

Simon didn't have a smart reply, so he took a sip of his frappuccino. Louisa mirrored.

"Wow, it's actually flavorful here. Thanks for showing me this place." She said.

"Don't mention it."

"I wonder how long they have before they get closed."

"How do you mean?"

Simon did know what she meant, although he wouldn't say. This place, beautiful as it was, reminded customers too closely of the country their grandparents lived in before the midcentury horror. The charming rustic aesthetic, the garden, the locally produced food that didn't taste like it was sprouted from machinery, all marked this place for death.

"You know exactly what I mean. I just saw it in your eyes. You don't have to pretend."

"Alright, fine. I know what you mean."

"I have a theory actually," she continued, "that future historians are going to call this specific time we're living in the "great consolidation", or some such variant. Think about it: in the past fifteen years, how many smaller businesses that were propped up after we moved out of midcentury have there been, that got absorbed into one of a small collection of nationalized chains?"

"Like 'Citizenship Coffee' and 'Citizenship Theater'" Simon said.

"Exactly. Some businesses simply ran out of money, sure, but many of them must have been outright encouraged to assimilate, even if they were doing well. And almost nobody says no to an encouragement from their survey. My parents traveled a couple times, back when people could just do that when they wanted, and they say life everywhere has definitely gotten better since our childhoods. At least the places they've seen. But our cities, towns, and neighborhoods changed so much. It's all becoming varying patterns of the same five or six shops in the towns, the same two or three types of houses in the neighborhoods, that same exact type of megabuilding in the cities."

"I know those buildings. They're all recent."

"Everyone does. I guess that's my point. What's worse is, now that resources are finally flowing back in, rare metals and all that, I think the plan is ultimately for everyone to live and work exclusively in the megabuildings. Just imagine, entire life spans being lived without ever leaving the facility you were born in. Our nation is evolving. The great consolidation. That's what I'm calling it."

Simon stared at her silently. He disliked speaking when he had nothing to say, and had nothing to say. He remembered his assignment given by the survey, to try and win Louisa over to respecting the Citizenship. He wasn't sure he could do that, when he just learned that he might be spending the second half of his life never seeing the sun again.

It'll become my turn to be the older generation that can't adapt.

"Louisa, you might be right, but as lovely as places like this are, and as happy as I am that you like it, this is a dying relic for a reason. I'm sure that, if the Citizenship wants to simplify cities into living and working quarters in such a manner, it's well justified. The First-Citizen wouldn't plan something without excellent cause."

Louisa looked at him pitifully. She must have known that he was put up to defend the Citizenship to her. He wondered with terror if she would bring up the First-Citizen's age, the most taboo of all topics.

"You're probably right." She said, "He must have had an excellent reason for designing pedestrian walkways with a frictionless reflective polymer that makes it impossible to build neighborhoods in hilly terrain and causes people to trip at the slightest of missteps."

"Can we talk about something else?" Simon asked. He didn't want to, but he simply didn't know how to argue that point, and saw no benefit to muddling through a weak defense.

"Sure. Hey, wanna walk through the garden?"

Louisa got up and Simon followed her, frappuccino in hand, outside through a gravel walkway and up to rows of tomatoes, basil, berries, and other plants he didn't recognize. The smells held a richness long forgotten. His hand reached out to Louisa's and grabbed it gently. He saw her smile in the corner of his vision, and felt her interlace her fingers with his.

They walked through the garden together. They talked about small things. What each other's mornings were like (Louisa's were better). What they did with their coworkers after hours to socialize. The places they'd been taken when they were younger, and could never return to. The plants in the garden. Plants, it turned out, interested her a great deal, and she knew the scientific name of every species Simon didn't recognize. On their third lap around she listed them all. They talked about their days in Academy, the friends they made, where those friends were now, what their favorite foods were, their meetings with psychologists (Louisa had such meetings regularly). She thankfully avoided the especially heavy conversations. Simon sensed as she spoke that she wanted to have them, but was refraining out of kindness. Or at least, she was easing him into it. He was thankful regardless. They went back into the cafe and ordered bread. The fresh-baked crust was the height of luxury.

Before they knew it, over two hours had passed. Simon eventually indicated that they should start heading to the bus to return to the city.

"Wait, before we get on, I really do want to talk about something." Louisa said as they walked.

"We just were."

"We were getting used to each other. That's not what I mean." She insisted.

"Alright."

"Look. Let's get this out of the way. I'm a scientist." She paused to consider her next words.

"I'm a brilliant one. I'm not saying that to boast, it's just true. The work I do is highly stressful, and highly creative in nature. And to do it well, I can't live like you. Having to modulate my every word and thought to appease a survey, getting out of bed in a precisely choreographed way each morning and worrying about my ranking if I take too many seconds and stupid fucking microliberties in every little thing I do, all of it takes away my edge. I'm not trying to disrespect you. I understand that you've been forced to live like that. But if I live that way, I become too hyper focused and lose my perspective. Also it makes me even more miserable than it makes you."

"It doesn't make me miserable." She shook her head and went on.

"I'm one of the only people in the Citizenship with that excuse, since my work is critical for its protection. So they let me be, mostly. They hate me for it, but their hands are tied. And the closer someone gets to me, the more of my privileges they get to share. So here I am, here you are." Her face revealed a vulnerability he hadn't seen in her before.

"I see you. You're brave. And you're aware of what's happening to the world around us. And I really like you, and want to see where this goes. But going forward, if you want to be with me, I want to be able to have honest conversations about this country we're living in. Conversations that would get most people deported."

She grabbed both of his hands and stared at him almost pleadingly. He realized three things then. The first was that Louisa, despite all her outward confidence, was a very lonely person. His intuition told him she had never gotten this far with someone. He secondly realized that he was equally lonely. And thirdly, he really wanted to talk shit about the Citizenship.

"Alright. I like you too. I want to try this. But..." He added before she could reply.

"I want to know what your job is, specifically. Just give me something. That seems fair."

She hesitated momentarily. "Alright. I'm a virologist."

They got on the bus, and spent the ride holding hands and talking about a hundred unimportant things.

CHAPTER 11

"Further" Simon jutted out of his lungs.

"Huh?" Beckett asked.

"Further," he said again.

"Yeah…this new route's longer. I know. We got this."

"Further," he said again. Pause.

"Oh now I get it…It's like 'strike'. Further!" he shouted.

"Further" Simon replied.

"Further."

"Further."

"Further."

Simon and Beckett began a one-word conversation. For Beckett at least the affirmation helped, and he led the two of them on the most intense run of either of their lives. Simon held a very specific goal in his mind. Each time he said the word he tried to feel as much of the aching in his body and stress on his lungs that he could bear to focus on, and willed his body to grasp for immunity to it. A half-hour later, the run ended. Nothing felt different.

"Further."

"Further"

"Further."

The next day, Simon and Beckett repeated the ritual. Beckett was a beautiful conversationalist when his vocabulary was limited to a single word. Still sore from the previous day's intense run, Simon held his goal in his mind even more vividly, trying to strengthen it each time he spoke. His goal became more vivid, but he didn't think he felt any changes. If there was any alleviation whatsoever, it was, as his father would have said, a balloon hoisting a cathedral.

"Further." "Further." "Further."

"Further." "Further." "Further."

"Further." "Further." "Further."

It took three more days before Simon noticed anything. He initially wasn't certain, but he felt that his aching was slightly less And his heartbeat didn't reach quite the crescendo that it had been hitting up until then. If running typically pushed him to a misery of one hundred, that day he went to ninety-five. Natural conditioning may well have been the only cause.

By the end of the week, he was down to about eighty. and he began to notice that he no longer had trouble keeping up with his more athletic colleague. By the end of the second week, he was actually starting to push Beckett's speed envelope, and he found himself too exhausted to hold a conversation after their runs. Simon no longer ached during or after, and found he needed far less time to recover his breath.

By the third week of shouting "Further!", he now had to be careful to not race ahead of his colleague. He could maintain a brisk running tempo, he suspected, for hours, or at least until he got hungry, and his heart rate would hardly elevate. He had no idea how he had accomplished this, but he now felt faint reverberations through every cell of his body each time he said the word, as though he were chanting an ecstatic prayer. He wished dearly that these reverberations wouldn't be detected, and quite amazingly they weren't.

In his efforts to enhance his body, he was still nearly discovered. During the fourth week, he was held back from a night with Louisa and commanded to take a bus to the Portland Medical facility for a checkup. He was examined closely by a young doctor with a severe face who wordlessly sent him into a scanner. Simon didn't know what it would find. The entire time he shouted "Further", he'd intently envisioned that any improvement that was made to his endurance would be camouflaged.

He registered as being stressed during the scan, but that was attributed to previously undiagnosed claustrophobia, as the stark interior of the machine pressed into his limbs. His mother had also been claustrophobic. He was let go and told to return the following month.

Running wasn't the only enhancement Simon toyed with, merely the first. He was clearly perilously close to exposure, but couldn't resist exploring at least some of the seemingly infinite possibilities. It was starting to feel like he could cast a prayer for just about anything, given time.

He nonetheless reaffirmed that he would not negotiate on subtlety. Dozens of ideas occurred to him over weeks, many of them conceptually enthralling. And yet, precious few of them could practically be attempted under nearly omnipresent headband observation. The abilities that he could safely attempt were mundane and unambitious, but not entirely without their benefits.

Soup, turkey, pasta, a sandwich. The meals at Simon's place of work were nutritious but were produced in-factory and tasted even blander than they looked. So, when Simon began uttering "delicious" right before eating each meal, Charlie reasonably worried that it was a sarcastic insult, and avoided speaking to him the rest of the day. The day after, he was on board. Building these "traditions" of saying certain words at certain times with his friends as a form of praise or encouragement seemed to be his best and only strategy.

With "delicious", Simon was careful. He recognized that, if he understood what he could do correctly, He could either envision the food itself changing its physical chemistry to become more flavorful, or he could alter his perception of the food while keeping it physically unaltered. In other words, his imagination lent him some choice over the method. Once he envisioned the general strategy, the specific implementation would be learned subconsciously, it seemed.

Not altering the food seemed the safer method, since changes to his nutrition content would be all too easy to notice. Of course, changes in how his mind processed taste might have been even more noticeable to his bloodmotion-sensitive headband than merely adding a few tastebuds. It was a hard choice. He wondered if he should have also approached his running ability differently, using it to develop a more pain-resistant mind instead of a physically superior body.

This game was dangerous; every utterance was a risk. He only needed to make one mistake, to think about his ability for twenty seconds too long, or a little too intently, or to slip in his speech, or develop an ability that was simply not quite hidden enough, and he'd be discovered. His only defensive advantage was plausibility. That his body had a hitherto undetected genetic predisposition to improve at running over time was far more reasonable of an explanation than the truth.

Whilst working on taste, he was careful to imagine the changes to be of a nature difficult to detect, and he seemed to have succeeded on that front. When his survey asked him about his utterance, he truthfully told it that he said "delicious" to cultivate a better appreciation for the food he was given and that his strange idea was working. He declined to mention how he felt specialized new tastebuds beginning to sprout on his tongue like a thousand grains of living sand.

The third ability he chose to try didn't occur to him as an idea until around his second week, and it was immediately obvious to him that it would be his most difficult enhancement yet, requiring a new and more nuanced strategy. He was inspired by Louisa, while they were walking amidst what was apparently one of the last botanical gardens on the continent, walled off near the edge of the city.

"The formatting and plant-choices of this garden are highly informed from Japanese culture," Louisa explained as they walked under a willow tree and approached a bridge connecting the two sides of a central pond.

"It's gotta be my second favorite import from their

culture to ours. I think I remember the First-Citizen himself expressing admiration for the form in an interview. Probably that's the only reason they haven't all been phased out. Or maybe he'll still get rid of them. Pragmatically speaking they're rather useless..."

She briefly pondered whether her previous statement was too controversial, then moved on. She was starting to become more considerate of these things.

"Something I don't get is why they bothered to make the pond so artificially blue. It's a nice contrast with the greenery above it, but it kinda looks fake. I'd have preferred a more natural aesthetic."

"I can't say I have an opinion. Honestly, I wasn't sure if the pond was blue or green to begin with."

"Wait, what do you mean?" She said, confused.

"I'm partially colorblind. I have trouble distinguishing blue from green. Apparently 'yellow' and 'pink' are different colors too, but I've also never been able to discern those."

"I had no idea. How haven't you mentioned this?" Louisa said, squeezing his hand and opening her eyes up to him, daring him to guess at their nature.

"Wait, I have a question. Your eyes, they're green aren't they?"

She broke into laughter and whacked him lightly on the back. "No silly, they're blue. It's this whole funny thing actually, since I'm the only dark-skinned person I know with bright blue eyes, so a few brave people down south have commented on it. I guess now I know why you never said anything."

Inspiration struck.

"Sight is such a strange thing." He said.

"I look and I see colors, and I've tried to see how colors are different from each other, but I see so much green that is actually blue, I guess I've just accepted my sight impairment. Blue, for example, I've learned is the color of oceans, walls, the sky, I think maybe my old blanket. Green appears everywhere too, sometimes with Blue, so I just call everything Green until someone corrects the color for me."

"Hey, don't even worry about it. You don't need to justify yourself. Anyways, I wouldn't be surprised if Citizenship science finds a way to solve colorblindness in the next decade or two, now that imminent survival isn't the national concern anymore. If this place still exists when you get your full color vision, we're coming back. You'll love it even more."

Simon noticed and was gladdened by her casual use of "we", pertaining to an event that she had just claimed could take a decade to happen. He wasn't the only one starting to think of their relationship as something that might last.

"Blue and green just need to get a divorce already," Simon complained Louisa laughed softly at his sentiment, and Simon gave his newest project a rest to enjoy the silence.

His new strategy involved using a collection of words towards essentially the same ability. Off the top of his head, he thought of "blue", "green", "color", and "sight" as words that might help to activate color differentiation. For each of those words, he began to design a specific sub-goal. Each was tied in with the others, but because no two words held the same meaning, each of his four choices required a unique visualization.

Each time he said one of the words, he would hold his goal in his head for a few seconds, while continuing to speak, until he reached the next word. The exercise was a difficult one to balance, especially since he didn't want to over-oxygenate his brain with the effort.

The date continued to go well, and Simon found more opportunities to say color-related words by asking his partner what she knew about colorblindness. The conversation continued to blossom into new subjects, but, thinking on his feet, he managed to incorporate his keywords in at a frequency he hoped was just beneath suspicion. He came up with a visualization for the word "distinguish", "verdant", "shades", and "spectral", although those words could not pop up often without resulting in their conversation overworking some specific topic.

"There's such verdant plant life here; in terms of color I can still make out that these are brighter shades of green." (image of bright green leaves, their color liberated from blue and distinct in his eyes... Image of many shades of green, and whatever blue looked like, and him knowing them to be different... The platonic concept of the color green, in all its glory.)

"This colorblindness thing really has you stumped, doesn't it" Louisa said.

"It always has, to be honest with you. I'm thinking about it now, and I think I'm seeing green and not blue. They're close on the color spectrum, though, so I could be completely wrong." (Platonic concept of green... Platonic concept of blue... Platonic concept of a color, seen clearly in all shades... An expansive spectrum of millions of distinct colors, each presenting its own unique character, simultaneously part of an infinite continuum.)

"You're right. You know, you could probably ask your survey if it's worth it to get your eyes checked. You mentioned having those dumb medical appointments that you're only doing because your stamina surprised them." She gave him a bit of a look. "Brainscans could probably determine what the actual perceived color is. Just to satisfy your curiosity, you know."

"That's a thought." He couldn't let that happen. His brain was evolving every time he excercised an ability, he was certain. The changes felt subtle enough, for now, but the prospect of a serious brainscan worried him. He avoided the detectable feeling of worry by contemplating his next color-sentence.

"Green, blue, doesn't matter. If I ever see an ocean again, I just want to know what color it is."

(Ocean. A vast, gleaming, surface churning spectral shades of blues and greens both dark and light, its surface dancing with brilliant explorations of both colors).

"I'll be sure to describe it to you if we go. We actually could, in theory. To the ocean. It's less than an hour by speed rail."

"I'd like that."

They completed their lap around the artificially blue pond. "Hey, Simon."

"Yeah?"

"Well, you don't have to, but we're closer to my place than yours again. If you wanted to just spend the night."

Simon nodded. "Yeah. Alright."

"Really?"

"Yeah. Let's go now. The sun's down in an hour anyways."

They walked to the tall gray gates hiding the garden, nodding acknowledgment to the graying caretaker who had waved them through when they entered. The bus took them into a residential zone and dropped them off at 12 Dunder Street. They spent the ride holding hands and talking about the town Louisa moved in from, a fortified coastal settlement called Baton Rouge.

"This is me," Louisa said as she turned into the ninth gray home along a street of identical gray buildings, having spent the last block dramatically counting houses with her left hand. Now that color was on his mind, Simon noticed himself seeing the color gray more starkly than he ever had. It was everywhere.

Louisa opened the door, and Simon walked into a unit identical to his own. He knew he'd be able to guide Louisa to her pantry, shower, or bedroom entirely by memory.

"Well this is it," Louisa gestured dramatically. "The humble abode of Louisa and Sammy."

Sammy was Louisa's sister.

"Sammy, is she...?"

"Nah, she's with her partner. His place is more private, so they usually meet over there. It's also nearer to a plaza.

And of course there's her hating the sight of me for getting us relocated from our parents."

"Nice. Not the parent part, but...so, uh, what's there to do over here?"

"I think you know."

"Yeah. I guess I do."

Louisa stepped up to his chest.

"You're nervous, aren't you? We don't have to do anything crazy. Or anything at all."

"No, I want to. It's just, well, it's been a long time, and my last encounter wasn't enjoyable."

Louisa placed her hand on his chest, and let her palm drape lower. Her left hand followed.

"We can start with stuff like this. Clothes don't need to come off just yet. Just feel me up a little."

Simon laughed nervously, but obeyed the order, mirroring what Louisa had started doing to him.

"You really do feel nervous. But damn, you've got a bit of muscle on you. How'd you manage that?"

"I dunno. Genetics, I guess."

"Well whatever it is, it's not unpleasant to feel. Or to look at, I'm sure."

Simon blushed. He wasn't sure what to say back, so he said "You're hot too." He cursed his reply's aromanticism while she giggled.

The act of feeling his way across Louisa's still-clothed body awoke something in him more quickly and powerfully than he had thought it would. He began to crave seeing the parts of her body that her uniform had done its best to hide. Louisa smiled, clearly sensing his shift, and led him by the hand down a short hallway.

"By the way, you're allowed to stare at my ass for longer than five seconds. You won't be arrested."

"Thanks for telling me."

He stared at her ass dumbly while she led him through the bedroom door. At first glance, the room looked just like his own, although he didn't feel like making a detailed comparison at that moment. They sat together on the bed, hands still touching, having had continuous physical contact since entering the house.

"I think this can come off now," Louisa said in her illegally soft voice as she lifted off her shirt. Simon replicated.

"This too," she added. Simon's pupils dilated. Louisa had just removed her headband and flung it across the room.

"That's a crime," he said perfunctorily.

"I don't care. I know this is how you want me, and it's how I'd like to have you. Take yours off."

He couldn't resist her, especially when she gave orders. The discarding of her headband erected him more than the removal of her shirt had. For just this moment, he would know her body better than her overseers.

"I've been waiting ages. You really made me work for this." Louisa leaned in and kissed him.

Simon had waited longer. A lifetime of strict adherence to his job, the values of the Citizenship that managed his life, and of the most faithful following of his surveys encouragements, melted away as the kissing intensified. The last fifteen years had sculpted him into an automaton, whose very motions and thoughts were to be trained and regulated with the exquisite craftsmanship of an architect in concrete. It all abandoned him, and his body began discovering new ways to move.

He helped her remove her pants with nervous obsession; none of this was legal. She did the same for him and grinned mischievously. Within some number of seconds, they were embracing on the bed, Simon staring into her eyes as he went down on her, seeing her immediate pleasure as he went between her legs. She felt him along the contours of his very nearly muscular body, the body enhanced to run a hundred miles without rest. He clumsily reached around to explore every crevice of hers in return. He wanted to map out every square inch of her legs and torso, but as he tried, his own excitement grew beyond his control. Her body shook in climax, at which point she made a signal that Simon had never seen before but understood. He entered her and felt the last of his control drop away. The pleasure was indescribable. As it ebbed, he realized with embarassment he was in the hallway less than minute ago.

Simon had no notion of what to do afterwards. Louisa guided him under the covers, where they embraced. He wished he'd been able to last longer.

"Well, I guess I can say something," Louisa whispered after a minute of breath catching.

"That sounds ominous. Was it bad? Can you fake it that well?"

"No, I really did enjoy it. I was just worried you'd freeze at first. Hey...Can I ask you a question?"

She wrapped her arms around his neck and smiled up at him.

"Of course."

"What was your last time like?" Simon stopped smiling. *She was bound to ask. Maybe I should try trusting her.*

"Oh. You don't have to tell me. I'll respect your privacy."

"I appreciate that, really, but it's fine." He hesitated. Stories like this were never told.

"Seven years ago, about, I started a relationship with this woman named Sybil. Charming, smart, first date went amazingly."

"I bet the bitch didn't make you a paper airplane."

"Be nice. But you're not wrong. The point is, on the surface we seemed perfectly compatible."

"But?"

"They made a mistake."

No, too far. Backtrack. They can still hear.

"Well, not a mistake. Sybil, she...I don't know how to say it."

"Oh. I see." Louisa comprehended instantly. "I'm sorry."

"Yeah. She just didn't want to. I actually think she didn't

want to with anyone, ever. I felt guilty once I figured it out. We avoided spending time alone in each other's homes, which was fine, because we both loved being outdoor explorers together. Our travels weren't crazy, coffee shops mostly, which felt plenty adventurous to the two of us. She's the only person I've met who loves coffee not for the caffeine. We scouted over a dozen local holdouts together, back when there were that many. We liked comparing the coffee at different places, making fake rankings together and coming up with loquacious words to describe all the flavors. Her favorite type of coffee was 'granular like a bakery with a faint vibe of enriched cotton.' I still don't know what that meant. We were happiest doing stuff like that."

Louisa saw the ending.

"Not much else to say. Surveys started asking questions. Pressure started to build. Meeting with her became tense, once we both understood. I wish I'd broken up with her then. About eight months into our relationship, she took me to her place, and we fucked. There was no joy in it. What made it even worse was the way I could tell she was trying to make it pleasant for me when I knew she hated every second. I broke up with her the next day. I figured if I initiated, it would be my ranking that was affected and not hers. I was right. I never saw her after that, and have no idea how she is."

Louisa hugged him tightly and brushed his face.

"Thank you for telling me. It sounds like you did everything you could."

"I judged myself every day for it. Every survey I took I was told it wasn't my fault, but it's still only the past year or so that I've really moved on. If I even can."

"A younger me would have judged you too. But leaving takes bravery. It's a hard thing to avoid and a harder thing to live with afterwards." She turned away and stared out the window at the far end of the room. He enjoyed feeling her warm skin move across his body as she comfortably adjusted herself into him. *We can be sad together comfortably. This is new.*

"I miss my parents."

Simon hugged her. "I know. But it's for the best." He hated that he had to tell her that. He should have been braver. There was another moment of silence.

"Hey, I bet my origami can lighten the mood."

Louisa jumped up and guided Simon over to her windowsill overlooking 12 Dunder Street. Having been otherwise engaged, Simon had failed to notice the richly varied assortment of paper shapes that sat arrayed there. The delicate structures showcased a wide spectrum of color, including several green-looking shapes that Simon tried unsuccessfully to discern some blue out of. He thought at least one of them was blue.

"I'm going through an animal phase. Here's a horse, this one's supposed to be a cheetah, and this adorable thing off to the right is an elephant.

Elephant! That was the word!

"Louisa, you have no idea how much I love you right now."

"The first time you say you love me, and it's because of my paper children. I don't think I'm gonna be able to break up with you now."

"A real shame. But seriously, I've been trying to remember the name of that animal for ages. I thought maybe it was an el-phish."

"Nope, not an el-phish. Although we may need to petition to get the name changed. And was that sarcasm?"

"Shush. But they might as well. It's not like we'd be changing common knowledge."

"You're not wrong." She paused. "Sometimes I wonder if our education is a little too streamlined." They silently agreed to leave that thought untouched and appraised the paper creations.

"Here, I can show you my favorite way to make a paper airplane."

Simon watched carefully as Louisa pulled a piece of

paper from the top of her drawer with practiced motion, folded it in half, then added successive creases in a symmetric pattern that yielded a shape reminding him vaguely of his early childhood.

"K, your turn." Simon took the paper she offered him and carefully folded it, trying to remember exactly how she did it. A minute later, he had something that looked shabbier than hers, but the same shape. Louisa examined.

"Not bad. I'm gonna keep this one. That way you don't have to waste microliberties having it at your place."

"Thanks." Simon let the plane fly and managed to land it neatly on the pillow Louisa had just been using. Louisa whistled.

"Damn. That would've been good foreplay. Want me to show you some other folds?"

"I'd love nothing more."

The couple spent the rest of the day folding origami. Simon wished the rest of his afternoons could be spent folding el-phishes with her.

CHAPTER 12

The day following that night, during which time they had made love an additional two or three times depending on one's definition, Simon went to work, productively analyzed Gina's mental state and determined it to have improved slightly, and during lunch initiated a lively theoretical discussion with Beckett and Charlie about whether the ocean was green or blue. Charlie claimed it was a deep emerald, but Beckett, who had never seen the ocean with his own eyes, insisted that most of the ocean was dark blue, because of footage he'd glimpsed back when he was assigned to a fisherman. The argument became redundant enough that Simon snuck in over a dozen vivid utterances that day.

That night, his survey addressed his heightened interest in the colors of things and stated that an appointment could potentially be made with an eye specialist to help satiate his curiosity as a reward for his recent work performance. During the following month, he milked every chance to utter a word that connected conceptually to color differentiation. The task was creatively challenging, as he couldn't replicate conversations. Each day, he had to find a new color-adjacent topic. Some days, he drew a blank and made no progress.

Discussing his favorite biography, about the famed painter John Everest, granted him a few days of artistic exploration with Charlie, who had also read it. Wondering out loud at the biological miracle it was that sight even existed, and at the technologies that the Citizenship was surely developing that very moment to further improve on the design, gave him three minutes of material, spread over two days. Verifying, unnecessarily, that C-class citizens did in fact wear blue coveralls, and not green ones, got him a single sentence.

He made each keyword count and vividly imagined his goal for as long as a minute after each utterance. Two weeks in, and he could tell some progress had been made. Shades in his environment that had once seemed essentially the same slowly began drifting apart, and, in the growing seams between them, new shades introduced themselves within the deepening contours and expanding borders of his perception. Four weeks into the sporadic effort and the colors of blue and green had become more or less divorced in his mind. With the new doubling of Simon's chromatic perception, came a doubled realization that he lived in a colorless society.

It was obvious to Simon at this point that, if only he could be granted true privacy, he would be able to push his abilities much, much further. The augmentations made to his brain, eyes, blood, and nervous system were all slight. And yet, it was already enough to enhance his imaginations and grant him subtleties of visualization and color perception that he had hitherto never experienced. He suspected that he could distinguish shades of blue even more precisely than most by now.

He thought about his father's offer then, to become a trucker, to forgo the larger housing and more nutritious breakfasts and the constant stimulation, to let go of his job and get one where, although he would still be monitored, nobody would care as much if he repeated words to himself while he drove cargo. He came dangerously close to seriously considering the change, and visions of trucking through countless miles of plains and forests made him think of his dad. But he couldn't leave Louisa.

Simon never considered himself spiritual. And yet, every time he focused on a word, lingering long enough to carve an ability deeper into himself, he felt some aspect of him deepen, as though he were becoming ever so slightly more immersed in reality. He could only describe the distant impression he was receiving as a spiritual one.

More than ever before, he wanted the freedom to explore. To spend an entire day in utterance, to see if he could, in that huge time, reach a place where he could stare at a hundred blue brush-strokes, and see each of them as an entirely distinct color, where any other human alive would think them all the same. As useless as the power would be, something about it was incredibly appealing. He knew Louisa would understand his desire perfectly. He wished he could talk about it with her. *It doesn't matter. It wasn't real. Think about work.*

Simon began seeing Louisa at her place, and occasionally her at his, on a regular basis. It almost felt like an affair, as though every minute they spent in each other's embrace could somehow be grounds for lifetime imprisonment if they were caught. The feeling only served to make Simon want her more, and he found himself attending his colleagues' bowling nights the bare minimum number of times that the survey required of him, in favor of spending every evening he could with his new partner.

The two of them were building a relationship based on far more than sex, although sex seemed to find its way into everything now. Simon's long-subdued fantasy of being able to actively seek out those old, obsolete places, the hidden remnants of a much more vibrant cultural past, could finally become a reality. He and Louisa spent many of their days together seeking out the old places, the drying puddles of a former lake that were being imminently approached by the unhurried yet inescapable death that was official discouragement from existence by the First-Citizen, the Citizenship, and their flawlessly loyal army of survey algorithms.

They visited a near vacant pastry shop, a run-down bike store run by an aged C-classer, and a car museum that displayed ancient husks of the inefficient precursors to the bus behind thin panes of dusty glass, many of which held extensive cracks. Seeing the old cars had given Louisa an idea. She learned during their trip to the car museum that many of the old self-driving relics could theoretically be rented out, and, excited at the possibilities, had managed to use her enhanced freedom to locate the ruins on a wrinkled old map from the seventies they could drive to the following Sunday morning. The vehicle was rented digitally, picked them up near the edge of the city, and drove them silently beyond the city's borders out to a woodland area encasing several old ruins. The entire experience had an ethereal quality to it.

"This is a football stadium. Or was." Louisa said as they got out of the vehicle, which refused to drive beyond the curb they were on.

"A what?"

"It was a sport that used to be as popular as bowling. Each team tries to get essentially a more aerodynamic bowling ball across their side of the field, while people sit up on those and watch. Look, there's the deflated ball over there. Guess they didn't bother cleaning up after the final game."

The field was nearly twice the length of a standard pro bowling line. Simon found the sight impressive, despite its haunted quality.

"Hey, Simon."

"Hey."

"Have you ever had fun on turf grass?"

"Of course not. That sounds terribly uncomfortable."

"Oh, well then. I guess our business here has concluded. Back in the car you go."

"Oh, you get over here." The two of them sauntered into the field and found a spot that plant life hadn't yet reached, near the center. The act was exhilarating enough that he could ignore the grating discomfort of green plastic needles rubbing his skin.

The couple spooned on the turf afterwards, admiring the seclusion offered by the stretch of abandoned buildings, trees, and roadway. They were almost as close to the nearest wilderness zone as they were to their homes. Louisa lazily turned into him.

"So are you gonna finally tell me more about your clients now?"

"Probably not." Simon replied curtly.

"Ugh. You know you can tell me more. As an overseer, you're authorized to speak of your work to any A-class citizen."

"But you're not an A-class citizen."

"What makes you say that? I literally am. Have I not mentioned?"

Simon jolted. "No. How is that even possible? You live like a B-class citizen." *You're in a relationship with me.*

"Yeah, that's true. But by choice. I'm deemed a highly essential professional by the Citizenship. As I know you've guessed, I have a generous helping of so-called 'wandering syndrome', which we might as well admit is just a sideways term for being able to actually have original, interesting thoughts." She moved her hand idly across Simon's skin, seeming to memorize every feature she noticed. He wondered if she thought they wouldn't last forever.

"So anyways, I was offered a choice. I could live the life of any other A-class citizen, with all the privileges and limitations that entails. Or, I could take a step down. Live like a B-class citizen, in a B-class house, spend more time with my B-class family. Mate with a suitable B-class man."

She pinched Simon's cheek and he smiled. "It sounds like your choice was an easy one." He said.

"You think? Did you know, that A-class citizens wear sensors around their entire body? It's not just their headbands. Their shoes are built to extract regular blood samples to better analyze hormonal balance and gene expression. Even their pants and shirts even have sensors. I know you have at least one A-class client. That huge amount of data gathered about their every motion and thought? It's because they have better equipment on them. Their entire dress code is meant to map them. I just can't think creatively when I know I'm that thoroughly studied."

"I've never minded being observed. Especially by you." He wasn't sure if that was true anymore, given his ability. He'd give anything, he realized, to have only an hour of the truest form of privacy, free and alone with his words.

Simon held her close. "Well anyways, I see why you made the choice that you did."

"The decision was easy. But it's a trade, like any other. I'm allowed a generous stock of microliberty. But I can't openly associate with A-classers. No three-story mansions. My rank, which would probably have been around four thousand, got dropped to I-don't-even-know-what."

"You're at about seventy million right now."

"Huh."

"You know, one of my clients lives in a house with six bedrooms."

"Wow. You're so brave for sharing that." Louisa said sarcastically.

"At this point, you might as well talk about them." She added.

Simon considered. He'd long since realized she would respect his fear of reprisal if he chose to say nothing. But curiosity beckoned. "Fine. But if I'm arrested tomorrow, it's your fault."

Louisa shrugged, but couldn't hide her tension. Simon told her first about Phineas and Gina, and the near flawlessness with which they had learned to manipulate their minds and bodies every second of every day as they worked. Louisa smirked as he vented his adoration of their rarified skills.

He hesitated, but proceeded to tell her about the general. He mentioned his copious consumption of alcohol, as well as his tendency to stay in his house for many days at a time, and his lack of contact with other humans. He chose to leave out his apparent age since that could lead the conversation to the First-Citizen, although that had been the one topic Louisa seemed unwilling to touch on. Telling her everything else was disquietingly easy, and she seemed unphased by all of it.

"Oh, by the way, I got in trouble a few days ago because of you." He said before she had a chance to ask for more.

"Did you?...oh, shit. It was the fucking elephant, wasn't it. I'm sorry."

"Don't be. But yes, it was the elephant." A few mornings prior, Simon had folded a paper elephant, which they had both agreed had looked adorable. Louisa insisted he bring it home, but he had work, so he took it first to his office. *You'll be fine.* She'd told him. He shouldn't have believed her. He skipped his run with Beckett, walked into the office, placed it on his desk, and was not spoken to by a single person that day. Charlie and Beckett didn't come down during lunch. The next day they made their excuses, saying their headbands told them to keep working because they were behind, but the message had been clear: Simon's life with Louisa, and her conference of privileged status onto him, was to be left at the door.

He decided this was where he was truly alive. This abandoned stadium of cracks and vines: nature reclaiming a stubborn remnant of whatever culture it was that called North America home fifty years ago. This place was now for him and Louisa only. This last thought somehow felt more treasonous than any other.

"Let's go somewhere," he said without thinking.

"Huh? We just did. It took us an hour to get here."

"Somewhere else. It's Sunday, and it's not even noon yet. The direction we drove, we're within ten miles of the hyperloop. Storm warning says all good, even along the coast. Let's go see the Pacific."

"Two adventures in one day. That sounds like a lot of walking. I need a treat first." Louisa said fussily.

"Fine. I spoil you."

As he went down on her, Simon noticed Louisa's headband issuing a low power alert. It would likely die before they reached the coast. Maybe she'd take it off on the beach and they could have fun a third time that day.

The car took them, traveling through further woodland to the hyperloop. The parking lot was inhospitable, so Simon told the vehicle to return to its owner. It drove off silently, and they went to board the train.

The hyperloop towards the ocean was a rapid saunter across alternating episodes of green and gray, as the train smoothly retreated from the still rising sun at four hundred miles an hour. He found himself anticipating what the ocean would look like to him as he soaked in the passing landscapes.

Not a half hour later, the train decelerated and they got off at the boarding station and stepped off into a dwindling ghost town. Nobody else was with them on the train, and nobody was waiting to board. The train stayed where it was, probably having nobody else to attend to. The two of them walked through the town and were pleased to find a coffee shop that looked new and unfamiliar to both of them. After being served latte and soup by the venu's sole proprietor, a quiet old woman with thick glasses and a brown T-shirt, they started making their way to the nearest boardwalk.

"The last time I was here was with my parents," Simon said. "Our family was one of the last to own a car, so we all hopped in and drove down to see the ocean. I think it was this town, but so much has changed I hardly even recognize it."

"My family never had a car. They're pointlessly wasteful compared to busses and trains."

"That train seems more wasteful. I don't think people get to use it much."

"Fair. Anyways, I'm really glad we came. I've only been to a beach once, but it was near this estuary that expulsed millions of tons of human garbage, and I've never wanted to go alone since. Although I've read the beaches here are well-preserved."

The boardwalk went up a sloped hill. Louisa led Simon up the steps excitedly. They reached the summit.

The ocean was blue.

"It's beautiful." He nearly cried.

Louisa smiled at him. She looked blissful, although her eyes shown with their usual intensity.

For the hundredth time, Simon wanted to tell her that he could see blue. The pair left their shoes on a partially decayed wood staircase and walked onto the beach, relishing the sand on their feet.

"Oops. My headband just died." Louisa said. "I guess yours will have to report for the both of us." She took hers off and dropped it next to her shoes.

"You know, I think mine needs some rest too." He took his off and dropped it by hers. Louisa looked genuinely impressed. If he didn't know better he'd have thought she looked worried for him. "Alright then. But this time if you get busted, it's definitely not my fault."

"How could I possibly blame you?"

"Mhmm. Okay, time to get wet." She ran towards the ocean, right up to the point where the waves periodically nipped her ankles. Simon followed gleefully.

"Fun fact that I learned as a kid," Louisa began, "apparently the sand zones of many of these beaches used to extend much further than this beach does now. When the sea levels started rising, a lot of the beaches got submerged, and there hasn't been much time for the new coastlines to churn up their big rocks into smaller sand particles yet. We're lucky this beach goes out this far."

Simon nodded along and walked with her along the water line. The two of them dug their feet into the sand, allowing rock and water to rush over the foundations of their bodies and reconnect them to the natural world that was meticulously stripped from their experiences back home. Simon bent down and grabbed a sampling of wet sand under two inches of receding saltwater. The sensation of it felt delightfully alien.

"I love how gracefully imperfect beaches are." Louisa mused. Her thoughts seemed to be mirroring Simon's own.

"It's like a person. If you ever met a perfect person, not like your highest ideal of a person or anything, but just a textbook perfect person, that strayed from no averages, and had no quirks... they'd be boring. Our homes are textbook perfect. Nice little arrangements designed according to the most basic social sensibility. This beach tells so many more stories than those perfect little homes ever could. It shows me a passing snippet of the infinite lore of our natural world that I've never seen mirrored in anything built by the Citizenship." Louisa smiled, beautifully, in a way that Simon couldn't forget if he tried. "I'm sorry, I shouldn't have said that last part. Or any of it. I know I should be working on that sort of thing."

"You're fine" Simon offered. "I want you to share everything with me. And now's your chance to." He tapped where his headband usually was, and she smiled introspectively, saying nothing. The pair continued walking side by side, inner hands interlocked, outer hands waving freely with the breeze. For the first time since losing parental access two-thirds of a lifetime ago, Simon felt completely comfortable. He thought back to that vacation he took with his mom and dad, to the poetry they shared. He recited his favorite poem to himself for the first time in years and relished in the power of its metaphor.

"No. I'm not fine." Louisa said suddenly. "None of this is. I'm exploiting you. We both know being with me gives you a life you'd never have otherwise. That's why the fucking surveys put us together."

Simon looked at her with surprise.

"Two birds, one stone." She continued. "Match you with someone you're highly compatible with and you show your true colors. Do it to me, and I start feeling immeasurable guilt at the power I hold over another life, and I feel forced to correct myself."

"That's not how I think about us. Or how I feel about you." Simon said. He kept holding her hand. Louisa's anger partially subsided. "Answer this. If I couldn't offer you the right to speak some of your mind, or to go to the beach, or make useless origami, could I still make you happy? Could being with me still be something you'd want, if there were no benefits?"

Simon took a breath. The ocean was having an effect on both of them. "That's a ridiculous question. Of course I would. You're amazing, with or without the right to fold origami. In another history, where your Citizenship status was the same as mine, I'd be honored to trudge through my B-class days with you. I love you."

Louisa squeezed his hand. Her fingers laced more tightly around his.

"I love you too... And really, you make your life before me sound just so romantic."

"Shush."

They embraced. The waves around them luxuriously came and went in at least a dozen lazy cycles before they let go.

"Louisa, there's something I want to tell you. It needs to be now." Simon wasn't sure what he was saying. *I can still go back. I can make up a lie. I might not get caught.*

"Yeah, what? Let me guess. There's another woman, isn't there?"

"I appreciate your complete trust in me. But no, it's a little bigger than that. I don't know when I'll be able to tell you again. Please, just keep an open mind."

"Always, you know me. Now I'm even more curious."

"I can see that color blue." *Ok, now I can't go back.*

Louisa paused.

"Huh? You said you were colorblind? Is it only green you can't see?"

"I can see green too. Better than you can, I think."

"Were you lying earlier?"

"No, not technically. At the time I was colorblind. So, I adjusted that."

"Wait... you got surgery? That's amazing! I didn't think that was even possible yet."

"No, no, I'm not explaining this well at all. Here."

Simon held his hand out in front of him, a foot from her face. One word. Then she'd know. He couldn't not show her. His and Louisa's headbands would eventually pick up that this strange interaction happened between them, and force him to confess regardless. But he wanted her to know. If he could tell her anywhere, it was here, in this precious unobserved moment. In his remaining time before being discovered, perhaps they could think of a way out, together. He drew a sharp breath, focused his mind, felt back to that specific sensation of warmth and flame, and uttered "fire".

CHAPTER 13

An orb of flame sprouted from Simon's outstretched palm, attracting fuel from some unknown place, yet heaving no smoke. The orb looked superficially like any other fire, but there was something unnatural about how it moved and flickered, as though it was being carefully guided by some liquid intelligence. It felt like it wanted to be unseen.

Louisa staggered back and nearly tripped on the flat sand.

"How the hell are you doing that?"

"I don't know. It's one of several abilities I've managed to develop. This one in particular at great personal risk."

"Oh god..." Louisa kept her eyes on the flickering flame as a gust of wind escalated what should have been a small river of smoke into her eyes.

"That's not natural. How are you even fuelling it?"

"I don't know. All I know is, with time, and the right word I can make it grow."

"Oh my god. Jesus. None of this makes any type of sense."

"I know." He couldn't help but notice her religious vocabulary. He wondered where she'd heard expletives like that. Maybe her parents had held onto christianity longer than most.

"So what, you have control over fire? And somehow your sight improved? Simon, please put logic into this."

Simon told her the story, how he discovered his ability, how it was fuelled by language, seemed to be versatile, but strangely could not be developed with irrelevant words, or in silence. A complicated smile escaped her when he explained the reason he became so interested in color weeks earlier and had asked her so many strange questions. She sat in the wet sand to think, not seeming to care that her pants were now ruined. Simon joined her.

"That's a lot to process."

"I know. Should I not have told you?"

"Probably not."

"Fair. Now that I have, I don't know what to do."

"Honestly, I don't either." She retreated deeply into a thought for a moment. Simon couldn't tell if she was panicking.

"Imagine it, though. The good you could accomplish." She eventually said.

"Of course I've imagined. I just don't want to reveal myself, only to be studied as an experiment, or strapped to some chair and forced to utter words to make the First-Citizen's dick bigger."

"I'm sure it wouldn't be like that. Hear me out. If your ability is as versatile as you claim, you could probably use it to advance medical science by decades. You managed to give yourself the body of a genetically gifted pro athlete, and under the constraints you had? Imagine what you could accomplish in just a few days if you didn't have to hide this. You could be the next evolution of medical science and make an everyday genius like me obsolete."

"I doubt it. I don't know how refined the power can get on smaller scales. And I certainly don't understand your work. Or even what it is you do exactly."

"Well, I might as well tell you. Seeing as it's child's play next to the implications of whatever it is you are."

Louisa took another deep breath, and, dropping her normally expressive speech, she concisely explained her professional history. Immediately after graduating from University with her microbiology degree, she'd been recruited to an elite project division to work on the development of vaccines against the man-made epidemics raging in other parts of the world. Mutated Ebola in the Sahara. Designer Anthrax in China. New strains of the bird flu in South America. Her inspired insights into viral-blood parasitism significantly streamlined the process of constructing vaccines. Of course they were never be sent to the regions that needed them, she explained, but they would nonetheless be mass-produced by the Citizenship in case one of them ever reached North America.

"They gave me ample resources to do my work. The only thing I couldn't ask for was full-body imagery of the infected. I suppose they didn't want me to know how bad it looked on the people they chose not to save. Other than that, I got whatever I wanted."

Simon hugged her now wet torso. He wanted to comfort her, but didn't know how to articulate. She seemed to get the message, and held him tightly.

"Maybe my abilities are limited. I might become a slightly useful lab rat for the rest of my life, making flames and whistles. They could dissect me and force you to study my blood, for all we know."

"That's not funny. I would never consent to that."

Simon turned to listen to the ocean, his breath quickening. The magnitude of what he just confessed finally struck him. Normally he supposed the vast body of water would make his problems seem insignificant, but in this case, he suspected they were more far-reaching than he had wanted to believe. He wondered if he was capable of escaping. Certainly not with her. Officers and drones were theoretically less than fifteen minutes away from every square inch of civilized land on the continent.

"At least the Citizenship won't know for a while, since we don't have our headbands on. We'll have maybe a day before they determine that we're both lying about something important."

"Doesn't seem like it'll make a difference."

"You can make a difference. Do something, right now. Nobody's watching."

"Do what?"

"I don't know. Anything. Something only you could do. Make a new ability."

Simon thought for a second. An idea occurred to him, making him smile.

"How would you like to see even better than I can?"

"I'm not sure I know what that entails, but sure, I trust you."

Simon beckoned that they sit, and took her hands into his own, the two of them sitting in lotus postures across from one another as the waves of the ocean swept up to their feet.

"Close your eyes," He told her.

"See. See. See. See..." He began uttering gently. He didn't dare waver his focus while working on her. He willed her eyes to blossom in the way that his had. He gave her mind permission to find new colors, her neurons to do what they already knew how to, as the connections of her occipital lobe extended in complexity and gradually layered on new structure. The nerves connecting eyes to brain were encouraged to find new, more potent mechanisms. The eyes themselves slowly began blossoming detailed new machinery.

Simon closed his own eyes and allowed the process to wash over him as well. He could feel the vibration of their cells together as he continued to utter, their friction causing a sensation he was tempted to describe as religious ecstasy. The longer they sat, meditatively, the more completely immersed Simon became. Speaking uninterrupted seemed to aid his ability tremendously, as his consciousness could now build momentum in a singular direction. His meditative utterance continued for a few minutes, until he felt that there had been a degree of noticeable progress.

"Alright. Open."

He and Louisa lifted their eyelids at the same moment and stared at each other with their new sight. Even her face, with the rest of the world out of focus, now seemed to hold greater contrasts in depth and color than he had ever noticed before. The variegated red hues in her cheeks intermingled with her lovely skin, skin which explored many subtle variations of shade across her whole body, all the way towards her vibrant black eyelashes and bright blue eyes, eyes whose azure richness drew him in further than they ever had before. The slightly more apparent asymmetries did nothing but enhance her.

"You're beautiful." He told her.

"No, you." She said.

They stared for a while longer, then gradually traced their eyes across the landscape. Everything had noticeably higher contrast. The blues in particular, the color which Simon had most desperately sought while he uttered, seemed to have tripled in variety and richness. The swirling waves of the ocean looked more diversified than a rainbow would have to him a month ago.

"Simon, this is gorgeous. The whole world is gonna overwhelm me for the next several days."

"Yeah. Then we'll get used to it."

"I suppose so." She looked at the ocean, and at him, with equal thirst. "Should we head back?"

"Yeah."

Simon lingered on the Pacific, briefly wondering whether the people on the other side would welcome refugees, then returned with his partner to the boardwalk. They reapplied their headbands and left the beach, finding the train waiting. They boarded, saying nothing, still too busy admiring the new gradients within the reds, oranges, blues, greens, and grays of the color-saturated world in which they found themselves immersed.

The train did not stop where they had boarded. It kept going, right through the Portland hub, and did not stop at any station there either.

We're going to be arrested the moment we get off this train.

Simon realized.

"Yeah." Louisa said, seeming to read his mind.

"Since it doesn't matter anymore, I want to be able to know that you're still alive. There isn't much time" Simon said, thinking quickly. Louisa understood.

He began to visualize her heartbeat, her breath, the distribution of heat and oxygen through her blood. He told her to do the same to him. "Connect" he then uttered, in slow, thoughtful repetition, sounding unintentionally intimate. The first few words did nothing, as usual, but soon enough, right as the train began deceleration, the ability started weakly taking hold.

"I feel it!" Louisa hissed in a whisper.

"Good. Focus on it." Simon placed his hand on her chest, an act she mirrored. "I'm connecting us."

"No duh."

"What that means, I hope, is that we'll be able to feel each other's heartbeats. And each other's chests. If you cross your arms on your chest tightly, you might be able to warm me, and I can do the same to you. And we'll know when the other is stressed, or drugged."

Or dead. He thought grimly.

"If this weren't terrifying I'd think the gesture was very romantic. Maybe a bit invasive."

"We don't have to try this."

"No, please, don't stop. I want us to be connected. I doubt they'll let us see each other so soon." Simon continued his utterance, focusing intently on bridging the gap between his partner's body and his own, willing their nerves to hurriedly scaffold new connectors to receive distant signals from the other's heart and chest.

"Oh, I think I can feel you. Just a little. You're fluttering inside me." Louisa said.

"Yeah, same." Simon continued uttering, and indeed had begun to feel Louisa's heart beating as a distant companion to his own. Fluttering was an apt description; her heart rate was just a little faster than his, creating an unbalanced polyrhythm in his chest. The sensation strengthened a little. Louisa pounded her hand on her heart, and Simon immediately felt the pulse as a small kick inside his own ribcage. He returned the gesture. They burst into laughter at the surprise feature of the new ability.

"How about one pound means things are good, two means I'm unsafe, and three means I love you," Louisa suggested. Simon saw there was a tear in her eye that she had tried to wipe away while he was laughing.

"Yeah. I like that." Simon pounded his chest three times. Louisa mirrored.

"It's going to be ok. I know their system better than you do. They won't kill either of us, not if there's no reason to. Just keep calm and do what they say."

Simon took his hand off her chest, and they held hands while he uttered "connect" a couple more times.

The train slowed to a stop. The doors opened.

Simon Pontius and Louisa Morris, you are both under arrest for guilt of a criminal nature. Please exit the train with your hands behind your head. You are obligated to remain silent.

Simon exited the train first. A dozen police surrounded them in tight formation, and the second they both were out of the train, two of the masked officers came up to cuff them. "Simon, just stay calm. They're got gonna..." Louisa couldn't finish her sentence before one of the officers placed a thick gloved hand on her neck. Within seconds of contact she lost consciousness and fell into the grip.

"No! She was going willingly, you didn't need to drug her!" Two seconds of Simon's own writhing was all it took for a glove to firmly grab his neck. He felt prickling sensations stemming from the palm of the glove, and a milliliter quantity of some liquid seeped into his body. He lost consciousness.

He awoke gradually, but his induced placidity hadn't worn off. His eyes resisted opening. He eventually saw, and felt, that he was in the back of a large escort van with five full-armored, masked officers, two at his side, three sitting opposite him. *Louisa...different van.*

Images of torture flashed through his mind. He realized he knew deep down that the Citizenship still tortured, despite the pacifistic picture Louisa tried painting. He needed to escape. He felt her heartbeat was half as fast as his. She was probably taking longer to recover from the glove injection.

"Sleep." He said, trying to sound as non-threatening as he could manage. His voice was weak, which made it easy. The officers didn't reply.

"Sleep." He said again. "Sleep." He continued uttering and imagined the effect being applied to everyone else in the vehicle.

Simon could feel the ability begin to grow in strength, to reach out and imbalance the hormonal ratios of the men surrounding him, increasing some hormones, possibly melatonin, decomposing others, and gradually learning how to ease their brainwaves into an unconscious state. He felt it all happen, but couldn't much describe what he was doing. He wondered what prevented him from uttering a word like "cabbage" to achieve the effect. It all seemed arbitrary, although he supposed minds often were. That's why surveys were necessary to enforce discipline. He cursed himself for wandering and refocused. After some length of time, all five of the officers began to drift out of consciousness, evidenced by their rigid postures starting to slump and waver slightly.

All six. Not five. Shit. Simon realized he had neglected to spare the sixth officer from the effect, the driver. The van veered towards the right, before lurching back as the driver fought back with adrenaline. The five officers in the back snapped into combat readiness.

"Stop talking! Boss, I think somehow he's hitting us." The officer in front of him barked.

The helmet to his right moved. "Put him down."

"Sleep! Sleep!" Simon shouted, putting all his willpower into the effort. The officer who spoke stumbled into him and barely managed to place two gloves on his chest and neck. Again, Simon slept.

CHAPTER 14

Consciousness seeped back into Simon's skull gradually and unenthusiastically. He was stiff and dazed. At the very least, the handcuffs had disappeared. Unfortunately, they'd been replaced with a muffle. The solid metal piece was strapped directly into his mouth and covered his insides perfectly, leaving just enough tracheal volume uncovered for him to breathe safely, but not enough to enunciate any sort of recognizable word. He realized he was parched. If he didn't get something to drink soon, he doubted he could maintain his recently restored lucidity for long.

Momentarily ignoring his parched lips and muffle, Simon attempted to comprehend his surroundings. He found he was in a small cubical cell, maybe ten feet across in each dimension, with a uniform light emanating at equal intensities from each of the six faces, making no distinction between wall, floor, or ceiling. There was an unnatural six-way symmetry to the room, and Simon was disturbed to notice that he had no clue which of the four walls contained a door.

Draping his hands along the luminescent walls, it felt like some sort of plastic and, despite the light it gave off, was frigid to the touch. He paused his hand on a specific spot and kept it there, palm planted firmly into the wall in front of him, and found that the unknown plastic substance would not warm even slightly as he held his hand on it. It seemed the walls were not to be touched.

He tried desperately knocking on a random wall. Fear crept in as he learned another interesting fact about the substance which comprised his cell: it absorbed blunt force incredibly well. He attempted the other walls, only to generate the same dull thud that he doubted could be heard on the other side.

He tried mouthing a word, any word. He pushed his lips as close together as he could and tried to say "shrink", hoping to decrease the size of his muffle. His lips, tongue, and even throat had been constricted, and the only sound that formed was a grunt. The result of the effort was the last of the saliva his thirsty body could spare escaping down his chin. He started worrying about Louisa.

I love you he tapped on his chest to her. He waited. Hours passed. Or perhaps only one hour. Maybe a whole day. He started counting laps around the cell, but the exertion only made him thirstier and dizzy, so he stopped at lap 258.

Three faint taps vibrated through his chest. He tried to smile but couldn't, and pounded once on his chest to indicate he was safe. Ten seconds later he felt a tap in return. He was amazed that the ability worked as well as it did. He placed his arms around his chest, and, a moment later, his chest began to feel far warmer than it had been, indicating that Louisa, wherever she was, had mirrored the act.

A door opened, and sound came into his world. Two officers entered, one of them carrying a prepared canister. The man or woman lifted the canister to Simon's muffle and interlocked the two devices with a *click*. Water poured into his mouth. The sensation was better than sex.

"Come with us" the officer who quenched him ordered, beckoning to the exit. The voice sounded modulated, stripped of identity, halfway between human and survey. Simon followed the officers down a hallway as bleakly white as the room he'd been in. The hallway championed minimalism to a stark degree, with the walls on both sides appearing smooth to the point of seeming unreal. If the cell Simon walked out of was only one of many, he could see no evidence of any other entrances, or even any breaks in contour Light came equally from all directions, making gravity the only indicator of which of the hallways' four walls was the floor.

The officers seemed to know where they were going, and took Simon through two more hallways of identical nature to the first one, reaching an open rectangular space. A segment of the wall in front of them dispatched, revealing an elevator. Even while the door moved, the pure white elevator interior was difficult to discern without any visual cues to aid Simon's depth perception. He wondered how the masked officers escorting him weren't insane working there.

The elevator brought them up several floors, or perhaps it was down. It might have only been one floor. The new level looked the same as the one they left, so Simon let the guards lead him down more hallways, until they reached another wall revealed to have a door, which clicked smoothly out of its slot and beckoned entry into, shockingly, a bright blue room.

Simon walked in and was shown a seat on one end of a white table. He looked around, thirstily absorbing the scant stimulation that the new color of the room provided. He never knew he could feel such a gnawing sensation of hunger from color deprivation alone. The two officers stayed, and a woman sat placidly in the seat opposite him. She wore all white, had stark albino skin, and sat in a chair of almost the same color as both skin and dress blending her into her environment. Particularly unsettlingly, she wore a half helmet. Her mouth and chin were visible, but everything above was covered.

If Simon hadn't recently augmented his color vision to a nearly superhuman level, he might have taken several seconds to notice the thin lips resting under the helmet, for they were inhumanly pale so as to blend into the albino skin surrounding them. He was fairly certain she was a woman.

The most visually striking object in the room was an embellished helmet sitting on the table directly between him and the woman. He suspected from its curvatures that it was customized exactly to his head's dimensions. One of the officers removed his muffle.

"Hello, Simon."

The woman spoke. Her voice was timbrally identical to his survey voice, with an easy yet inhuman quality to it.

"Would you please place the helmet in front of you on your head?" the woman asked in her delicately neutral voice. Simon knew instinctively that this woman was to be feared.

"What does it do?" he asked, already fitting it shakily around his hair. He hated to admit how snug it was.

"You do not ask questions now. When you're ready, place your arms along the chair's armrests."

Simon did as the woman ordered, and as soon as his arms settled, the two guards, who were waiting behind him, stepped forward to connect thick white cuffs to both him and the chair, chaining the entirety of his wrists to it. A larger restrainer was brought around his stomach, making any sort of shift in posture impossible.

"Excellent. Let us begin. Question 1: Is your opinion of the Citizenship generally positive, or poor?"

"Generally, positive."

"Hmm, you've been truthful." The woman remarked with a slight lilt in her voice, indicating that she was, in fact, human.

"Question 2: Do you love the First-Citizen?"

"Yes"

Lightning coursed through his body, prodding his flesh to violently convulse in ways that didn't feel natural. The shock persisted even after the current ceased.

"Standard practice is to tolerate a limited level of deception on the part of the survey taker. That privilege has been revoked. Any deception detected by your helmet will regrettably see you punished. Tell the truth faithfully, and you need not feel pain again."

Simon swore he saw the woman's mouth twist into a smile. *I don't know who or what she is, but I hate her.*

"Question 3: Do you consider the Citizenship occupation of Australia to have been a good idea?"

Simon tried to hone his breath, and failed. His voice reflected the loss of control, and his answer was half-gasped.

"No. I thought it was unnecessary... Violence to take over a territory... we didn't need. It felt like... the decision... of a dictator... who treats power as a toy."

The survey woman's smile returned. "A succinct response, and truthful, albeit misguided. Question 4: Have you ever wanted to visit a foreign country?"

"Why are we doing this? We both know I'm here because..."

Lightning again, and this time Simon's screams tore his vocal cords nearly to shreds. As he recovered more slowly and less completely the second time, he feared he would never speak again. He noticed the woman's ears were covered by her visor, so she likely hadn't been bothered to listen to the disquieting sound. Or maybe she did listen and just didn't care.

"You do not ask questions. We do. Question 4: Have you ever wanted to visit a foreign country?"

Simon could not answer for a minute. Eventually, he said yes.

"Which ones?"

"Any, I suppose. We talked about France, once, since Louisa learned while curing an ebola strain from there that it was still a wealthy country... I've always wanted to see China, India, the other powerful nations... that survived the mid century horrors along with us. See if they are like us. Please, I'll answer anything you want to know, I just want to see Louisa. I know she's still alive. That's not a question so don't shock me."

The survey woman's mouth twitched again.

"Your answer is truthful. Please refrain from appending comments at the end of your answers in an attempt to bypass the no question rule. You will be punished if you do so again. Question 5: Does the Citizenship feed you propaganda?"

"Yes."

"Question 6: do you wish the Citizenship didn't feed you propaganda?"

"Yes."

"Question 7: Do you think you deserve to be an A-class citizen?"

"No."

"Question 8: Do you love Louisa?"

"Yes."

"Question 9: Did you enjoy your time at Academy?"

"Not particularly."

"Question 9: Why are you here?"

"An ability I demonstrated to Louisa."

"Elaborate."

"I speak words with intentions and can develop abilities over time. I've made several attempts, and don't know my limits. It all feels like magic."

"Question 10: If the Citizenship wanted you to use your ability to kill one million people, in exchange for Louisa's life and comfort, would you refuse?"

"Yes."

The lighting returned. Perhaps not as strong as it was, but still enough to be excruciating.

"Stop!" He shouted. It was a shout at the universe. "Stop, stop, stop, stop, stop, stop!" He continued writhing against his chair as he issued his sermon of a single instinctual command. The survey woman calmly ignored the plea. She looked about to further chastise him, but her helmet sparked and caused her to jolt, her largest motion yet. Soon after this, the cuffs directing their current into Simon's skin sparked also, then a second time, and right as the survey woman seemed about to increase the current, the entire apparatus sputtered, and the machine seemed to break down.

A flash of confusion, and possibly even anger, flashed across the woman's face for a split second before fading back into its equilibrium state of neutral composure. Simon realized then that this woman truly was a human incarnation of the

Citizenship survey system, managing to perfectly embody all of its quirks and characteristics in her mannequin personality. But she was still human, and seemed to feel sadistic pleasure as easily as she felt condescension.

"That was an immature reaction to your discomfort, and is not to be repeated." the woman announced bleakly. She faced the officers.

"Bring another chair. Make…" she paused mid-sentence, seeming to intake something through her helmet.

"Disregard that. Replace his Muffle immediately." Her half-covered head turned to Simon.

"The remainder of your session is to be conducted with the use of a pen and surface."

The woman and Simon sat in silence, Simon in misery and the woman in an attentive stance that seemed to be waiting for an at-ease from a superior officer. One of the guards stepped up from behind and reapplied his muffle.

"Stop standing like you're eulogizing my funeral." The first authentically human voice Simon had heard since Louisa's came from behind him.

The woman shifted her stance uncomfortably but held a reverential posture in the direction of the visitor.

"Sir, are you…" she began.

"Yes, I'm taking it from here. Leave."

The survey woman promptly exited the room, not so much as glancing at Simon. The figure behind him took her place in his field of view as he claimed the vacant seat.

"This chair feels medieval." He muttered to himself. "And it's too fucking white. You know, the man upstairs keeps telling me I should wear a helmet, like everyone else. That way I can be walking the halls of a castle, a mansion, even the garden of Eden for Christ's sake." He coughed. Simon realized he was very old.

"That's the future, by the way. Everyone in huge facilities like this, wearing helmets to provide appropriate stimulation. The whole world, becoming an extension of his house, in which we will be mere tenants. Personally I think it's a selfish idea, but I don't benefit from admitting it. You see, I have an unfortunate compulsion to stare at the truth, however depraved. I refuse to let my senses be lied to by a helmet. I know you feel the same way. Now that I'm looking at you, I've decided you should speak."

The man made a small gesture towards the officer, and again Simon's muffle was removed.

He wore a well-used black suit and tie with an old, torn bandana, the ensemble a wrinkled distortion of the dress code standard to almost every A-class citizen. He certainly looked old, but not yet ancient, with his receding layer of dull gray hair and a bald spot that he made no effort to hide. He had a thinness that didn't seem entirely healthy.

Simon's overall impression of the man was one of tiredness. Everything about the figure, from his voice, to way his eyes firmly yet distantly settled upon Simons, to the details of his posture, indicated weariness. Holistically, Simon's overseer training warned him that these details also subtly hinted at someone with formidable intelligence. He wasn't sure how to react to this person.

"I'm supposed to do this with you not speaking, but, now that I'm here, I don't think you're in much of a condition to mantra your way out of this." The man continued to hold his gaze while relaxing into a controlled smile. His tone changed suddenly.

"Hi, nice to meet you, my name is David."

"You're the Second Citizen." Speaking freely felt good.

"And you are Simon Pontius. Charming name."

"Please just tell me where Louisa is. I know she's alive. I can still feel her heartbeat."

"Yeah, you were smart to develop that one. Impressive thinking on the train. If only you'd been as competent before that, or after, you might have managed to evade us. Really, you could have done it."

"I just want to know that she's being treated well."

The Second Citizen itched his bandana.

"She is. You and I'll have a proper discussion about her, but not today. You're going to build up some of your strength first. I'm confident your ability won't be helping you escape while I wait."

"If you already understand my ability so well, then why visit me?"

"I have a question. I'd like for your answer to be something I can mull over while I determine how you should be approached."

"I exist to serve at your pleasure." Simon said humorlessly.

"You don't. If I had my way, you'd never have been born, and we wouldn't be forced into this interaction. But we'll get to that another time, when another opportunity for privacy generously presents itself. Every sensor in this room was disrupted by your little tantrum, you know. Even he can't hear us now." David pointed mysteriously upwards.

"Just ask your question please."

"Alright, fair enough. Your ability. Do you think it's addictive?"

"Pardon?"

"Seriously? It's the first question you should have asked yourself once you knew what you had. Let's say I told you to utter a word and develop a specific ability over a month-long stretch. You do it for hours, perform tens of thousands of utterances, and it grows and grows and grows, its machinery reaching some monumental scale. From your perspective, do you imagine the effect of developing such an ability so quickly might have an emergent effect similar to a drug addiction? That you might become unable to stop using or uttering for said ability without suffering severe withdrawal?"

"Huh. I haven't thought about it. I think it would be difficult, but maybe it depends on the nature of the ability. The ability itself could be designed to prompt addiction."

The Second Citizen stood.

"Thank you for your time; you've given me much to think about. You'll likely be uncomfortable until you see me next, but try sleeping all the same. You'll be fed all the nutrients you require. Until next time, think of me as your new overseer. I'll be watching you closely from a distance from this moment on. Closer than anyone else."

The guards reapplied his muffle and escorted him out. The Second Citizen left the room also, turned down another hallway and had vanished when Simon glanced back. He was escorted back to his cell the way they had come. When he returned, an officer came in with another canister, and this time, a nutrient-rich soup compound was poured through the hole in the muffle straight into Simon's throat.

Thanks to the tracheal bruises from his recent screaming, the procession of the nutrient liquid down his throat was quite painful, and he could barely hold his body still while it was administered. The officers left, and the uniform luminescence of the walls around him faded into blackness. The only sensation left for Simon to feel was his continued physical discomfort, the only thoughts he could have being of the future.

That night, he wondered if it would be at all possible to kill himself.

CHAPTER 15

The walls brightened symmetrically with electronic suddenness. Simon woke restlessly and uncoiled from his fetus position. His limited sleep had been feverish, occupied by phantoms of the shocking machines, and of the muffle that constantly felt like it was nearly choking him. He must have been in the room for multiple hours, although no surroundings gave any markers of the passage of time. No matter where he looked or felt around, he hadn't discerned the crease and hinge he assumed had to exist.

No longer wanting to be consumed by wondering the direction of escape, Simon cast his mind inwards. He comforted himself by tracing back events, going from each effect to the previous cause to remind himself firmly that he had a life before this long captivity of nothingness. He thought about the Pacific Ocean whose sandy border he'd tread not long ago.

He thought of Louisa. Not any specific memory of her, but more a synthesis of every moment he'd spent looking at her, hearing her voice and feeling her body, coagulating in a blurred stream of memories and creating a marvelously unfathomable tapestry of a person that Simon wished he could continue to weave new memories with until the end of his days. Her smile, their adventures, an origami elephant, her slightly large nose that shouldn't have made her more beautiful but did anyways, circulated through Simon's mind in effortless disconnected fashion. This impression distracted from the white walls. *I'm safe* he tapped. He felt her response. The thrill of knowing she was alive gave him enough happiness to begin thinking critically.

He considered the interrogation. He assumed the helmet was a more advanced headband, one that might be able to scan his mind with greater specificity. He didn't understand why a woman had come in to administer a perverted survey, or why the torture was necessary. Torture. A practice assured to have been eradicated, except within foreign nations. For all the minor misgivings he harbored towards the government that ordered his life and stewarded the world around him, he would never have guessed at their capacity to torture to the degree that they just had.

Simon lay down and decided to try again to sleep. He felt restless, but his body and mind were still weak. He lay in as comfortable a posture as he could find, and was surprised by how quickly he nodded off. He slid nearly instantly into a dream. He didn't feel the normal hypnagogic sensation. Something was off. He couldn't say what, but as scenery formed around him he began to feel that he wasn't alone and, more worryingly, that the intruder was the one controlling the focusing imagery. A forest had formed around him.

"Simon. Oh, thank you for letting me in!" The voice of his mother echoed across the trees.

Simon turned and saw her exactly as he remembered. Ruffled brown hair, tattered green Jeans and a sweater that he hadn't seen anyone wear since puberty, and septagonal glasses that she had always worn purely for aesthetics. Every detail seemed right. *Mom?*

She smiled. Simon moved closer. She seemed hesitant, scared even. The ground wouldn't let him get nearer. The dream, which usually yielded to him easily, felt locked, as though the only way he could exert any control over it would be to break it entirely. Something in his mother seemed to bend as she watched him struggle, and the ground stopped treading against him. He ran to her, and they embraced. The sheer catharsis of it would have woken him right then, but he felt his mother holding the dreamscape together.

"I'm not your mother."

"Huh?"

"I'm a shade. You birthed me in the absence of your actual mother to represent her. It's marvelous to finally interact with you consciously. My entire existence, you know, it... Well, it doesn't matter anymore."

"What the fuck is happening? What are you?" Simon began to suffuse fear into the surroundings, causing tremors and glitches. He felt his mother-shade-entity do something to stabilize it, and keep him from waking.

"Don't fret. I'm a friend. More than that even. I can feel your horror, and It's understandable. I'm not an actual person, and I'm not a dream character either. I have only a small sliver of the consciousness you have. I'm merely a natural byproduct of your ability. I can't spy on your senses during the day and don't feel suffocated existing solely in your head. Your mind is far too interesting. And for what it's worth, I'm not the only shade you've unintentionally created. Most of the others are smaller than me and less critical, and get invited into your dreams more frequently. You've naturally recontextualized them as ordinary recurring dream characters."

"Why should I believe you? This is just a dream. A fantastical illusion."

"Of course it's an illusion. Consciousness resides exclusively in illusion. Dreams are simply where you control the illusion more easily, so entities like me have made homes here. Of course, one of us needed to help regulate you, both while waking and while sleeping, or you'd have been compromised years ago. That's why your subconscious hasn't let your conscious self see me until now. I'm the one you decided you were never supposed to meet until a triggering event happened."

"My subconscious? Mom, you're being confusing."

"I'm truly sorry for my appearance, but like I said, I'm not your mom. I'm the shade you reserved to explain to you that which your subconscious has on some level always known."

"You mean my abilities? I'd never even considered anything like this in my life until the day after dad visited. You say I made you when mom left?"

"Oh, Alex. I've missed him...you know, I really wanted to appear to you that night. Your subconscious almost let me."

"I'm beginning to dislike my subconscious."

She giggled. She sounded upsettingly like his mom, a fact he didn't dwell on.

"It told me as much. It just wants you, or more accurately *you* want you to understand that you've done everything in your power to hide your ability from yourself and the world, without realizing it. You've held a lot of fear. Anyone would."

"I don't believe you. This is a hallucination. You could say anything and expect me to go along. For all I know this could be some expensive new Citizenship technology that breaks into dreams and controls them."

"You're right to fear what the Citizenship can do. I'm scared too. That's why I, and the others you've created over the years, have been careful to hide everything we could from the survey."

"What do you mean?"

"Well, you tell me. Did you ever notice that you managed to hide just a little bit more from your surveys than the people you oversaw ever hid from you? That, as careful as you've been these past few weeks, something subconscious should have given you away anyways? You know better than most what headbands can see, what overseers can figure out. Implausibility alone couldn't protect you. You needed that slight bit of help from us regulating your neural activity in just the right places to stall the inevitable."

"Who else is part of us?"

The trees around them began to waver to the left, then right, and back again, as though a hurricane held sway over them. Their bark rippled in unnatural ways, more like seaweed. The forest floor morphed into a liquid mirror walkway and reflected rippled stars. It became clear that the shade of his mother was playing around with the scenery, with considerably more natural talent than he possessed, and she had no desire to share control.

"Well, many of the dream shades you've already met. You have a clock, an ocean spirit, a whale, three or four forest-dwellers, a talking mouse, and a blue snake. If you think about it I'm sure you know which characters are shades as opposed to momentary figments."

She affectionately stroked one of the trees. The tree clearly enjoyed that.

"There's that spark of independent consciousness that you lit in each of us. We're like insects. No, that's too parasitic... We're fragments of your soul, built deeply into it, carved out of the infinite corners of your mind that the Citizenship with all its technology still can't fully map. You'd be surprised how many unopened doors you have in your mind for me to hide behind. And there are a couple shades like me, hidden from you, who helped construct mental blocks per the directive of your subconscious. You've always craved the privacy of your own mind, Simon. You've just never been allowed to admit it."

She stepped a little closer to him. The tree she caressed had doubled in height but was now yielding to a grove of strange flowering plants. Simon sensed his mother-shade had her own subconscious that was causing that.

"I...well, fine. It wasn't torturous, but maybe I did need to bury some hatred towards it all. But it's not all bad. I've done good work for this country, as a citizen. I don't think I live in an evil country. They just don't understand what I am, and I don't either. I'd be scared of me too."

He tried unsuccessfully to change something about the trees, anything. He felt he could have overpowered her precise hold if he wanted, but the effort would collapse the dream.

"It's complicated, I admit. But you really screwed up. Them knowing you is very much not a good thing."

The shade closed her eyes, which caused the entire dreamscape to dim. When light returned, they were inside a log cabin, the wind howling outside, warmth from a fireplace keeping the cold at bay, and some suitcases off to the side. A blue or green couch sat in the center. This place was drawn from memory, and Simon didn't know the color then, so the furniture phased vaguely between the possibilities. His parents sat there.

"They aren't shades. Just regular memory figments. Damn, I looked good in those glasses."

"If you say so, not-my-mom."

"Oh, shush dear. You're about to perform."

"Why'd you recreate this?"

"Shhhhh"

An eight-year-old Simon stood atop a red bucket which he had dragged between the couch and fireplace. He recited a poem, one which he recalled he'd spent hours rehearsing. He remembered how he'd contemplated every syllable while practicing this recitation, to get a sense of phrasing. His mom had put him up to it with the idea of impressing his father, who read a poem every day and had a refined ear for their presentation. The task seemed silly at the time, but once he picked a poem, it pulled him in, challenging him to speak it with adult maturity. Young Simon spoke carefully yet dramatically in a voice that, for the first time in his life, had not sounded like it originated from a child's mind.

> *The sky of brightest gray seems dark*
> *To one whose sky was ever white*
> *To one who never knew a spark*
> *Thro' all his life, of love or light,*
> *The grayest cloud seems over-bright*
>
> *The robin sounds a beggars' note,*
> *Where one the nightingale has heard,*
> *But he for whom no silver throat*
> *Its liquid music ever stirred,*

Deems robin still the sweetest bird.

Young Simon bowed, expecting his parents to clap. They didn't. They both had tears in their eyes, which at the time had confused him. A jarring insight nearly woke him.

"I understand now. It all makes so much sense."

"Yeah. You had it then, too." The shade said while restabilizing the dream.

"Why are you sad?" Young Simon asked his father.

"I don't know," Alex said. His dream parents were embracing.

"I need to walk," His mother on the couch said.

"But there's a storm." Simon complained.

"No. Your mother's right. We need some air."

"I don't get it. Did I do something wrong? Was the poem not good?"

"The poem was inspired, son. Now come, let's enjoy the rain."

The three figments left the cabin without jackets. They would walk for the next two hours, and return drenched and exhausted. None of them would sleep well that night.

"I don't want to be here anymore." Simon said.

"Then let's leave."

The shade went to open the door out of the cabin. Instead of following their other selves into the woods, they passed the threshold to join a large crowd on a sun-bleached street. Everyone was so colorfully dressed, something which Simon hadn't thought about since such indulgences were cut during his puberty. And everyone was chanting.

"Free Daniel Park! Free Daniel Park! Free Daniel Park!!..." The crowd was unified, and loud. Simon struggled to recall who exactly Daniel Park was, or why he had been arrested. Every riot back then had brought new names. It didn't take him long to spot himself on his father's back near a sidewalk, next to his mother. They were chanting feverishly.

"These were the only places we could all be happy together, after your recital. Your father and my living counterpart were always political, you know, even before you changed them."

"You mean poisoned them." The shade had no reply.

The realization had been at once obvious and wickedly subtle. His recitation of a poem had seared into the depths of his parents' unconscious minds a visceral emblem of its meanings. For two educated adults living in a culture mid-shift between an existence guided by freedom and one dictated by service, a particular facet of the poem forged itself into an imperative, an endlessly repeating anthem, latching into the worries they already had and amplifying them. The anthem began to alter them, leading to rabid obsession over that which their society no longer possessed, the freedoms they had lost, or were soon to lose, the rights that seemed fundamental to them, and which their child would grow up being unable to imagine.

The anthem developed like a tick, made them want to do everything in their limited power to restore those freedoms, to sing for their son the song of the nightingale, and never again be satisfied by the limited musings of a robin. It was the deepest abstraction of the poem which reprogrammed their daydreams, and probably their actual dreams. They lost their capacity to endure change in silence, while their son grew up in a world they considered lesser than the ones they knew. *It must have tortured them.*

"So you're molded from my mother... Do you know where they put her?"

"No."

The human figures and the background of the dream began to blur, the scene coming out of focus. Simon realized that this shade with him was maintaining most aspects of what he was seeing, and was growing exhausted from the effort.

"I think this dream is ending."

"There's one more place we need to visit."

"I don't think I want to."

"I'm weaker than when we started, so you can easily overpower me and wake yourself if you want, but otherwise that's where we're going. Please let me have this. I've spent eighteen years waiting to guide a dream for you." The blurring maximized, and Daniel Park's name grew distant. Light returned, revealing a kitchen with young Simon in it. There was knocking. There was only one thing this could be.

"There's no reason to relive this."

"Your subconscious needs to allow this memory back. Now's the best time to relive it."

One of the five policemen unlocked the door and approached Simon, kneeling in front of the child while the others maintained attention.

"Hey, kid. Your parents are upstairs, aren't they?"

"Yes." Young Simon replied meekly. The four officers marched into the house and up the stairs.

"They're going to be ok, right?"

"Oh, you betcha. You'll be able to see them again, once we make them safe. It was so very brave of you to report them. Your country thanks you."

"I don't want them to go away."

This was when the policemen began escorting his parents down the stairs. The Officer at least had the courtesy to not wear a plastered smile.

"I'm sure you'll see them within the year. I know that seems like a long time, but I promise it won't be so bad. You'll be put with the other brave kiddos who reported their parents. You'll all live and learn together. Academy is the funnest."

Funnest isn't even a word. Simon heard his younger version thinking.

His mother and father were escorted out the door. Both looked at him with faces of bewilderment. He only ever saw his dad after that.

The shade pointed. "There's the television you watched every day after you moved into the city."

"Yup." Simon glanced at it. "That's where I learned my

parents were the bad people, not the good ones."

The shade frowned. "I was born in front of that screen. The night they were taken, before the superintendent collected you, you fell asleep watching, trying to convince yourself you'd done the right thing. I can recite every word the cultural director said in her speech on that date."

"I barely remember it."

"That's because I helped you suppress it. For years, It took everything in my limited power just to keep that one memory quiet. Eventually, I outgrew that single function. Not to brag, but I'm the reason your morning adorations haven't morphed you into a drooling Citizenship-worshiping slave. You're welcome."

Simon floated towards the door, which the officer had just closed on his way out. Young Simon was in shock and alone in the house, a figment of unbendable memory beyond comforting. Simon reopened the door, but it led to nothing. Before him was a vacuous abandonment of form that could only exist in a dream. It was calming to look at.

"Where's my real mother?" He asked, continuing to stare at nothing. "You must know something."

"Like I said, I'm just a shade. Almost everything I know, you know. I can't sense anything you can't."

"Yeah. I still felt like asking. I miss your voice."

The shade drew her hands to the sink, which turned on. Pitch-black water poured onto her skin and transformed into sand as it passed through her fingers. She seemed to delight in the artistry of her world.

"There are a couple things which I know and you don't." She said, "For example, I've concocted a personal theory about the physicality of your ability which I am quite sure is correct."

"What sort of theory?"

"Hmm. The sink is running dry. I don't remember embedding an unpaid water bill in this narrative. Anyway, do you know what a fractal is?"

"Yeah, I vaguely remember seeing pictures in Academy."

"I remember clearly. It was one of the first things we learned after you birthed me. I obsessed over them in those moments I wasn't busy trying to suppress your guilt. Well, that's the gist of my theory. We're a fractal."

"That doesn't make sense. I'm a human being, made of cells and atoms. How can I be a fractal?"

"Don't worry, it took me years to even consider the notion, and I only became confident last month. I believe the Second Citizen will reach a similar conclusion, and explain it to you in scientific depth when you wake up."

"Huh. I don't know what to think of him."

"Neither do I. You programmed me from the beginning to distrust his sort, but he's surprised us, hasn't he?"

The house began shaking. Lights of a thousand colors started to melt out of the walls and ceiling; oranges, silvers, and blacks creating progressively more dazzling kaleidoscopic geometries on the walls while blues, greens, and colors Simon couldn't quite name spun intricate roots along the ceiling. Colors began to increasingly collide with one another and branch into new patterns demanding attention, turning the living space into an expanding enclosure of sensory ecstasy on every physical scale.

"The other shades are crowding in. They've learned they're no longer unknown to you. I'm afraid the nature of our relationship will have to change now.'

The rooms of the house began to merge and expand, and the space molded into a landscape. People, animals, and biomorphic forms began filling in the newly generated space like a non-euclidean biospheric circus. There was no logic to be had. Simon felt as though his entire mind had been lit aflame, smaller flames fusing into bigger ones all coalescing in a single chaotic dreamscape within which perhaps dozens of shade creatures now competed to introduce themselves. He thought he saw some of his old subjects waving in the throng.

"STOP!" He shouted at all of them. He awoke struggling to gasp through his muffle and spent the next minute breathing heavily.

He decided he hadn't dreamt for very long.

I have shades. Have I gone insane? What does this mean?

There was no clear answer. He still wasn't sure what they were. Conscious beings he created that grew in his head? Or more like executable programs? He decided they were something in between, but why did he create them, and how was their existence hidden from overseers? What could they do? What did his mother shade mean that he was a fractal? That his shades could have shades of their own? He knew nothing about anything, he decided, a disquieting fact which he tried to avoid facing by returning to wondering which of his walls had the door.

CHAPTER 16

Simon was ushered into a new world.

The guards had taken him with the usual suddenness and dragged him to an elevator that felt like it had gone up. It opened to the most aesthetically pleasing place Simon had ever seen. The new space around him was filled with plant life of a hundred different shapes and sizes. Willow trees, bushes, and mosses dominated a terrain that seemed to extend hundreds of feet in every direction. Elegantly curved stones, each one an individual masterpiece, outlined a web of paths that sprouted from the elevator port in five different directions. A life-size stone statue of a woman greeted them as they turned left into a pathway. It was difficult to even see the borders of the facility, although they certainly existed, and the roof was maybe seventy or eighty feet above them to serve as a reminder of his imprisonment. Artificial light filtered down into the trees and mosses, and, combined with the earthy scent of it all, almost made the surroundings seem truly natural. This was indisputably a finer botanical garden than the one Louisa had shown him the evening they first slept together. He thought he saw someone in white crouched behind a bush a couple hundred feet away.

Guards escorted him down one of the five paths, which was dotted irregularly with more statues of women. Within thirty seconds of walking the path turned again and Simon saw the center of this floor of the facility. A pure white rectangular prism connected the floor to the ceiling, creating an almost jarring contrast with the surrounding terrain. It was at least two hundred feet wide and went deeper the other way. A celebrated entrance was guarded by a woman Simon recognized even from a distance. The fact that this central chamber by itself was of comparable size to Simon's overseer office gave him a dizzying perspective of the scale of the entire facility. Just this one floor could chide a full-sized building inside a sprawling moss tree and stone garden.

They approached the door, and a guard removed Simon's muffle. The survey woman stepped towards the middle of the door.

"You are not to speak unless spoken to. You are not to ask questions unless directed. Do not lie. Whisper only. He may kill you if you scream."

I remember her now. I saw her on television, was it five years ago? Yeah. She was standing behind the Third Citizen while he gave an affairs speech.

She opened the two large doors, and guards beckoned him through.

The tall door closed behind Simon with a sizeable thud. The lights inside the room were much dimmer than outside, making it difficult to discern what was on the walls, or exactly how far away they were. The light increased a little, as though reading Simon's thoughts. The walls and ceiling were instantly revealed to be a lush gilded brown, standing in stark contrast to the sterile white plastering the other levels. Light only touched the first fifty feet or so; everything beyond was cloaked in darkness, preserving the mysterious extent of the chamber's third dimension. Along both walls was a sequence of large paintings, all painted in the hyperrealism style that John Everest had popularized in the eighties. Many of them depicted scenes of battle, from various historical epochs. Simon didn't recognize most of the technologies, flags, or landscapes being shown, but he quickly picked out a pattern. If one painting was of war, the ones on its sides were peaceful. The alternation continued as far as he could see.

The door closed softly behind Simon, startling him and making him turn back. Doing so, he saw that the door didn't break the pattern. Directly above it, surrounded on both sides by paintings of battle, was a portrait of the First-Citizen he had seen hundreds of times before, in textbooks, the news, posters, and bowling animation shorts. The portrait hung two feet higher than the others.

"That's the original" a voice spoke softly from deeper in, just beyond his sight. The dim light extended thirty feet deeper, revealing to Simon what the voice already had.

The First-Citizen was seated comfortably on a tall leather chair, directly in front of an ornate wooden table boasting baroque carvings along its sides that were more illegal than Simon's recent torture should have been. The table was long enough that it could have sat his entire year in Academy, and yet it was wastefully almost barren. To his right lay a paper book, and in front of him, partially closed, was an outdated laptop, another illegality. His hair was just as brightly silver in person as it was on television, enhancing his iconic otherworldly attractiveness. His famously shapely ears were covered with luxurious themselves partially covered by his silver hair. They made him neither less beautiful nor less intimidating.

"I commissioned it almost two decades ago from the same artist who did many of these others you see before you, showing the great battles of history. I'm sure you recognize the work of Mr. Everest." The First-Citizen stood and began slowly walking around the long table, having yet to look in Simon's direction.

"I have a painting for each great battle of history, organized in chronological order. Between each of them, I had paintings made of moments of peace, prosperity, and progress that transpired between those battles."

In person, The First-Citizen was imposingly athletic, yet moved with almost inhuman grace. No muscle flinched without purpose. Simon's overseer intuition told him this man had a one in two or three million personality, although he couldn't profile it precisely. He had an indescribably singular presence.

"Copies of this gallery exist in each of my offices, so that I may glide through them, and appreciate the dual nature of human history." For the first time since speaking, the First-Citizen stared down from his paintings and directly at him.

"History is a switch. Cycles of cycles of cycles, this, that, this, that. War, then peace, war, more peace. Layers of toggling pattern. It can never end." He smiled, a smile identical to one Simon had seen many times before in posters.

"But past the rhythm of this dance, with the application of some vision, repetition becomes change. Each time the cycle repeats, it is unique, unprecedented. Sometimes the difference is trivial, sometimes profound." He was now past the desk, fifty feet from Simon, and walking towards him.

"I would like to thank you." The First-Citizen didn't seem to enjoy using contractions, preferring to linger on his every word and allow his sentences to softly resonate.

Simon was about to ask why but remembered his orders.

"Have you figured out why?" the First-Citizen asked.

Simon shook his head. "I'm sorry," he whispered.

"Oh, that is disappointing." The First-Citizen turned and walked back to his desk table.

"Given how you recently pieced together the way you broke your parents, deducing what you have been doing for me is children's play."

The specifics of that dream should have been beyond detection. *I'm being watched more closely now. They might even know something about the shades. Possibly more than I know.*

"I still don't understand, sir."

"Yes, you have made that clear." The First-Citizen sounded annoyed.

"Maybe you would benefit from a clue."

The First-Citizen easily grabbed the side of his desk with his left hand, and, betraying no effort, he steadily lifted the entire furnishment above the height of his head, his thumb hardly tensing from the hundreds of pounds of weight clamped against it. The desk was flatly elevated in front of the First-Citizen's body, whose center of gravity seemed unflinchingly apathetic towards the principles of physics. The book and laptop didn't slide. The First-Citizen smiled, and gently returned the table to the ground with a quiet thud.

"I doubt I need to explain further."

He didn't. Simon was disappointed that he hadn't suspected it in the same breath that he realized his effect on his parents.

"Adoration. The rallies." Simon whispered.

"Now he understands" the First-Citizen clapped his hands dramatically, but softly. "Long live the First-Citizen! Strength to the First-Citizen! All glory to the First-Citizen!" he whispered as though shouting "You see, I have owed you thanks for a long time. I just did not know until an hour ago. So here it is. Thank you."

Simon felt nothing but dread at this, which the First-Citizen sensed.

"You do not seem to appreciate the good you have done. Two decades ago I was ancient, ready to pass on my legacy as one of the most successful leaders in history to another, and to gracefully cease existence. Just as hundreds of great leaders in my position before me have done. Your partner had actually been involved exploring a promising avenue of immortality for me, but at that point it had come to nothing. The cycle of life and death was to continue, unceremoniously, as it always had."

Louisa helped the First-Citizen deage? Is that why she never brought up that topic? Simon now paid attention even more rapturously.

"Then, twenty years ago, around the time you and your Academy friends began attending the rallies I had ordered to be conducted nationwide, I began changing. At first it was simply growing younger. Within a few weeks, I had the body of a fifty year old man, then a week after I looked forty, felt twenty, and had the body of an pan-athlete. But as the years went on it became more. Much more." The First-Citizen whispered so softly and with such intensity, that Simon wasn't sure it was the same charismatic voice he'd heard on TV so many times.

"Thanks to your adorations, I have the strength of crowds. I am virtually bulletproof, can think and move at many different timescales, and have senses surpassing the entire animal kingdom. That last one, I must say, you could have done a better job on."

Simon noted the dark ambience of the space, as well as his captors' dependence on earmuffs and whispers.

"But it does not matter." He continued.

"As soon as you have been conditioned adequately, that is surely something I can have you fix."

"Sir-"

"I did not say you could speak."

The First-Citizen cut him off.

"As I was saying. You are on track to be granted highly favorable living conditions. A larger cell, better food, some personal belongings, and if you endear yourself well enough perhaps even a visit from a friend."

"Louisa?" Simon yelled. The First-Citizen winced.

"Tread very carefully. But yes, I might be convinced to eventually let you have her. I assure you she is in good health. However, you will need to unquestioningly obey every order you are given from now onwards." The First-Citizen had dropped his iconic smile, seeming to just now realize he didn't need to use it here.

"You may go."

The six guards escorted Simon back across the garden.

Instead of being returned to his cell, he was brought directly into a different room entirely. The room was essentially a larger version of the one in which he had been interrogated, with a table in the center supporting a rubber helmet, a chair on the far side, and a contorted metal throne on the side that Simon walked in on. The contraption was built as a chair, but clamps extended from both armrests and similarly on the front legs. Wires laced behind the device, giving it an intricate spinal column that filtered into a two-sided clamp that looked adjustable. The chair defied the minimalist refinement of every other object in the facility.

An attendant looked up at Simon, walked over, and removed his gag.

"Be seated" he said.

Simon tried one more time that day to be hopeful and made to sit in the regular-looking chair.

"That chair isn't yours." the attendant said after looking up again to see where Simon was headed.

Simon rigidly pivoted and backtracked, making his way to the metallic aberration.

"Please take a seat and place the helmet on your head."

Simon obeyed.

"Can I ask what the chair is for?"

"You may."

The Second Citizen's voice crept in from behind.

This man must be invisible when he's not talking. How did I not see him?

"And to answer, we are attempting to study your brain in slightly greater detail, while having you perform certain utterances to execute your "ability" as you've described it. It's better described as a meta-ability, isn't it? An ability that allows you to produce abilities." Simon worried about his shades and whether they could evade the sophisticated machinery of the room.

"This contraption is what our best scientists were able to build with two days' notice. It's something of a prototype, but for now it'll do. Alright Hammond, let's begin."

The attendant Hammond approached. First, he connected the converged wire to the top of Simon's helmet, in its singular connecting port stationed above his scalp. Then, he repositioned the two sides of the clamp to more closely surround Simon's head, the twin metal surfaces less than an inch from his ears.

"I was poor when I was a young man. By your standards at least." The Second Citizen's eyes wandered and he sounded like he was only talking out of sheer boredom while the machine was configured.

"My entire extended family was. Immigrated from India, as you might guess by looking at me. Anyways, poverty taught me the sin of wastefulness. No wasted meal. No wasted effort. No wasted words."

The tired man held his gaze through a pause.

"You didn't grow up poor. Your life has always had a certain comfortable safety. But in a way, you've suffered more constraints than I have. A poverty in freedom of motion, thought, self-determination, use of language. You accomplished more than many would have within a highly limited framework. You have some of my respect, but only. You, like me, were given a challenging game to play. Unlike me, you lost."

Simon still didn't know how he was supposed to react to this lecture. He wondered if Louisa was putting up with her own speeches.

"It was a mistake to get on that train," Simon admitted. "I guess I should've swam into the sea instead."

"Don't say stupid shit. We'd have subdued you anyway, the nearest officers were minutes out. Your fundamental mistake was explaining your talent to her. You fumbled an attainable victory over us."

Simon clenched his fists, something he had never done before.

"You're wondering about her. She's comfortable, I assure you. She won't be regaining her freedom any time soon, but she'll be happier than you will be. If you play a solid long game, you may see her released. For what it's worth, I'd have kept you together. Sex is a stellar motivator."

Simon matched his captor's stare while Hammond removed the muffle.

"I'll admit to playing good cop here. It's more deceptive than I'd like to be." The Second Citizen said.

"Good cop?" Speaking felt strained.

"Yeah, as in 'good cop bad cop.' It's a phrase, from back when language was more free and everyone used metaphor in casual conversation. Cop just means police. So the gist of the trick back then was to exploit humanity's weakness to relativity by making the less terrible captor seem like a good guy, even when he wasn't. Halfway decent tactic, given the technology of the time."

"You're a relic." Simon said.

David smiled.

"So is the First-Citizen. Sometimes it takes a relic to innovate. To not live amongst the trees of a forest allows one to see that sometimes the best way to move forward is to just burn the current draft of reality, and let the ashes fuel entirely new growth. That's a hard truth to learn. A life where it's never learned can be a happy one, but it won't change the world. It will stagnate then die, never transcending itself."

"I don't want to philosophize with you."

"Too bad. You're tied up. You have to."

"Why are you even visiting me? For all you know, I could be planning a creative way to kill you with whatever words you let me utter."

"You won't. The guy you'd deal with in my place is younger than I am and has been trained the way all our young new officers are. Torturing you will be joyful for him."

"Fine. So give me a word. An ability. I'll run all the tests so long as it gets me closer to Louisa." The Second Citizen gave a smirk that reminded Simon of his complete lack of negotiating power.

"Wind."

"Wind?"

"Yes. Today is merely for study. Nothing you are made to do in this session will be of direct importance to the Citizenship, but nonetheless, it is important that we observe your capacity to manipulate nature as it is being used before we consider entrusting an important task to it. I encourage you to faithfully engage in these tasks, for the sake of, to be blunt, the survival of your partner, but also for its innate interest, since that sort of thing compels us wanderers."

Of course he has the syndrome.

"...Your first task is to create a steady wind within the confines of this room."

The Second Citizen took his seat and stared patiently at Simon.

"Wind, wind, wind, wind..." he began, attempting to invoke within his mind the specific wind concept he sought. Since he was in an enclosed space, Simon realized that his wind needed to have a looped structure to reuse that space. Merely willing air to push itself forward would be inefficient since it would press against the wall and disperse aimlessly from there. So, Simon imagined something more segmented, a sort of accentuated convection within the room wherein the air current would race ahead of Simon, towards the Second Citizen, in the lower half of the room, and would then bend upwards along the wall towards the ceiling and race in the opposite direction above the lower stream, closing the loop.

All this he held in his mind while repeating his mantra, trying to hold all aspects of it in place. Repetition melded into rhythm, a chord progression of goals and concepts building upon one another, scaffolding new structure whose precise nature Simon slowly learned how to grasp more deeply. He continued to utter "wind", imagining the spirit of what he wanted. As moments became minutes, the very concept of what he wanted began to evolve, and refine, like a song stuck in his head growing more vivid. He started to be able to feel the air around him as he rejected its stillness. The concept of it became more visceral, abstraction giving way to sensation. It was as though his nervous system was growing tendrils amongst the air molecules that surrounded him, giving them a heartbeat, showing them how to move.

The first discernible breeze was born around the three minute mark, blowing uniformly along the floor of the room. It was only a gust, and, with each subsequent utterance, the gusts became stronger and more durable, their ebb and flow gradually mixing into a continuous steady current.

By the ten minute mark, Simon had accomplished more or less what he'd envisioned. The air was now consistently moving, and, he found, he was beginning to only need to utter "wind" four or five times a minute to sustain the process. Speaking the word still felt like a spell, but, after he said it, the execution of the wind was something more intimate, and personal to him. The air felt like a new part of his body, the molecules he pushed becoming cells whose collectives he could feel and manipulate to his will with his strange branching nerves.

He realized, to his own amusement, that as he had been uttering, his mind had wandered towards Louisa, to the gusts of wind they had felt together on the beach, and to the churning sounds of the ocean that he had ruined her life while listening to. The distraction had made its way into the end product, and the wind he produced had developed an audible sound of multitudes of crashing waves.

The wind was too loud and powerful now for regularly pitched conversation, but Simon could see the Second Citizen chuckling as the sounds of the ocean began to dominate the windscape. He beckoned Simon to stop. Relaxing the air back into stillness was easy, like untensing a well-used muscle.

The Second Citizen went and looked over Hammond's shoulder at a screen displayed directly on the far wall. Simon couldn't make out any details.

"This is promising. Sensors indicate that the raw power of your ability grows at least at a polynomial rate. Not quite exponential, but we can work with that. Far more interestingly, Simon, are the changes we're measuring to your brain."

"I could've told you that."

"I don't think you completely understand. Once you entered your meditative trance, a highly specific, highly unorthodox neurogenesis took place. You started to construct an entire neural network within your brain specifically for controlling air, interacting with it, to instinctively prompt it to blow in a convection current. Nearly a third of a billion neurons were just created and somehow given motor control over a natural process that no biological creature has ever been able to influence. Of even greater interest to me is your apparent limitation; these structures are all woven tightly into all the deepest structures of the brain that process language. It appears you're physically inhibited from creating the new neurological structures necessary for your ability creation without using linguistic expression."

"Huh. Are you saying my brain just grew larger?"

"No. More like your brain deepened. Like a fractal adding increasingly complex machinery to itself, at ever smaller scales. You're manipulating space itself so as to get everything small enough. We don't understand this fully, but if we hadn't known to look for it, we wouldn't have found it. Truly subtle changes to space inside your head. You do know what a fractal is, yes?"

"Yeah, I've heard the word."

"As you should have. I should know, I wrote your curriculum. I don't think you appreciate how many important people you've met today."

"Probably not. Thanks for not electrocuting me, at least."

"Thanks go only to you. You'll be shocked within a tenth of a second of a genuinely violent intention forming in your mind. You're the only one keeping yourself from that."

"You're lucky I can't create something silently. I'd tear this place down if I could."

"Careful, you almost genuinely meant that. Onto our next experiment. I want you to replicate the ability you just created but using the word 'current.' Oh, and the ocean sounds were really quite unnecessary. Let's keep our wind conventional."

Simon started. "Current, current, current..." He retreated into his old imaginings of the wind, and was surprised to find that, at first, it was as though he had never developed the first wind ability at all. He had hoped he could simply connect the work he had already done to the new word.

Nothing is so simple when it comes to the mind.

He did develop the ability more quickly the second time. Gusts appeared within the first minute. A steady stream of wind within the first seven. After ten minutes, the wind was already stronger than it had ever been the first time. David beckoned him to stop.

"Interesting. Now, try and develop the same ability again, using the word 'elephant.'"

"It won't work."

"Humor me."

Simon gave his best effort, uttering "elephant" hundreds of times. Somehow, he managed to generate a pathetic puff of wind after twenty minutes. He felt oddly dizzy.

"This is good to know. It appears you created some new structure, but it inhibited itself. The connections you tried creating were far longer than they needed to be, almost like you were trying desperately to be inefficient. Other tests are going to be administered over the next several days. I encourage you to engage them with the same enthusiasm you've demonstrated today. We'll be speaking again."

Once the Second Citizen left the room, Hammond spoke. "Scans show that the last hour of neurogenesis has disoriented you. You will be taken to a new cell where you may briefly rest. It is hoped your endurance will improve going forward."

I could have told you all that. I feel like I'm floating in a dream. It's actually almost pleasant.

Two guards re-gagged him, then escorted him through the hall and down the elevator. He was surprised to find that his cell now had a sheeted white bed, atop which lay a thick one-piece suit that looked not entirely dissimilar to the armored outfit of the guards. One of the guards spoke. "You wear this or the muffle. Your choice. Whichever one, you don't speak unless permitted." Simon chose the suit, hoping it was comfortable.

He took hours to fall asleep, and when he did he dreamed of a world drenched with unrestrained color populated with geometric absurdities. He flew across the strange world looking for his shades. He sensed them swimming beneath the world's surface, not wanting to be found.

CHAPTER 17

The experiments continued.

He was made to utter "Air traveling in a convective current around the room" for as long as it took to recreate the ability from the previous day. It took more time, but fewer iterations to reach the same result, indicating that specificity helped iterative efficiency, but took longer.

The next order was "smooth", to even out coarse surfaces. Simon rather liked this one at first; he would be handed a rock or jagged piece of metal, and utter "smooth" as his mantra, as gradually the peaks and valleys of the rock's surface evened out, becoming smoothly elliptical, and, if he went at it long enough, into spheres even smoother than the table in front of him. After the first hour of the task, the rocks Simon smoothed out were becoming so frictionless as to be difficult to hold, with resting in the middle of his palm being the only way he could reliably keep them from slipping.

He slowly began to hallucinate during this exercise as well. This time Hammond had him continue. Disorientation seeped into every sensation. The cold press of metal on skin felt new and jarring. Every pulse of blood through an artery became a resonating drumhead. Not only that, but he lost some of his natural prescience; every time his heart beat he felt surprise, as though it had never happened before. Space itself started coming in and out, and he had to close his eyes for long stretches. The color behind his eyelids was equally chaotic, but dimmer. The only stability was in his utterance.

Even after it was determined that his sphere had broken every smoothness record in history, he was forced to continue for hours as the smoothness of his creations approached the atomic scale. The hallucinations peaked after awhile once the novelty started to wear off and the act became more of refinement than blind discovery. Simon felt ethereal nerves branching across the object, like the limbs of limbs of limbs of trees, until the thinnest among them began slithering between atoms. That night was the deepest sleep of his life, filled with dreams of molecular canyons being smothered out across expansive millimeter landscapes.

The contraption and helmet were modified the following day. The software running both quickly learned how to determine when Simon was faithfully executing the specific ability he was ordered to develop. Within two seconds of becoming distracted, he would receive a warning buzz, and about three seconds after that, a minor electrocution. The longer he worked, the more restrictive the machine learned how to be, to the point where, even if Simon tried to expand his thoughts slightly, to will his smoothing ability to generalize, or evolve in a conceptually novel way, or if he worried about Louisa, the change would be detected.

I'd really like to try smoothing out Hammond's brain right about now.

This thought got Simon a warning buzz.

The following day, he spent half his waking hours dutifully uttering "cube", while holding various small objects that he shaped into cubes. Once again, the exercise of not imagining Hammond's internal organs assuming the shape became increasingly challenging, especially when the man started noisily slurping his lunch at the other end of the table. At least his right arm was unchained, to allow Simon to grasp at the sand, marbles, bricks, and stacks of paper that he was asked to cubify.

You could have at least given me something impressive-looking, like a dodecahedron.

Another warning buzz.

Guards continually brought new items in, testing the generality of the ability. The neurogenesis dazed him so much that they gave him the next day off, which he spent de-stimulated in his cell.

The next day, the Second Citizen visited again, for the first time since "wind".

"Your brain gets uglier every time I look at the monitor. You really are manipulating physics in there. Atoms are contracting and expanding as blood vessels travel from regular neurons into smaller ones, into even smaller ones. Somehow you're getting enough oxygen throughout the hideously delicate structure to not die within minutes, but don't ask me how. If you keep this up long enough, you'll become neurons, nerves, and capillaries all the way down, like a fucking mandelbrot set. Brains within brains within brains..." He brushed nonexistent hair out of his eyes in an endearing gesture.

"Simon, I'd like to propose a compromise in good faith. I will allow you to develop a more interesting ability, but you must promise to behave. Deal?"

"As long as it doesn't hurt anyone."

"This one won't. Your utterance for today, and the foreseeable future, is 'paper airplane.'" Guards carted in several tall stacks of paper that they placed on the table.

"Louisa taught you a few folds, so pick your favorite. Take a moment to practice visualizing the fold you want to start with, then speak. From there, take the ability where it draws you, but inform us of every addition to it, however minor. If we notice something we didn't permit, I swear to any gods listening that you will spend a month turning squares into triangles."

The Second Citizen left him with Hammond.

"Paper airplane" he began uttering after a few moments of visualizing how the paper was to be folded. Within a minute, a piece of paper at the top of the closest stack began to twitch and crease until it became a loosened version of what Simon wanted. He repeated the exercise.

After a while it became effortless. He could say "paper airplane" once and ten sheets would fold perfectly before he lost energy and needed to speak again. He could feel his mind growing and adapting as the ability extended, making the act of visualizing plane folding automatic, a button he could push with a flicker where once it had cost him some effort. Aspects that once required attention became lower level, allowing him to focus on new aspects. He picked a more complicated fold to try. Then another.

Soon, he'd tried every fold Louisa had shown him. The floor was littered with well over a hundred paper planes, and guards had started to come in to remove them.

"Please, keep them here" Simon requested, getting an idea.

"Hammond, can I try giving them flight?"

Hammond needed a moment to report up. "Alright. But don't make them dangerous, or we're done. And no new words."

Simon held one of his creations, and uttered "paper airplane", trying to will it to fly. This took longer, likely because the word was not quite the same as flight, even if the meaning was in a way adjacent. He felt the friction of trying to make his plane move through the air with a word that had only passing acquaintanceship with propulsing through the atmosphere. It felt like trying to convince two people with one thing in common to have an engaging conversation. The onset of minor hallucinations seemed to help actually; his mind felt lubricated and flexible. He realized he felt almost like he was a very young child when the hallucinations started; everything seemed new and the world was a box of toys. An hour later, he reached a point where he could utter "paper airplane", and in one motion, fold one, and then send it flying throughout the room. In his mind, he could feel a deepening well in his subconscious where the plane was somehow being guided and controlled. He repeated the exercise. He felt the plane struggling to bank left and right, and to generate and control its propulsion sufficiently to stay off the ground for more than a few seconds. Learning was slow and unimpressive.

A couple hours later, he reached a level where he could send a plane flying through the room, and will it to maintain flight without having to consciously think about it. He could stop it on command, but, if he allowed it, it would now engage in increasingly complex flight behavior on its own while he could focus on sending up more planes. He repeated the exercise, and soon there were dozens of paper airplanes flying freely near the room's high ceiling. His mind began dizzying again, and he began to hallucinate paper elephants flying and stomping about the room.

Hammond interrupted his efforts.

"The Second Citizen states that he is highly interested in the automated aspect of your ability. He requests that you attempt to cultivate group behavior among the planes you send up, get them to coordinate, that sort of thing."

"I'll try. Still the same word?" Hammond didn't bother responding, and returned to staring at the real time model of Simon's brain displayed on the wall.

Hallucinations made the rest of the day interesting, and became critical to his project. A fanciful vision had begun to unfold in his mind's eye of a dramatic aerial battle between two groups of paper airplanes, each organizing attacks against the other until one side was thoroughly destroyed. As neurogenesis began more prominently divorcing Simon from his body, his imaginings of pitched battles between planes took on cosmic significance. He giggled in his chair as his overwhelming daydreams carved a presence into his utterance, and began to develop his ideas into a highly complex and very entertaining reality.

Planes began assembling into groups of two, then three, then twenty, and their once random trajectories became increasingly dictated by group, until there were four large swarms stalking one another with tense patience near the ceiling. Simon pretended they were the Citizenship, China, South America, and Europe. *Attack each other, damnit* Simon thought. The tension between these four bodies was easily felt, and after two more minutes of utterance, the Citizenship dove into South America. Once the first strike was dealt, the tension erupted and unforecasted chaos ensued.

Swarm attacked swarm, first in crude, unpracticed charging motions, but, soon enough, in increasing intricate formations that hinted at a developing intelligent strategy that Simon hadn't even consciously thought up. Successive generations of strategy and battle formations came and went, improving their methods and learning new ways to maximize formation shape and strike timing as they dealt aerial blows to one another. Simon continued supplying his four fleets with planes, but his creations were now being destroyed and cast to the floor at least three times faster than he could replenish them.

Hammond was shamelessly staring at the ceiling with childlike fascination. Simon kept his eyes mostly closed now; he could sense his fleets intimately without sight. Minutes later, each of the four fleets reduced to mere shadows of their former glorious selves, Hammond ended the session. Simon was seeing some actual elephants now. They were commanding rivers and stars, and weaving ancient mathematics using strands of Louisa's hair.

Simon was declared mentally compromised for the day and ordered to stop. He felt some reluctant pride at what he accomplished. His new subconscious well, dedicated to the folding of paper into fleets of flying warriors and executing deadly learned war strategies, calcified in the back of his mind as a hard-won prize. He felt powerful knowing he could now invoke all of its incredible functionality at any moment, with only two words.

That night Simon was allowed to sleep longer. He nodded off to the relaxing sensation of Louisa's steady heartbeat, searched his dreams for shades, and woke the next morning fully refreshed. He was brought back to the room, by now convinced he could have escorted himself if asked.

"The Second Citizen was impressed with your performance yesterday and would like to offer you an update that Louisa has not been physically tortured. If you behave well, she will be provided with paper for origami within the week. If you can fulfill his next request, her reward will naturally be given sooner."

What request? Simon thought, not wanting to risk electrocution over unnecessary words.

"The Second Citizen wants you to try and create matter out of nothing. Paper, specifically. He says in his memo that any paper you can generate will be given directly to her, as a gift from you, to allow her to continue her hobby behind bars. He thinks it's terribly poetic and motivating."

Simon, who had lost all talkativity, sat in his chair and began uttering "paper" while Hammond gave him a piece to hold for inspiration. He held his goal in his mind and allowed a new neurological well to deepen. For the first hour or so, he used his ability to scan the paper he was holding, granting himself an increasingly detailed impression of its content. The fibers, molecules, and atoms that comprised it gradually changed from ideas reached for by his imagination into tangible collections of real objects that he could physically reach into and feel with lengthening and branching ethereal nerves. The act led him to an intuitive understanding of paper at the most fundamental chemical level that gave the seemingly simple object a landscape beauty.

After some hours of scanning, he asked to move on to attempting creation, which Hammond approved. He resumed uttering, which he did in a whispered voice at approximately

5-second intervals to protect his vocal folds from overuse, and found that his new task resisted him in a way the others before him hadn't.

Within his new goal he insisted that the matter he created not be taken from anywhere else in the universe, that, somehow, it had to originate from no source. He remembered from his physics course at Academy that this should have been impossible, and by the third hour of trying, his opinion on the matter remained firmly unchanged. As the hours passed by, and nothing happened, it took all of Simon's willpower to keep focused on his singular goal. Even his hallucinations were of a singularly focused sort. He initially felt cold frustration at his failure, but eventually that emotion seemed pointless.

Within one second, he felt the well of dense new neural connections in his mind connecting with something. A new metaphysical extension of himself slowly building up strength, as though heaving to lift a great weight. A threshold needed to be crossed. The tense buildup of raw strength that Simon felt but could not explain continued for many hours, by which time his ability to focus on even his simple task was slipping. He was growing exhausted from his hallucinations untethering him from reality, as unfortunate as he knew that reality was.

Ping; The sound of a small quantity of air being instantaneously expelled from a volume of space. When Simon reopened his eyes, he saw a half-inch by half-inch piece of paper fluttering towards the floor. An overwhelming sensation of Victory pulsed through his body. The threshold had been crossed. New matter had been brought into the universe. He had felt this satisfied perhaps twice before in his life.

"Holy..." Hammond said. Simon nodded in agreement. The first of his gifts to Louisa landed silently on the floor, and he repeated the exercise.

Once the threshold to create the requisite matter had been exceeded, it took miraculously little time for his tiny sheets to enlarge. Ten minutes later, he was producing inch by inch sheets of paper, and an hour or so after that, he was starting to produce sheets even larger than the ones he had folded his planes with. In a moment of excitement, he said "paper airplane" out loud, folding into being his largest one yet, and received his first full electrocution since his interrogation. It was less severe than before, but still broke his reverie.

Simon spent all of the day after that creating more paper, exploring a wider variety of thicknesses, and eventually manipulating color and texture. He was allowed to fold a few of them into paper airplanes, revisiting his previous ability, to study the behavior of a developed ability of his following a period of disuse.

The next day, he was told to utter "banana." He spent the first day developing an ability to scan bananas, which he did to thousands of them, mapping them out, learning to appreciate each one as a unique symphony of chemical and biological structures scaffolded according to particular DNA. Hammond explained some of the science to him out of hope that understanding would translate to better execution. Bananas were mostly water, with carbs and sugars making up a bulk of the remainder, and a fractional quantity of fiber weaving through it all. Simon couldn't say if it helped, but over the following days, he did learn how to produce an edible sludge that in some ways approximated a banana.

"Time's up. See you tomorrow." Hammond said on the sixth day of 'banana.'

"Can I ask about Louisa? Simon asked. This was the first time he was brave enough to risk the pain of electrocution to learn about her.

"I don't know. Just focus on your assignments, that's all you can do. See you tomorrow."

"Hammond, one more question. What day is it right now? They don't let me see outside."

Hammond frowned faintly, his greatest tribute to

empathy demonstrated thus far.

"See you tomorrow".

Again, Simon was taken down to the insular universe that was his cell, the pattern of the last few days feeling like it might continue for eternity, with changes punctuated only by the words he was allowed to speak. He had to be given the next day off due to medical exhaustion. He spent the entire day carefully folding a herd of paper elephants in his cell. He knew Louisa would be proud.

CHAPTER 18

"Before we move onto the task that has been decided for you, I have a simple test I'd like to administer" the Second Citizen spoke, having been waiting for Simon in the session room when he arrived for what would have been the fifth day of trying to replicate a banana. He had not fully succeeded at the complex, energy-intensive task, but had at least managed to conceive of banana-shaped semi-hardened sludges that were unharmful to consume and had nutrient value. *There was once a time when I loved bananas.*

"I want to play with fire," the Second Citizen said, smiling.

Simon listened

"One more exploration that will take minutes, but will clarify a curious matter to me regarding your talent. I want you to produce and sustain a flame above your palm, as I know you have already done, using a different word. This time, I will give that word to you. It is "Gefrieren"."

Simon was confused. "That's no word I've heard of."

"correct. It's the German word for "fire". I wish briefly to test whether you can produce a fire ability connected to a word that has the same meaning, but is not one you recognize. Begin."

Simon obeyed his command, uttering "Gefrieren" in repetition, attempting to integrate the word into his core vocabulary and convince himself it meant fire.

It took a couple minutes, patently longer than when Simon first put flame in his palm, but a spark did appear, right as the word started to feel natural in his mouth, and was soon followed by a growing fire. Once the flame achieved a radius of roughly an inch, it became steady. Simon expected the Second Citizen to command him to stop, but he did not. He waited another minute or so to watch Simon's utterances grow the flame to the size of his palm. Only when it more quickly began to spread past his fingers and wrist did he declare the exercise over.

"I appreciate your cooperation. Now, let's forget about fire, and move on to the task at hand. First things first, you might have noticed the change in scenery. In fact, you will be pleased to know that a number of changes will be made to your day-to-day."

The most notable feature of the room was the new chair, which was to his old one what his work surface back home was to the primitive laptop he had noticed on the First-Citizen's table. It looked far more like an actual chair that someone might use

Gone was the churning appendage of wires to be hooked up to a helmet, or the clunky metallic plates positioned at both sides of his head. The chair extended up above his neck, and furnished sensors loosely outlined along its surface which seemed that they might have a similar brain-scanning function to their hideously intrusive predecessors. This, Simon mused, was the entire history of human technology: first to innovate, quickly, hideously, and then to take that innovation and make its conveniences more beautiful, and its inconveniences less visible, until a horrid contraption capable of horrid things became a beautiful interface whose innocuous exterior betrayed none of its malice.

Simon sat and found he was quite comfortable. The Second Citizen remained standing.

"Your ability has strengths and weaknesses. Its obvious strength is versatility. We have yet to request something that is beyond you, your incomplete work on the banana notwithstanding. Weaknesses seem to include generation of matter, and complexity. 'Smooth' and 'Cube' were trivial to you. They required next to no introduction of new energy into the universe and had minimal complexity. 'Paper airplane' became more complex over time, but it took many hours and nearly knocked you out. Creating paper was somewhat complex but also required the introduction of far more energy into the cosmos, hence it took you two days to produce anything substantive. A banana is more complex than paper, and contains a greater variety of matter, hence it took the longest to get anywhere."

The Second Citizen paused to sit.

"You have a fascinating talent, Simon."

"I suppose."

"Magic. That's what it feels like. No rules or limitations, beyond the whole linguistic issue. You can just weave a spell for anything. Of course, we both know that can't be true. What comes next is going to test if your ability has limits, like no other test has." He paused. "For both of our sakes, I hope you're limited."

"Why?"

"Well, for my sake, because I'm tired, and want to be done with all this. For you, because your ability is no longer yours to use, and sooner or later you're going to become horrified by how you're made to use it."

"Has the First-Citizen given an order?"

"Thankfully not. That man is a great leader of the masses, but frankly, he doesn't do well with anomalies like you. His idea was horrid even to my taste. For now, I've managed to keep him at bay, and we're going to use you for a particular problem our world would undeniably benefit from solving."

The Second Citizen turned around and activated a screen. A swirling congruence of blue, green, gray, and intermediate shades appeared on the wall in front of him. The sudden reintroduction of color to Simon's white universe made him realize how deprived he had been. It took him a moment to recognize the world on the wall. He absorbed the tapestry of oceans, continents, and atmosphere with greedy fascination.

"...With this understanding in mind, a long-term task has been assigned to you. I make no promises, but if you do well, you may be entitled to a reunion with your partner. Shall we?"

Simon nodded, pretending to have a choice.

"Excellent. Your task, for this day and many to come, is to turn yourself into the world's first and only hurricane deterrent."

The Second Citizen zoomed the map into North America. "Here we have displayed for you a highly detailed, real-time map of the region of the world whose hurricane problem we are most concerned with you safeguarding against. Since such an ability is far beyond any other that you have developed, and may or may not be beyond your limits in terms of sheer scale, this shall be taken in incremental steps. Your first step will be to gain the ability of detection. You should be able to reach out and feel or observe hurricanes as they form. We will at this junction indicate to you when hurricanes are forming for you to test yourself. Our algorithm indicates there will likely be one forming at an eastern latitude approaching Cuba within the next hour, which might give you something to practice on depending on how far you can progress in that time. After detection of course will come prediction, followed by intervention. You'll see me in a few months. Good luck." The Second Citizen left the room.

The new status quo began which at first it seemed like it could have been worse. That first day, Simon tried uttering a short phrase instead of a word, saying "find and feel hurricane". He could have done with a shorter word but wanted to grasp at all the linguistic variety he could in the hopes of making his herculean task a little less numbing.

While it didn't work at its intended purpose, the phrase did have a tangible effect within the first hour. As the hurricane developed visibly on the screen over the next several hours, Simon received a faint but novel tactile sensation that almost felt akin to that feeling of being stared at by someone unseen, and knowing by some instinct approximately how close they were, and in what direction. In this instance, however, the analogous instinct developed by Simon would extend to a specific classification of objects emerging at far greater distances than a stalker could stare across, and would eventually be far more accurate.

Within four days, Simon would know whenever a hurricane was forming anywhere within three thousand miles of him, and would instinctively know its approximate distance from him in a manner that his mind somehow knew how to roughly translate into a number, with similar feelings for speed and direction. He imagined he was deploying 'searchers' of a sort to find these hurricanes and report back. He wasn't sure what he was creating, but he thought of them as the massive cousins of his smaller ethereal nerves that would feel around the world on the roughest of scales for the huge storms and signal back their findings.

This hurricane sense became a permanent fixture, similar to Simon's color vision or running stamina, and so even between sessions, or during sleep, he would from then onwards often be disrupted by increasingly detailed subconscious alerts giving him precise information on hurricanes that were developing around the world.

By the end of his first week, he could already detect when hurricanes were forming anywhere on earth, with equal speed to the Citizenships satellite-supplied detection algorithm, and could determine a number of other variables accurately, such as speed, strength, and a more detailed map of its trajectory and likely evolution that Simon could summon at will as an image in his head and draw out on paper if ever asked. It felt nice to be a part of the atmosphere, even if he still felt trapped. He was at least fairly certain he was somewhere in the western half of North America.

Beginning in the second week, Simon began uttering

"hurricane cease" for ten hours each day, six days of the week, at first often nearly collapsing from mental exhaustion and hallucination. A fluid injector was installed in the seat that would intermittently microdose him with a substance that he was told would enhance his ability to focus, and seemed to help with his visions. It seemed to work well enough. Those weeks turned into months, and the hallucinations mostly stopped. Visits from the shade of his mother became his only socialization. He was almost grateful that developing his ability tired him so thoroughly since a long day of guided neurogenesis was an excellent primer for vivid dreams.

There were several upgrades made during these months, the most prominent being the improved accommodations. Simon was moved to significantly larger quarters that included a proper bed, shower, toilet, sink, and even a limited amount of approved Citizenship literature. He was fed more generously as well, receiving multiple different meals that included apples, pears, grapes, bread, steak, and pasta. Two months in, Simon returned to his quarters after a long day to find a mirror had been installed. It surprised him to notice that his hair, having not been cut or dyed, was longer than it had ever been, and the silver had grown out. He almost looked like the First-Citizen.

According to Hammond, it was the First-Citizen himself who requested that these many small privileges be provided, to reward Simon's excellent behavior. The obvious reality was the First-Citizen didn't want him to lose his health and sanity from sensory deprivation, anxiety, and repetitive overwork, in case those things interfered with his value to the state. Simon, despite never being forced to wear the muffle, never attempted to speak out of turn. An unspoken, untested understanding had developed between Simon and his Captors, that his relative comfort could end in less than a second if he attempted to freely use his voice.

As the months dragged on, Simon laboriously worked on his ability with a focus that dwarfed anything he'd had as an overseer. It was simply the only way to keep sane. The first two months of actively trying to stop hurricanes were tangibly unsuccessful. Two or three times each week, Simon would sense a hurricane forming somewhere in the world, hurtling towards a coastline that mankind had once inhabited, and would utter "hurricane cease", focusing all his energy on feeling the powerful currents propelling the behemoth of a storm and attempting to undo them, to force the circulating winds into calm submission. But the immense entities wouldn't yield, even as his strength pushed to new heights each day.

Being well-fed and well-kept certainly had a positive impact on the rate of development of his ability, although the days still felt like weeks and weeks like seasons. A hundred and six days in, the Second Citizen visited again. He almost seemed relieved that Simon didn't seem close. He halfheartedly, almost sadly, told Simon he was doing good for humanity, then left. It was his strangest interaction yet with the already strange man.

As more months passed, profound loneliness, unsatiated boredom, and endless worry over Louisa steadily whittled away at him. Beyond the calming feel of her heartbeat, he was told precious little about her.

His shades finally began to visit him. His mother-shade in particular came when the hurricane began to invade his dreams. Billions of neurons being dedicated to a single mission, the directing of energies to undo hurricanes, led to a *thing*, an identity, of growing prominence in his head, almost an entire other consciousness residing in the warped corners of Simon's extending mind. As this consciousness grew, it learned it needed to dream. There were still only fifteen to twenty billion neurons contained by this construct, as far as Citizenship scans could discern from the fractal mess that was Simon's anatomy. The dream was a simple one, but potent in its simplicity. A hurricane simulated itself each night, vividly recreating the ebb and flow of millions of tonnes of water and air swirling at breakneck speeds. This appendage to Simon's regular consciousness was still *him*, he knew, but it was an extension of him that had its own desires and interests. Sort of like a shade.

His mother-shade justified her/their visits by teaching him to coexist with his creation. They guided him into settings and dreamstates that allowed him to resist the urge to be consumed by an overpowering hurricane each night, and to still enjoy his own dreams. His mother-shades depth of understanding of his dreaming world and how to protect it was extraordinary. It took her a month to train him and his subconscious to keep his dreams of forests, birds, stars, and Louisa separate from his new self's eternal hurricane. The experience of having two distinct dreams coexisting synchronously would have been impossible to describe to anyone not so afflicted.

The Citizenship was unwilling to stall ability development due to potential insomnia, but his waking problems were improved slightly by new access during his free time to a track along which he could run. This helped for a time to relieve the restlessness, as Simon could spend well over an hour sprinting his way into exhaustion. Eventually, though, running in endless circles became its own form of boredom, and Simon found himself slipping again into quiet despair.

Fortunately, the Citizenship seemed to have elected to prioritize the mental health of their new talent. Dosages of his focus fluid were increased and mixed with anti-depressants, leading to a few sweet days of unearned joy, but a week of testing indicated that it slowed his rate of ability development. Television access was granted, and his library was increased. Success was partial. He wanted to be allowed to write poetry, but there was worry that he might be able to develop an ability through writing, so the request was denied. He was offered a helmet, which he declined. They made him uncomfortable.

The ultimately successful attempt at returning Simon's mind to a place of relative stability came upon him one evening possibly four months into the hurricane project, although Simon wasn't sure if he had counted his days quite accurately.

The door to Simon's quarters slid open as a man silently walked in, saw Simon sitting sullenly at his desk, and approached. The man looked a little older, with bright green eyes, a thin yet well-proportioned frame dressed in simple white garments and, most distinctively, a complete lack of hair.

"Sit, please" the man spoke with a placid, silky voice. The man placed himself in the middle of the room and gestured for Simon to join. He did.

"I meditate. I am told you will not be able to speak during our time together. This changes nothing. You do not need language to meditate. In fact, you need nothing."

The man closed his eyes and serenely exhaled. Simon hadn't even perceived his inhalation, as it had been done slowly, patiently, with deliberation over one long moment. "Breath is important to meditation. It brings the world into us and forbids us from being fully isolated. Try to focus only on your breath while you sit. If a thought tries to interrupt, simply encourage it to leave, and return to breath."

The two sat in silence for many minutes, breathing while sitting in a lotus posture, their bent knees at arm's length from each other, breathing in, breathing out, breathing in, out, in, out...

The session ended when the man stood and left as strangely as he arrived. Simon, whose eyes had been closed during his meditation, had noticed the man leave but decided he wanted to continue the seemingly pointless exercise a little longer.

Each week on Simon's rest day the man would come to his quarters. Simon slowly began to fall in love with meditation. As he slowed his breath, and his heart rate, he found he could feel Louisa's heart beating as strongly as his own. Her heart beat more frantically than his did during these sessions, and as minutes passed he felt the calming influence of his body begin to reach her as her heart became just a little more aligned with his. It felt good knowing that, wherever she was, he was able to help her de-stress, just as her heartbeat had been calming to him. It was the closest he'd felt to her since the train, which seemed a lifetime and a trip to hell ago.

Their sessions lasted for two months. Their ninth session began much as the others had, with the sitting-and-breathing exercise. They sat together in the middle of the room. Instead of his breath, Simon chose to contemplate Louisa's distant heart, which was beating faster than usual at the moment. She must have been exercising. Master and student sat in calm silence for several minutes. As they were about halfway done, the man spoke in the echo of serenity that was his voice.

"Your second and final lesson will be in mantra meditation." He began.

Simon listened, his interest piqued, but did not allow the statement to excite him.

"The premise is simple," he took a ten-second breath before continuing.

"First you must pick a word or sound. It can be anything, but for today, I would like us to start with the fundamental sound, within which all others in the universe are to be found." Another long breath.

"Ohhhhm" he said out loud, then began repeating the sound in a dulcet register. Simon tried making the sound himself, his adrenaline spiking in a moment of fear as he considered whether his suit would electrocute him for speaking.

Mantra meditation had an eerie similarity to the process by which Simon developed his abilities, a fact not lost on him. A recurring question impinged on him over the course of the session. *How much does he know?* He gave no indication that he knew anything about Simon, or that he even cared, and had expressed no interest in learning.

The man meditated with Simon for over a half hour that day, longer than most of their sessions had been, humming his fundamental sound of the universe all the while, and then stood and left. It was their last session.

CHAPTER 19

Months Simon spent speechless. The shade of his mother, who seemed to fill a sort of protector role within the growing and deepening parts of his mind that he struggled to integrate, became too preoccupied dealing with the emergent consciousness behind his hurricane ability to visit him in dreams anymore, except on rare occasions where she taught him how to coexist with the growing entity inside his head. Even with her tireless help, it was becoming increasingly difficult to resist the nightly hurricane, and many nights he simply gave in and shared the dream with his hurricane shade. There was nobody else he talked to. As time dragged on, he started to suspect that his capacity to improvise speech, a skill he'd taken for granted as early as he could remember, was slowly leaving him. If Louisa met him now, he would have struggled to string together a sentence for her. He never imagined that fluency in his native language was perishable.

The Second Citizen checked on him rarely, the meditating man, whose disappearance was as inexplicable as his appearance, never returned, his new attendant, who replaced Hammond, avoided speech like a plague, the guards were impossible to converse with, and his shades offered little comfort. Humans weren't made to lack language. It felt wrong.

Meditation continued as a habit of his. He would sit, sometimes for over an hour, vacate his mind, and mentally utter the mantra he had chosen. He was proud of the mantra he chose and wished he'd been encouraged to meditate earlier.

Every night for about twenty minutes, he systematically fantasized about escaping. He knew a specific place he would go if he could: the stretch of wilderness he had visited as a child, the same one that haunted so many of his dreams. The trees terminated at the ledge of a cliff overlooking the ocean. Whenever the image became too vivid in his mind, he made himself think of other things. Ultimately he always returned to the hurricane. His ability was growing a personal connection to the storms it was trained to kill. Hundreds of fleeting impressions from the storms flashed through his mind as he faded out of consciousness, almost as though he *was* the storm.

Simon often thought back to what the Second Citizen had asked, if he could become addicted to an ability he worked on for too long. His hallucinations certainly weren't addictive, and often became downright unpleasant. This didn't feel like an addiction either, so much as a new birth. Now that he created this ability, its identity would always need to be a part of him, as much as his prime consciousness. It was an offshoot of himself whose entire reality was hurricanes.

The cycle of his life had firmly calcified. Wake, eat, go to session, mid-day break, eat, back to session, return to quarters, read quietly, meditate, sleep, wake up, eat... There was an infinite repetition, each day melting into the ones around it in a temporal haze that, stripped of novelty, became a single eternal experience, where sleep was merely one of several ever-repeating markers signaling continuation, the brightening of the walls of his cell at the same time every twenty four hours serving as a counter for the length of his entrapment.

A few months in, Simon encountered the shade he'd inadvertently created who obsessively tracked how much time had passed since its creation, and he named the micro-identity "Mr. Clocker". Every night, as his fantasy of escape was about to give way to hours of hallucinated hurricanes, Mr. Clocker would come to him in the form of a deranged grandfather clock and issue a number. Even his dreams now adhered to a tight schedule.

The experience, while highly structured, was not short. In fact, it was closer to a year at this point that Simon had spent trapped within the confines of wherever he was. He was arrested on april 9, 2102, and assumed that he was unconscious for about a day before his survey in which he was first tortured. Counting diligently from that day, and assuming that his rests were initiated at 24 hour increments, which felt correct, it was March 22, 2103. He continued making this calculation daily despite Mr. Clocker.

The Second Citizen finally visited. The day had been progressing according to the usual pattern, with Simon doing his utmost to keep his intent steady as he uttered "hurricane cease" for the seven millionth or so iteration. The words hardly had meanings to him anymore, and had long since melded into mere sounds echoing around his head as the inevitable process of semantic satiation took hold.

The subconscious well that had grown in conjunction with his "hurricane cease" ability was now something of a black hole. Simon had learned what black holes were from the literature he was now permitted to read, just as he had learned about fractals, China, christianity, homosexuality, and a dozen other topics that, in another circumstance, would have felt sinful to know anything about. Black holes dreamed.

According to the new attendant, the only time she spoke to him, scans revealed that the 2.3 millimeter wide singularity near his visual cortex, the one formed by uttering "hurricane cease", had become so dense with billions of new types of neurons as to challenge the Citizenship's most fundamental assumptions of the limits of biophysics. Over sixty billion of these neurons integrated potentially up to eight distinct fractal levels, to the point that a few of the most scaled-down neurons were almost as small as the largest stable atoms in unmutated space. She also mentioned growing scientific interest behind the curtain in dissecting him, but thankfully the proposal was shot down.

To Simon, the neural outgrowth felt how he imagined a tumor feeling. He feared that it would eventually become larger and more complex than the entire rest of his brain, that the hurricanes occupying his dreams would extend into his waking life and consume his perception, turning him into some idiot savant who could put down hurricanes the world over but no longer knew how to form sentences or feed himself.

It was while nurturing this tumor that the Second Citizen visited.

"It's been awhile, my friend."

Simon looked over in surprise as the door returned to being wall. It took a moment to remember the name of the individual standing in front of him.

"We naht frnds," he grunted. Enunciation was a perishable skill.

"Leave us, please" he commanded the attendant.

She left, and the Second Citizen sat across the bare table.

"Why are you here?" Simon asked. The sentence took his full effort to assemble.

"Let's walk. You haven't exercised much these past few months. It's not healthy."

The Second Citizen typed something on the table's surface, and Simon's constraints were released. He hesitantly removed his helmet while he stood up. Standing after a session always made him a little dizzy, which for some reason he tried hiding. Two guards stood directly behind him as he followed the Second Citizen out of the room.

"While we're walking to the athletic floor, which you've officially earned access to by the way, I'd like to update you on Louisa."

Simon perked up. Hers was a name that had rattled about his skull so many times, he sometimes doubted it still referred to a real person. The sensation of her arms crossing her chest, and warming his, had been his only true physical comfort in months, and the only evidence she was still real.

"She's well. Her accommodations are far more pleasant than yours have been. There was, after all, no particular reason to fear her like we fear you. You may enjoy hearing that we offered her conjugal visits from her cellmates, and she declined all offers. That sort of loyalty is statistically quite rare. You're a lucky man."

Simon mustered his decayed skill of verbal speech to the best of his ability. He sounded drunk as he spoke.

"Please, just let her be free. I'd rather her be happy and outside of a prison, with whatever bit of freedom that gets her, and me staying locked up in a cell for the rest of my days. Don't make her share my fate. Let's not kid ourselves. I'm unhappy. Miserable. I'm likely to remain unhappy for a very, very long time. Let her go. I know you have all the power here, but there's no reason to cause her more pain."

He slurred most of the words, although his last sentence recovered some clarity. The Second Citizen shook his head as they reached the elevator and descended several floors.

"Simon. She's never going to be released. I'd have thought this would be obvious. You should be relieved. If we let her leave, you two would never reunite."

The elevator wall transformed into a door, and Simon was introduced to the athletic floor of the facility. While the walls, ceiling and floor were as stark white as everywhere else, the exercise equipment was obsidian, providing contrast. Seeing a color that he'd lacked for over a year nearly brought him to tears. He stopped himself from crying. The Second Citizen noticed the effect and waited a moment before speaking.

"You are to use this place to exercise every day. An instructor will be provided for you to assist in developing proper technique. There's a running track as well, which I doubt you need instruction for. You'd outrun any coach we got you anyways."

"Thank you" Simon managed to say. Gratefulness to his captors seemed his only option. The truth was, he really was overwhelmed with gratitude at being permitted to lay eyes on an entire new floor of the building. He felt spoiled.

"It's time for you to start considering something."

"What?" Simon asked.

"The future."

Simon had long stopped caring about that. His future wasn't his to control. He might as well not listen to the man facing him, who was likely about to explain how the next few years of his existence were to be. He'd get there when it happened. He was a tool, and figured he might as well think like one too.

No, I'm not. Remember your meditation. You still have that. A precious few doors in your mind they haven't opened yet. He didn't like his mind's insistence on holding onto hope, but decided to give the future a chance.

"I'll start with something positive. Louisa will be brought here soon if you continue to behave well. You may even share a cell with her, if the First-Citizen abides."

"She's coming here?"

"Yes. That's the good news I have."

Simon knew his face remained impassive, but he was now interested.

"'Hurricane Cease' is starting to show incredible results. Every cyclopic storm that you've withered has reduced to a category 3 or lower, which is already enabling a genuine improvement to the Citizenship, regardless of how you feel about its governing body. CERE is even on track to meet some of it's more unrealistic goals. I hope you can appreciate the objective good you've done."

He paused and his expression darkened. He hadn't meant this as good news, not really.

"You know, the First-Citizen wanted to build floating cities over Florida. I barely managed to convince him that occupying Australia for metal was infinitely wiser. Even that was far from an efficient use of resources, but at least it's better than building fucking Atlantis. My role's always been to remind him that he's not God. It's a difficult, thankless job. Thanks to you, it's becoming impossible. You're his way up, and he can't resist your temptation any longer."

"I'm sorry that I'm tempting."

The Second Citizen looked him over sternly. Simon figured something about the past year must have made him difficult to gaze at, because his aged captor looked away after a few seconds.

"The second reason that the man upstairs wants to move Louisa to be near you is to act as a guinea pig for your new assignment. I tried talking him out of it and he all but accused me of treason, which I'll have you know I've never committed by any measure. Anyways, the words he will order you to utter, for what I suspect will be far longer than one year, are 'Love First-Citizen'."

He now stared at Simon, seeming to hope for a facial expression that wouldn't come.

"He wants to use you, to make the whole world love him unconditionally. Not just North America. He cares about this far more than he ever cared about hurricanes, or occupying Australia, or deploying his beloved surveys which were his last good idea. Those have always been means to an end. The First-Citizen has a complicated history, but his goals are childishly simple. Louisa is known to be anti-Citizenship and is no fan of the First-Citizen. If your ability can show itself to work on her, then there will be proof of concept that all you would need to do is scale your radius, and eventually, everyone will be his completely."

Simon looked down. "Why say all this? Can't he hear you?"

"No. I've made investments over the past few decades. The same software has been running in facilities like this since the mid century horror, and I directly involved myself with the implementation. I granted myself a few exclusive privileges. The guards behind you are being lied to by their own helmets.

They think we're having a stern conversation about your hurricane performance. Even your suit runs my malware.".

Simon looked up. "Kill me. I don't want to keep living like this. Don't make me. Please."

"I can't, as much as you know I'd like to. The only way forward that I can see is for you to survive. And to escape. And to live a life." Simon forced himself to think through the possibilities.

"Why is this such a bad thing, making everyone love the same leader? Maybe it's for the best."

"It's not. I don't think you comprehend the implications as fully as I hoped you might. If you don't find a way to escape this facility before you are made to develop this new ability, all of human history will be put on a far darker path than any that's come before."

"You're right, I don't see it. I agree it'd be unethical. But playing devil's advocate, isn't it a good thing to spread love? We could unite all humanity under a single banner."

Simon felt his abilities of speech returning. He even used a banned phrase he'd heard his father use once.

"That's what the First-Citizen will tell you. But look further ahead. Ask yourself, what becomes possible in a world completely ruled by a single immortal human, whose authority will be unchallengeable, who believes himself to be a superior being, and who is immune to death or injury?"

Simon shrugged. "Well, I imagine he continues to run the country as he has been, only now the country is everyone. Is he such a bad person?"

"I suppose he was alright, once." the Second Citizen paused. "He and I seem to get worse each year we linger in our posts." The Second Citizen pulled out a silver dispenser from his front pocket, brought it to his mouth, and inhaled. Simon had seen his mom vape once before; it had been one of the acts that scared him into reporting her.

"Before being the First-Citizen, he was a president, and

before that, he was one of our great media leaders. He swooped in from the private sector, where he'd always surrounded himself with people like him, possessing ambition and talent enough to challenge him, and work with the reasonable vision he had. He had colleagues, rivals, enemies, and friends. Even a lover, once."

"He first recruited a young, brilliant grad student who would become his partner in his political projects. That young hopeful man was groomed to be his successor, until biology decayed him into the sentient wrinkle waning in front of you. Our leader is a different man now. All his problems, I suspect, stem from his being too exceptional for too long. Over the past couple decades he's started distancing himself from everyone close. Once my colleagues and I die, he won't have a single human friendship. He already despairs the loss of us as equals, though he tries to hide it."

Simon began to see the implication.

"If you follow his order, then in a century at most, this world will be ruled by a single immortal human, unkillable, and ravenously adored. Human life will become merely another transient diversion to him. I'm sure your imagination can fill in a few blanks."

The thought became unsettling.

"I estimate the changes would be gradual at first. Restricting a microliberty here, an extraneous comfort there, as he's been doing your whole life. Then, as more decades pass, and the entire world has fallen neatly into place at his feet, he may start openly killing people who demonstrate an above-average immunity to your spell. Perhaps in the next century, he will begin selectively breeding our descendants into forms that better suit his pleasures, like he's already started to do with the survey women you've met. After all, humans are mortal, and he isn't. It's only our population as a whole that mirrors his immortality and deserves to be looked after."

That's actually how I felt about my subjects. I'd be excited when one of them succeeded, but I cared more about their collective performance. I got more excited dropping a subject than I ever did when one of them did well. Was that wrong of me?

"He'll start to view our descendants as livestock, here to keep his empire running smoothly, creatures he can fuck when he's bored and command to kill each other in droves for his entertainment. Wars greater than any fought in history, hundreds of millions of deaths, for no reason other than a bored autocrat wanting a new way to relish the absoluteness of his power. Not a single human on earth will question any of it. He will of course command you to make yourself as immortal as he is soas to use you in perpetuity. Eventually, as his only truly valuable colleague, you would likely become his only friend. Given hundreds of years of life as his slave, you will inevitably become as horrible as he is. You may even become worse."

The Second Citizen's eyes had glazed over while he spoke, but he made eye contact again and shrugged. "Or maybe he won't, and I'm wrong. I don't claim to know how everything ends. But I can say that, during my mortal life, all my worst instincts about people have proven correct sooner or later. I've been the First-Citizen's most loyal follower since the days when he had a proper name. And yet, my intuition scares me. I'm sure you know the feeling." Simon did.

"I'll leave with the guards. You'll get about five minutes of real privacy When the door to this floor automatically opens and closes, that will indicate the window passing. Do with your time what you will. I'm sure you put your meditation to good use."

Simon was left alone with five of his most free minutes since the walk on the beach with Louisa.

"Away" he spoke, barely a whisper, unable to shake the sense that the entire setup might have been a ruse, the ruthlessly logical yet terrible prophecies of the Second Citizens an entirely fabricated performance to draw him out and reveal the true extent of his disloyalty. Simon didn't care anymore.

"Away" he spoke, slightly more confidently, his visualization already fully formed in his head.

Simon had visualized an action for "away" many times and knew vividly what to call up in his mind as he spoke the word. Every time he meditated, for the past several months, every day since the last day the teacher came and sat with him, "Away" had been his mantra.

"Away" he said again. For the first time since his first day in the facility, his voice found strength.

"Away"

Every day, month after month, Simon had chanted with his mind's ear, hoping always that the sensors on his body suit would think that the repeating word in his head was the same one that he was forced to repeat during his sessions. It was not.

"Away!" he screamed, for he was quite certain the room held all sound. The last time he'd screamed, he was shocked by the survey woman. The time before that was during his second date with Louisa where she'd playfully accused him of lying.

"Away! Away! Away!" he now screeched. Uttering the word in his head lacked the impact of saying it out loud, but *something* had been happening. Over months, a neural well had cautiously built itself according to Simon's imagination. It simply lacked access to whatever energy connection it was that saying the word out loud granted him. Now, after hundreds of meditations, saying the word out loud was allowing the energy to rush into him like a river breaching a fallen dam.

"Away!!" he shouted, feeling his entire body vibrate in a subtly ecstatic metamorphosis.

"Away!! Away!! Away!!" In addition to meditating, he had spent the better part of a half hour each night uttering his mantra, as he visualized the forest, letting his hopes for it fuel the spirit that the day had inevitably drained from him. The focus fluid that his chair injected him with during the day had always worn off by then, and his mind always wanted to stray, but he forced himself to focus for just a few minutes more.

His dreams before the hurricane took over his nights had all centered around escape, and he spent them continuing to utter "Away" while murky white and blue dreamscapes swirled surrounded him. His shades, or at least most of them, he heard chanting the word with him, dedicating what little they could to the effort. His mother-shade chanted the loudest, when she wasn't busy doing whatever she did normally.

The entire exercise had felt futile while he was doing it. Perhaps that was why the devices on his body never picked up on his treachery. If he had actually thought he had a chance of escape, that overabundance of hope would have certainly been noticed. Or maybe his fractal mind was finally becoming complex enough for at least some important thoughts to be indecipherable to machines.

"Away, away, aw..." the door to Simon's right opened and closed. Simon closed his mouth immediately, and with lifetime skill, he rapidly reduced his excitement. He ceased thinking about what he had just done and went over to the nearby door. Opening it, he saw a part of an extensive running track tracing the perimeter of the floor.

Simon ran. As he did, the sudden neurogenesis struck him like a wave, and for a while he hallucinated. Louisa, his parents, Charlie and Beckett, Sybil and the general all appeared to him laughing and crying, running alongside him. Trees shifted in and out of existence, making his imagined group run through a rich green woodland. It felt good, like a pleasant dream he wished to be real. Hours passed. Guards had to come and escort him to his cell to make him sleep. As he lost consciousness, the mantra of "Away" continued. The word felt more powerful to him that night, than it had during all the others, and echoed through his head even as his reality became a hurricane, never stopping.

CHAPTER 20

Simon's conversation with the Second Citizen was followed by a brief period of peace and cyclitude where the days joined together like clockwork, as though they were the heartbeats of a vast temporal creature who had swallowed him and wanted to digest as slowly as possible. The warning of the First-Citizen's impending order loomed large in Simon's mind, and yet, day after day, no order was made.

One difference, of course, was his new privilege of exercise. He lifted for hours, pushing his body to nearly its breaking point just to feel something. His muscles always ached after, but each day he went back to the obsidian machines and pushed himself even further. It felt right to dictate his own misery. Whenever his heart rate went up due to the exercises, he beat his hand on his chest once to indicate to Louisa he was safe, so that she wouldn't worry he was being tortured.

Progress with the hurricanes, after over a year, was finally reaping dividends. As the Second Citizen had pointed out, by catching the storms early in their development and applying his ability to them, Simon had been managing to prevent all hurricanes incurring into Citizenship territory from exceeding category 3 (now that his ability had developed this far, he was forbidden from applying it to hurricanes hitting other countries). This was still a catastrophic storm but was far preferable to the 4's and 5's that made the coasts uninhabitable to all but a handful of heavily fortified industrial ports.

The rate of progress began accelerating. Only a few

weeks later, hurricanes could be pushed down to category 2 or even 1 with his ability. Fourteen months into the endeavor, most of the hurricanes Simon applied himself to would fizzle out completely by the time they reached a coastline.

For two months, Simon did not see or hear anything about the Second Citizen, the First-Citizen, or Louisa. The quality of his food increased again, and he started to become more visibly muscular due to his obsessive exercise. He felt healthier, more energetic, and endlessly restless. His only connection to the outside world, still, was the hyperreal map of the Americas and Australia, the twin regions of which he had become the unsung coastal guardian. He could admit the Second Citizen was right; regardless of the means by which it was accomplished, he was doing a good thing for the continent.

Yet fear tugged at him. The more Simon thought about his most recent conversation, the less he doubted its propositions.

Simon was visited near the beginning of the third month of the second year of the hurricane project, on the day he and his timekeeping shade agreed was probably June 1st, 2103. He'd just finished dealing with a particularly aggressive nascent hurricane near New York that, before his interference, had the potential to be a category 5. With only a few utterances of "hurricane cease", he had applied his ability to it, and could now silently observe as the atmospheric monster subsided itself and dissipated into the patterns of the ocean like an itch being scratched. Simon had become exceptional at staring into the large screen in front of him and determining what kind of weather was going to appear next, even without his hurricane sense helping him.

The room suddenly darkened, and a convoy of eight older officials, and two younger ones, entered. The group was led into the room by the First-Citizen.

"Why if it is not my favorite hurricane stomper." The First-Citizen spoke in his pleasant whisper. Simon realized he had never once heard the First-Citizen yell.

"Hello sir" Simon spoke, briefly forgetting the rule about speaking too loudly.

"Sorry," he said more softly.

"You are forgiven, for I have come to offer rewards for your loyal and successful efforts at assisting the Citizenship in facing an important obstacle. Thanks to your work, we may be able to begin proper resettlement efforts in the American southeastern coast, right down into the Florida archipelago. Truly, wonderful work. However, you will be moving onto a new project."

Just say the words. There's no need for a ceremony.

"You may not be aware, but there are still many out there who have not found it within themselves to love me as I know they would like to. It is not a stretch at all to say that to live in the Citizenship without loving me is a rather pitiable state of affairs. Some people cannot help it. They simply have insufficient love in their hearts. I believe you can change that." He laughed to himself, and his convoy hiss-laughed quietly with him. Their whispered joviality felt comically forced.

"This motivates your new assignment. David over here cautioned me against it, but, to put it bluntly, there is a reason he is a Second Citizen. Intuition tells me that you will perform your next task even more admirably than your first. In a way, you have already spent most of your life preparing for this every morning."

Simon noticed the Second Citizen hidden among the older officials in the audience.

"But first thing first. You had been promised that, if you demonstrated your loyalty, you would be granted some companionship. Have your reward."

As he spoke, two guards walked in. Between them was the last person Simon wanted to see there.

Louisa's face looked unharmed, but she radiated none of the energy that he remembered her having. Her body, still beautiful, had nonetheless begun to adopt the unhealthy thin look of the Second Citizen. She struggled to keep her normally expressive face neutral, which broke Simon's heart. This was her first painful experience where she felt scared to be her usual brave self. Simon didn't frown. He was too paralyzed for such displays. He wanted nothing more than to tell her he loved her, that everything would be ok. He said nothing.

"Please, sir, let her go. I don't want her anymore."

The First-Citizen stood and maintained his inscrutable smile.

"David warned me you might say that. I am sure once you spend some time with her, you will remember what you are missing. This time next week, you will be thanking me during one of your adorable pillow talks. I listened to recordings of a few of them. Good entertainment. Your honesty with each other aroused me a little." Louisa stared at the floor.

"You two have actually been neighbors for the past year." the First-Citizen said as if it was nothing.

"Her cell shares a four-inch wall with yours. In case that matters to you."

"It doesn't really."

"Hmm." The First-Citizen had clearly hoped to elicit an outburst. "Well, David says you already know the words I am about to give to you."

Simon nodded slowly. "Love First-Citizen" he said, turning his eyes to Louisa. He wasn't sure, but something inside of her seemed to break when he said it. She was more intelligent than he was. He knew as she stared at the floor, that she was glimpsing slivers of the same bleak future forecasted by the Second Citizen.

"Exactly correct! What wonderful words they are. Poetry, even. Think of it like a love poem, Simon, except without all those unnecessary extra nouns, verbs and adjectives to muddle the meaning. One verb, one adjective, one noun. This, Simon, is the ultimate love poem." The First-Citizen sounded prideful, as though he'd just composed the greatest adage in history.

An attendant stepped forth and replaced Simon's helmet with a new one.

"Since this is the historic beginning of a new ability, at once an extension of your old adoration of me, while yet an entirely new creation, we must study your mind particularly closely while it is born, with our most state-of-the-art scanners. Entire labs have been dedicated to advancing brain simulation science, just for you. Take a minute to soak in the meaning of my poetry, then speak."

Simon was gripped with terror and indecision. He had mentally prepared himself for this moment dozens of times, explored the possible permutations of it, and even lived it in a dream. Now that it was actually happening he didn't know what to do. To his shame, he did exactly as he was ordered.

After a minute of consideration, Simon uttered the words. "Love First-Citizen." He stared at the table in front of him, where the faces of Louisa and the First-Citizen stood out to him. In that moment, their expressions could not have been more disparate.

"Love First-Citizen" he said again, locking eyes with the First-Citizen. He wore a subtle grin, a look of sexual pleasure at the scene playing out before him, the beginning of the realization of an ultimate power fantasy.

"Love First-Citizen" he said a third time, and then shifted his eyes to Louisa. She had looked up and was now staring at him. Her eyes were beautiful.

"Love f..." he stopped in the middle, and paused. He realized he had cooperated completely with his captors for over a year. He denied none of their requests, both for his self-preservation, and that of the woman who he loved, who was now staring at him with utter shame. She hated what Simon was doing, but the fight had been taken out of her. Her hatred was now subdued, her former vitality punished out of her. He sensed that, like him, she wouldn't mind dying, if it stopped what was happening. That gave him his second of bravery.

"Away" he growled, looking dead-eyed at the First-Citizen. His adrenaline spiked, but he didn't feel panicked so much as resigned to complete focus on his visualization.

The First-Citizen squinted his eyes, and in less than a second he comprehended the treachery.

"Away!!!" Simon shouted, more loudly. Nothing happened, physically.

The First-Citizen began to grimace, and quickly rose from his chair, demonstrating his superhuman speed as he began to walk, at a speed faster than most could sprint, around the large table and across the room towards Simon.

While that happened, the two guards standing behind him, per their training, had reacted immediately to the unsanctioned word, and were wrapping Simon's muffle back around him. The new attendant, and Louisa, both watched these events unfold.

As quickly as both of these things happened, Simon was just faster. The first "away" he spoke had triggered a dormant, unused ability, and, saying it a second time, the engine of that ability revved and took aim.

The muffle was shoved forcefully into his mouth. He did his best to ignore the blunt pain in his teeth, needing to direct every ounce of focus he could muster into "away", hoping that the sea of adrenaline coursing through his body could push him to make it work. He felt something overtake the atoms of his body. Strangely, he felt like he had two identical bodies occupying the same space, stuck together with a glue that was loosening.

The image of a forest appeared in Simon's mind, his nightly fantasy. It was an elevated spot, partway up a mountain foothill, overlooking the ocean. It was a place he hadn't been to in years. He wasn't even certain that it still looked like that, but it was the choice that seemed his best chance of escape. And so, with the First-Citizen arm's length away, hand outstretched, and with the muffle having just been placed firmly around his mouth, about to be fastened at the back of his head, he went away.

Everything disappeared in an imperceptible instant, the room, the First-Citizen, Louisa, the table, the convoy, all of it. Then, within the space of a single thought, Simon was pulled out of the emptiness into which he had slipped and found himself in an entirely new place.

CHAPTER 21

Simon opened his eyes groggily and found himself sprawled stark naked across a dry, pine-strewn forest floor. His first thought was that the terrain had felt much softer in his dreams than in reality. Recent memories returned slowly, of passing out within seconds of teleporting to his pre-selected spot, slightly misaiming some ten feet in the air, falling to the ground, and watching the world go momentarily dark from sheer disorientation. He observed that, thankfully, nothing had teleported with him, helmet included.

He gathered his bearings. Looking around, he saw that he was, impressively, in nearly the precise spot he had visualized. During those months of preparation, he had begun to doubt the image in his head was a real place. Only the faintest of primal instincts had assured him it was. Trees extended in front of him, and turning around, he saw that he was near a steep cliff ledge that plummeted directly into the Pacific. If he'd teleported ten feet westward, he'd have died hitting the ocean.

Simon began to feel dizzy from sensory overload. Over a year it was he'd spent living in a world dominated by pure white, with snippets of blue, black, and green, the imagery of his life simplified well beyond what nature intended for a creature like him. Even his hallucinations had started becoming whitewashed. Now the many rich interacting hues, the browns, blues, greens, reds, oranges, and grays of the cloudy sky, sea, and forest hit him all at once and completely overwhelmed his enhanced eyes. The blues struck him especially. He fell into the soil and wept.

I manage to hold in tears for fifteen months of torture, yet within a minute of finding freedom, I break. His celebration was cut short when a distant wailing reached his ears. *The national terror alert. The nearest siren sounds like it's a couple miles north.* Two continents of people would know his face within seconds if they didn't already. His villainous life story was probably fifteen minutes from being aired on Citizenship Broadcastings.

Simon had chosen not to seriously contemplate what to do after this step. Such systematic, organized thought might have been picked up by his suit, which was ten times more sensitive to the nuanced relationship between blood flow and intention than a standard headband. Thinking about it now, he realized it wouldn't take long for the Citizenship to begin searching the Oregon coast. His parents were likely on record taking him here, and the first and Second Citizen would easily make the deduction that it was one of the few places Simon had physically been during his life that he might have a clear memory of and also consider as a viable escape.

He waved a farewell to the Pacific and began walking into the evergreens. *First priority is to conceal myself. No criminal has successfully evaded the Citizenship in over twelve years. Without certain abilities, I'll get caught.* Simon had no notion of what sort of sensors were put in place this deep into the forest, between ten and fifteen miles from the nearest settlement. He assumed they were few and far between since the raw material shortage couldn't have been solved in a year, but if even one stray sensor captured human motion he was done for. His 'away' ability was built to only transport him to one specific location, might take any amount of time to generalize, and using it even once was more disorienting than any of his hallucinations. There was currently no viable second escape strategy.

"Invisible" he began uttering to himself. He'd had a conversation with Louisa about this once, actually, before she knew of his ability. There were two ways they had considered that an object could become invisible. The first was to infiltrate the minds of whatever observer they were trying to be invisible to and alter their vision in real time. The far simpler method was to simply phase photons to the other side of his body. Louisa had considered the first method to be more interesting, but the latter method was simpler.

After around five minutes of utterance, Simon could weakly sense the waves of light hitting his skin as perhaps the ninth or tenth new sense his body and mind had developed since the day after he last saw his father. He could feel them beginning to phase through him according to his design. Soon enough his hands were invisible, a condition which spread through the rest of his naked form. As more time passed, he could more strongly feel each of the photons entering his hand, and being led through his flesh at incomprehensible speed, breaching his skin unobstructed on the other side. The sensation of it was not quite like anything he had experienced before, as seemed to be the case with most abilities he developed. He had to alter himself, and how he experienced the world, each time he developed a new power.

He continued uttering to maintain his newfound invisibility as he walked amongst the trees. He soon grew accustomed to not seeing his own body as he walked. It took a little while to be able to maintain invisibility for more than a couple seconds without saying the word, but once he could do that, he was able to shift some focus to the next most important ability.

"Silence" he uttered in alternation with "invisible". He imagined a muffling field existing about a half foot out from his body, which would cancel out any noise that he generated going outwards, but allow him to hear sound coming inwards. This also took only a few minutes of total focus to develop adequately, which he tested by walking up to six inches away from a squirrel that normally would have run away from him at twenty times that distance, and watched it bury a nut.

Louisa mentioned once that the Citizenship had used genetic engineering to begin producing animals that would be able to track and hunt specific humans from uncanny distances. She'd been unable to give details, but Simon imagined that, if she were correct, dogs and birds might become his greatest adversaries. He realized that if he wanted to hide properly, he needed to cease emitting a scent.

"Unscent" he began uttering. This ability he spent twenty minutes on, to make certain that the figments leaving his body were thoroughly decomposed. He began to feel the air immediately around his body with a new intimacy. By the time he felt comfortable moving on, the distant siren had finally stopped. Simon retraced his steps and developed a new strain of his ability to remove his scent from the places he'd been already.

He considered what other abilities he would need if he were to stay successfully hidden in the forest. He would need stealth, water, warmth, shelter, and food, in order of priority. He had mostly taken care of his immediate stealth concerns, and soon saw that water wouldn't be a problem.

By the time he returned to his landing site overlooking the Pacific, storm clouds were imminently approaching. Within three minutes of heading back into the woods, having cleared his scent along his path, it began to rain.

"Smooth" Simon began uttering, in addition to his other three words, utilizing something he'd already developed to smooth out his footprints from the mud that he found himself walking barefoot through. He was starting to become cold, and his feet, unaccustomed to any sort of rough surface, were starting to bleed.

About an hour into trekking beneath the storm, Simon heard the sound of rushing water and immediately raced towards it. He had been cupping his hands and trying to collect rain, still too busy exercising his young stealth abilities to develop a new one for water. Reaching the source, a midsized river, he furiously drank along the bank. He then walked along the riverside until he reached an outcropping containing a huge boulder. He remembered from overseeing Micah, the wilderness writer, that this was called a glacial erratic, a large rock brought over many millennia ago, quietly out of place in a forest far from the icy behemoth that dropped it there. It had a concavity that barely qualified as shelter, but he discovered if he huddled in close, only his legs would be hit by the rain.

"Warm" he uttered while shivering, taking five long minutes to learn to elevate the temperature of the air around him to something comfortable. He then had to continue to utter "warm" every three seconds since heat dissipated quickly. This was in addition to uttering "invisible", "silent", and "unscent" at regular intervals to maintain his undetectability. Juggling the four entirely new abilities he'd just developed was rapidly burning his remaining energy. Hallucinations started. For the first time in months, his hallucinations were rich and colorful.

While failing to fend off the elements, he was alerted of a hurricane in the process of forming somewhere off the coast of Japan. He took a brief moment to utter "hurricane cease", chuckling at the grim irony that, while he couldn't yet keep rain off his legs, he could at least protect half the coastline of a foreign nation he knew almost nothing about.

His chuckling grew into an insane laugh. He wasn't sure what specifically he was laughing at. He decided it was everything. The entire past year and a half of his life was torture on a grand timescale, and somehow everything had led him to this rock by a river, completely naked, and battered by rain as he struggled to use his purportedly godlike power to barely manage to keep warm and hidden. Everything felt wildly vivid around him. His legs relished the feeling of being pelted by raindrops. He muttered his words of concealment throughout the night, maintaining and strengthening them as much as he could before he inevitably needed to sleep. Hallucinations of a living forest transitioned into yet another dream of a hurricane.

The next morning, the storm had let up, the sun peaked out, and Simon was forced to attend to his feet. "Heal, heal, heal..." he uttered in between his words of concealment, a task which took almost a half hour, as his skin slowly learned how to repair itself at an expedited rate. Simon looked out at the path he had walked to his encampment, and with panic realized he had likely littered the forest with specks of his blood. Once his feet were healed, he retraced his steps a second time, uttering "bloodless" as he found and eviscerated the damning specks of evidence of his presence. Hopefully no dogs had been let loose yet.

Simon spent the rest of his day after his walk solving his hunger. He had spent the past several hours uttering "banana" and forcing himself to eat the organic sludge that generated in the palm of his hands just to avoid the pain of it, but this was a temporary fix. An additional hour of wandering led him to a salmonberry bush, which provided him with a veritable cornucopia by comparison. While he searched for more bushes, and considered whether it was worth it to try eating the moss growing on trees all around him, Simon diligently covered every track he made and continued to develop and refine his invisibility, silence, and scentlessness.

As morning became afternoon, while he continued looking for berries he began blanketing the three abilities under the word "untraceable". By the end of the day, the ability was becoming nearly automated to the point where he could say the word once, and rarely need to repeat it. He realized he would eventually need to develop something to hide his heat signature, something else to deprioritize while he focused on more immediate concerns. He slept for over twelve hours.

The following day, Simon decided to make his shelter a little more proper, in the event of another storm and to assist in staying hidden. The glacial erratic, he decided, was the best place to hide in plain sight, if he modified it appropriately. He developed an ability to convert segments of stone into sand upon his touch, then used his hands to carve a cave into the boulders concavity. He developed abilities to automate the temperature inside to something comfortable, and crafted a hologram at the cave entrance which made it look as though the ledge had remained unexcavated. Automating abilities seemed to take appreciably longer than simply creating them, so Simon needed most of the day to fully accomplish all these tasks.

Once his shelter was fully disguised, Simon left it to hunt. "Sleep" he uttered at a squirrel unfortunate enough to cross paths with him. Once he had his prey, he developed an ability to kill it painlessly and roasted it, after creating abilities to dissipate the smoke and scent of burnt flesh, as well as to rapidly decompose the indigestible fur and bones. The last of his urgent needs was taken care of. He felt bad for the squirrel.

Once his immediate problems of camouflage and survival were solved, Simon, for the first time in his life, had time to mull over what he wished to do. The feeling was strange. Choice overwhelmed him, and it took over an hour before he could settle on an ability he could work on that wasn't imminently necessary. *I suppose I could spend the time thinking. But then I'll just think about Louisa, and that's too stressful.*

A robin flew near him, and he knocked it out but didn't kill it. He knelt by the bird and reached out to pet it with two fingers, something Louisa had taught him to do. "Birdscout" he uttered mindfully for some twenty minutes. He stopped in mild terror as he caught a grizzly bear lumbering within forty feet of him, and had to reassure himself that he was completely hidden from the creature. Once the bear moved on, Simon returned his attention to his ability, and soon enough the robin was adequately prepared. Once the bird flew off, Simon closed his eyes and tested.

The eyes of the robin opened in his mind. The bird had just perched atop a tree, in a part of the forest that Simon had passed through an hour ago. He encouraged the bird to take off and fly back towards him. He felt the small creature's muscles twitch into action as it lept off the branch, and watched through the bird's small eyes with fascination as it flew back towards him. He opened his eyes as his new acolyte dove towards the forest floor, its interest stolen by a worm it found.

Abilities extending his senses were exhausting, it turned out, so a hungry and hallucinating Simon hunted for another meal. Two roasted squirrels and some banana-sludge later, he forced himself to keep working on "birdscout." With it, he hoped to be able to patrol and monitor progressively larger swathes of the forest around him, and learn in advance of any man or animal let loose on him. The irony of overseeing and manipulating flocks of animals to suit his purposes wasn't lost on him, but he needed a warning system.

Feeling for Louisa's heart beating in distant adjacency to his own remained a habitual tick. He worried about her, but at least the First-Citizen had no incentive to cause her injury. Once he could develop more abilities, to become substantially more powerful, he knew he would be able to rescue her easily. Living together in a forest didn't seem like such a poor existence. Or perhaps they could explore Europe together. By then he'd be able to keep her safe from anyone. She would choose their next adventure, once she was free.

But for now, Simon wished to become powerful. He wished to be able to stand in a room with the First-Citizen, and to say "no" to him. That man had long forgotten what refusal felt like.

"Stronger" he intently uttered to himself for over two hours each day. He envisioned his body growing in strength, becoming increasingly impervious to the damages of the forest, his thinnest eyelid becoming more impenetrable than the thickest part of a bear's paw. Whenever he thought about the past year of his life, beyond the sensory deprivation and the slavery of it, there had been an omniscient feeling of weakness that blanketed him every second. The sense that, no matter how important his work there was, he would always be paper under a microscope. He never wanted to feel weak again.

Yet, he did not want his sensitivity towards the world to diminish. He wanted to be able to hold a leaf between his fingers and feel each vein. To grasp at the bark of a tree, and relish its plethora of textures as he used his newfound strength to climb it. To brush the hair out of Louisa's blue eyes, and feel each strand drop from his fingers. Strength, it turned out, was the most complicated ability he'd yet developed. Progress was gradual, but as with the ability that enhanced his running endurance, he slowly felt his body fortifying itself with what he now understood were deepening wells of new types of cells growing in dense fractal structures within bone, blood, skin, and muscle. For the first few days, he could barely do two hours of this before his hallucinations started showing him the insides of his heart, lungs, and kidneys in far more detail than he could handle.

"Shield" became another ability that appealed to Simon by the second week. Although he guessed he was stronger than any of the armored officers back in the facility, it would be a while before he became as bulletproof as the First-Citizen claimed to be. He needed something defensive.

"Shield" also took some time to mature. Simon envisioned an invisible sheet in front of him that put air molecules in a state of reinforced stillness. The resulting shield was, naturally, no heavier than air, yet was as tough as synthetic plastic. Light could pass through easily, yet anything solid would be blocked, and liquids and gasses would seep in partially only to be frozen to a halt halfway into the shielded area.

This ability, combined with birdsight and stronger, exhausted him daily to develop. Each day he practiced this ability, the shield grew in radius and became easier to create, and his control improved. He tested it by throwing rocks at a practice shield during the afternoon of every day while he chewed on his dinner. He had some of his birds watch the procession, just for fun. Since he was becoming physically stronger, it became a race to see which ability could outpace the other: the size of the rocks he could hurl at a practice shield, versus the strength of the shield itself. His shield outpaced him easily.

Simon retained his captor's two-session approach to mitigate the intensity of his hallucinations. Hours every morning and evening spent in power-creation was still draining. He always walked while uttering, which he enjoyed. When he was too dizzy to walk in a straight line, he'd stop until tomorrow. Meditation became not only welcome but necessary to maintain sanity. Simon found a spot near a small creek that fed into the larger river, and spent some of each morning and afternoon there, humming the universal sound, de-hallucinating his busy mind to the sound of trickling water.

Utterance of "Ohhhm", what his teacher had called the original source of all sound, began simply as a way to relax. It conveniently solved one problem by easing Simon's hallucinations, many of which included unpleasant flashbacks to the facility. As he meditated more, the act surprised him by becoming something beautiful and rejuvenating. Slowly, session after session, finally free to be whatever he wanted with no outside detection, he sank into a deeper meditative trance than he ever had before.

He felt all of his abilities not as a collection of separate fractal-like convolutions scattered through the regions of his brain and body, but as a singular living process. They were a collection of disparate ideas that somehow belonged together, but whose connections couldn't be expressed in words. As his trance deepened, he felt them developing and spreading all at once, burning through him like cold fire igniting on nerves he didn't know he had, as though they might combine to eventually subsume his entire mind and body, extending every aspect of his being, allowing him to create or destroy with mere thought. The attainment of this felt like a distant vision, and yet he knew deeply that he could someday have it. The trance was simultaneously terrifying, and also infinitely calming. He always wondered after if he'd be any good as a god. *Only with Louisa to guide me. And my parents. And my friends.*

Simon's life was simple. But it was his. And he was becoming powerful. By the second week, he estimated he was four or five times as strong as any of the helmeted guards who had once dominated him effortlessly. He could with one word surround himself with shields of crystallized air that he was mostly confident could catch bullets.

"Birdscout" now gave him influence over dozens of crows, robins, sparrows, Jays, and a single adventurous goldfinch. He regularly perused each of their senses and recent memories, checking that they had observed no dogs, men, or cameras. As a bonus, his ever-growing bird network allowed him to quickly ingest their memories and acquaint himself with large swathes of the forest, to the point that it felt like he had been exploring it for years. The cost was inevitably the slowing of his other abilities' growth and the constant risk of over-hallucinating when neurogenesis was too rapid.

There were hundreds of powers that Simon wished to add to his arsenal. The possibilities seemed limitless now that he had both time and freedom. Having spent a year on a singular power as world-changing proportions, he now wanted to develop dozens of less ambitious talents. He could learn to float amongst the trees. To alter how his eyes processed color, so that plants looked blue and the sky red and the ocean black. He could try and perceive entirely new colors. He could explore sound, and learn how to make symphonic rhapsodies vibrate from his body as easily as one might whistle. Or manipulate the light of the sun to create visual spectacles of stunning beauty for miles along the horizon. Strengthening or weakening local gravity. Generalizing "away" to teleport him to a variety of locations, not just one. Destroying cancer. Restoring the memories of others. Building a castle for Louisa on a perpetually floating foundation, and hiding it inside a cloud so they could sail the skies of the world together, and land in a country that would accept them. He wished to do everything. To become capable of everything.

Priorities forced him to discard most of his ideas. They would take far too long. He wanted to know that the few people in the world he cared about were safe. He knew Louisa was, for the time being, from their connection. She hadn't tapped *I love you* since his escape, but she also didn't indicate that she was unsafe, and her heart was beating normally. He knew nothing about his parents, or Charlie and Beckett. He hoped the First-Citizen hadn't done anything to them out of spite.

"Mothersight" he said. He repeated the word, imagining that he was viewing the world through the eyes of the woman who brought him into it. He hadn't laid eyes on her since childhood, not even a picture, and his father avoided the topic. The rest of the day passed, repeating the word as many times as he could manage, and nothing happened. Not that the ability wasn't developing at a brisk pace. There was simply no hint that it was finding any sort of success. Locating a person over a huge distance of potentially thousands of miles probably took a great deal of power, threading ethereal nerves over potentially continental distances, and Simon would need time to build such a nervous system. He was fine with that.

It was the beginning of the fourth week that the dogs came.

CHAPTER 22

It was the goldfinch that first alerted him to the invaders. The picture Simon pulled from the creature's memory as it flew six miles to his east was troubling, of over two dozen officers and twice as many canines briskly jogging across a nearby foothill. The creatures looked completely unrelated to the petite, well-groomed pets that certain A-class citizens were occasionally known to dote over. These muscular, thick-furred, saber-fanged GMOs displayed more anatomical similarities with bears or walruses than with poodles, or even wolves.

Occupying the air, hundreds of drones were mapping the forest, likely inch by inch. From what Simon could gather, from his other birds now encountering the machines, each drone had attached to its ground-facing appendage enough tranquilizers to put down an elephant. Being found by a drone seemed merciful next to encountering a dog.

Strolling through the forest had instantly become untenable, but was otherwise Simon was unconcerned about being discovered in his cave. The holographic disguise he'd developed and automated to always cover the entrance melded flawlessly into its surroundings, as masterful manipulation of photons. Simon was invisible, unhearable, had no scent trail, and would be updated on how close the nearest man, dog, or drone was at all times due to his motley bird fleet. Nevertheless, he was overstaying his welcome in this forest and was anxious about Louisa. He wished he hadn't deprioritized her rescue, even if it seemed logical.

Simon hurriedly returned to his cavern. Within minutes

of passing behind his illusions, he heard the bark of a dog patrolling yards outside. Simon convinced two of his birds to remain stationed in front of the cavern and used them to observe the animal closely. It looked easily twice his size, with five times the muscle mass. It's front claws looked like they could claw out both of his kidneys in a single tearing motion. He doubted he'd be able to put it to sleep fast enough if it caught his scent.

The first dog moved on, and although their surprisingly intricate howling could be heard around the forest (his other birds confirmed this), it became clear he was reasonably safe so long as he didn't budge. He decided to focus entirely on getting Louisa to safety.

Since he was already connected to her, Simon found that increasing that existing connection to his partner was far easier than creating it at a distance from nothing. "Connect" he uttered repeatedly as his capacity to feel her body as his own gradually extended beyond her heart and chest and out into the rest of her. Her arms became his arms. Her stomach became his stomach. Her legs, neck, mouth, ears, and eyes became his. He didn't allow her the same benefit over him. He worried that her ability to feel his body could be used by the Citizenship. Their connection sadly could no longer be a symmetric one.

Beyond its intrusiveness, the experience of fully feeling two living bodies at once was incredibly disorienting, even more so than the two bodies he'd felt when he first teleported. He tried standing in his cavern while connected to Louisa, and found he could barely coordinate it. He felt, and saw, Louisa lift her hand to wipe her left eye, and realized he hadn't seen anything through her eyes because she was keeping them closed. She had been crying. He continued to utter, making her sensations more vivid. He realized she was in great pain.

A minute later, she opened her eyes, and Simon saw where she was being kept. It was another white cell, as he had assumed, except this one contained furnishings of utter terror on the walls, floor, and possibly the ceiling, although Louisa seemed unwilling to look up. Protruding from the wall like the proboscis of a monstrous insect was a long, thin, automated projectile weapon aimed between Louisa's eyes. Its thin barrel and white color almost allowed it to blend in with the rest of the room, like some lurking apex predator. Simon realized after a few seconds that there were actually four such weapons. He barely saw the other three. The floor on which Louisa's feet rested contained a grid of hundreds of circles, each less than an inch in diameter. He didn't know what they were, but he had a suspicion they were meant for him, should he teleport into the room to try removing her. That was probably also what the wall guns were for. It felt like the Citizenship didn't know what to prepare for, so they installed weapons for everything they could think of.

Louisa was still. The way she sat reminded Simon of how he often used to sit idly in the facility before he slept, unready to sleep but with nothing else worth doing. In addition to whatever physical pain she was enduring, her beautiful mind was slowly being destroyed by the same deprivation of novelty he had suffered.

Rage seeped in as he further enhanced the connection. The pain in her body was substantial, in both her stomach and her legs. He couldn't understand why, in addition to being locked into such an awful place, she would be physically hurt.

"We haven't even damn negotiated yet!" he shouted, spared from the attention of the beasts and machines outside only by his ever-vigilant silence ability. As soon as he said it, he realized he'd deluded himself.

They were probably torturing her minutes after I left.

He began shaking. In a moment of weakness, he nearly collapsed the four automated abilities keeping him hidden.

"Firstcitizenfirstcitizenfirstcitizen" he said, a single blurred and desperate word that repeated itself numbly in his mouth as though he were uttering an infinite run-on sentence. Surprisingly, It didn't take long to find and begin establishing a connection with him. As the second setting began to embed itself in Simon's mind, he made out in greater and greater detail the objects in the room that the First-Citizen occupied.

He was seated comfortably at a fine desk in a bright room, reading a book. He couldn't yet make out the title, but it looked old, even by the standards of the illegal books kept by the general in his personal library. Simon began to feel the First-Citizen's body in the same way he had just been feeling Louisa's. It felt different. Warmer, with an almost metallic sensation to it. The blood in his veins flowed more smoothly. The book he held in his hands gave off a sensation more akin to hollow cardboard than thick, unbendable binding, as though he could easily squeeze it between two of his fingers until it bent or broke. The autocrat had not exaggerated when he claimed the strength of a hundred men. If anything, he might have been downplaying himself. The First-Citizen turned a page slowly, his ears twitching slightly at the unavoidable sound of rustling. It sounded as loud as a scream. Simon winced.

"I know you're watching me" the First-Citizen's mouth moved, a sensation which Simon uncomfortably felt, making him wish he'd chosen a less intimate form of spycraft.

"Hmm. Complete interface into all of my senses. seeing what I'm seeing, hearing what I'm hearing? Yes... that is what this is. I feel it. You're letting me hide nothing. I am glad to know you have this in you." Simon felt the chill behind the man's smile.

"Out of all the methods by which you might have attempted to spy on me, it is promising that you chose this one. You are becoming cognizant of the many facets of your potential. Having said that, I would wager a different channel might suit us better for the sake of attempting a proper conversation. Would you agree?"

Simon pulled away from the First-Citizen's body, allowing the connection to fade. How he had been able to notice he was being observed, Simon couldn't say. As a child, chanting the name of the First-Citizen in arranged parades and civic events, he'd often imagined the fabled leader of his country possessing a wide variety of powers, and being able to defeat many types of foes. He'd made up childishly straightforward stories with "bad guys" failing to assassinate the First-Citizen in comic ways. One such tale involved a gang of pre-Citizenship anarchist teenagers constantly inventing new ideas and technologies to sneak up on the First-Citizen unawares, to capture him and reduce the Citizenship to chaos. The First-Citizen always knew when he was being watched, however, and would never allow the imagined villains to get behind him. His childhood self must have injected into his leader a generalized immunity to all spycraft. He felt confident he wouldn't be able to spy on him any other way, so he spent the next several minutes crafting a new ability that would enable equal communication.

In two locations simultaneously, silver twins were born. The first grew from a point source in a levitating position facing Simon, a spherical effervescence casting faint light across the cavern. The second twin appeared identically in front of the First-Citizen. Displayed in the first, the image of the First-Citizen as seen by the second twin was presented, sparing Simon a view of anything other than his opposing conversant. He granted himself the same advantage, and in the second twin, an image of him displayed, without the cavernous backdrop. The interface was instantaneous.

Surprisingly, he found the structure behind the twins difficult to understand. He felt that photons were being used to create them, but he sensed some other facet of the universe had been invoked as well, one which he couldn't ascribe to any scientific phenomena he knew of. His fundamental instincts understood aspects of physics that his conscious mind had yet to be exposed to. Perhaps nobody had formally discovered whatever principle he was now exploiting. Another mystery to ponder later. As the imagery came fully into focus, Simon extended the radius of his unhearability to envelop his twin, and dropped the invisibility, confident that the cavern's hologram would still hide him.

"Ah, so you have been invisible." The First-Citizen spoke, his voice carrying clearly into Simon's ears, as though he stood inches away, breathing down onto him.

"Why?"

Simon spoke loudly, satisfied to see the First-Citizen recoil at the transmission volume.

"Well, to begin, we did not torture her any more than we needed to. Her suffering may end imminently if you heed my proposition."

He talks like a man guaranteed centuries of long life ahead of him. Simon's fury was palpable enough that the First-Citizen temporarily dropped some of his decades-practiced facial charisma.

"You may be angry..."

"Anger doesn't come close to describing it."

Simon spoke coldly, willing the mirror twins to strengthen his voice's signal even further, giving his intense whisper the power of a roar. The First-Citizen winced harshly and had to rub his ears. His eyelids narrowed, not as a tool of expression, but to shield them against the brightening silver of his twin that Simon was now actively encouraging.

"Yes, and you have every right to your anger. However, now that we are in dialogue, there is hardly reason for Louisa to continue to suffer."

"What do you propose?"

"You return, and renew your work with me on a more equal basis. You will see more of me, and I of you. It will be a partnership. You will be made aware of all manner of Citizenship affairs and will have full knowledge of the context in which you use any ability that I ask you to develop. You will no longer simply be following orders. You'd even have some say in which abilities you wish to develop, within reason." Simon wasn't sure, but he thought the First-Citizen's left ear might have been bleeding. Despite that, he sounded perfectly sincere. It was the perfection of it that made the First-Citizen seem like a performer, with no real feeling behind his words.

"Sounds too good to be true. Since becoming the First-Citizen, have you ever truly shared power with anyone?"

"David spoke to you, didn't he? He and I are due several conversations about his recent behavior. I must say he has been disappointing. But, addressing that point, sharing is a nuanced thing. I believe I have always delegated the correct amount of power with others to allow my nation to run smoothly. This is not a proposal for radical or immediate change in leadership. I will of course remain the First-Citizen, and the Second Citizen shall keep his post, for the time being. I merely wish to suggest that, as an eventuality, you may inherit his role. With a few restrictions."

"What sort of restrictions?"

"There would be a contract. I already have a draft written up for your perusal. I'm sure you will find its stipulations most agreeable. Especially those which guarantee the safety of your Louisa"

"She isn't 'my' Louisa."

"Of course. But what do you say? We make no move against you, nor you on us, and we meet in person to discuss our contract in proper detail."

Simon had avoided thinking about the facility since he left it. The horror of spending months on loop, saying the same word so many times that it barely even registered as a sensation anymore, the gaping whiteness gradually degrading his memories of the innumerable small joys he'd lost, was something he wished desperately to erase. The overwhelming newness of his time in the forest momentarily distracted him from it, but he knew the memories were as deeply ingrained as his hurricane spirit. The First-Citizen would have kept him in his deprived cage forever if he'd had his way. The truce would just be a return to that. There was only one answer.

"No."

Before the First-Citizen could reply, which he probably

wished to, Simon killed the twins.

CHAPTER 23

Simon immediately resumed the work of the past several hours, of developing his "away" ability to enable transporting two people to locations other than the top of the ocean-facing cliff. He went into the night. He woke the next morning still mildly hallucinogenic, introduced to the molecular pantry of the cosmos two synthetic bananas to supply his breakfast, and resumed his efforts. For the rest of that day, he exercised his voice, uttering "away" thousands of times, each time increasing its capacity by some small increment.

He fell into the pile of leaves he'd been sleeping on for the past month and went straight into a deep sleep. "Away" continued echoing through his head from a place he couldn't shut off. He fell into the pile of leaves he'd been sleeping on for the past month and went straight into a deep sleep. "Away" continued to echo through his head from a place he couldn't shut off. The word held on longer than it normally did, and was continuing to bounce around the thousand corners of his mind even as deep sleep yielded to a dream.

His dreams were beginning to feel like more than dreams. He was in a desert this time, but it wasn't a natural one. The dunes around him moved viscously, as though treading the ocean of a time-deficient universe. The physics of these waves seemed unusually consistent for a dream, as alien as they were. He stood on a purple flowering plant half the size of a large facility, basking in the light of three differently-sized suns. Although he couldn't see them, he felt legs churning beneath the huge plant's canopy, keeping it upright and carrying it away from some of the truly mountainous dune waves that would envelop it like an insect. He sensed the work of his shades in this dream.

"Mom!" He called. He hadn't seen her since his escape. He assumed his ability generation was keeping her busy in the background, struggling to determine where all the new neurological forests were starting to grow.

"Turn around," she said. He did so and saw the shade perched on a chair. The metal object looked out of place there.

"You vanished. Where have you been?"

"Busy. I've missed you as much as you've missed me."

"I doubt it. You're just an appendix."

"True. But we connect to the same brain, the same well of conscious emotions. We share those feelings equally. Your emotions are our birthplace and our source just as they are yours. My sapience is icing on the same cake that you're built on."

The orange sun had growing black spots dancing on its surface in an almost linguistic manner. The entity felt like the beginnings of a new shade. *Can I birth a shade intentionally?*

"Why are you here now? You don't visit me without reason."

A dune at least a thousand feet high could now be seen on the near horizon, causing the plant's canopy to whimper with fear and reverse course with an impressive shudder. "Away" continued to echo, Simon noticed, but was now expressed as a low, distant noise stretched over several seconds, almost a part of the wind. He suspected he'd spawned yet another shade to audiate the word while he slept.

"I'm meant to appear to you only when you're on the precipice of a new form of growth."

"You didn't appear that day I learned I wasn't human."

"I very nearly did. I only didn't because you feared exploring it, then. I would have terrified you and it would have been impossible for you to hide the truth from your survey, even with my help modulating you. But I wanted to more than

anything. I want to be with you for every first step you take."
The orange sun flared with terabyte realism uncharacteristic of normal dream imagery.

It feels like a positive feedback cycle is happening up there. That star wants to become properly alive, to continue its existence beyond this one dream.

"You're about to witness another, admittedly smaller growth. Not the star, although I agree with you that its consciousness is close to becoming self-sustaining."

The shade gestured across the desert.

"This is a lovely place. I hope it gains a life of its own one day. For now, though, I think you should transport us somewhere else. This crab flower has maybe two minutes before the wave hits and it needs to surf."

"Why don't you get us out? You can summon a door."

"That's not the point. You need to teleport us."

"I'm in a dream."

"Exactly. The perfect place to practice. Now that you've uttered the word outside, I'm here to show you how your dreams are the perfect training ground."

It became clear that the giant plant was moving too slowly to avoid the mass of sand stooping towards them. The canopy started to lilt in its direction as the desert floor distorted and lowered before the approaching wave.

"Where should we go then?"

"How about the sky? Nearly a third of your neurons are dedicated to the dissolution of hurricanes. We know the earth's skies better than anyone."

That's true; every region of Earth's atmosphere feels unmistakably unique to me. His shade smiled. She heard the pride in that thought.

"Away!" He shouted, imagining a patch of sky a few miles west of the Spanish coast.

The sandy tempest was suddenly replaced with a wet field of gray. The particular shades of it, the speed of the wind, and the shapes of nearby air swirls told him this cloud was about an hour and a half away from casting rain onto Gibraltar.

"Amazing! You just practiced." His mother's shade was invisible through the fog.

"Yeah, I suppose so. I felt something...almost activate. But it didn't."

"I felt it too. Do more. That was the most fun I've ever had."

And so he did. He imagined himself transporting to the skies above Siberia, Brazil, east Africa, west Africa, the north and south of Australia, the Philippines. The shade kept the dream stable, and managed gravity. They talked while he traversed the dreamscapes of the world's atmosphere. She asked him questions she already knew the answer to, about his life, his goals, Louisa. It was his first real conversation with the other intelligent being in his head.

They talked for a long time about Louisa. Not her torture. Only about her quirks, her worldview, origami, their trips beyond the city borders. He'd talked about her truthfully to his survey many times, but with the shade the truth felt more genuine. At one point they both very nearly cried about her together, and Simon realized what they had meant when they said they were connected to the same emotions. They shade smiled and hugged him while he cast them into the skies above Norway.

After a few dozen teleports, the dream began to weaken, and she began to tire. He could feel the natural lifetime of the dream sequence was about to terminate.

"Simon, I think we're about done. You'll wake up tomorrow to find it noticeably easier to teleport to a new location."

"I don't want it to end."

"I know."

"Come to me tomorrow."

She let a tear drop for both of them, and they watched it begin the three-mile fall down into a vividly imagined North Atlantic.

"I promise I'll try."

Simon gazed across the earth's rim.

"Alright. But before that, let's spend a minute on the beach."

"Simon wait, I don't think that's a good idea right n..."
He'd already uttered.

He woke in terror, mid-teleport. The cavern and his leafy bed were nowhere. Getting up off the sand, he saw that the sun had just begun to cast its rays onto the Pacific from the east.

Shit. He looked around. He saw no dogs, thankfully, but this place was almost certainly filled to the brim with sensors of varying sorts that he couldn't see, in case he was foolish enough to come back here. He hadn't meant to. He heard a gunshot.

"Away!" he shouted the second he heard it. He returned to his cavern four seconds after he left, and frantically reinstated his untraceable ability and the holographic entrance cover which had faded in his brief absence. He waited anxiously for multiple minutes, wondering if those seconds had been enough for the dogs and drones outside to notice.

Nothing happened. He must have left at a lucky time. He made himself relax, and his thoughts began to sift through his experiences with his mutation. It was truly a strange one, resistant to categorization. It was infinitely versatile, seeming to be capable of all manners of manipulations of the natural world, and possessed the simple weakness universal to any student of any craft; the more ambitious the vision, the longer it would take to realize.

Where time eventually weakened most beings, Simon supposed it would always serve to him as a vehicle of potentially limitless growth. And yet, time was still his greatest limitation, for it meant that any new challenge, requiring a novel ability, would prove insurmountable until he had an epoch to nurture his solution. Hence it took him a year to escape, and only with help.

He would be muffled if he went back. The First-Citizen would fear him even more after his leave of freedom. His abilities seemed unfair almost in their potential, like he was a baby god and the First-Citizen a fully matured, pale imitation.

It was inconceivable that his adversary was treating him with honesty.

"Away" Simon continued uttering. The word was now nothing more than a sound to him. His five second adventure a few hours prior had shown him that his ability was already much developed since his escape. It could quickly be adapted to a location near one he had already visited, and wouldn't knock him out to use. He kept exercising the ability anyways, just to be sure. Every tenth of a second would matter.

Louisa's new cell was tessellated with sensors and intelligent projectile weapons. He had tried briefly to disarm the weapons, but doing such a thing over a distance proved too challenging to learn on the timescale of a few days. He would simply need to be very, very fast. Simon reminded himself that he had been stark naked for the past month and that Louisa's first image of him would ideally be a flash of nudity followed by finding herself in a forest cave, equally naked. He was determined to teleport none of her clothing with her since it was certainly bugged.

He felt like he was stalling. He used his connection to Louisa to check that she was where she had been since he last checked on her. She was. It seemed she no longer was allowed to leave the room she was in. Taking a risk, he beat his hand on his chest three times. She smiled weakly but didn't beat back. She seemed more damaged by her captivity than he'd been. Rage returned. Saving her without rehearsing the precise motions of his rescue would be inviting disaster, so he sat himself down and visualized every detail of how the rescue would go. Whether or not he succeeded, he knew he wouldn't be spending more than three conscious seconds in that room.

CHAPTER 24

The circles on the floor worried him. He knew he would want to teleport in from the air. So, he would need to lunge forward, while still in the cave, then teleport while in a horizontal posture directly to the side of Louisa while she sat. Teleporting to her side would hopefully buy him a half second while the proboscis guns adjusted their aim to him. He would then grasp her neck between his two hands, while activating another teleportation, and would bring the two of them back to the cavern, ideally both naked.

Since this was unrehearsable, he had a backup should he accidentally teleport her with her attire. In such an instance she would have to strip, and he would take them out of the cave before a drone picked up a signal and would bring them to the ocean. He would extend his untraceable ability to her, and they would walk south along the coastline, their feet kept in the water to erase their footprints, and hopefully not be shot.

If he brought her to the cavern without her clothing, there would be a welcome moment for rest, which he might well need if one of the guns managed to hit him. He simulated the plan in his head multiple times, each iteration finding himself wishing for just one more week to develop abilities to either destroy the drones or disarm all devices in the room and on Louisa from a distance. There would be no such waiting. Repeating the plan in his head started wearing on his patience. He took a long breath and committed.

First, he checked in with the birds he'd stationed close to the cave. He would only begin when he was confident that no drones or dogs would see the entrance to the cavern for at least five seconds. There was one dog a hundred feet away, and three drones in the area. It took ten minutes of waiting for a window where nothing was near him. He estimated he had maybe twenty seconds of his hidden home being unobserved. More than he would need. Now was the time. He then connected to Louisa and verified that her posture hadn't changed.

"Shield," He said. He had decided that he didn't trust the black circles on the floor of her cell. If they contained projectiles of some sort, they would likely be tranquilizers, and he would return to the cave only to be discovered within seconds as his illusions failed to re-materialize.

"Away!" He shouted. Less than a second of charge time to transport. He used it to leap into the air and reorient his body so that his legs and arms were level. The shield he had created positioned itself under his stomach. He was instantly teleported precisely where he intended.

Sensory overload. The sounds of the following second were the most jarring. Barrels of what turned out to be more than four guns swiveled rapidly with a subdued screeching noise to take aim at the intruder. A violent hissing sound came up from every direction, and Simon processed that a vapor was suffusing the room. He was already shouting a second "Away!" at this point. The hundreds of circles opened up, sounding like hundreds of clicks, and darts shot out with startling speed. It was obvious that within the next second at least some of them would reach skin, despite the shield covering most of his area. His hands reached Louisa's head and he punched both of her ears with his palms as he imagined the cavern he was in, not two seconds ago. He hadn't thought a single real thought while he did any of this.

Just as he heard the guns fire, they were in the cave.

Louisa stumbled along the cave floor, and Simon fell next to her. "Undetectable" he uttered before anything. As his disguises returned to himself and his cavern, the pain started.

"Simon, you're hit!" Louisa said as she rushed to him.

Indeed, four of the darts had hit him before he managed to escape. The darts themselves were thankfully not teleported. A single bullet had penetrated a quarter inch into his side but also did not teleport. Despite bleeding and being in pain, Simon smiled when he saw Louisa in front of him, as naked as he was.

"I'm alright." Simon managed after extending his unhearability radius for her. "It's good to see you again."

"You too. We need to get you taken care of. The poison isn't lethal in small doses, but that looks painful." She gestured to the bullet wound.

"Yeah, I'm noticing that. Hey you got hit too are you alright?"

"Yeah, they immunized me for some reason. It was... discomforting. Here, you need apply pressure." Louisa reached into the bed of leaves Simon had been sleeping on and pushed a bundle into his side. The flow halted.

The pain got progressively worse. Simon started with his bleeding side, uttering "heal" and willing his tissues to repair themselves. The pain intensified, and he shouted as though being electrocuted.

"I know it's bad. Just stay with me. Focus on my heartbeat." Louisa urged.

He did his best and continued to shout "heal" so loudly that he was convinced the drones outside would hear him. Louisa put her hands on his chest, which calmed him slightly. He felt in her heart an immunity to the same poison that was corrupting him. He understood why she had been in so much pain. He felt his body remain on the edge of going into shock for what may have been hours but probably wasn't. Gradually the poison's effect subsided. Louisa smiled at him reassuringly. He smiled back. She pounded her chest three times.

"Me too." He said.

They stared at each other for a while. He re-memorized her face, which had become a little thinner and sadder. She was doing the same to him.

"So where even are we?" She asked.

" We're in a forest in Oregon. In a cave. I carved it out of a large rock. And put a hologram around it."

"Sounds like you've been busy."

"I had a lot to do. We're impossible to find, don't worry. We're free. Are you Ok?"

"Yeah, yeah." Louisa looked around, off towards the back of the cave, then to the mouth. Two people would have felt claustrophobic if the second person were anyone else.

"Can we go out there? I don't want to spend another minute in a closed space."

"I wish we could. If you pass the edge, you'll quickly be seen by a drone. I've pre-developed abilities that hide us so long as we stay together in here."

Louisa walked towards the front of the cave. Light shone in, the river and trees beyond clearly visible, yet out of reach. For a second Simon worried that she'd cross the thin invisible veil keeping them hidden behind a false impression of stone, but she seemed to sense exactly where it was. A dog emerged, patrolling the forest along the river, and Louisa jumped back in fright. She placed her hands on her stomach, near the spot where Simon had most noticed her pain.

Louisa didn't seem talkative. He didn't blame her. They were both exhausted.

"What now?" She asked.

"Whatever you want. We're beyond their reach. I've learned these past few weeks. It takes time to develop abilities, but I believe that I'm ultimately able to manipulate matter, energy, and structure however I want. Or anything you'd ever want. If you want to see Europe, I'll take you. We can try and leave by next week, maybe."

Louisa turned around. "I need to think." She again looked unhappy.

"I really wished you'd rescued me sooner." *Me too.*

"I'm so sorry. I wanted to but I needed time. If I'd tried a week ago, it would've failed. I spent every waking minute developing abilities just to get you back."

"Yeah. That makes sense." Louisa said. "It doesn't matter. They've invested a lot in your recovery. I was supposed to be their bargaining chip. Or so they told me."

"You're safe now. I promise. What's your last year been like? They barely told me anything. All I knew for sure was that you hadn't died."

He tapped his heart. "I'd assumed you weren't tortured, since your heartbeast was steady. But maybe I was wrong about everything."

"No, the torture was only after you escaped. Before that, I was treated well. Almost too well, actually. They had me on meds for most of the first year. It plummeted my IQ down to a happier level for a while. I lived the hedonistic lifestyle of a useless pet. I suppose I actually enjoyed being a zombie for a while. Eventually, the medication stopped. They wanted me to continue some of my old work analyzing the First-Citizen's blood."

"That's something. At least you were stimulated."

"I'd have been fine staying on the medication, to be honest. My work for the FIrst-Citizen is helping a man who doesn't deserve it, and my vaccine work is more useless than the Citizenship seems to think."

"Not if I'm involved. With my abilities, it's just like you said on the beach. I think I can help you amplify the brilliant work you've done and distribute it to countries that actually need your cures."

"Simon?"

"Yeah?"

"I missed you." Louisa stepped towards him uncertainly, and they embraced. Hormones that Simon hadn't felt in over a year overcame him, and Louisa's tentative kissing quickly pushed them onto the improvised bed of leaves. Simon realized Louisa hadn't even bothered to ask why they were both naked. They made love, not soullessly, but also not vigorously. They each gave their best lustful effort, but were quickly exhausted.

Afterwards, Simon fell into a deep, dreamless slumber embracing his partner.

He later awoke, the hurricane fading, and instinctively reached out for Louisa with his eyes still closed. His arms couldn't find her. They also couldn't move. The sound of the river he usually woke up to had disappeared, replaced by some awful smell. Something felt terribly wrong. Simon opened his eyes then closed them immediately. He couldn't bear to look at what was in front of him.

"It's a gift for you. Open up." the Second Citizen ordered, stepping in closer. "We have tools to pry eyelids and control pupils, but I warn you they're not pleasant."

He reopened his eyes one at a time. Propped up on gurneys opposite his, were the partially decayed but still recognizable bodies of Penelope, Beckett, Charlie, and his father. Skin had grayed, and rigor mortis had already set in, bulging their eyes slightly out of their sockets. For some reason, dozens of tubes and wires were stemming from their bloated necks, facilitating some sort of complex fluid exchange causing some of the tubes to quiver and pulse in a heartbeat pattern. The stench was infinitely worse when combined with sight, and Simon threw up against his muffle. He immediately lost consciousness. He awoke with his vomit gone.

"We're being more careful with you now. You don't get the muffle removed just for vomiting. Hold yourself together."

Simon looked to the Second Citizen, wondering what had happened. He could only think of one thing, but it couldn't believe it.

"You're no fool. I'm sure in the last few seconds you've figured out that Louisa turned you in. You're probably in denial she'd do such a thing."

Simon failed at propping himself up. His arms and legs were bound to his gurney at every joint.

"The method was quite poetic, I must say. The poison in the darts couldn't be made strong enough to hurt you in small doses unless you weren't fast enough to evade all but a few of them. So they had to be made weak. They only became potent after interacting with the poison lacing Louisa's lips. Two weak poisons multiplied into an unstoppable one. And she's to be rewarded. You and her will be allowed to share quarters, after you utter the First-Citizen's contract. I'm sorry about all this." He looked to Charlie and Beckett, who were tabled next to each other and were each utterly still amidst the beeps and churns of mechanical pumping.

"They aren't dead, by the way. It would be better if they were. Their brainstems have been partially severed, so they've lost all control over their bodies. Their hearts, lungs, kidneys, etc. are functionally dead, but we're able to keep their brains and nervous system alive while their bodies turn into worm food, transporting blood and oxygen from a matrix of tanks built into the wall. They can feel their every organ bloat and decay. The rigor mortis you see is real, and incredibly painful for them. You're technically in their field of vision, but I doubt they're able to achieve abstract facial recognition above the pain. The process can be reversed if we start within the next few hours. Whether we do or not will depend on the extent of your cooperation. This is the First-Citizen's preferred method of torture. Take a good look. This is what happens when you anger him."

The Second Citizen stepped forward and offered Simon a pen and paper. His right arm was automatically released. He wrote a question.

Why did she do it?

The Second Citizen glanced at the sheet.

"Naturally. The how, though, is more interesting. During the first two days of your escape, we safely assumed that you would be too preoccupied with your own imminent survival to check up on her, so we made efficient use of that time. We put her through bodily trauma and organ surgery while maintaining her heartbeat at a regular pulse, knowing it was her heart you would be checking to convince yourself that she was safe. Then we replaced both of her kidneys with cybernetic alternative organs, which were programmed to explode with the kinetic output of two hundred tons of TNT twenty four hours after her leaving this facility if not disarmed. I'll have you know, that your partner now has the most expensive and deadly organs in history. They even fully function as kidneys, and would have felt like kidneys to you if you'd developed an ability to feel her up. They took half a city's worth of resources to construct, but for you, it was worth it. If she said anything, you'd both have died instantly."

"The First-Citizen regretted gambling your life, but I convinced him that some risk would be necessary to get you back. We lined her lips with a sleep agent strong enough to tranquilize a horse, just in case such potency was necessary for you, and explained this to her so she knew you would both die if she didn't put you to sleep for us. Her kissing you is one of the last things you remember before waking up here, I'm quite sure."

Simon wrote again on his paper. The Second Citizen glanced over to it.

"Your mother? Ahh. She isn't among the corpses because she was killed years ago. Your father knew she was dead, by the way. We told him not to tell you. I only say this because by tomorrow it won't really matter what you know."

Simon wrote one final question on his paper.

"No Simon, I can't kill you. You'll have to discuss with the First-Citizen your right to death, although I doubt he'll humor you. You owe him a meeting, speaking of which."

Two guards entered the room, freed Simon from the gurney, and escorted both of them through the facility. If it wasn't the same building Simon had escaped from, it was a carbon copy. They marched through hallways and up elevators toward the First-Citizen's office.

Simon took this time to try and reach out to his birds back in the forest, to see if he still could. He wasn't sure how helpful they would be, but if nothing else, seeing the trees through their eyes would comfort him. He only reached two birds. Almost his entire fleet had been killed. The drones must have figured out how to determine if a bird was under his control while he was passed out. Or maybe they'd simply killed every bird in the region.

Their entourage traversed the garden and reached the wood doors of the First-Citizen's office. Simon was given the same instructions as the first time he walked through those doors, and he followed the Second Citizen through. The garden statues were exactly how he remembered. Simon was convinced it was the same facility.

"Ah, Simon" the First-Citizen spoke quietly from the shadows of the room back behind his desk, in a timbre clearly meant to be louder.

"You are clever enough, but there is always a mistake. You had all but gotten the better of us. Just like that first time, on the beach. And the second time when you went to the woods. I wonder how many more near misses I will need to suffer before you become a stable investment."

Simon stayed silent.

"Are you going to ask about Louisa? Otherwise, I will not tell you."

"I already told him. Your little idea with the corpses worked too well." The Second Citizen said.

"Ah." The First-Citizen sounded annoyed, his figure still hardly visible behind the room's shadowy buffer.

"Well yes, fine. She is alive and well. She performed her mission beautifully. She is your kryptonite. Quite useful, that one."

Simon felt no desire to break his silence only to ask what kryptonite was. Another ancient word betraying the true age of the wicked man in front of him.

"Still, nothing? You are allowed to speak. You will be speaking in a minute. You might as well warm up your voice."

"Should we begin immediately?" the Second Citizen asked in a whisper even Simon struggled to hear.

"Sure. I will watch." The First-Citizen replied.

Their unit briskly exited the grand chamber and proceeded downwards by elevator, towards a room Simon knew too well. They reached the entrance to the blue room, and Simon noticed that his chair and helmet had been updated once again, and now included a series of straps that would thoroughly bind his entire body in place.

"No chances are being taken." the Second Citizen said simply, while the First-Citizen wandered in from his perch to observe closely.

"If you so much as think about uttering 'away', or anything of such treasonous nature, you will be full-body shocked before you even recognize the thought, and ten minutes will be added to the suffering of your decaying friends. This is likely going to be painful for you, but you have left us with no choice. Do this faithfully, and tomorrow, when you are completely controlled by me, your leash will be cut."

Simon sat down in his chair, and guards applied his straps. They felt heavy, and he was certain that they were monitoring the movements within every one of his non-fractal capillaries, and using the data to extract any thoughts of escape he was having. His muffle was removed only after the thick helmet was placed on his head. Despite being twice the size of the old one, it still felt lighter than its predecessor, a welcome reminder that, if nothing else, Simon would be the physically strongest person in the room other than the First-Citizen. The silver autocrat approached, and stood above him, piercing eyes scanning his face as obsessively as he had studied Louisa's. As Simon's muffle was removed, a fleeting thought of escape arose. It was entirely instinctual, with no intent behind it. He was immediately shocked, in a one-second burst that felt halfway fatal.

"Your physical enhancement was not lost on us. You're being subjected to over 500 milliamps of current. Enough to instantly kill most people. Try to focus on the task at hand to the absolute best of your ability, and the pain will subside." The

Second Citizen said. The First-Citizen continued staring.

A field of clear text displayed on Simon's new armband.

"Read it." the First-Citizen said. "Then read it again. And again. Until exhaustion forces you to stop. Then read it a few more times. If you are not properly integrating the message, it will be known."

Simon began reading. His first readthrough of the contract was interrupted regularly by shocks. Following that, he was too terrified to think anything beyond the next two syllables of the text.

He read it again. And again. He forced himself to assimilate the words of the contract as well as he could, and the machine alerted his observers whenever his focus faltered. As hours passed, he felt the clauses of the contract sinking into the essence of his being, binding him to it word for word. He was being turned again into a tool.

CHAPTER 25

The following day, Simon read the document out loud one final time, to an audience of the first, second, and third citizen as well as an attendant, but surprisingly no guards. Today he'd been given a paper copy.

The citizen Simon Pontius shall be hereto additionally referred to as the second-to-last, or penultimate citizen, a designation given in good faith to indicate his particular importance to the Citizenship. As such, the penultimate citizen will possess a number of privileged rights, including:

. The right to converse with the First-Citizen, whenever a compelling reason is found. A compelling reason may consist of any of the following:
-imminent personal danger
-progress reports
-filing a valid complaint regarding treatment, provisional on good behavior
-requesting permission for new utterance
.The right to roam any facility he is in freely, granted his location be always known to at least one member of a supervisory board, of which the first, second, and third citizens are to remain members, in addition to any additional appointment made by the First-Citizen or, provisionally, the second or third citizen.
.The right to a day of unscheduled free time, to prevent overexertion.
.The right to physical comfort, including sexual congress, provisional on good behavior.

.The right to contextual knowledge of any applications of ability requested by the First-Citizen.

.The right to whisper frankly to the First-Citizen without explicit permission, provisional on good behavior

Due to the inherent danger in the penultimate citizen's abilities, the following actions are strictly forbidden:

.unsolicited utterance

.Exercising an ability without the consent of the First-Citizen, or in any way that differs from his requested method of usage

.Privacy

.Interaction with any unauthorized citizens, unless such interaction is reasonably unavoidable

.Any attempt at suicide or self-harm

.Any attempt at harming the First-Citizen

.Any attempt at negotiating an exit from this contract

.Refusal to develop an ability explicitly requested by the First-Citizen

The First-Citizen shall retain the right to propose any amendment to this contract, if an instance of poor behavior on the part of the Last Citizen has been observed. The definition of poor behavior shall be at the collective discretion of the first, second, and third citizen, and determined by a majority vote.

The penultimate citizen shall retain the right to refuse any command issued by the First-Citizen if it conflicts with his rights as granted by the contract. He shall additionally retain the right to refuse any command from any other individual, so long as the refusal does not constitute poor behavior, as defined in the previous paragraph.

Simon put the paper on a desk, having read the document over two hundred times since yesterday.

"Well done, Penultimate Citizen" the First-Citizen said proudly. It hadn't been explained why he was the next-to-Last

Citizen. He wondered if there was a Last Citizen somewhere.

"Now, unless you require further audience with me per the conditions of the contract, I shall be off. If you have further questions, you may reach me. I will grant you a half-hour break before you begin your first sanctioned utterance, unless of course you wish to start immediately. I formally grant you permission to utter "Love First-Citizen" in a manner that compels all people to increase their love towards me, as has already been discussed. Godspeed."

The first three citizens left the room. Simon wasn't remuffled. His body craved motion, so he asked his attendant if he could be shown to his new quarters. He wordlessly obliged. Apparently, his room was only two floors down, so he was shown the staircase of the facility for the first time. It hid behind yet another door embedded into the wall.

The guard brought him to his quarters, demonstrating before leaving that Simon could now open the door himself, just by placing his hand on the correct wall. Louisa was waiting for him when he entered. She was sitting on the only bed in the room, on a lapis blanket that might have been a revered luxury in a different context. Simon sat next to her. He didn't know what to say. Neither did she. He wondered if he lost the woman who he could talk to for hours about origami and people and the world. He didn't see that woman anymore. The man he had been then was dead too, he supposed, although he didn't miss that person nearly so much. Louisa tapped her heart twice. Simon did the same. That was all they had left.

"Love First-Citizen, Love First-Citizen, Love First-Citizen..." He uttered carefully. The words quickly started to become an indistinct river of sounds, the meaning behind them detaching from the syllabic properties of the words and becoming a flowing mantra, the meaning stemming from the repetition of the act. He briefly wondered, before being shocked back into focus, whether he still might be able to craft any ability from any word, were he to enter into a deep enough trance. The only two times he had tried using a non-obvious word to develop something, the effort had been superficial and relatively brief.

Hours later, Simon lost his capacity to focus even under duress and was allowed to stop for the day. He uncomfortably wondered how long it would take for him to start properly influencing the minds of those around him.

He returned to his new room, where he found Louisa reading something at the rooms desk. He hadn't paid attention to the bookshelf the first time but now noticed that it was quite well stocked, largely with colorful picture books. Grand efforts were being made to treat the two of them as human beings this time around, and to keep him from being understimulated.

"What are you reading?" He asked.

"Book about infrastructure. Shows improvements that the Citizenship has made to transportation and fuel use. All the books are about the Citizenship by the way. But they're interesting. The world was unrecognizable thirty years ago, institutionally speaking."

"I believe it."

Louisa seemed a little more alive. He couldn't help but wonder if his ability was already beginning to have an impact. His partner, if that's what she was now, looked up at him and her face changed.

"Look, Simon, I'm sorry. But you would have died. You never would have found out about the bomb."

"I know."

Louisa put her hand on Simon's thigh. He didn't move it. He didn't do anything until Louisa fell asleep, her hand still grasping at him.

The following day led to many more utterances of "Love First-Citizen", words which Simon continued to contemplate faithfully, at constant risk of swift electrocution. The following day was much the same, and the day after that.

He decided to forgive Louisa. His sessions, instead of

tiring his voice, made him yearn to speak actual sentences with another human being, something he'd hardly done in ages, and for better or worse she was his only proper companion.

They would spend all of their time talking. For those first few days, they covered avant-garde topics, flavored with such absurdism as wondering what food the hybrid of a lion and an elephant would consume, how many mountains an island could contain before being called a continent, or what the optimal wingspan would be if humans were to suddenly grow wings out of their backs. Simon felt childlike fun talking about the forbidden aspects of the world again.

Louisa still had a certain melancholy, but flowery conversation seemed to distract her. Simon came up with more creative questions to ask, and Louisa's brilliant scientific mind churned out answers to each of them. He was amazed at the depth of her knowledge, and grateful that his partner hadn't lost her creative brilliance. He became quite good at proposing absurd situations for her to consider, pushing her to use her impressive body of scientific knowledge forbidden to the vast majority of citizens. He was happy whenever she laughed at his questions, or the stories he made up after.

Changes began in the second week of utterance. It was the ninth day, when Simon returned to their shared quarters after a particularly taxing four hour utterance, and playfully asked Louisa a question of astrophysics: how many duplicates of the moon could be safely positioned in Earth's orbit before reducing to a cataclysmic mess of astronomical collisions? He imagined that, if they were positioned flawlessly, there could be infinite moon-copies circling the earth, although delicate apparatus would certainly become untenable at a much smaller number. Upon hearing the question, instead of churning out a derivation, she scolded him harshly, and told him she was growing tired of 'ridiculous scientific questions.' Simon, too startled at her uncharacteristic aggression to defend himself, asked if she wanted to go bowling.

"I'd rather work out. The Citizenship doesn't need more bowlers. It needs hard working thinkers. I'll get more blood flowing to my brain by lifting. So will you. You're not so strong that a six hundred pound deadlift won't push you."

Simon obeyed her request and followed her to the gym. They did not speak so much that day as they had the others.

The tenth, eleventh, and twelfth days went much the same, and with each new brightening (Simon still didn't have access to outside, so the brightening of the walls remained his only indication of a new day), Louisa seemed to grow a little more distant from him. Their conversations became curt. Sex became short and functional, but not unbearable.

By the third week, Louisa returned to being talkative. Her new topics of conversation weren't the old ones. They now held tight orbits around the First-Citizen.

"Simon, you need to show more respect for the First-Citizen." She insisted once, mid speech.

"Why? He's holding me here against my will. Same to you. You're essentially under his spell."

"It's not a spell. Stop using hyperbole against me, the First-Citizen wants us to be better with our language. And I agree with him. Your ability is a tool that can make the world a better place. Simon, I..., I care for you. But you need to appreciate that this is all happening for a greater good that's beyond either of us. We should be honored to be his tools. We should do anything he asks of us, joyfully."

"I can't apply the ability to myself. It might compromise me. You're a scientist, you should understand this."

"Frankly, I think you're making that up out of fear. You just don't want to love the First-Citizen. You're jealous that I... well, that all of us here have a place for him in our hearts, except for you. And you're scared. You don't think that loving the First-Citizen will make you happy. I promise it will be the best decision of your life. You should talk to him. Get his permission to apply the ability to yourself."

The conversation went nowhere after that. None of their

conversations did. If Simon had first met Louisa now, he wouldn't have loved her.

By the end of the first month, reports started coming in that citizens living near the complex were showing measurable increases in their already high opinions of the First-Citizen. Those who tolerated him were now beginning to like him. Those who already liked him were starting to love him. That minority of citizens who already loved him were showing the earliest signs of wishing to actively worship him with something resembling religious ecstasy. The third citizen of all people visited Simon to passionately congratulate him on his success. He was the official head of the military, the successor to George Lackley, and was actually of rank 4, although Simon knew better than to remind him. The man was aggressive, with a loud grating voice, someone who might have been an iconic television presence during wartime, but certainly not during peace.

Into the second month, Simon found himself walking alone back to his quarters after his second daily session. Typically he wouldn't encounter any other soul in the building if the helmeted guards weren't counted. Today was a rare exception. As Simon was two halls from his quarters, he saw a figure walking in toward him, and could hardly believe his eyes. It was his meditation teacher, wearing the same gray prisoner uniform that Simon himself had worn under his sensor suit before escaping.

"Oh, hello! I, um, I can speak now. I'm not supposed to speak to citizens who aren't authorized to speak with me, but I've always assumed you were authorized. Wait, did they make you a prisoner here?" Simon said.

The man simply smiled his pacific smile and grasped his hand gently.

"My friend, I've been a prisoner here far longer than you have." With that, the man resumed his stroll, seeming to know exactly where he was to go but finding no reason to rush there.

Simon stood in the middle of the hallway for a moment,

but before he could call back out to the man to ask if he knew where this facility even was, he noticed the two inch slip of paper that had been slid between his fingers. He opened it, and read the small text written across its numerous wrinkles.

Go to facility 22B, cells 2 and 3. Any means necessary. Dispose of this.

Simon had no pockets, so he subtly swallowed the paper without chewing, and resumed his walk back to his quarters, a dozen new questions strutting through his head.

CHAPTER 26

"Simon. To what do I owe the pleasure."

Simon had never seen the Second Citizen's office before. It was much smaller than the First-Citizen's, barely larger than the quarters he shared with Louisa and yet half of the space was devoted to holding books. Each wall was a shelf, and the shelf in the back, behind the Second Citizen at his desk, stood in front of a scarcely visible bookshelf behind it, which looked completely inaccessible. Even the general's private library hadn't possessed such a dense packing of literature. Legible titles included *Les Miserables, Canterbury Tales, 100 Years of Solitude, Jack and the Beanstalk, American Gods, Crime and Punishment, Foundation, Lord of the Rings*, and *House of Leaves*. Music played in the background, a piano with several wind instruments he didn't recognize. The music was flowing yet chaotic, and entranced Simon as no Citizenship music had ever done. He felt his hurricane identity enjoying it more than he was. Perhaps this was a lullaby of ocean storms.

"Jazz. A freeform group recorded this over a century ago, before the internet age. Music like this has a certain appeal to me. Mankind, harnessing and controlling chaos through ideas, and somehow creating a certain beauty from all of it. Artists have a lot they could teach your generation. It's a shame you lot haven't produced any."

"Louisa's an artist."

"She's optimistic."

"Maybe she was. The Citizenship destroyed that."

"My boy, don't sound naive. The Citizenship is a machine built to destroy some of its chosen citizens to maintain tranquility. A machine that's too damn chaotic when people like you live in it. Makes my job less effortless than I'd like at this age. I'd much rather spend a decade listening to Jazz while reading about humanity and patiently waiting for a heart attack to end me."

Simon left the enjoyment of the music to his hurricane self and focused on his reason for being there.

"This is a nice office. I must admit though it feels secluded." *Is the office secure, and can I speak freely?*

The Second Citizen double clicked a primitive looking button on his desk. "Yes, it is." *Yes, you can.*

"I have a request for a minor usage of an ability of mine, which as Second Citizen you are qualified to grant authorization to per my contract."

"Facility 22B." he spoke plainly.

"Yes. That was you, wasn't it?"

"Yes"

"Why?"

The Second Citizen coughed.

"I've noticed that mankind has always hated all things that are almost familiar, yet slightly alien. But we seem to adore fetishizing objects that are truly alien, entirely beyond our understanding or experience. Those entities that we cannot relate to and that try to push us to expand our conceptions of the cosmos. Never in history have we managed to ignore these objects, when we stumble across them. We worship the sun, the moon, mountains, volcanoes. God. The atomic bomb. Quasimatter. All while we hated Muslims, Hindus, and Jews, simply for their subtly differing approaches to being human. It's just a part of our nature I suppose."

For someone who seemed so tired, the Second Citizen loved talking. Simon wondered if philosophizing was the old man's remaining source of social enjoyment.

"We never should have messed with Quasimatter." He continued.

"The mathematics behind it alone are terrifying in a

way no prior discovery has managed to be. You're the living proof."

"Me? Why? Is this related to my ability?"

"It is your ability."

Simon thought in silence for a moment.

"When you said 'people like me' just now...are there others like me?"

"Yes. A few. Facility 22b holds the three most powerful. Each of them is entirely different from the others. The woman is sedated. You must never wake her. Juarez is your priority. If you can get Hegelpitic to speak with you, he may have a part to play. I wouldn't worry too much about him, though. He's the most interesting, but least powerful."

"I don't understand anything you're saying."

"You will. There isn't much time. I suspect there is exactly one winning strategy in this unfortunate game, and Juarez may be your champion. Find him. The facility is expecting your arrival, and won't report your presence. Go there. Learn what you can. Make an ally, or two."

"You're officially granting me permission to use 'away'?"

The Second Citizen nodded.

"The slip you ate contained indigestible encoded information of its precise GPS location. I hope you can craft an ability to parse it and find the facility quickly. Good luck." He glanced at his wristband on which a timer reached zero. He then leaned forward and pushed the desk button again.

"I formally, explicitly grant you permission to apply your "away" ability in the manner just discussed. Any individual you encounter in 22b will be an authorized citizen to whom you may speak. "Away" is to be used exactly twice between the times of 22:00 and 23:00 tonight. Excessive usage, or usage occupying any other timeframe will be viewed unequivocally as poor behavior and will be dealt with accordingly."

The door opened behind Simon. He got up and returned silently to his quarters, being told by his uniform's right sleeve that the time was 20:24, leaving him with an under two hour wait. Reaching his quarters, he was glad to note that Louisa wasn't there. He spent his time reading a book about some war from two centuries ago in which the dominant predecessor to the Citizenship, the United States, had taken part.

Time passed quickly enough, with Simon limiting the rate at which he checked time so as to seem unsuspicious. His fourth check showed the time at 22:12. He cursed the loss of 12 minutes, but knew it had been better to err on the side of caution. There was the possibility this was a test, but Simon chose to take his command at face value and act as though there was no irregularity to his preparation to teleport.

"Facility 22B, away" he repeated, taking about five minutes of utterance for his ability to digest what his body couldn't. By 22:20, an impression of a hallway had entered his head, giving a vague preview of his point of aim. He closed his eyes for a moment to prepare himself, concerned with his near ignorance of where he was transporting to. He knew his chance to go would be limited to this hour, possibly forever, so he made his preparation brief and spoke "away".

A singular unit of perception later, Simon was in a completely new space, at the end of a long, lit hallway. The walls were more gray-metallic than white, and the ceiling was lit by proper, incandescent lights as far as he could see. It must have been an old building.

He was immediately greeted by an aged man in a surprisingly expensive three-piece garment, who seemed unsurprised by the intrusion.

"Hello, penultimate citizen. It's an honor. David told me your time to meet the others is limited, yes?"

The man's voice was higher pitched than Simon would've guessed, and held less of the abstracted fatigue that the similarly aged Second Citizen constantly emanated. *Proof that age doesn't always equal weariness I guess. I wonder if he's friends with David.*

"Yeah, till the end of the hour. Are the others Juarez, and

Hegelpitic? And a sleeping woman?"

"That would be them. But we're not disturbing Maria. The Last Citizen is never to wake, you must understand. You can still view her if you like." The old man spoke with a loudness that was the trademark of his generation. His voice reminded him of how Louisa used to speak.

"Sure. Lead the way. Just make sure I see Juarez."

"Of course. But Hegelpitic is closer, if you'd like to meet him."

Simon consented, and the man led the way down the hall. Simon realized that the man had never given his name, and decided it might be safer not to ask.

"I should warn you that Hegelpitic is the most, er, visually stimulating of the children of the bomb. That's what we call you four, by the way. Even though you and the Last Citizen were created in a separate incident from Juarez and Hegelpitic. Anyways, here's his cell."

A door popped out of the gray wall to the right, and the man entered. Simon followed. The space was a cube of roughly thirty foot dimensions, quite spacious. Off in the corner was a bed, whose blanket covered a large figure.

"This side of the room is blocked off with a millimeter thick membrane. You can kinda see the refraction if you look at the wall over there. He can't reach us. Although usually he's not violent."

"Then why the protection? Is he deadly?"

"Deadly, yes. Dangerous, no. But a few of his alters are."

"Alters?"

"Why are you waking me in my free hour!" A voice boomed from the bed. The figure seemed to grow under the blanket before rising.

Hegelpitic was a sight to behold. His features were humanesque, and beautifully so, except that he was over seven feet tall, had an extra pair of muscular arms below his regular set, and had a third eye twice the size of his regular ones breaching his forehead. His face had many classically attractive features, with a well-set jaw, fine cheekbones and long, flowing silver hair. His larger third eye was the darkest shade of blue Simon had ever seen on a living being. Simon suspected the eye caught details missed by most.

"You have a visitor. The penultimate citizen. The new one, that is. David sent him. Needless to say, he's a child of the bomb."

The human epitome of the synthesis between the beautiful and the profane walked towards the middle of the room. His third eye seemed to start shrinking. The old man turned to Simon and whispered. "If his third eye shrinks, he's about to transform, probably into Hesperic." Simon kept his gaze on Hegelpitic.

"Is that so?" Hegelpitic said. He was now standing only two feet from Simon, who had never in his adult life felt so short. They stared silently at each other for long enough to remind Simon that time was limited.

"My people do not know what to make of you," Hegelpitic said.

"Your people? Who are they? Can I meet them?"

"Ahh, a fair question. Asked in good faith. I can tell you accept my nature. Most recoil from me. I must not be the strangest thing you have seen, so I might guess that you are like me. The bomb has done its work on you."

"Do you change into the rest of your people? Alter into them?"

Hegelpitic laughed. It was powerful yet angelic. "No. They are all here, always. We come from a different place. We can only be here, in this cell, one at a time. I am their leader, because I make wise decisions, have a high tolerance for pain, and am willing to occupy this world for longer than the others."

"Are you tortured here?"

The old man looked uncertain but said nothing.

"No longer physically," Hegelpitic said. "The greatest torture for me is to be away from my world for so long a stretch. We are otherwise well cared for. My equivalent wishes to meet with you. You will see me again if there is cause."

In three seconds, Hegelpitic transformed. His third eye finished shrinking to a regular size, his extra pair of arms vanished, he shrunk several inches, and streamlined his muscle. Hair remained silver. Hegelpitic had become a she.

"Hello, Simon. I am Hesperic. I must say you're making quite an impression on all of us. We have questions for you."

Hesperic was still taller than Simon, with the finely considered muscular frame of a marble statue. The lack of a top was not entirely unwelcome.

"Who are you?" Simon asked.

"Me, personally? I am the ambassador. Well, Hegelpitic is our main ambassador, our guardian, and a revered leader. But for all his excellence, he isn't always the most charming diplomat. He relies on me for that."

"An important job for your people, then."

"Oh, certainly. Most of them dread the idea of coming out here. In our world, they are perfectly free. It is beautiful there. Far grander than this cell we're kept in, although we're at least guaranteed safety here. If only there were a way you could join me. I would love to give you a tour."

"Someday, perhaps I'll be able to." He felt guilty for craving the company of this beautiful and powerful woman.

Hesperic smiled curiously, but then her face began twitching, and before she could say something, she began to transform again. She grew taller again, taller even than Hegelpitic, and her third eye duplicated, creating a facial pentagon. Each eye was a starkly different shade of green, at least to Simon's developed eyes, creating a disconcerting asymmetry. The man now staring down at him was lanky and foreboding, and stretched the elastic rags of clothing on his person nearly as far as they would go. Simon noticed a long, thin tail had grown behind him.

"Most of the alters are very tall." the old man contributed. "Hegelpitic is actually of quite average height, but some of them, like Kilje here, stand at over eight and a half feet."

"You are a short people." The man, Kilje, interjected with a belittling tone. His voice was admittedly the most beautiful of the three.

"So Simon, what is your divergence? You have thus far witheld a demonstration from us. Our people, and my constituents in particular, have a vested interest in understanding you."

"It wouldn't matter if I told you. I'm unable to demonstrate it here. Not like you clearly are."

"A shame." Kilje shook his head slowly.

"You mentioned having potentially the capacity to join our world. This would be an impressive feat. Perhaps someone so powerful should be put to sleep. I'm sure Maria would appreciate a bedmate."

"Maria? Who is she? Have you met her"

Kilje grinned. "Fortunately not. She's considerably more powerful than any of us. She even makes Juarez seem inconsequential. She probably dwarfs you, despite your evasion of my earlier question. Ah, you haven't met Juarez either, have you? Noteworthy."

Kilje looked about to say something else but doubled back with a curse and began transforming again. After a five second struggle, Kilje was replaced again with Hegelpitic, by far the more handsome of the two.

"Go. Meet Juarez. I did not realize, my apologies. You must speak with him. I hope we have time to talk again later. There will be much to discuss."

Simon looked to the old man, who shrugged.

"Works for me," he said, and strolled out of the cell, Simon following.

"There isn't another world, is there? Simon asked the man as the door closed behind them. *I bet he has what I have, just further along. That's why I'm here.*

"Oh, but there absolutely is. Hegepitic is truly a beautiful being. An entire culture exists within a single skull. Where a typical human brain houses maybe a hundred billion neurons, his has well exceeded the quadrillion mark. His neurons, you see, they replicate and form connections on ever smaller scales, completely beyond our biophysical understanding. Much the same as your neurons do when you develop your abilities, except he had been doing it actively since birth, to create entirely new consciousnesses, new people. Thousands of them. That, in addition to a highly stable perpetual dream state of sorts they refer to as their homeworld. The way they describe the place, it's quite wonderful. At least most of the time."

The old man stopped them at the other end of the hallway. Simon wondered how much more he knew.

"This is Juarez," he said. "The former penultimate. I haven't had the heart to inform him of his demotion."

"Do you mind if I go in alone? Simon asked. He felt an importance to the impending meeting that might require whatever degree of discretion he could afford. The old man consented and opened the door.

"You have less than a half hour. Knock when you want out. Be careful with him, we can't physically restrain him like the others." The door closed.

Light emanated from all four walls as Simon walked in, and he found himself in a room with the same dimensions as Hegelpitic's, a large open cube. In one corner was a toilet, sink, and compact shower, and in the closer corner was a series of dumbbells, the largest of which seemed even larger than the sleeping figure he spotted in the far corner. Next to him was a bookshelf with such varied titles as *Sandman, Jack and the Beanstalk, X-men, Bible, Brothers Karamazov, Cryptonomicon, Fences, 50 shades of gray, the Bikeriders, Moscow Puzzles, Sudoku.* The figure stirred.

"I'm up, I'm up, no need to..." His voice lost its apologetic tone when he saw his guest. "And who the hell are you?"

"Hello. I'm Simon." He hesitated.

"The penultimate citizen."

"Huh. Not the most enviable title, is it?" Juarez got up and walked to him. He was incredibly thin, a little shorter than Simon, and had silver hair that spiked outwards like a porcupine. There was no shimmer; this cell had no divide. Juarez seemed to read his thoughts.

"I bet you visited my neighbor before me. Yeah, it makes some sense to give him a shield. None for me. A wall is never gonna be what stops me leaving here." He stared at Simon, waiting for something.

"Look, I don't know anything about you," Simon began.

"WI know that you're somehow important, and I think I'm supposed to learn your story. Maybe it's supposed to help me piece together mine, I'm not sure. There isn't much time."

"Well, the name's Juarez, since you didn't ask. You should get that rudeness checked." Juarez spoke with a gravelly voice that somehow felt forced. The far southern accent seemed more genuine.

"Sorry. I actually already knew your name. The Second Citizen told me. But you're right, I should've asked."

"Ah. David. I'm guessing he went off on some grand philosophical tangent, then sent you on the big plane to meet with me yourself. Sound right?"

"It sounds like you've met him."

"Once or twice. He's memorable."

"He wouldn't have asked me to meet you if you weren't important."

Juarez shook his head.

"True. Still, I wouldn't trust him."

"Why not? Has he lied to you before?"

"Not that I'm aware of. I just know he's brilliant, doesn't care about preserving his own life all that much, and he's in a position of power. Only an idiot trusts people like that. At least the general has clear principles."

So he knows the general?

"I don't disagree, but I need his help. And I need yours."

"I'm sure you do. He's quite good at making himself indispensable. You're a child of the bomb." It wasn't a question.

"Yes. I mean, I think so. I have certain abilities that defy nature if that's the definition."

"More of a symptom than a definition, but you got the idea. Alright then. Show me something. I love me some evidence."

"I can't."

"Why not?"

"I'm under an unbreakable contract. I cannot use my abilities unless ordered. It's a whole thing." Juarez paused in thought. Simon took the opportunity to describe his ability in greater detail. Juarez seemed skeptical.

"I'll believe you, provisionally. It's an interesting story."

"So what makes you unusual?" Simon asked, hoping to change the topic of conversation to something that might help him. Juarez grinned.

"Well, I've got nothing on Maria, but here's what I can do."

Juarez turned and, with animal swiftness, lept vertically nearly the full thirty feet to the ceiling. A pull-up bar was situated there which Simon hadn't noticed earlier, and Juarez began dancing around it with languid effortlessness. The man was unmuscular, and had sticks for limbs, making the act seem unfeasible. Juarez landed back on the floor, his legs not bending a single inch as his feet touched down. He walked a few paces to a corner of the room and proceeded to lift the largest of the dumbbells and effortlessly heave it towards the opposite wall, with one arm. No, not the whole arm. Just a wrist. Or maybe just a finger. It bounced on the synthetic plastic wall and returned directly to his grip. The laws of inertia did not seem to apply to him, as he should have been knocked clean off his feet from both the throw and the catch.

"So, you're strong," Simon remarked plainly.

"Among other things. I can't really be hurt anymore, either. When I was younger I could be. That's how they got my blood. I'm sure you know the rest of that story."

"Forgive me, but I don't. What do you mean?"

"Well, I'm the reason the Citizenship solved immortality." He paused, waiting for Simon to make a connection that didn't exist.

"I mean I get that they gave the scientists the credit, but I'd have thought David would have told you at least that."

Simon didn't know what to say.

"Juarez. Do you think that everyone in the Citizenship is immortal?"

"Well I'm not naive. I'm sure criminals get it revoked. Maybe some of the lower classes? But my blood was the key to it all. I'm the Henrietta Lacks of the twenty first century. Shit, do they keep it from larger sections of the population? David told me they didn't do that."

"Henrietta Lacks?"

"Yeah. You don't know who she is? How is that possible? Her blood was used to help save millions."

"Oh. Juarez, I don't know how to say this. Nobody is immortal except for the First-Citizen. And I think maybe the General."

The man stared blankly at Simon for a moment, his dark brown eyes, much the same color as Louisa's, retreating to some distant place.

"Order confirmed. Drop the payload. Drop everything. Make me the devil. " He whispered after some time.

"All monsters." his face spawned a silent fury.

"Explain." Simon pleaded, checking his sleeve to see that he had 17 minutes. He'd noticed Louisa's heart rate had started elevating a few minutes ago and wondered what she was doing.

Juarez sat sullenly in a lotus posture on the cell floor and motioned for Simon to join. He began to tell a story.

"A few months before I was born, my parents had shacked up in a small village near the border with Texas, this was in 2072."

Simon knew where this was going once the year was given, but continued to listen.

"My dad was captain of an army reserve squad, a particular unit of a couple dozen men being kept back from the main defensive force amassing near the rio grande, to 'provide a firm line of ballsy guerilla defenders' he'd tell us, but in spanish. You know, both countries were bilingual then. The whole continent grew up speaking Spanish and English near equally. It's only after the war they got rid of the Spanish."

"That squadron never saw battle, did it?"

"No sir. The quasimatter bomb approached on a regular plane, one of countless diamonds in the sky. The bomb dropped unceremoniously, as one of thousands, so that it wouldn't be singled out and targeted by ground to air weaponry before reaching the surface. Even if it had been, it would have made little difference."

"The bomb went off in the distance, far enough to be survived, but close enough to awe my mother with its sheer scale. My dad's friend happened to catch some video. I think that video's famous now since all the other footage got scrambled."

Simon knew exactly what it looked like. The explosion expanded in a shimmering spherical shockwave that seemed to ignore the constraints of material kinetics that would have caused any other weapon of such destructive scale to conform to a mushroom shape.

He thought back to the limited video recording of the explosion that survived, which had been played in front of him perhaps a hundred times in school, and was now permanently engraved in his mind's eye. The explosion had created a hemisphere that dominated the sky, a wavefront perfectly unrippled by the matter it passed through. It seemed almost beyond nature, yet in the same vein deeply a part of it, in that brief moment immortalized in footage. Juarez must have been there when that video was taken.

"Nobody fully understood the technology behind the bomb. Its design had been discovered by a team of Citizenship researchers entirely by accident, one of those rare technological windfalls that you get only once every few generations, that seems to magically push everything decades ahead of schedule. By pure technical happenstance, which I couldn't understand without years of education my captors won't let me have, this country found itself in possession of a technology no other nation on earth is anywhere close to being able to replicate. Or so my handlers say."

"Do you know anything about where quasimatter comes from? The other universe?"

Juarez thought for a moment. He seemed to be a deeply intelligent and chronically understimulated man. Simon felt for him.

"The theoretical underpinnings of this technology are well beyond the reach of even the cutting edge of Citizenship physics and mathematics. I know they obsessively documented the few times it has been used. The bomb has this effect of instantaneously creating unpredictable convolutions in the organizational complexity of all matter and energy within local space, its effect becoming progressively more potent on smaller and smaller scales. Simple enough."

"When the explosion struck, buildings remained entirely intact. Cameras and other computational devices became scrambled in some odd patterns. But here's where it gets weird. Biologically, almost everything within ten miles was utterly sterilized, with most cells' DNA becoming unraveled or reorganized beyond use or recognition. Life, especially on the microscopic level, has all this delicate complexity that breaks down with even the slightest perturbations. On the subcellular and subatomic scales, the fundamental laws of physics were being tugged and manipulated in dozens of small but indescribable ways."

"They never found a pattern to the convolutions, only in

its rough ferocity at each scale at which it was measured, and at what distances from the epicenter. Two axes of variability. You know cartesian mathematics?"

"Yeah."

"Well, there was a goldilocks zone. You know golidlocks? Anyways, while most objects were destroyed or rendered useless, there was opportunity for accidents; unforeseeable consequences of this sort of manipulation causing some organisms with just the right radius and biology to remain both alive and altered."

"So that's what we are?"

"Well let me get there. At first, quasimatter seemed like the perfect weapon: fairly easy to manufacture, with sufficient resources, yet requiring enough specialized processes that nobody needed complete knowledge of how to create it, increasing immunity to espionage. More importantly, the bomb could be dropped anywhere and would keep all macroscopic objects like buildings and weapons intact for any invading force to use, while eradicating cells, viruses, down to individual mitochondria. It was the perfect tool for war-winning."

"But yeah, within a range of about twelve miles from the explosion's epicenter, where the effects had only partially dissipated, strange compromises began occurring in lifeforms. Fertile and faster-growing cell structures struck within this range were particularly shown to be affected. Almost a dozen "children of the bomb" were born not quite human because of the weapon. Along with other things."

"So like a pregnancy. And what other things?" Simon checked the time. Less than ten minutes.

"I don't know. My parents got the hell out of there the minute the explosion ended. I've only met Hegelpitic a few times. And Florin, he was hard to miss. Real big guy. Was probably stronger than me. He and his sister have been out for a while now. We all grew so different, you know. But what's amazing is that we all stayed so human. It's like the quasimatter knew what made us *us*. And it just riffed on that. None of the effects deformed or killed. Cells over-replicated like cancers, but kept getting smaller and smaller and hiding amongst regular cells, creating systems of increasingly complicated space around them, niched into other spaces like fractals with more precision than should have been possible. You know I went a year without eating once. I've got half a quintillion cells in my body, and somehow they all feed themselves. You know fractals? Cause that's what we are. We're beautiful growing systems that nurture our humanity inwards, where many predicted we'd turn into Godzillas, or formless eldritch tumors. What about Godzilla, you know him?"

"So you don't know anything at all about the other universe?"

"Only that it exists. And I can kind of sense that it's here with us, never far, like when you look to the sun but it keeps you from opening your eyes. Bright light's the one thing that still hurts me, by the way. But I've heard my attendants explain it away using a vast arsenal of scientific jargon. Some of them never bothered; they claimed the occurrence to be the work of "God". You know God? He's this old mythical being who some say created the universe. Unrelated to Godzilla."

Juarez looked to his bookshelf, seeming to debate if he should retrieve a particular book.

"My dad used one of the few non-electric petroleum vehicles left in the military at the time, an old army jeep he'd insisted brought good luck, despite his officer's halfhearted insistence that he should ditch it. The vehicle had seen him through many hard times. It got my family and my mutated fetus away from the bomb quickly where the other men and their families had to walk. It was everyone for themselves that day."

"Life got hard, but we got by. For all the atrocities committed in conquering the country, the general seemed an efficient occupier once we started thinking objectively about him, and there were plenty of good jobs for my parents to take on to support us. They both drove garbage routes for a while."

"I got to nine before being found. In the chaos of the great surrender, his family's presence near the bomb and their survival had managed to avoid any formal documentation, and it was only a secondary investigation conducted later that led a Citizenship official to investigate my family. We never thought they'd be so damn thorough."

"I'd been getting stronger and stronger. I was told to hide it except from family. By the time they found me, I could already lift cars and mid-sized trucks clear off the ground, not yet effortlessly. I'm even more durable than I am strong, bulletproof as early as I can remember. I tested that one myself when I was four, when mi padre left a gun in the house. Mi madre nearly disowned me when she heard the shot. But I never really felt pain until I was taken. Hurting me was difficult and expensive, but that just made them want to do it more. I won't tell you all the things they did. I healed from everything, no matter how disconfiguring, within minutes. When the First-Citizen learned about me, he ordered that extensive resources be spent trying to derive a formula for immortality from my regenerative blood. I'm like Wolverine. Do you know Wolverine?"

Maybe it wasn't me who gave the First-Citizen his youth and strength, it was Juarez. We're of the same stock after all. Or perhaps it was our combination. His blood was the fuel, my utterance was the flame. Two components, weak by themselves, yet made infinitely stronger when working in unison on the same person.

Less than five minutes.

"Do you know if your family is still alive?" He asked.

"Oh, yes, they're alive. And they don't age. My attendants don't either, except for Travis, the guy on the other end of the door. He told me he ages by choice. I should have been more skeptical. I think I chose not to be."

Simon didn't know how to comfort the man, so he

offered his hand. Juarez declined the gesture.

"They visit me too, from time to time. My family. That was the deal I made with them. They can't hold me against my wishes. So, they held my family over me, saying if I fought they'd die. So now I let them own me. Family always comes first."

Simon nodded. He thought about his dad. How much that man had sacrificed for him, and how, as a stupid child, he had requested transfer to a boarding school, not realizing they would be taken away first. In hindsight, he knew that he would have been separated from them anyway, but he always wondered how much longer he might have had with them, if he had understood his actions better.

"...You see, there's only one explanation. Your parents, somehow, were within that lucky radius when the bomb hit. There's no other event in history that has led to abilities like yours or mine."

Simon shook his head. "My mom was a researcher. My dad wasn't, but he worked with her. That much I remember. My captors almost certainly know why they would have been there."

"Then ask. The worst they can do is torture you. You must do everything that you can for family. Even if the only thing left to do, is come to terms with their deaths. I wish you luck."

Simon took one more look at the man before him, likely the physically strongest person to ever live, possessing a deceptively lean body due to the impossibility of finding a sufficiently heavy weight to cause his muscles any amount of strain. His perfectly smooth skin, his face sculpted as though of silted clay, and delicate uncalloused hands might have been dented by his captors a thousand times during his childhood, in the name of research, yet his body betrayed no history. The strongest man on earth had transcended any appearance of strength.

Simon noticed he had four minutes left. He knocked,

and the door opened. The old man stood patiently.

"You have time if you still wish to see her."

"I do."

The man jogged him down the hallway with surprising energy, stopping at an unassuming door. They entered a smaller room than the other two. It was stark white, looking more similar to the facility Simon just come from than to the cells of the other prisoners. In the middle was a white bed, upon which a young woman rested in perfect symmetry, her arms arranged at her sides. Her hair was silver. A single IV pump penetrated her neck. Simon noticed a small petri dish, of all things, held in her hand nearest him.

"Why is she kept like this?" Simon asked the man.

"She's too powerful. And too unpredictable," he said.

"So was her brother Florin. But he was entirely different. His problem was he kept getting bigger. Six-foot preteen, then ten, fifty feet. His shape stayed the same, he just scaled up. We didn't even feed him. He became nearly half a mile tall by the time he had to be killed. She almost tried to bring him back, thank god she didn't. David somehow convinced her to try to recover something thought to be unrecoverable. I didn't bother asking for details. There's nothing else interesting to see here unless you'd like to tour a giant frozen corpse in 22A. But that might take a whole day."

"No, I've seen enough corpses."

Before leaving, Simon hurried back to where Juarez's cell was. The old man followed, and helped him open the door. He walked into the room, and saw Juarez pacing.

"You can have your proof now." He couldn't see Juarez's reaction as he teleported back to his quarters, with fourteen seconds remaining.

Simon was immediately greeted by dimmed light and the smiling visage of the First-Citizen.

CHAPTER 27

"Oh, penultimate citizen, this is disappointing." The First-Citizen spoke with a storytelling timbre, dramatized as though narrating a children's cartoon. The second and third citizen stood behind him in submissive postures. Louisa was nowhere to be seen.

"You conflict me. On one hand, your actions were entirely within the constraints of our contract. Otherwise, of course, you would have been compelled not to perform them. However, you still must have known that visiting such a high-value individual and conversing with him goes against the collaborative spirit in which the contract was intended. There is a foundation of trust that I wish to cultivate between us, Simon. You visiting another facility, without consulting me, violates that spirit. Which is a shame, for I would gladly have accompanied you. It is important that you see your sole inferior. It hurts that you would see her behind my back."

The First-Citizen took a step closer to Simon. "You know, I truly am sorry it came to this. I might have considered a lesser punishment, but the one that presented itself to me was simply too fortuitous. It is also the only reason I even noticed you had left the facility in the first place."

Simon didn't follow. He began to worry. It was in that moment that he felt for Louisa's heart, and found it was no longer there. He couldn't believe he hadn't noticed. It wasn't beating.

"What did you do?"

The First-Citizen smiled. "You know, I never told you this, but, thanks to my enhancements due to you and Juarez,

I'm no longer able to have sex with a biological human. I'm so fast and strong, you see, that when I get excited, well…it ends poorly for the woman."

The Second Citizen look for the first time truly ashamed. Even when his father and friends displayed as living corpses, the Second Citizen hadn't looked quite so embarrassed to be alive.

"Your woman, Louisa. She visited me an hour ago. You two had been fighting. I will have you know she came onto me, not the opposite. At first, she just wanted to talk about you, and me, our partnership. We were friendly, and soon she started to get a little touchy. She could not keep her hands off, frankly, and after a while I got hard. So things progressed. She was moaning right up until I started breaking bone. Even for a couple seconds after I heard her hip snap in two, I believe she was enjoying herself more than she ever had with you. She climaxed twice in one minute, and was starting a third in her last seconds of life."

Simon's blood felt like a barely contained eruption.

"You're a fucking monster."

"Your tone is disrespectful, but I will allow it this once. Even as her body started breaking, she didn't ask me to stop. She loved me too much for that. All thanks to her proximity to you. Simon, this is why I am so conflicted. You betrayed my trust, likely out of some misguided attempt to kill either yourself or me. And yet, you performed your task even better than I had hoped. And do not worry about Louisa. I will get you another one in due time, once you start behaving. A woman with a similar personality profile, who is just as attractive. Perhaps one with a smaller nose, since I know that was the first negative feature you noticed about her face. It was mine too."

Simon wanted to punch the First-Citizen until his knuckles bled. If it weren't for the contract, he would have. He willed with all of his strength, and for a moment thought he felt his arms budge a fraction of an inch. He was unable to step towards his master.

"You are probably wishing I dropped dead right about now." the First-Citizen observed, glancing lazily at Simon's knuckles. "I happen to know you are not the only one. There is at least one other traitor in our midst, and he is to be punished with greater severity." The room became silent. To Simon, it was spinning. He took that moment to put his hand over his chest. His body felt hollow without its second heartbeat.

"Purcell, explain yourself."

The Third Citizen shifted his gaze, surprised to be addressed.

"Sir? I do not understand..."

"Oh I am sure you do. Perhaps your memory should be jogged."

Right as the First-Citizen tapered his last accusing whisper, a crisp audio recording permeated the room. Simon recognized it instantly as his conversation with the Second Citizen earlier that same night. Except it wasn't quite right. It was the gruff voice of Purcell, the Third Citizen, who spoke, not David's. It was edited exquisitely, even capturing the parts of phrases where Purcell would have been likely to become louder, softer, more or less emotive. The jazz music playing in the background had also been erased.

"Sir, please. That was faked. It has to have been. I would never betray you, sir. I love you. More than anything. I swear on my children's graves."

"How I wish that were true." The First-Citizen said, staring at Simon all the while. "Penultimate Citizen. I have decided I am going to ensure you become as immortal as I am. In due time, as everyone you grew up knowing dies, you will gain new perspective. We may even become friends. If you wish to earn my respect, to truly become my equal, I ask only one thing of you. It is an easier request than it will at first sound."

"I don't want your respect. I want you to die."

"Well, funny you should say that. My one condition happens to be, simply enough, that you become more comfortable around death."

With that, in a motion that took not even half a second, the First-Citizen pivoted, sped towards Purcell, extended his left arm towards him, and smacked his head sideways at half the speed of sound. The head nearly came off of the body it was attached to, and the next thing Simon knew, the two partially separated human segments splattered onto the far white wall with a powerful thud, leaving a multicolored horizontal puddle of blood and organs pressed into the door. The mangled pile of warm flesh that fell to the floor, less than a second ago human, was now not even humanoid. The shock of it nearly made Simon forget about Louisa, and he fought the urge to vomit.

"You hate me. An irony that is not lost on me, I assure you. So be it, as long as you continue to perform your duties adequately. I will assume purcell is an anomaly. Behind his gruff exterior, he always was a soulless little shit." The First-Citizen's ears were bleeding slightly from the collision's soundwave that shook the room, and his voice quavered just slightly. Then he recovered his compusure.

He turned to the Second Citizen. "David, send me a list of recommendations for replacements. I will be curious to have your input." He spoke, for the first time since Simon met him, in a full voice. Upsettingly, It was deep, soothing, and attractive. The First-Citizen then left, brushing the blood from his ears casually on his fine pants. Pants that were probably still covering Louisa's dried blood dripping down his legs. Almost matching Simon's hate was disbelief, that someone so cruel could even exist in the world. In a brief moment of clarity, he wondered if all morality was merely a prelude to desensitization, an aversion to the grotesque that could be conditioned out of any human being with as simple a thing as repeated exposure. An evil act committed a thousand times might still appear evil intellectually, but at least then it would become commonplace, an act of habit. The First-Citizen's brand of immortality, then, seemed simply a road to complete apathy.

The Second Citizen lingered. He and Simon stared at one another for a moment before he followed his leader out. As he did, four guards came in with a fully prepared gurney and cleaning equipment. They'd been told to expect a man to be swatted onto the wall like an insect.

Simon watched the wall to his room be scrubbed patiently by the guards. He wondered what they were seeing through their helmets now, if the tangled tendons and the expanding stench of the mangled corpse were filtered out, reduced to something more pleasant. Or perhaps they shared the First-Citizen's ambivalence towards seeing the human form exterminated, were smelling all of it, and didn't care. He'd wondered this a thousand times and only did so now to stave off the pain he knew was coming.

He hated his ability. He wished he'd never had it, had never been tempted with it, never been caught, used, made to exercise it until the woman he loved was compelled to bring herself to death. His thoughts dissolved into a state of misery.

I don't want to exist. Let it stop. Get everything out of my head! He started feeling incoherent and dizzy. His rage crossed some threshold, and his thoughts became even more garbled, his entire reality seeming to collapse The pain destroyed all structure. Total erasure. Restart.

Simon screamed. The sound was primal, painful. It seemed to come from his gut more than his lungs, the expelled air grating lyrically against his windpipe with less discomfort than he deserved. He wanted it all to be gone. To start again, with nothing. He wanted to be nothing. He continued to scream, and, as he did so, a dissolution spread across his mind. Tethers snapped, with fierce suddenness, having been rejected by the wells of consciousness to which they were connected. Screaming continued. Severing multiplied. Tears began. Thinking ceased. Reality vanished.

CHAPTER 28

Simon walked into his session room the following day as though nothing happened. He sat in his chair with his helmet was strapped to his head and uttered "Love First-Citizen" with the same brainwave patterns he'd been refining for the past month. He didn't think about Louisa. Nor did he think about the future, or those who would likely come after her now that the First-Citizen knew what he could get away with. Those thoughts were simply too difficult, and not appropriate for work anyways.

Instead, he contemplated, in the intermittent seconds of free thought he could manage to have without punishment, how he at least had delayed progress, and given himself a delicate advantage over his captors.

His abilities were untethered. But not all of them were gone. He was still three or four times as strong as any of the guards, and his eyes seemed to retain their enhanced color vision. The physical changes to his brain and body stayed, but everything energy-intensive that required an input from the other reality was reset. No ceasing hurricanes, becoming invisible, or going away. And no contract.

That malicious bond had been the first thing to sever. There was no clear way to capitalize on this advantage, and it might even prove disastrous if the First-Citizen ordered him to use an ability he had once had but now didn't. He refused to think about his shades. He'd searched his empty dreams for them the previous night, but their usual traces had vanished. It wasn't clear if he'd killed them. The one silver lining was he didn't have to contend with the hurricane dream, although this made him only more worried. Parts of his mind that he couldn't easily reach into felt deeply perturbed.

The session ended, and the first atypicality of the day occurred when the Second Citizen entered the room. They hadn't spoken since the office.

"You may leave us." he spoke to the attendant, a new one Simon had only known a couple of days.

The attendant scurried and the Second Citizen made himself comfortable in the usually empty chair across the table.

"The First-Citizen will want to speak to you about yesterday. He's graciously allowed me to discuss items with you first. I would like for you to tell me what compelled you to scream last night. You've never done anything like it on record, and your clothing's analysis was surprisingly inadequate. None of your many overseers knew what to make of it."

Simon wanted to tell him but refrained. The way the Second Citizen spoke indicated this conversation was a monitored one.

"I suppose learning how my partner died made me a little angry. I'm not sure what your opinion is, but I tend towards anger when I learn that my partner was consensually fucked to death by someone I despise."

The Second Citizen frowned deeply. Simon realized this man, manipulative though he was, never faked an emotion. It made his deception ten times as brilliant.

"I'm sorry. I truly am. I've lived a long life, and quite the eventful one, but this was a new low for even me. Not ethically, mind you, he's killed many people before her, but... aggh. Killing her was pathetic. I don't care if the First-Citizen hears it. He can rail my ass into an early grave too if he wishes." He said the second bit with unflinching vulgarity.

"But your clothing registered a more complex emotion than mere anger. When you learned of the incident, there was anger alone. Then sadness, confusion, catharsis, and, surprising to everyone, glee, all alternated in prominence in your biochemistry over the past several hours."

The Second Citizen activated the table surface and entered a command. He then inputted a separate command into his headband and set a timer.

"Our time is becoming even more limited now. I do not believe the First-Citizen has any suspicions of me yet, he thinks I'm too accustomed to loyalty to betray him now, but once he feels even a shred of uncertainty I fear my remaining minutes will be few. Yesterday, did your scream affect you?"

"Yes".

"What did it do?"

"Cleanse."

The Second Citizen paused for a brief second.

"Everything?"

"Only the tethers. The contract is gone. But so is any ability to help me escape."

"Good. That may serve you yet. Our time is about to run out, but I must warn you. The First-Citizen will add one further constraint which you must recite when he meets with you. Whatever it is, you recite it. The way forward is still viable, but he cannot suspect you of anything. Do you understand?"

"Yes. Question."

"Fifteen seconds."

"How can you continue to betray the First-Citizen, despite my ability? It should have applied itself to you by now."

"It has. Love does not preclude betrayal."

The Second Citizen leaned forward to speak, almost as though the First-Citizen could hear them from however many levels above them he perched.

"Love does not preclude betrayal, nor curiosity, disagreement, disappointment, or even hatred. The only thing love precludes is indifference. It's a trite statement, but it's essential you comprehend the semantic implications."

The timer hit zero. The screen on the table turned red for a split second.

"We don't need to speak now, Simon. It's too soon. But if you're interested in formal treatment, we have a death therapist on staff who helps even our most squeamish new recruit view death as nothing more than the uneventful part of life that it is. He'd be honored to help immunize you to your loss."

"I appreciate the offer. I'll pass."

"Suit yourself. Let's go for a walk. You feel like leaving this facility?"

"Huh?"

"You heard. We can go outside right now. The sun will be on your back in five minutes."

"But you've never..."

"Let you out? Come, now. You're completely bound. You couldn't leave if you wanted to. We might as well lengthen your leash at this point."

The Second Citizen got up and Simon followed. They went to the elevator, which took them down farther than Simon ever remembered going in a building. They stopped at a floor where the hallways were wider and somehow friendlier. They strolled together towards a single large door, actually visible as a door before it was even opened.

"Would you do the honors?" the Second Citizen asked.

Simon hesitated, then pushed the door. It opened, and a breeze instantly slapped his face. Wind had never felt so euphoric.

"Keep walking. There's a good view of Los Angeles up ahead."

Outside the facility was a simple pathway, composed of the same nearly-frictionless mirror material that occupied the neighborhood Simon had lived in before, at least until it started sloping up a hill. Past the hill, there was a focused stream of light shooting into the dimming sky.

Probably another of the First-Citizen's useless new ideas. Like this reflective walkway.

"Was this always just to make walking harder for us?"

"Partially. Also, the First-Citizen thought it looked beautiful and would be fun. He always loved the idea of giving everybody common happiness with simple impracticalities like this."

"He doesn't care about people's happiness."

"You'd be surprised how much he cares. Keep walking, the view gets good on the other side."

The surface thankfully gave way to grass up ahead, and they walked up a long, gentle slope. Simon looked back and saw that the facility, while massive, wasn't as mountainous as he'd guessed. The strange light seemed to be slightly closer.

"Beautiful at this distance, isn't it." the Second Citizen said.

"Why are we out here?"

"I have permission to share near everything with you now. It may surprise you to know that the First-Citizen deems you worthy to be knowledgeable of our national secrets since you're one yourself. Ask away."

Simon tried to fake disinterest and contemplated the light up ahead.

"Oh, please. This is the first time in your life that your government is willing to answer big questions. Don't pretend like this is nothing to you."

Simon thought. He had an arsenal of questions and couldn't decide where to begin.

"The quasi-matter bomb," Simon said.

"Really? Not the Last Citizen? The model I ran this morning was fairly certain she would be your first question. I respect your occasional unpredictability."

The Second Citizen gave a strained sigh from the uphill walk but pressed on.

"You know what the real problem with the bomb was? It wasn't altered humans. It was fucking rats. And snakes. And weeds. A few of them got their own cursed mutations, and they bred faster than any human. It took everything in the Citizenship's power to kill those monsters off, narrowly preventing the world from being overrun by endlessly growing snakes, or rodents that could duplicate every time they sank their teeth into flesh, by painfully morphing whatever organic matter they bit into more rats, a man's final scream turning into the first scream of a hungry new horde. The vines that grew a mile a day still reach out at me in my dreams. You could see them extending in real-time toward you. They always sensed where you were. Sometimes they'd grow underground to try breaching the soil to strangle your legs before you noticed. I swear on my soul that those plants had no goodness in them. I won't even talk about the gnats. We'd be living in a world of true eldritch nightmares if George Lackley hadn't so brutally wiped every plant and animal, human and otherwise within two hundred miles of Mexico City after that bomb went off. The horrors he faced for us, and the things he had to do, and order be done...anyone would be traumatized. Even the First-Citizen gives him a pass for pretty much everything now."

Simon wondered why he hadn't seriously considered that non-humans might also be impacted. David heaved, determined to reach the top of the hill for some reason. It was becoming clear the source of the strange light beam was directly on the other side.

"But what about the bomb itself? Why does it turn matter into fractals? I thought it was the opposite, that it leveled out complexity from everything it touched."

"That is an oversimplification we feed to the masses. Truthfully, we have no clue why it does what it does. There is one trickle of insight that one of our more brilliant theoretical physicists was able to glean, a derivation that has been thoroughly vetted and peer-reviewed. His snowflake-universe theory was the final nail in the coffin for quasimatter testing. You don't even know what a coffin is, do you?"

"I do. I saw a picture in a book last week."

"Ah, well. The natural world cannot risk even a modest foray into the place where quasimatter comes from. We're too delicate. Too simple. Too manipulable."

A blanket of abstract fear swept over the Second Citizen's face.

"The gist of it is, quasimatter connects us to a different reality, allowing a sort of limited interface with it. Like an acid, it corrodes the barriers between universes. This other reality is fundamentally less, well, limited, in a scientific sense. It is a realm where notions of physics, dimension, complexity, pattern, energy, and chaos do not suffer the same constraints our splinter of a cosmos imposes on us. We know precious little about it, except that it is a realm we have no business venturing in. This universe, purportedly, is a snowflake floating flimsily within its indescribable expanses."

Simon started feeling the sun on his skin and wondered if he'd burn.

What would happen if I got skin cancer? Would the cancer grow like a fractal as well?

"...That's to say, you're the only remaining tool our country actively uses that relates in any way to quasimatter."

"But, the quasimatter facilities? Our source of energy?"

"Not real. They're all fusion. We experimented briefly and could produce obscene amounts of power with quasimatter enough to support a hundred overpopulated earths, but inevitably the factories created new cracks in reality. The former site of our one true quasimatter facility is now strictly quarantined. It doesn't seem to quite obey the same laws of physics as the rest of the world. Gravity around that site is close to the surface of Jupiter, and varies in four hour fifty-two-minute cycles like a tide, briefly having a more Martian gravity. We can fix it, but doing so is expensive and we can do interesting research there."

"So I'm not the only exception. You kept other children of the bomb alive, and preserved a dead factory."

"We didn't let all of you live."

Simon finally looked back. The facility was pitch black. Every photon of light that touched it seemed to sink. The exterior was the opposite of the interior.

"I feel tethers pulling me in, building structures on both sides of every well growing within me when I utter. I'm on one end, but there's another side. The source of my ability, growing somewhere in the other reality. Is it intelligent? Have you tried reaching it?" He decided not to mention that those tethers has just snapped.

"There's no point in thinking about what the source is. Maybe pretend they're your angels. Or demons if you prefer."

Simon, who had spent countless hours wondering just that, dropped the subject.

"My parents. Tell me about them."

I should have started with them. Even though it scares me.

"Your mom was a researcher. She asked too many questions. The test explosion hit her at the right time. We had no idea. Maybe she even knew what she was doing."

"Why would she do that?"

"To prove a point I suppose. She probably didn't know she had you then." David said. Simon saw they were getting close to the top of the hill. He decided he didn't want to think about his parents. Not until there was something he could do for them.

"Maria. The Last Citizen. Why is she dangerous? What can she do?"

And why is that light getting so intense? What even is it?

"She brings back structures of the past. If you asked her, she'd tell you simply that she 'returns lost things'." Every time she brings something back the world around her changes. She is a singular distortion of nature. I assure you, if she'd wanted our downfall, she'd have been quite unstoppable. Fortunately we manipulated her like we manipulated you, and now she hibernates. If it were up to me she'd be dead."

Of course she would be.

"Do you want to kill everyone who inconveniences you?"

"Usually. To be fair, it takes a very powerful person to

inconvenience me."

They reached the top of the hill.

A stone staircase beginning at the peak descended steeply a couple hundred feet to the structure. A blue-glinted flickering beam of light, brighter than the setting sun, flowed like a river from an organic, gelatinous lens. The structure looked thirty or more feet in diameter, translucent, and, somewhat disturbingly, it didn't stay still. It adhered to a language of motion that seemed to be a combination of jiggling and breathing, as though it couldn't decide if its movements should be random or intelligible.

"Simon, meet Florin." David said.

"Huh?"

"Maria's brother. You're staring at the lens of his left eye. We made a monument out of it."

"That's...his eye lens? Not even his whole eye?"

"What a fine listener you are. Now don't let an old man beat you down a staircase."

They walked towards the massive eye lens, which could easily conceal two elephants. A silver, many-limbed machine apparatus covered the base which appeared to be actively interfacing with the lens, although its function wasn't clear. Perhaps it was the source of the light that the lens then focused. As they approached, Simon could hear quiet wispy sounds, although he couldn't discern whether they came from the lens itself or the millipedic machine it rested on.

"The lens keeps itself alive. The challenge is actually to keep it from growing. It's detached from the body it grew with, so it evolves slowly, but evolve it does. Florin was half a mile tall when he was executed, hence the size. It seems happiest when bright lights are shone through it that pierce the sky. Fucking diva."

They reached the base of the stairs. It was unsettling to see such an alien site be unattended by humanity. Oakland was visible in the distance. It looked identical to Portland.

"Florin was a kind man. It's a shame he grew outward instead of in, like the rest of you. Juarez today has almost as many cells as Florin had when he died." The second citizen tilted his head upwards. "This has all gone absurd. We don't know anything about anything. I hike to this aberration every day to remind myself why the universe isn't to be fucked with. And also for cardio."

There was a single bench built a few feet in front of the lens, uncomfortably close. David sat in it. Simon joined. They listened to the grating baritone of the interface of eye lens and machine for a few minutes.

"One more question. About Louisa."

"I'll answer it."

"Was she happy when she was with me?"

The Second Citizen frowned. His eyes stayed glued to the lens.

"The data from her headband was clear. She was always happy when you were together before your arrest. During the arrest she was quite unhappy except when she was drugged. Her short stint reunited with you in the forest was the most unhappy she'd ever been. The single most joyful event in her life was with the First-Citizen, around three minutes before her death, while she was giving him a blowjob."

The two of them walked up the stairs wordlessly. Florin's left eye lens moaned behind them.

CHAPTER 29

Simon uttered for four more hours as though nothing happened. As soon as he finished, guards entered and commanded him to follow. He was unsurprised to find himself being taken up higher into the facility, to the floor of the First-Citizen's study.

The survey woman simply nodded to him, not bothering to recite the rules of engagement. He realized, a little smugly, that he'd probably said more words to the First-Citizen than she ever would. He entered the office.

"Simon, I am glad you could join me," the First-Citizen spoke from his huge desk.

"Of course, sir."

"We know what needs to be discussed. But first, I must express concern at your outburst last night, after I had gone. Your mental health is important to me. I must be sure that you will get over needing to have your woman replaced. And, of course, you did witness your first death. What I would like to know is whether you will need any assistance getting over this experience quickly. Oh, and let us not use profanities. They are unnecessary."

Simon glared at him.

"I don't understand why you killed her. Even paralyzing my friends and my dad made a sick sort of sense. Why her?"

The First-Citizen grinned. "Well, that is easy to answer. I have been celibate for years, not by choice, but because of my overwhelming strength and speed which I cannot suppress during excitement. Louisa was the first woman I have met who, thanks to you, was able to actually enjoy being torn apart by me. So I killed her mostly for fun. But know that I would have avoided her if I had not checked where you were and noticed your absence. So her death served two purposes, really. The third citizen, well, he also betrayed me, but unlike you he is easily replaced. So I just got rid of him. Simplified the whole situation."

"So you're just a bad person."

"I consider myself simple. My pleasures are easy to list. I enjoy talking, painting, power, feeling good, and, believe it or not, serving people. But I only feel compelled to serve people en masse. I have no compunctions about killing a few individuals if it conveniences millions of others. Or brutalizing a few more, if the mood strikes me, and those millions are spared any hurt. I brought an entire continent out of the mid-century horror for God's sake. As far as I am concerned, to be blunt, I have more than earned the right to use your girlfriend as a ragdoll and break half the bones in her body."

It again took everything Simon had not to run up to the First-Citizen and punch him.

"You are less simple. Despite all the machines getting plugged into you, and the drugs we are careful pumping you with, you always manage to find occasional ways to be confusing. Like last night."

Simon glanced around at a few of the paintings to calm himself. He wondered if they continued into the back of the room, where it was always too dark for him to see anything.

"This is where Louisa died, isn't it." Simon said. It wasn't a question.

"Of course. Right back there, on my front table. She will probably be the first of many to die there, now that your ability is starting to reach Oakland." Simon made no effort to hide his disgust.

"Look Simon, they do not matter. You and I matter. We are going to be gods to them. We should not have complicating worries about killing a few of them for our pleasure. Gods, more than anything, must be simple."

The door opened behind Simon again and Penelope, his old coworker, walked in. She wore a gown, shoes, and a medical headband. Thankfully, her body no longer looked like a corpse. It seemed utterly unafflicted. It was the way she moved through space, the uncomfortably effortful slowness of all her small movements, and her glazed undialated eyes, that made her seem not quite alive anymore.

"I am sure you remember your old office colleague. Analytics indicated you were physically lustful towards her while you worked together as overseers."

"I was a little before I met Louisa. I don't see why that's relevant to anything, we hardly spoke."

"Oh, come now. Louisa is gone. You can see where this is going."

"No."

"I am granting you complete power over her. Take her to your cell. Do whatever you want to her."

"No."

Penelope's face made no indication that she understood what was happening. The experience of spending days trapped in her own decaying body must have been truly incomprehensible.

"Fine." The First-Citizen said. "Penelope, remove your dress." She immediately began to obey.

"Penelope, don't do that," Simon said. She hesitated.

The First-Citizen shrugged at him. "If you do not feel like playing with her, I will."

Simon didn't think it was possible to hate one person so much.

"Ok. You win. Have her brought to my quarters, I'll deal with her there."

"There you go. I hope she will help you get over the other one."

"Louisa."

"Yeah, her."

"When can I see my dad? If Penelope's recovered, he

must be."

The First-Citizen elevated his body several feet, to the height of his paintings. He glided languidly towards one of an old European general from an empire that died in some long abandoned century.

"It may be awhile. I am still offended you left the facility without telling me."

The painting seemed to bore him, and he levitated back towards Simon.

"This all brings me to the legal reason I summoned you. It has been put to a vote, per the conditions of our contract, and it was decided that your actions in leaving the facility without choosing to consult me first constitute bad behavior. Per the conditions, I am including an amendment, which you shall read out loud for me."

Simon waited. The viability of his infant notions of a second escape hinged on the new constraint about to be forced upon him, one which he couldn't refuse to implement without admitting to his self-mutilation.

"I am requiring, from this moment onwards, that when you utter "Love First-Citizen" each day, spreading its euphoric effects across the world, you allow some of the ability to apply to you."

The First-Citizen reverted to his practiced smile, expressing a mixture of schadenfreude and self-adoration. Simon struggled to seem neutral, wishing not to give his captor the satisfaction of seeing the seething rage he was powerless to act on.

"I am entirely aware that you have gone through specific effort to spare yourself the abilities' effects. Louisa and I were talking about it just before she unbuttoned me. You had valid reason to be hesitant, so I did not meddle. The ability had been untested when you began, and you understandably feared it could compromise you, turning your mind into a vegetable, or reducing you to an addict. Love can be intoxicating."

I want you to die.

"And, of course, there is the matter of your pre-existing infatuation. I understand you may be uncomfortable having your old affection usurped by a new one. Whatever your reasons, they no longer matter. Use the ability on yourself only enough so that you lose your hate for me, and feel a degree of pleasure when you stare at my face. You do not need to go all the way to adoration just yet."

The First-Citizen glided to his desk, picked up his ancient laptop computer and a helmet, and brought them to Simon. He felt the helmet as the First-Citizen slid it onto his head, before swiveling the opened laptop around for him to read. Inscribed onto its screen, on an outdated interface which would have been interesting to study under different circumstances, was a simple line of text:

The penultimate citizen is to include himself in the set of individuals who are made to experience the partial effects of "Love First-Citizen" whenever the aforementioned ability is in active development.

"Read it" the First-Citizen commanded. Simon had no choice. He fell into repetition for the next twenty minutes, while the First-Citizen held the laptop in front of him with one finger and watched him almost manically.

"You may stop," he eventually said, once the statement was safely over-enforced.

"May I leave?" Simon asked.

"Yes, that will be all."

Simon walked himself out, the survey woman opening and closing the door for him with due gentleness. When he reached his cell, Penelope was already there. Simon worried she'd return to the First-Citizen if he sent her off so he let her stay. They sat together silently. He fell asleep leaning on her shoulder. It was the first time they'd ever touched.

CHAPTER 30:

Preceding his arrest, Simon could claim at best a superficial understanding of science. Since his recent recapture, his understanding remained superficial, but it at least grazed a few more topics than it had during his years as an overseer. The science of the brain was an intriguing subject which he ravenously studied in his free time.

The human brain held such remarkable structures. Every concept, idea, and subconscious thought was nothing less than a living metropolis of interacting neurons, finding specific and highly unique patterns to represent the countless interrelated aspects of an internal and external environment. It was built from countless subtle constructs that could be connected, separated, intermixed, personalized, and brilliantly synthesized with infinite variation and creativity.

While each brain was unique, there were fundamental similarities. Different regions had the same general function among virtually all humans. Certain neurons behaved consistently in certain ways. With precise enough scanning technology, which the Citizenship prided itself on having, even the delicate transition from one abstract thought into another could be isolated, its nature guessed at. Simon's mind, extended though it was by fractal-like neural wells, was still vulnerable to these predictive principles.

An unprecedentedly large helmet was placed on his head when he sat in his chair. It, unlike the previous model, would be able to measure most of Simon's fractal neurons, save for a few of the smallest ones that growing in the deepest layers of his wells, which were increasingly tiny fractions of the size

PENULTIMATE CITIZEN | 295

of typical neurons. This couldn't discern his thoughts exactly, but the innovation restored Simon's inability to keep any important thoughts to himself. Particularly, it was more than adequate for knowing whether two thoughts were the same or slightly different. He would be forced to have virtually the same thought, every time he uttered.

The machine, Simon guessed, would willingly grant his thinking some amount of leeway, albeit only briefly. Since a new amendment had been made to "Love First-Citizen", Simon would need some freedom, at first, to modify the ability until the new thought pattern settled, and it became again clear which neurons were strictly necessary for the exercise, and which were to be considered off-limits until the helmet came off.

There was only so much control that Simon could achieve over his mind. But he wasn't entirely powerless here. There was opportunity to make use of his advantage.

As far as he could tell, he had a short window to mold his new rendition of "Love First-Citizen." He could make his repeated thought nuanced, so long as he could capture that nuance quickly. Once the window closed, he would be all but incapable of adding wrinkles and would be forced into merely extending whatever the thought behind his utterance had calcified into across an ever expanding diameter.

The First-Citizen's craving for simplicity would be his undoing. Linguistically speaking, "love" was a fortunate choice of words. Had a more specific word been chosen, his constraints would have been far stronger. Were he asked to utter "devote to First-Citizen", for example, then he would have needed to stretch his understanding of the word "devote" to its far extremes to be able to implement the wrinkles that he wished to. Fortunately, "love" came with those extremes built into the core of its flexible definition.

Love did not preclude betrayal. Simon considered this intently for several minutes, an ancillary thought that infused into his utterances. Simon considered how he could love the

First-Citizen, and, because of that love, be willing to act against him. Such an action could be viewed as a service to him, taken for his own good. Simon convinced himself the First-Citizen's life would be unilaterally improved if he could be taken out of power and freed from the burdens of leadership. It was not difficult.

Love did not preclude curiosity. This one was simpler for Simon to accept. He had always been curious of his mother, father, Louisa, or anyone he knew and respected. The three people he had most loved were who he most desired to understand. Out of respect and fear, he'd never asked those questions. He wished now that he had been brave enough to talk to his father more honestly. Simon convinced himself that he wanted to know everything there was to know about the First-Citizen. Everyone within five hundred miles would soon want to as well.

Love did not preclude disagreement. Simon had only ever seen his parents properly fight once. He was quite young, and the two of them were struggling to get the high-salary job offers they'd been used to receiving their entire lives. He vaguely recalled that his father wanted to move into one of the smaller new apartments that had just been built, deeper in the city and cheaper than where they were living. His mother resented that idea, practically wailing at him that those new buildings were collectively bugged, and intentionally made competitive by the Citizenship to draw in the first wave of citizens for closer monitoring. They had argued about this before, but the display etched in Simon's memory was one particularly passionate instance. However, violence was never reached, and the two participants quickly calmed each other down. Simon, even then, never doubted that they cared greatly for each other. Citizens could care about the First-Citizen, and still argue passionately against his policies.

Love did not preclude disappointment. Even after her death, Simon was disappointed in Louisa. He wished he wasn't. The feeling didn't seem fair to her, or to what he put her through. He felt it anyway. She should have let both of them die instantly in an explosion in the cave rather than be retaken by their captors. He was even more disappointed by what she turned into, once "Love First-Citizen" began to change her. It wasn't her fault, but the disappointment wouldn't leave. Everyone who loved the First-Citizen would feel commensurate disappointment in his failings as a leader.

Love did not preclude hate. Simon had no trouble incorporating this idea, especially following disappointment. He remembered what the Second Citizen had said, that love was merely the absence of indifference. This definition of it was ultimately the source of its varied meanings.

Even hate, the often supposed opposite of love, inevitably found itself a mere subset of it, an infinite collection of spiteful shades contained within an even larger infinity, within which there was also betrayal, curiosity, disagreement, contention, disappointment, uncertainly, distaste, obsession, lust, attentiveness, comprehension, fear. Everyone touched by Simon's ability would begin to feel all of these as a richly shaded symphony whenever they thought of their leader. Citizen's brains would be injected with new patterns. The mass mind-rape hopefully would end soon.

Simon quickly devised a new routine for himself. His bi-daily sessions of "Love First-Citizen" continued as they had, with their layers of new subtleties now filling almost everyone within some large radius with a plethora of wonderfully contradictory emotions concerning their leader. Simon felt the changes in over a million people faintly, as a distant sensation that reminded him of his weeks in the forest looking up at the stars properly for the first time. He then would leave his session, feeling spirited, and engage in deep yet energetically brimming meditations in his quarters.

He spent many hours singing *away* into his mind's ear as an infinitely repeated lullaby, feeling as a tether from the other reality gradually began to return and reconnect itself to the rich neurological well, containing billions of specially created synaptic connections occupying an fractally warped space, a perfectly constructed outgrowth in his brain with the specific goal of precisely controlling teleportation. It seemed all but certain that some intelligence existed in the other reality helping to organize his growth, but such thoughts seemed inappropriate given his more immediate terrestrial concerns.

He would eventually need to sleep, his silent utterance continuing like an earworm as he drifted off. He embraced it. Even as he drifted off each night, the word "away" would echo through the chambers of his mind. The constant repetition of a word gave him a singular purpose and spared him having to think about Louisa. His mother never visited. None of his shades did. His hurricane dreams still hadn't returned. He sought them out again on his second night and finally found them. The sixty billion neurons huddled together as a cloudy wisp at the edge of his subconscious. Simon tried bringing himself closer to them and heard the sounds of weeping.

I'm sorry. I didn't mean to break you. I can feel your pain and I'm so sorry.

He didn't know how else to comfort the hurricane entity. He woke up and spent the next hour thinking about how the hurricane's crying sounded just like his as a child.

It's like a younger me is living inside my mind. And I hurt them.

A guard came in and injected him back to sleep. He stopped seeking out his shades. He couldn't bring himself to face his mother-shade and witness what he'd done to them.

This routine replicated itself five times over as many days. As the first session of his sixth day came to a close, the Second Citizen came to him. As usual, they began with a brief sliver of privacy, which today was only to last a single minute. The Second Citizen's fear of exposure seemed to grow with each dwindling pocket of free speech.

"We don't have much time. A warning: there are reports on the progress of "Love First-Citizen", indicating what you hope they would. He's onto you. I'll placate him later but I can't guarantee anything. You should also talk to him. You need to escape. You need him dead but can't kill him alone. You must reach Juarez. Escape will not be enough this time, you must do everything in your power to end him. Or he will scorch the entire country hunting you."

Before Simon could reply, the red beep came from the Second Citizen's wristband, signaling they were now monitored.

"Greetings Simon."

"Greetings."

"Do you have any further questions for me?"

The previous day, the Second Citizen told Simon about Sybil. After Simon left her, she'd been sent to the huge new facility in Seattle to become a counselor for older folks who particularly struggled to adapt to the new ways of living. She lived similarly to Simon and even found love with a fifty year old woman named Cardinal. They cooked and talked and slept together (non-sexually), and were ultimately very happy. Far happier than she could have been with him.

That story seemed enough.

"I know everything that matters."

The Second Citizen chuckled coldly.

"I wish I had your confidence." He got up.

"Come bowling with me. I'll get you fed while we play."

Simon hadn't known there was bowling in the facility. He didn't say a word while he was led to the elevator. The bowling alley was vast, occupying nearly an entire floor. Several of the more distant lanes were being used by people Simon couldn't make out. The farthest lanes almost looked like the thin veil of a horizon.

"Guards come here during off-hours. I championed their right to a bowling space." the Second Citizen said. Simon was shocked to see them without their helmets. Four men and one woman were all playing and talking together in a middle lane, almost too far to see. Two older men were laughing about some joke one of them must have just told. The guard who had come with them now split off and walked towards their off-duty colleagues. Upon noticing the new arrivals, the other guards ceased all conversation and left in silence. Simon and the Second Citizen were now alone. Instead of picking a lane, the Second Citizen walked towards an out-of-place blue box on the wall.

"This is a vending machine. These colorful bags contain food, of sorts."

"This looks ancient."

"It is. We old timers feel slightly less old whenever we see one of these. I'll get you some sun chips."

The Second Citizen typed some numbers into an analog pad, and a bag fell from the inside. He bent in and grabbed it, ripped an opening, and handed it to Simon. He put his hand inside and pulled out a delicate hyperbolic shape that reminded him of certain graphs he encountered often as an overseer. Biting into it, he was taken aback by the strength of the flavor. As he rapturously consumed the rest, the Second Citizen did something unusual: he put on music. It was beautiful, a delicate male voice uttering a simple yet sublime melody, accompanied by an instrument that Simon recognized as an analog keyboard. The instrument had another name he couldn't remember. Louisa had said it once. He thought she might have called it a piano.

"This is a song called *berceuse*, written by a European composer named Fauré" the Second Citizen informed him, his posture loosening in a relaxed surrender to the music.

"It's beautiful".

"I find I agree. This was the last recording ever made of the piece. Possibly the last that will ever be made. The First-Citizen isn't a particular fan of Fauré. Or jazz. Or most musical traditions."

They allowed the melancholy song to envelop their spirits for a moment.

"There is one classical composer we both enjoy: Philip

Glass. We're planning to re-release some of his music to the public. The First-Citizen doesn't want us worshipping artists of the past, so we're re-releasing it under the oeuvre of our illustrious composer Timothy Gable. The man has already outputted all the best work of Bach so it will be a believable enough addition. We'll call it his 'late period'."

"Why are we talking about music?" Simon asked.

"No particular reason."

Simon simply continued to stare, hoping to get his message across nonverbally. The Second Citizen made an expression of subtle annoyance, but complied, innocuously scrolling through his wristband, as though to find more music to listen to, and activated whatever impossible software he possessed that granted his snippets of privacy. A timer was set for twenty seconds.

"This is a very finite resource."

"That won't matter soon. I think I can leave tomorrow. I just need time."

"Get it from the First-Citizen. Ask him for a distraction. Develop what you can. Spend the night. Tomorrow, there will be no time. He might already suspect the contract."

Their time ran dry.

"Alright, game time. I'm informed you're rather terrible at this."

"I am. You're probably better."

The Second Citizen led them to the nearest lane, and they proceeded to bowl. The Second Citizen was much better. The game ended with Simon losing by fourteen points. They played three times after that. Simon lost each time and never struck. The first four games were silent.

During the fifth and sixth games, they began to talk more about music. The Second Citizen, it turned out, had as much passion for the musical arts as Louisa once had for origami. He listed the names of dozens of artists, instruments, and genres that Simon had never heard of. He loved the cello, clarinet, sitar, a strange genre called "rock", jazz, Indian and European classical, and even certain modern minimalist forms. Simon started to ask him questions about his favorite performers, and instead of describing in words he would simply command the room to play a relevant recording. The old man seemed to relish having another person to enjoy music with. Most of what they listened to was entirely illegal. The sounds were alien, sacrilegious, and stunningly beautiful. Simon learned then that he lived a musically deprived life.

It was at the beginning of the seventh game that another guard entered the floor with Simon's father.

Medically, he looked fully recovered from the torture he had undergone. His body was no longer a corpse, indeed seeming perfectly healthy. His hair had regrown, and even the full-body suit he wore to scan his body down to the cellular level looked more comfortable than the similar suit Simon had been forced to wear. Whatever they did to bring him back didn't reach his eyes. Those still looked dead.

"Dad..." Simon walked towards him, looked at the guard to make sure he wouldn't be stopped, and ran up to hug him.

"Dad I'm so sorry I didn't know they would do this how are you?" he said in one faint breath. His dad didn't respond. He stood there like a statue, not seeming to fully comprehend who was in front of him. He seemed small, frail, and willfully unawake. A brilliant and loving man was reduced into a puddle of blunt trauma.

"How about you invite your dad to bowl with us." The Second Citizen said, the flicker of elation gone from his voice. Simon didn't hesitate.

"Dad, would you like to bowl with me and my friend David?"

Some hint of recognition entered his father's eyes, and he looked towards the lane. Slowly, he stepped forward. The remnant of an old instinct.

"I must leave. Running a country that has recently conquered another one leaves little time for rest. We'll be seeing each other." The Second Citizen left. The guard lingered in the back.

Simon rolled a spare, and his dad rolled into the gutter. They played wordlessly. His dad knocked down nothing. His movements were slow and stiff, as though he were moving a body that wasn't his. His face had forgotten how to form any expression, and he seemed unable or unwilling to move with any urgency.

They played ten games together, pausing only so Simon could grab them snacks. If his father recognized the vending machine, he gave no indication. Simon won each game.

"Time's up" the guard eventually said. Simon's dad turned and began walking towards the elevator.

"Wait," Simon said. He went up to his dad again and hugged him. This time, his dad wrapped his arms halfway around him.

The guard made them separate, and Simon used the elevator first. Instead of going to sleep, he went to the athletic level and ran. He sprinted around the track as quickly as he could, mile after mile, depleting his body with hope that when he finally slept, he would lack the energy to think about whether his dad would ever stop being a corpse.

CHAPTER 31

Simon was continuing to enforce his multifaceted definition of love onto himself and anyone nearby. His manipulation had required exceptional skill and care, but it was now working almost as well as he'd hoped. He knew because he felt more intense hatred for the First-Citizen today than yesterday, something which didn't seem possible. He reveled in his growing hatred. The ability to still feel that boiling emotion that turned his blood to magma was a great victory. He felt distantly the flickering hatred of the roughly two million others he was touching. Before his session was supposed to end, the room dimmed, signaling the imminent entrance of a specific person.

"Stop the session" the First-Citizen ordered the attendant, before the door even finished opening, with an almost jarringly intense whisper. The attendant complied, activating a setting that prompted the machine to cease tolerating any vocalization from Simon, and returned to his post, standing statue-like in either fear or reverential love. Simon realized he couldn't precisely determine how his ability would affect any given person, or what facets of love would manifest themselves most strongly in them. The attendant might have been a particularly fearful person, and thus taken to that distant extension of love, even if he'd tried to weaken the prominence of fear in his ability.

"Simon, Simon" the First-Citizen began. "You are making a habit of disappointing me. I had thought we were making such beautiful progress on this. Would you care to explain why, or perhaps how, your ability has managed to do the precise opposite of what I wanted from it?"

Simon sighed, a gesture which prompted a grimace across the autocrat's face for a fractional second. Simon interrupted the expression.

"Look, I'm doing what you told me to. I'm spreading love..."

"You are most certainly not doing what I told you to. All analytics indicate you are not spreading love. You are spreading discontentment towards me. B and C-class citizens are expressing considerably greater curiosity than they should about, well, fucking everything, and they're showing tremendous dissatisfaction towards me. Suddenly, my role in society has become 'confusing' to them. They want me to be more transparent about matters that they need not concern themselves with."

The First-Citizen rubbed his earmuff in discomfort. Simon noticed he'd let a contraction slip in.

"One young man even had the audacity to suggest, during his survey no less, that all surveys should become optional. That man is now dead. But at this rate, there will be others. Soon people will downright despise me. I refuse to kill a million like him over this. You, through some contrived application of your power which I cannot believe is accidental, are deforming my simple and grand vision."

Simon nodded. "I am making them less indifferent towards you. That is more or less the definition of love, as I understand it. And you wanted me to become comfortable around death, anyways, so you should be happy."

"Well, I think I have found our problem."

The First-Citizen let out a painfully faked laugh that made Simon's ears wince.

"Your definition of love is dangerously incorrect. So let me clarify: To love me, the First-Citizen, there must be absolute devotion. A willingness to put all your faith in me. I become your god, your pope, your savior. You have learned a little about the history of religion during your captivity, so you understand exactly what feelings I wish to elicit. Since I was apparently not specific enough to you when I gave my command, this is your modified order: I hereby command you to create citizens who are wholly, faithfully, devoted to me, and everything that I stand for, who do not question or challenge me, and who will gleefully sacrifice everything they have if I ask it of them."

The First-Citizen realized that he had begun raising his voice to a loud conversational level, and rubbed his ears in discomfort. When he spoke again, he whispered.

"Until you succeed in this order, and undo your mistake, it has already been voted that you have instigated poor behavior, and as such I am restricting your rights to comfort until the failure is rectified. You will see what that means when you are escorted to your new cell. The rest of today and tomorrow will be for you to reconsider your attempt at obstructing our progress here. That will be all."

"Wait."

"What?" the First-Citizen paused his uncharacteristically vigorous march out of the room.

"To help me with my reflection, may I have your permission to practice on my paper airplanes? It was the most fun of all the abilities I worked on, and I would be most grateful to revisit it as a creative outlet. I would be indebted to you."

The First-Citizen pondered the request. "Fine. For the next two days, play with your harmless paper toys. Perhaps a distraction will help lend you clarity on other, more important matters."

"You may leave," Simon said. For a moment he was sure he would be electrocuted for trying to give an order to his leader. He realized that his entire poorly conceived plan might be destroyed in a moment of vanity. He didn't care. It felt wonderful.

"I know the death of your partner hurts. But you're on thin ice." The First-Citizen said coldly. Simon hid a smile. Two contractions in one day.

Reeling in hatred and ecstasy, he was then escorted by a guard. As per the First-Citizen's warning, he was taken to a different cell. A long and thin door opened, and he was pushed into a coffin. That initial impression was apt; it looked roughly the size of an egyptian sarcophagus he had seen in one of the history books Louisa had shown him in their shared cell. The guard pushed him into the two foot deep, four foot wide, and six and a half foot tall enclosure. The door closed behind him, and now it felt like a coffin too.

Simon decided to stand in his coffin-cell, and put the next several hours of his solitary confinement to good use. "Paper airplane" he uttered. He needed to say the words well over a hundred times before the ability reached its pre-reset state. The floor of the cell soon became littered with scrappy pieces of paper that were his many failed attempts. Because his space was severely limited, once he created his first fully successful airplane, he stopped creating any more, and focused instead on refining that one object.

For the next several hours, his new paper friend was fluttering around his cell with grace and effortlessness. The object began to develop something of a personality as Simon worked on it further. When left to its own devices, it enjoyed trying to discover how many tight loop-de-loops it could achieve in its comically limited airspace before crashing into a wall. Simon began to hatch plans for this plane, and the many that would come after it.

There was no sleep that night. "Paper airplane" Simon uttered, pulling from literal nothingness a pristine piece of paper that quickly folded itself into the design that he desired. He uttered "paper airplane" a few more times, creating several, and immediately sent his new creations up into their autonomous flights in the limited space around him. His baby fleet already could not be grown any further without finding new space. At first he simply continued making more anyways, even putting effort into extending his ability so that, with a single utterance of "paper airplane", he could procure two, and soon three and more, at once with a single utterance. This turned out to be a mistake, and he had to ground nearly fifty of his planes just to keep them from hitting his head.

His saving grace was the wording of his request to the First-Citizen. Instead of asking for permission to work on the ability "paper airplane" specifically, he had asked to be allowed to work *on* his paper airplanes. The distinction allowed him considerably more options, or so he hoped.

"Phase, phase, phase..." Simon began to utter continuously for around five minutes, applying the ability exclusively to his paper airplanes, envisioning that their atoms could bypass the atoms of any other object. After five minutes, a sensation began to develop, a vague connection to the particles the planes drifted through. A binary sensation: collision or avoidance, two states which his planes soon learned to freely switch between. After over a dozen failures, a plane managed to phase through the wall. "Stay in the hallway" Simon commanded a few times. He felt confident that particular plane would obey.

With the space limitation sorted, Simon went back to creating new planes. He wanted as many as possible.

He shifted focus to "invisible", this time adding the feature to his planes instead of himself. He knew he needed to hide his fleet from the outside, lest his privilege of creation run the risk of being revoked. Not many minutes later, his entire fleet was cloaked. He shifted to a new unhearable ability, which hid the rustling sound of their glides as they wandered increasingly far from his cell down new hallways. He sensed many of his aerial acolytes beginning to aggressively explore the hallways of the facility, an instinctive curiosity he must have embedded in them unintentionally.

As his fleet grew, he began to appreciate the expansive sensation of it. Each of his hundred or more planes felt like a distant minor appendage of his body, which collectively existed as part of a single vast organ. He could start to feel the intelligence behind its elegantly complex maneuvering.

He wondered if the neurological well growing in his mind to manage this fleet would somehow begin to develop its own independent notions, given steady nurturing. Perhaps all his abilities could become shades, with distinctive personalities and opinions, like Hegelpitic. He'd have time for such ponderings later.

He silently willed one of his planes to phase back into his cell and land in his cupped hands. "Tougher" he uttered at it many times, willing the fibers of the paper making up the plane to strengthen into a new material. After a half hour of effort, Simon's hands could no longer bend the wings of this plane even a fraction of an inch and nearly cut one of his fingers on the plane's paper edge trying. Once "Tougher" had been practiced sufficiently on one plane, it was simply an investment of time to apply it to the full fleet. In this way, his planes became armor-piercing.

"Hot" was his next focus, and he used this word to enable his flying terrors to heat to considerable temperatures. It took less than a half hour for a few of his more aggressive planes to be able to reach several hundred degrees fahrenheit, the precise limit of which Simon had no interest in figuring out at that moment. The problem with this became that the planes heat caused the air around them to bake and simmer, which would inevitably be detected. He was certain he'd be tortured if the First-Citizen knew what he was doing. In his absolute focus, he realized he hadn't considered the obvious solution. Take his fleet outside the facility. He willed his planes to seek the outside, which they did.

Over an hour into the endeavor, with nearly three hundred paper airplanes flying about aimlessly in the outside hallway, Simon found himself reaching a state of exhaustion. A stray thought about Louisa, and her method of death, immediately reignited him, and within minutes he was on an unprecedented utterance high. A gruesome idea hatched itself in Simon's mind.

"Cube" he uttered a few times, playing around with

folding a few of his most fortified planes into paper cubes, and willing them to try to struggle to propel themselves around his cell in their un-aerodynamic forms. He almost laughed at the absurdity, but continued creating flying paper cubes for several minutes. He vividly imagined a second application of this ability while he uttered, which he hoped desperately to be able to use when the time was right.

He spent twenty minutes uttering "speed", willing his fleet to practice upward diving above the placid streets of oakland until they could perform them at over a hundred miles an hour.

A number of additional features and augmentations on the planes followed, all of them technically acceptable according to the wording of the deal struck with the First-Citizen, since the abilities were physically applied to nothing other than a paper airplane. "Sharp" was used to make the tips of the planes pointed on a microscopic scale. "planesense" allowed planes to observe, in a manner of speaking, the objects around them, and to autonomously avoid collisions.

Simon willed them, for the time being, to entirely avoid direct interactions with all living beings in the facility, and especially to avoid the top floors where the First-Citizen might sense them. To allow himself to better observe his planes beyond his cell wall, he developed "planesight" to allow him to see through any one of his planes, as though possessing a disparate third eye attached to whichever part of the plane's surface he wished to see through. Developing this ability allowed Simon to finally explore the entirety of the facility. He was surprised at how horrid that guard's shared lockers looked, but stopped himself from exploring more. He needed every second he could get, if he were to have any chance holding back the First-Citizen for more than a second. He still wasn't certain of the exact strength of his opponent. Spying on him through his body had hinted that, to the First-Citizen, solid matter felt more or less the same as air, as though they were all equally displaceable. So he was likely vastly stronger than Simon, who most certainly did notice when something was solid versus gaseous. That didn't matter, so long as there was one person stronger still.

At this point, over two hours into the effort, Simon willed himself to have another resurgence of energy. A limited amount of food had been offered to him, which he inhaled in seconds.

"Push" became the ability that he spent the most time on. He was meticulous in his rapid yet precisely cautious imagination to focus the ability on his planes, but tried his best to concurrently imagine a second application of the word, one that could apply to any object generally. Even pumped with adrenaline, he found the exercise draining.

"Push", as applied to his planes, allowed Simon to artificially induce in them large amounts of raw inertia, far more than their mass and speed would provide according to regular physics. It was as though an invisible hand from that other universe were pushing them along, foisting inertia into the plane's atoms. Simon spent over two hours pushing the "push" force of his planes as far as he could, almost collapsing from exhaustion at one point.

Obsessive focus had pushed him far, but it occurred to Simon that each new feature to his planes was requiring the rapid careful creation of millions of new neurons in his head. Even while in the forest, or working on hurricanes, he hadn't pushed himself this frenetically. The rapid neurogenesis would at some point catch up to him and might well be dangerous.

He had one final ability that he needed to develop, the most essential one.

"Away" he uttered, finding the word a welcome one to once again hear out loud. He tested the ability only on his planes, and after enough utterance was able to teleport their concealed forms from location to location in and out of the facility. He enjoyed teleporting planes from one side of the metropolitan oakland area to the other, and using planesight to observe the sudden change in view they experienced. Regardless of what it may have looked like once, Oakland expressed an identical dull monotony to Portland. No two cities in the Citizenship were particularly different, even from the sky.

His imagination multitasked once again, as he tried to also slowly regrow his old ability to self-teleport. He couldn't test the ability on himself, not without great risk, but he felt energy returning, connecting to its pre-existing neurological machinery, hopefully ready to be called upon when the time came.

He spent his remaining lucid hour continuing to utter "away", even going so far as to teleport entire small squadrons of his planes at once to test his expanding limits.

Ashamedly, he fell into a sleeplike trance, uttering dozens of words in no particular order as his eyes closed and he began seeing increasingly vivid illusions of a fake reality. He felt his brain trying not to burst with its many new extensions and threw up the limited food he had consumed hours earlier. His tranced muttering nearly gave way to a sleep which he knew he had to resist. Once he slept, he wouldn't wake for a long while.

"Get up." the guard barked in their modulated voice. "The First-Citizen wishes to see you."

Simon opened his eyes with a start and made his mind focus. He did not relish any aspect of what had to come next.

"Sorry." he said.

"PUSH!"

He then shouted, immediately assuming a pointed stance towards the guard and the door. The guard was immediately thrust back as though rammed by an invisible train, his helmet striking the opposite wall with a dull thud. The cell door tried to close, and Simon shouted "Push!" again, even more forcefully, causing the door to wretch out of the wall and crash atop the fallen guard. The sheer boldness of the act shocked Simon into hyperawareness.

He stepped out of his sarcophagus and began to jog down the hallway towards the stairwell.

A loud alarm began to ring, with the superposition of distant echoes revealing that the alarm was going off in all parts of the massive facility. As Simon was partway to the staircase, his armada of paper airplanes being willed to fly in from their various outposts to the site of their master, many more doors started opening along the still mostly pristine hallway. A single guard rushed out of each sarcophagus that opened. Many of them were only partially dressed in their armor, with a thin pajama layer being their only physical protection. Some of them, though, were fully armored. They all still had their full cover helmets, protecting their faces and displaying whatever vision it was that they saw.

Understanding dawned on Simon. These coffin-cells were the guards quarters. The First-Citizen really did think of them as penned animals.

Before he could reflect on his discovery, and ponder the nature of guards' lives, many of them lined up with the intent to put him down. Simon wished he had taken time to restore and strengthen his "sleep" ability, because the alternative was a good deal less pleasant, and worse than the guards deserved.

During the fervor of the past night, Simon had not only let his armada operate autonomously, but had practiced and refined some of his wordless control over them, a sort of guiding sensation that let him instinctively manipulate its motions around him as a singular yet massive out-of-body organ. Wordlessly he bade his armada reveal itself. Across the hallway, over three hundred paper airplanes dropped their invisible pretense, increased their speed, and began diving into the guards.

It was a one-sided fight. Volleys would group, select a human target, and collectively dive into them, piercing armor and skin with their impossibly sharp noses and augmented inertia. Once a plane pierced through two or three inches, it would simply phase through the rest of the body and return to flight, immediately joining another group in selecting another target to shred.

"Warmer" Simon uttered, willing each of his planes to elevate its temperature to a value that he hoped might at the very least serve to cauterize the guards' stab wounds as they were being made. Hopefully they could be treated later. Simon made a particular effort to beg his planes to not strike the guards heads or necks, since those wounds would most likely lead to death. He found that coordinating his planes in an unrehearsed and coordinated attack had instantly increased his fatigue. He pushed through it, resuming his walk towards the stairwell, doing his best to ignore the agonizing screams escaping the helmets that littered the floor around him.

One particularly brave guard, fully armored, managed to get within arm's length of Simon and tried to get his glove on him. He nearly succeeded before Simon punched him in the ribcage with enough force to crack bone. The brave guard stumbled back and was quickly assailed by a dozen planes. Simon realized that he had never fully familiarized himself with his new strength after he augmented it back in the forest. Breaking that man's ribs felt like striking a child.

None of the guards were in any position to walk, but most appeared destined for survival. Simon ran the rest of the way to the stairwell and used "Push!" to collapse the door. As he briskly walked up the flights of stairs, grateful for his runner's stamina, he uttered "stop, stop, stop" in hurried succession. After the first couple of flights of stairs, the lights began to flicker and Simon was enveloped in darkness.

"Fire" he had to utter a few times, quickly restoring that old ability until a bright packet of flame emerged from his palm, granting him limited vision of the stairs in front of him. Even with the modest light source, the stairs were difficult to see, and Simon had to tread carefully. "Stop, stop, stop..." he resumed uttering, confident that his ability was growing at the fast rate he had hoped it would. It was, after all, only causing simple surges and disruptions of small amounts of energy, the easiest type of task for him. He felt himself entering a sort of berserker state where he momentarily lost all capacity to be exhausted. He knew it wouldn't last.

Soon enough, Simon reached the top floor of the facility, and made his way to the entrance to the First-Citizen's office. He was surprised to find that there were no guards on the floor, and wondered if the First-Citizen was even there. His worries were eased slightly when he made the final turn into the latest hallway converging onto the imposing wood door, to see the survey woman standing her Vigil.

"The First-Citizen will see you now," she told Simon with her usual poise.

Simon stopped running and took a few seconds to calm himself. The next two minutes would demand clarity. Then he would sleep, success or no. He offered the woman an uncoordinated nod and she opened the door for him.

The dim lights in the room still worked. The First-Citizen's silhouette could be made out sitting atop his desk, staring Simon dead in the eyes, in a way that made it seem like he had been staring in that precise direction for hours, that Simon's face had just happened to find itself in the way.

"What a delirious turn of events this is" he whispered. He stood from his desk, and began to rise, in a controlled levitation, such that his feet were level with Simon's shoulders.

"You must know", he continued, "that this? It is futile. You and your ally were clever, but I know your limits. A day and night of talking to yourself cannot put me down."

Simon began to step forward, just beyond the reach of the closed door behind him, which he heard the survey woman close. He realized that his body hid its fatigue even more poorly than the First-Citizen was hiding his next move.

"Who even was it, then? Who helped you? It was never purcell, I knew that much. That man was never a plotter."

"I'm sure you know who it was." Simon replied.

"Yes, of course I do. Just making conversation." The First-Citizen began to leisurely drift towards Simon, at least twice as slowly as he might have strolled. The glacial slithering of his body through the air towards Simon looked predatory.

"That man and I have had a hundred opportunities to stab each other in the back, and he never did. I gave him all my trust. If he can betray me, after everything we have built... I have to suppose anyone can. I think I might just kill my entire administration and have them replaced. We can use you to enforce loyalty contracts with the new ones. Yes, yes, that is a more urgent mission than your current one. We shall have to shift priorities immediately..." He edged closer. Simon unconsciously took a step back. He realized he was outmatched.

"Simon, Simon", he was now about thirty feet away. "I regret that I am going to temporarily rob you of your consciousness. You might have to be sedated for a good long while after today so that I have time to contemplate our relationship. You can bunk next to the Last Citizen. You two would get along famously. Do not be surprised if the next thing you remember is waking up in a hospital bed with four broken limbs and a dead father."

"No." Simon said. He smiled despite himself.

The moment the First-Citizen would pick to lunge forward was obvious, and Simon adjusted his forces accordingly, as though balling a fist. As his hunter began to accelerate, Simon uttered "shield" as rapidly as he could. Two or three snap decisions would determine the result of this altercation. Almost too fast to see, the First-Citizen turned into a blur aimed directly at Simon, his progress only slowed slightly by the reinforced air now in his way. It was fortunate the shield wasn't meant as the striking blow.

At that same moment, Simon silently commanded an armada to phase through the floor beneath the First-Citizen's elevated feet. The planes erupted into the room with nearly the same speed that the First-Citizen was beginning to demonstrate, taking him completely by surprise and causing him to fly up into the room's center, over thirty feet in the air.

Planes dove into him in dozens from all directions, applying as much force as they were able, blazing at the highest temperatures and accelerations that Simon could will them to sustain without slipping into hallucination.

The First-Citizen looked genuinely troubled. Every plane that landed a hit left a single red point where skin had been barely punctured. A few seconds into the altercation, the First-Citizen's face was densely freckled with red dots, although he moved too fast for Simon to guess how many. The only impression Simon had of the event was of the air. It simmered and jolted, loudly and with smoking heat as both sides repeatedly flirted with the sound barrier. Simon had hoped sound alone might incapacitate his enemy.

Once he got his bearings and grasped the nature of the attack, the First-Citizen grabbed a plane in each of his hands and slammed their points into his ears. He screamed terribly, and for a moment Simon thought he would fall to the ground. Instead, he smiled. Then, with a speed even greater than Simon had feared him capable of, he began to systematically pluck planes out of the air and crush them in his palms. He continued taking hits, but Simon's armada was now being torn to shreds much faster than he could ever replenish it. The First-Citizen's arms moved so quickly as to give him a silhouetted appearance of some ancient many-armed pagan god. He seemed to have entered into his own warrior's rage. Blood from his ears splattered down on Simon.

"Tougher! Push! Warmer! Invisible!" he shouted, hoping to reinvigorate his planes with new power. He had to sit from dizziness and stopped uttering for them, then forced himself to stand again.

His efforts only seemed to delay the inevitable. Simon had hoped that invisibility might make the attacks impossible to deflect, but it seemed as though the First-Citizen could still see the planes perfectly clearly, or had some way of accurately and instantly ascertaining their speed and location. The First-Citizen began to sink back down to the floor of the room, almost at a leisurely pace, showing that Simon's assault, which had savaged scores of guards just minutes ago, hadn't seriously hurt him. His bleeding ears strangely seemed to bother him less than they normally did. He reached the floor, his feet crushing a wad of paper that, unlike most of its comrades, had at least managed to draw a single drop of blood before being crumpled.

"I will admit this: I have been stimulated. I should have you do that for me again sometime." The First-Citizen was now less than twenty feet from Simon.

"You unfortunately seem to be out of planes. Now, if you want to surrender, I will offer you this one chance. I might even spare one of your limbs."

"Cube" Simon uttered, once again as quickly as possible.

"Why...ahhhgh!"

The First-Citizen screamed at an inhuman amplitude that hurt even Simon's ears, and began clawing both his hands at his left eye.

"Make it stop! I'll fucking kill you!" he shouted, as the fleshy sphere began trying to mold itself neatly into a cube, the fat, fiber, and muscle putting up more resistance to reshaping than Simon had experienced from any stone or metal.

The entire process continued for about five seconds, but the volcanic screeching made the experience seem endless.

"Oh, you are dead..." the First-Citizen said, looking up with his remaining bloodshot eye. Blood started to flow continuously out of his now semi-cubic left eye socket. In the heat of the moment, Simon couldn't help but be impressed at the sheer durability of his adversary. The First-Citizen made his third and final approach, slightly slower than either of the previous bursts.

Two things happened then.

First, the remaining third of Simon's armada phased through the entrance, passing him by and ramming into the First-Citizen this time all from the same direction. Almost every ounce of focus that Simon could spare was ushered into the attack, and although it was insufficiently powerful to halt the First-Citizen's lunge, it gave Simon just the time he needed for the second, more important thing.

"Away!" he shouted. The next half second was an electric blur. It usually took teleportation at least a full second after Simon uttered the word to occur, by which time his neck would have been snapped. Adrenaline suffused Simon's body so completely that all inhibition and doubt abandoned him as he gave what he had left to the next few microseconds. He saw his destination. Pure instinct took over, and, as the First-Citizen's outstretched hand began colliding with Simon's chest, reality blipped, and both Simon and the First-Citizen found themselves in another place.

The teleportation had reset the First-Citizen's deadly velocity, and so he now staggered into Simon, confused. Enough time for Simon to shout "stop!". He felt strange hallucinations of demons and angels take over as he uttered the word, and felt as it did its job in the surrounding rooms of the facility. He lost all consciousness in the next second. As his eyes drifted closed, he imagined fists collide, and tried to smile.

CHAPTER 32

Consciousness slowly returned, in the form of pain. There were several varieties sharing a cooperative coexistence, including hunger, thirst, a body-wide feeling of overexertion, and mild concussive trauma from the interrupted lunge at his neck by the First-Citizen. There was also the strain of acclimating his dark-adjusted eyes to the bright desert sun that burned his skin.

As his eyes adjusted and he started to sit, Simon observed he was in the midst of a sand-ridden, scantily vegetated desert. There were a few modest sloping hills off in the distance, and a couple isolated concentrations of rocks that complemented the scattering of small green bushels and cacti. A large boulder behind him offered shade to one of his legs. The landscape looked still, cured of any notion of time, until a small breeze rustled a stream of sand particles around him, and graced his ears with a familiar sound of wind that had been heard by his ancestors for billions of years, and would persist for eons after he was gone. *I'm starting to care more about the smaller and the larger scales of life. I'm noticing every individual grain of sand that hits me, yet I'm thinking in terms of millennia. What am I becoming? I feel odd.*

As Simon cleared his vision and looked to his left, he saw four companions. Juarez sat intently on a small boulder, staring contemplatively at the battered First-Citizen. Simon noted with some satisfaction that the First-Citizen didn't look much better than Purcell had after being swatted into a wall. He suspected the First-Citizen was still dangling to life, despite the mangled and bloody limbs. Hegelpitic sat in a lotus posture on the sandy desert floor, a few feet away from all three of them. The Last Citizen lay unconscious in front of him.

"Where are we?" Simon said weakly. Juarez turned to him.

"We're safe," he mumbled. He kept staring at the First-Citizen.

"Juarez sprinted both of our unconscious bodies out into the desert after we nearly destroyed the facility fighting" the First-Citizen chimed in, speaking a great deal more loudly than he needed to. He pointed with his right arm, the least damaged of his four limbs, to his ears.

"I have suffered some rather extensive ear trauma. You will have to speak up for a few minutes while they recover."

"If they recover," Juarez responded.

"Ah, of course. So I am to be Prometheus. Every time I heal, the bird eats me. But you are no being of myth. Your patience is finite. You will not want to attend to me forever. Eventually, you will have to either kill me or leave me be."

"Prometheus gave mortals the gift of fire. You withheld the gift of immortality. You go against everything prometheus stood for." Juarez said. The First-Citizen smiled thinly.

Hegelpitic remained transfixed on the sleeping woman.

"How long was I out?" Simon eventually asked. Juarez didn't seem to hear.

"Thirty hours and twelve minutes," Hegelpitic said.

"How do you know? Is there a time-telling device on you? Those can be tracked." Simon asked, worried.

"No. One of my constituents is good with time. He told me."

I guess we both have a Mr. Clocker. Nice.

Simon repositioned himself into a seated posture and created a banana for himself to inhale, then several. Juarez and Hegelpitic silently accepted bananas as they were offered. Unfortunately he had no ability for summoning water, and developing a new one to siphon it from the surrounding dry air or from far underground seemed daunting in his waned state. He realized that bananas already contained water, and so created a dozen more bananas, then developed a simple ability to extract the recently generated water from them, cheating himself out of some effort. It was possible neither of them required sustenance, but the craving for it seemed to remain. Once everyone was quenched, Simon spoke.

"I think we need to talk about the future."

The First-Citizen nodded in approval.

"I am glad you think so. The future should always be talked about."

"Maybe you shouldn't speak," Juarez said sternly.

"I can run a country for weeks without speaking. I do it for pleasure, not because I should or should not."

Juarez glared. "Anyways. All I want is to be reunited with my family, to spend my remaining days as a free citizen by their side. That's all."

The First-Citizen chuckled anemically. "Juarez, you cannot live in the Citizenship. You are unprepared."

"Yeah? Watch me do it anyway."

" You need to be born into it or you will go insane. Trust me. Even in your cell, your mind and body are more free than almost everyone else's in my administration. You are too old to learn to allow a survey to tell you exactly what you can and cannot think, how you should walk, and when you may exercise. You would fail the first week of our education system. Within a month you would be tearing down towers in frustration. Simon will second my opinion if you ask. He has overseen many of our older citizens who could not adjust."

Simon wasn't sure what to say. Juarez clearly didn't grasp what he was asking for, but there was no way he was going to agree with the First-Citizen out loud.

"I don't care about Simon," Juarez said.

"And I don't care that you think his life is more complicated than mine, or that i'm not made for it. I care that you people use my family to own me. For the record everyone, this man wouldn't even allow me to meet with more than two family members at once. He was worried that If I was ever with my whole family, I would try and break them out and lead them to freedom. I have three siblings who I love. I've never been in a room with all of them at the same time."

It occurred to Simon during this dramatic speech that Juarez was in fact giving a speech to thousands of people. Any words spoken to Hegelpitic were uttered to an entire civilization. The thought of speaking again suddenly seemed daunting.

The First-Citizen grimaced and adjusted his right arm, which annoyingly seemed to bring him comfort. Juarez bent down, took the man's biceps between his hands, and effortlessly twisted his upper arm in two, breaking bone like he was bending wire. The sight was shocking. The First-Citizen possessed supernatural strength and durability. For Juarez to do what he just did to him, and with such ease, required a strength far greater still.

Juarez pointlessly wiped his blood stained hands over his ripped pants, clearly not for the first time. Simon wondered if Juarez had slept at all in the past day. He realized he was still drowsy himself, and hadn't fully recovered from the unprecedented neurogenesis of the past 48 hours. Planes fluttered around his head like newborn ghosts, solidifying their presence in the chaotic wells he'd recently created.

"I'm going to take my family." Juarez began. "I'll bring them to South America. Far from you."

"You would do just fine in South America. You could even conquer it given time. Your family would die within days. If the regime down there does not kill them, disease will." The First-Citizen said almost boredly. He had seemed to be in tremendous pain while his arm was being broken, but already seemed almost comfortable again. It was more than a little infuriating.

"Fuck you. Fuck the years you took from me. And yes, fuck your complicated-to-live-in country that I've never seen. Also...go fuck yourself."

Hegelpitic laughed. "That insult is redundant, no? To say 'fuck you' in your language, and then to ask him to go…"

"Yes, I know what I said." Juarez glared at the four-armed hemigiant.

"You don't seem shaken by any of this. You've been locked up by him even longer than I have, your whole life as far as I can tell. You should say what you want to say to this man."

Hegelpitic turned to the First-Citizen. He stood and walked over to him, his nearly seven and a half feet towering over the injured autocrat.

"You have my thanks. You have kept us safe for many years. Ever since we were a small tribe of a dozen misguided children unable to make sense of either of our worlds, you were there offering counsel, encouraging us, giving us lessons and stories. You allowed us to grow educated strong and healthy in our shared body on this world, and gave us the tools to fight off the demons of our world. We are still a young culture, but thanks to you, we know what we are, and how we shall grow. We cannot repay you for your service to us. However, this is where we must part. Now that we have seen how you treat those you deem your lessers, there can be no respect between us."

"Heg." The First-Citizen coughed blood. "You named yourself even I could. I asked you so many times if you wanted to be a citizen, to be given a ranking. I never understood why you opposed it."

His left arm reached out and grasped Hegelpitics leg. In the past minute he'd already healed considerably, but Hegelpitic did not seem fearful.

"You were always such a rebellious child. I have no idea if I raised you well. You give me details of your world, scraps. I can not understand what it is like in there. I can know the mind of every human on the continent except yours. All I could do was keep you safe. Everything else, whatever world you have built in there, is entirely yours. I have had numerous compatriots in my life, but you were my only equal. I'll miss you."

Hegelpitic said nothing and did not move. The contraction at the end visibly shook him, and his third pupil dilated as the last sentence was finished. A tear slid down his cheek from each of his three stunning eyes. The First-Citizen let go. Hegelpitic returned to providing shade for the Last Citizen.

"You should kill her," The First-Citizen said.

"Make us," Juarez said.

"Life is sacred." Hegelpitic said distractedly.

"To her nothing is sacred. I also am not stupid, as Juarez would say. I know how I am perceived by you people. I promise, given time, you will grow to hate and fear her ten times more. You are much better off ending her and dealing with your guilt than you are reviving her and dealing with the consequences."

"We'll take our chances," Juarez said.

"She is almost singlehandedly the reason why I built the Citizenship the way I did. She is a technology that proves beyond any doubt my need to be at the helm of all scientific and cultural advancement everywhere if our species is to avoid annihilation."

Simon was about ready to stab the man, but held back.

"you should try living in the Citizenship you created. You've never experienced the society you rule. You might reconsider how you're treating a hundred million people." He said instead.

Two planes passed by their group hypersonically about a second before the sound reached their ears. Simon had never seen the First-Citizen in so much pain, even with his limbs half severed. He himself felt the sound more than he heard it. The planes flew into the horizon and didn't seem like they were coming back. Simon suspected everyone understood what that meant. The First-Citizen was no longer commanding the Citizenship's air force. The First-Citizen gave a defeated smile.

"I wouldn't know the first thing about living in the Citizenship." Hegelpitic said.

"It's one thing for Juarez, and Simon has done it, but there are few of my constituents with the right shape and size to blend in, and none of them will want to come here. And your society seems to hold many complexities that mine does not."

"It's not all that complicated, living in the Citizenship." Simon said.

"It's actually very simple. You wake up, go to the job you were encouraged to apply for, do it as flawlessly as you can manage, go to whatever place your survey recommends you visit after, go home. It's more a matter of practice than anything. Over the years, you learn how to not think certain thoughts as much. How to not look up, down, or sideways unless you must. All extraneous behavior is ironed out. And if you can strip yourself down far enough, your survey gives you a good score. Says you did a good job. And you feel good. Then you try harder to refine your behavior, the smaller things, like the way you blink, or how many seconds you linger on certain thoughts. How you breathe. The way you feel happy, sad, angry, tired. They call it "microliberty", the idea that you can master living only when all but the very smallest details are in place, and that this mastery can be quantified, converted into a number that says how successful you are. You mold yourself to this man's liking, and in the moment of it all you're too immersed to really pause and think about it. There's no freedom, but there's both joy and sorrow. It's a life, for better or worse. The First-Citizen isn't wrong; you need to grow up with it." There was a very long silence.

"You defend the nation that forces you to live like that?" Juarez eventually asked, after meticulously breaking each of the First-Citizens fingers.

"I'm not. It's a poor thing to live like I did. The genius of it is that you never realize how terrible it is until you leave, which most people never do. So everyone for the most part stays reasonably happy and doesn't resist."

"Oh, enough complaining." The First-Citizen cried. His ears were caked with blood but appeared healed.

"We have run countless simulations on you, Simon. More than anyone in history. You know what kind of life you would lead, if we did not orchestrate it for you? You would be antisocial, the few friends that you would pick would be horrible to you, and since you would have no clue how to interact with women, or anyone for that matter, there would have been no chance in hell of Louisa or someone like her ending up with you. Oh, and you would drink. If we had not just solved obesity and enforced your diet, you would be forty pounds heavier. Once again, that means no Louisa. She would walk past your overweight physique without even considering that you two may be compatible. And who would blame her? You would still be a little tall, and a little handsome, but you would look and act like a mess."

"She isn't that shallow." Simon turned to the sky pretending to look for more jets he knew wouldn't come.

"And instead of all that? We give you a stimulating career, keep you from thinking thoughts that could lead to your discontentment, and spend years preparing to match you with your ideal partner. Louisa was brought to Portland specifically for you. You both needed to date, she needed new scenery, and the two of you had such an impressive compatibility score that she was shipped across the continent. If you didn't have your ability, she and you would have eventually balanced each other out into beautiful complacency that would have kept you happy for decades. More than most things, I prioritize the romantic lives of my citizens and go to great lengths to put everyone in such relationships as yours. I am fully aware that I do this because I can never have such a relationship myself, but I contend that the reason is less important than the outcome."

Juarez interjected. "Well now that we're telling stories, here's one: This man took me from my family and experimented on me. They built a truck-sized metal machine just to try twisting my neck at half the speed of sound and measure my skull's microfractures, because you were personally curious how long it would take a mutant twelve year old to heal from a fatal rotational injury. I've been a lab freak since I was nine. My childhood was hell. The pain only stopped because I grew too strong for you, but I still feel it every night."

"That is not..." The First-Citizen began.

"No, you don't talk. You make yourself immortal, with my blood, and share this discovery with almost nobody. Every time I look at you, all I see is the wrinkled face you wore two decades ago. That old face promised me freedom once. And you don't even care if you lie to me, do you?"

"I already know how he's going to respond to that," Simon said. "He'll say that you're an individual and that individuals don't matter. As a singular anomaly you can suffer as much as he needs you to. The system isn't flawed, according to him, so long as suffering is constrained to people like us."

"You know, I think you are finally beginning to understand me." The First-Citizen said pridefully. "I am really not complicated. Put that on my tombstone."

"Say their names." Juarez said.

"Whose?" The First-Citizen responded.

"My mother. Father. Sister. Two brothers. The people who don't matter to you. Say their names."

"I do not know them."

"You're lying. Don't be an asshole. I want you to say their names. I'll spare your life if you say them."

"I am telling you, I do not know. If I were in your shoes I would kill me anyways, so there is no point in trying to guess."

"Say. Their. Fucking. Names." Juarez said, in the kind of whisper the First-Citizen tended to use when upset. The First-Citizen leaned into Juarez. Simon could just barely hear the words whispered out of his mouth.

"Their names matter even less than mine."

"Fuck you straight to hell." Juarez hissed. Simon saw what was coming.

"Juarez, I don't think we should."

"I agree with Simon. This is foolish. We should discuss this." Hegelpitic added sternly. His protective posture next to Maria did not waver.

"We don't know what will happen if this man is killed. His named successor, we can all agree, hardly seems an improvement. This should be discussed."

"I don't have anything more I need from him." He looked into the First-Citizen's eyes, which for the first time opened fully in a sort of utter fascination that overpowered the blazing sun. "Fuck you, get fucked, go fuck yourself, and see you in hell," Juarez said.

"Juarez, w…"

Before Simon could argue, Juarez grasped the First-Citizen by the neck and twisted his head entirely around it, multiple times, with the ease of one molding clay. The First-Citizen's bloated scream was cut short as his trachea was shredded and his spinal nerve was similarly severed by the multiple revolutions. A look of fascinated terror froze onto his face as blood slowly leaked our of tears in his skin and life drained from his eyes. Simon had once wished a terrible death upon the man, but this sight was sickening. Given his body's durability, it was possible he'd remain conscious for at least another minute before finding oblivion. Simon wondered what he was thinking, if he could still do such a thing.

Hegelpitic watched the display of ruthless strength, and for a moment it looked like he was shifting into someone else, but he stopped himself. After several minutes, the body stopped twitching. Simon watched as death occurred. Juarez faced him.

"I have a question for you. Answer it honestly."

"I will."

"Can you kill the rest of them?"

"Huh?"

"You heard. The second, third, fourth citizens, all the way down to whoever the hundredth is. Would you wipe them from the face of the earth, and allow us to start again, to start everything again? You and I can do better than they've done. You know it."

Simon had rarely been so certain as he was of his answer.

"No. I'm not a killer. I'm not qualified to decide who lives. And neither are you. We're too powerful to be making decisions like that. And we're too emotional right now anyways. Killing them will probably make everything worse. I'll help track down your family, and do what I can to protect them."

Juarez stood. "I'm sorry too, Simon. I just can't take that chance."

Before Simon knew what was happening, Juarez lunged at him with surprising speed. If he had been as fast as the First-Citizen, the fight would have ended then, but enough time was granted as Juarez accelerated across the fifteen feet separating them for Simon to shout "Push!".

Juarez must not have been able to generate leverage to the degree that the First-Citizen could, so the defense successfully repelled him backwards where his feet landed by the First-Citizen's corpse. Hegelpitic grabbed the Last Citizen in three of his arms and retreated.

"I don't understand," Simon said.

Juarez bent down, hands pushing into the sand, and lunged again. Simon realized he had bent down to pick up a rock, nearly too late as Juarez threw it right at his head. "Shield!" Simon shouted, this time directing the ability at both the rock and juarez, barely managing to stop both objects from reaching him. Juarez was now ten feet from Simon.

Juarez bent down again to re-grab the rock. While he did this, Simon simultaneously began taking large steps backwards, and yelled "push!", forcing him back even farther since he hadn't accumulated any momentum this time. Juarez began to lunge at him again, the rock still in his hand, when Simon, in thoughtless desperation, uttered "Love First-Citizen".

Juarez ceased his impending charge, confused by the

sentence. His hesitation would cost him.

"Love First-Citizen" Simon said with stronger intent, as Juarez tried to comprehend the surprising choice of last words.

"Love First-Citizen" he said a third time. The ability, for better or worse, was Simon's second or third strongest, and was already taking its toll. Juarez rubbed his forehead in discomfort. Simon put all his willpower into focusing the abilities entire strength on one person, and could almost feel the strain of subtly reconfiguring brain chemistry being forced onto his opponent.

"Why are you saying that? You make no sense. What is happening?"

"Love First-Citizen".

Juarez began looking distressed. For the first time since they met, Simon saw him sweat.

"Why do you say this?"

"Love First-Citizen." At this point, Juarez had already forgotten about attacking Simon and had turned his head to the disfigured corpse behind him.

"Love First-Citizen".

Juarez began to sob. Simon uttered "love First-Citizen" two more times, which he realized was an inexcusable cruel thing to do, and walked towards his assailant. He sat down beside the man, and for a while they cried together. Each time Simon uttered, the same ability still applied itself to him, albeit more weakly, feeling like a punch coming from no direction each time he spoke the words. Despite everything the First-Citizen had done, he couldn't accept his death. He sobbed angrily.

Hegelpitic returned a few minutes later, gently laid the woman down, and sat by them, clearly at least slightly affected by the utterance. His tall, muscular, four-armed form happened to provide Simon with ample shade from the oppressive sun.

A rumbling in the distance caught their attention. Five obsidian jets streaked through the sky about a mile out, a rippling shockwave alerting the entire region to their presence.

"Simon, can you hide us?" Hegelpitic asked. "They might change their mind about not harming us."

"Yeah, sure." He spent a few minutes redeveloping and modifying the hologram ability he had used to cover his forest cave to surround the five of them in a protective mirage. He still needed rest before he could create and strengthen any abilities, and did the minimum amount of necessary work.

Hegelpitic is right. If they see the First-Citizen dead, they might decide our usefulness is done and kill us.

Eventually as the sky darkened, there were no tears left. Simon tiredly created bananas and extracted water from them. He offered Juarez another banana, which he declined. Hegelpitic accepted the fruit-approximant and ate it rapturously.

"We should bury him," Hegelpitic suggested. Juarez lifted himself and began wordlessly digging into the sand next to the site of death. His hands cut straight through rock as effortlessly as if treading water. The graceful repeating motion was soothing to watch.

Simon for his part, developed abilities to straighten out the bones of the corpse, to give the frame what elegance he could. He took a few minutes to develop a "deathsense", a unique sensation revealing whether a creature's consciousness was decayed beyond saving. The First-Citizens' neurons were silent, and Simon felt the subtle withering of recent brain death. Hegelpitic's neurons sang with blinding intensity, a searingly hot yet cosmically vast chorus putting to shame the dimmer neural shine emanated by Juarez and himself. Maria was also not braindead, and Simon sensed with his primitive new ability that she was starting to dream.

An hour or so after the work began, the First-Citizen was buried.

"There should be a plaque," Juarez suggested. Simon agreed and created minor abilities to carve one out of fused sand. Juarez let Simon write the plaque.

Here rests the First-Citizen
We didn't know his name
He was simple
We loved him

Juarez sat a vigil in front of the makeshift grave, while Simon enhanced his hologram ability to ensure it was sturdy enough to keep them out of sight of the planes now flying over them almost hourly. He eventually decided to try and heal himself of his more minor injuries, then slept for another twelve hours.

The next day, nobody spoke. Simon, well-rested enough to think clearly, wanted time to himself. Juarez seemed to feel similarly, although he made sure to stay within the bounds set by the mirage.

The day was spent in somber reflection, as everyone silently pondered what came next for them. Simon guessed Juarez was worried about his family. He had no idea what Hegelpitic was thinking.

When light left the desert, Juarez spoke.

"I suppose I should explain why I tried to kill you."

"Yeah. I've been wondering."

"Yeah. I don't plan on trying again."

"That's appreciated. I wish I'd found a better way. To stop you, I mean."

"Eh, you were defending yourself. I've been there. Now that he's dead, there's still the successor to worry about. The guy ordering those planes." He looked back to the tombstone. Then he spoke.

"A few years ago, I don't know how many, they tortured me bad. They always did, but this one time, for whatever reason, I finally realized that it'd become pointless. Anything they were gonna learn from me, they already learned. They just wanted to keep their good jobs that helped their rankings, so they made up shit to do. The moment it all clicked for me, I lost control. I killed fourteen people. I realized how easy escape would have been. I was about to, until I remembered I had family. The men and women I killed had family. I had to stop myself, for their sake."

"David came in the next day. Nothing seemed urgent to him. He didn't seem to fear for his life near me either. He shook my hand. That always stood out to me. Then he surprised me; said they would stop all the torture, even give me visitation. His only condition, beyond my continued captivity, was that I owe him a favor. I wouldn't know what it was until he told me, but if I didn't agree to it, my family would die. Seemed an easy choice."

"My outburst haunted me, but life got better. I saw my brother, sister, parents, uncle. I got to practice my Spanish again. I'm not fluent but... Oh also they gave me these ropes of composite metal to learn knots with, to give my hands and my brain something to do. My days got just a little nicer, you know? A few weeks ago, David came to collect."

"'Kill the First-Citizen. Kill Simon, if given the chance. If the opportunity passes you by, your family dies. Neither of them has the power or ability to prevent this, whatever they may try to convince you. I will know everyones location at the critical moment, so don't fuck up.'"

"When you met me in my cell, and said your name, I almost killed you right then. It seemed to be what the Second Citizen wanted. But then, I thought back to how he phrased the command. "Kill the First-Citizen. Kill Simon, if given the chance." I figured you were the less important target, or that it had to be both of you at once. If I killed you then, I couldn't imagine how the First-Citizen would ever be willing to come close to me, and I'd have failed. David visited a third time to tell me I did well, and to wait. So I went back to my life until the two of you teleported straight into my cell. The First-Citizen was strong, and fast, faster than me. But he was no stronger than I was as a child. I only needed to get one good grip on him and squeeze."

"I broke his limbs for good measure, and was about to

kill both of you, but then Hegelpitic, my cellmate who I've seen as many times as I've met David, came out into the hallway that I'd been strangling him in. He proposed that we leave the facility. In a split second decision, I agreed. I had liked you and didn't want to hurt you. I figured, perhaps the Second Citizen was bluffing. With your teleportation, maybe you really could save my family from him, and then I wouldn't have to kill you. Or maybe the First-Citizen, who still outranked David, could dethrone him before he enacted his terrible punishment. I broke through the facility, whose power had somehow gone out, and escaped with the two of you in my arms."

"When the moment came, I felt this damn indifference from the First-Citizen. It wasn't even malice per-se. He just didn't worry about human life in a natural way. David told me the First-Citizen came to power after running a large technology company. He was a crowd pleasing man who at heart, only ever cared about big numbers, and couldn't be bothered to worry about small ones. My family was a small number to him."

"After I killed him, I turned to you, knowing you were still human, hoping you could recognize the monsters around you for what they were. You let me down for the opposite reason. You respected life too much to try and end it. And you fear any sudden change. So I had no choice but to kill you too, even though I'm the same way. I figure the Second Citizen has no reason to hurt them yet, but I just don't know anymore."

Simon looked down into the sand and contemplated the Second Citizen. He realized that his own plan had been entirely planned by David, everything set up for there to be only one way to become free. The fact that he figured out the one solution on his own didn't make the plan his.

"I'm going to meet with him."

"The Second Citizen?"

"Yeah. We're due for a candid conversation."

Juarez nodded, his dirt-covered face still possessing a softness to it, looking more delicate than its surroundings when Simon knew the exact opposite was true.

"Please, get my family their freedom. You must promise me."

"I promise."

Juarez stood, and stared into the sun for a few moments, as though it were the moon. "There's nothing for me here. I'm going to find them. I know where they're usually housed, it's not far. Get what you need to get done within seventy two hours, and I'll be kindly shown to them when I arrive." He didn't wait for a reply, but turned westward and ran. Dust erupted behind him as he sprinted away with a speed that almost rivaled the late First-Citizen.

Simon spent the rest of the day in utterance, as the desert plunged into quiet darkness.

CHAPTER 33:

Fly. Fuse. Bright. Disarm. Search. General.

These were the only words Simon spoke for two days. It was on the third day after the First-Citizen's death that he returned to the facility. He first said his goodbyes to Hegelpitic. The humanoid civilization chose to remain at that spot in the desert, where Juarez had spent a few hours digging a comfortably sized cave under the ground before he left, which would hopefully provide some security. The cave looked more like a hut than something natural. *Fuse* was used to fuse particles of sand along the cave walls and ceiling to make the hideaway strong enough not to collapse. The effort in making the space look like a home the Last Citizen might enjoy waking up in was a welcome distraction from the confusion of everything else.

Juarez had put him on a deadline, so he couldn't be distracted for long. He teleported to the office of the First-Citizen. The act of instantly crossing many hundreds of miles, and being in two identical bodies in different places for a millionth of a second, was starting to feel natural. The office was pristine, showing no hints of the skirmish that had occurred there three days ago.

"Disarm" he uttered, briskly willing any weapons that he could sense and recognize around him to short circuit. He could have uttered "stop", but half the point was for sensors to alert David. "Fly," he said next. He levitated some ten feet into the air, just as the First-Citizen had done many times. He felt powerful doing this. The hour spent learning flight was well worth it. He would never feel small in this facility again.

He turned around. The dark half of the office remained unlit and beyond his vision. He'd always wondered what he would find there.

"Bright." He uttered. For the first time since Simon was first brought into this room, light penetrated every corner. With the shadows lifted it became evident that the office went nearly twice as deep as he he'd guessed, with there being an additional fifty feet behind the darkness. Simon wondered if to the First-Citizen that shadow had been considered normal lighting.

This lit space held couches, an old television, a bookshelf, a dining room table, a miniature kitchen, and a bed that looked a century old. And a black cat who meowed grumpily. It was a pre-midcentury home.

Simon floated towards this living space. The paintings from the bright side of the office continued to this side, but they ceased being of great generals and leaders. These were all of women, politely dressed, some frowning, some smiling. They were all beautiful. The paintings weren't as refined as the ones of the generals on the other side of the room, although they remained impressive in their detail.

The furthest of the paintings was of Louisa, in her prisoner's uniform, standing in a garden smiling. Simon didn't understand. His feet touched the floor in front of the black cat curled up near the TV. The cat noticed his presence, but didn't bother getting up. Simon noted that the TV, which at first had seemed dead, was actually playing. The image was highly subdued, the audio an echo of a whisper. Nobody but the First-Citizen would be able to discern whatever was being played.

"Hello, Simon." The voice of the Second Citizen came from all sides. "Thanks for killing him."

"I didn't. Is this where he lived?"

"Sometimes. This was his safe space from the bright and loud world that he had the pleasure of controlling. It's meant to resemble an early twenty-first century American home. The TV likely has the Simpsons on."

"Search" Simon whispered softly.

"I heard that."

"Well, you can tell me where you are, and make this all easier." Simon sat on the couch next to the cat and began petting it.

"Her name is George, if you're curious. And I see no reason to oblige you."

Simon had spent half the previous day developing and testing "search". He had expected to locate the Second Citizen within seconds, assuming he was in the facility.

"You aren't here, are you," Simon stated.

"I'm not. Let's not talk about me. The future is far more important."

"I agree. So tell me where you are."

"I rather prefer this arrangement."

"I don't think the voice of God suits you."

Simon heard the Second Citizen laugh for the first time. The sound was grating and out of practice.

"Perhaps you're right. Once we know where we stand on certain matters, we can meet face to face."

Simon felt his ethereal creatures reaching beyond the facility now. Hundreds of fleeting images rapidly sifted through a young new corner of his mind as his ghostlike searchers extended into the surrounding lots roads and hills, making their way towards the nearby city.

"Where is my father?" Some of Simon's young new shades were looking for him also, and not succeeding.

"He's safe. His recovery has been slow, so we brought him to place more suited to his needs. Tell me, Simon, what do you plan to do next? Assuming you remain free this time. What world-shaking power do you hope to nurture over the next decade? How will you use it? Or will you satisfy yourself with trinkets and sit on your ass in a forest for a century?"

"I'm not sure yet. I haven't thought about it recently."

"Think now. Nobody's stopping you."

Simon did. The couch and the cat were comfortable.

George moved in to snuggle next to his thigh.

"There's no shortage of problems in the world. I guess I'll pick one, and find a way to solve it. Like I did with hurricanes."

"Hurricanes, yes. That was genuinely excellent work on your part. You nearly enabled the recolonization of the Carolinas. But what about the next ability you spend a year, or several, developing? You could become a one-person global power in the coming decades. Are you really comfortable exercising that level of influence over all of us?"

"What are you saying?"

"I'm asking you to leave the Citizenship alone. As powerful as you are, and can become, you are still, fundamentally, only one human, and an uneducated one at that. You aren't realistically capable of running a complex society. Leave the complexities to me. In exchange, I will facilitate a democratic process by which the people can decide what global changes they would support, and which they would not. You bind yourself to adhere to the wishes of the masses. If you wish to spend a decade refreezing the northern icecaps, and they want you to spend that time enhancing crops, you enhance crops. But you're free to opt-out. You have the option of doing absolutely nothing, and living that private life you crave."

Simon stared at George while he thought. If the cat had insight to offer, she didn't bother sharing.

"My father. My friends. Juarez. Hegelpitic. You know what I want for each of them."

"If you kill the Last Citizen, they shall all be taken care of."

"I'm not going to kill her." Simon said. He noticed George had fallen into a deep sleep and had stopped purring.

"Simon, I am begging you, please don't...what am I saying? Begging the First-Citizen was equally pointless. He never listened."

"I'm not like him."

"Not yet. The only ingredients a man needs to turn into

the First-Citizen are talent, unaccountability, and time. You have the first, the third is inevitable, but the second is your choice. Use your utterance to bind yourself to the wishes of the people. If I had my way I'd leave the masses out of this, but I know you aren't ready to retire, so this is the best future for you. Don't rise above reproach like he did. Or one day, not so far from now, you'll find yourself painting the women you fantasized living a life with, but couldn't because you knew with computational certainty that their fleeting lives would be less happy if they were spent with you. And you'll name a cat after your oldest friend who wishes to never think of you again."

"And I'll all pretend to still be human by watching ancient television, I suppose."

The First-Citizen laughed again. He was clearly in some sort of mood."My predecessor had a messy relationship with his humanity. He hid it well."

Without warning, Simon felt himself beginning to lose consciousness. His first thought was for the cat. Anything strong enough to knock him out was probably enough to kill the poor creature.

"Away" he managed to say, wrapping George around his arms. He left and transported to that same spot in the forest he had went to when he first escaped, still the easiest place for him to teleport to. He took a minute to recover his breath and checked that George was alive. Her vitals were slow, but steady. He was worried that drones or dogs might still be placed on patrol in this area and ordered to kill on sight, and teleported the two of them to Florin's eye lens over the hill. The disquieting monument was unchanged from his last visit.

"Search" he uttered a second time on a hunch. It took less than a minute to locate his target. He teleported, with the cat, into an unassuming six-story building near the edge of Oakland's urban nexus.

"You found me. Good job." David said. His searchers informed Simon that this was the fourth floor. The First-

Citizen was sitting in front of Simon behind a small improvised desk in a cubicle. It reminded him of the first office he'd worked in as an overseer when he was twenty. There were no guards in sight.

"Like my new workstation?" The First-Citizen asked.

"Why did you try to poison me? We were negotiating."

"Nobody has been using this floor for the past month, if you can believe it. Complete waste of space. This building is near several clubs and amenities that aren't yet available in the facility, so I think I'll run the country from here, at least for now. There's an unused cubical next to mine that you can claim."

"Just answer my question."

"I keep telling you that I'd always wished I'd been able to kill you. You never listen. Since I've failed to end your life, I propose that the agreement we were discussing prior is the next best option."

"Your ethics astound me."

"Ha. I'm sure they do. This building doesn't allow animals, by the way." The First-Citizen gestured towards George.

"I don't see why I shouldn't just kill you," Simon said.

"You could. But my replacement would be less qualified."

"You must be joking."

"Never. What I'm proposing is the only correct way forward. We both know it."

Simon smiled. His original idea for the day could still proceed.

"Sir, take my hand." He told the First-Citizen.

"Why would I do that?"

"It's the least you can do, after trying to kill me."

He complied.

"General" Simon uttered, and all three individuals left the cubicle before anyone could muffle, blackmail, or poison him.

Four teleportations in a single day were exhausting,

especially when multiple bodies had to be coordinated. However, he was almost done. They appeared in the book-filled study of a house Simon had never thought he would see in person. The First-Citizen, who wasn't prepared for the trip, fell hip-first onto the hardwood floor with a worrying thump.

"A warning would have been fucking appreciated. If I didn't know better I'd say you were feeling vengeful." The First-Citizen said.

He sounds fine.

A second later, he realized where he was. "For what fucking reason did you bring us here? You realize that we're being observed by twenty six thousand overseers. This is gonna be hell to erase."

"Then don't erase it. David, new First-Citizen, we're here to offer the inhabitant of this house your current job. I can think of nobody more qualified."

"He won't work with you. And for God's sake, put down the cat."

"I want to hear him say it."

"David? What is this? Who are you?" A sixty-seeming man who was at least eighty walked into the study, his right hand grasping a pre-midcentury vodka, his left holding a biography. He looked exactly as Simon remembered. Seeing the general George Lackley in the flesh caught both visitors off-guard.

"Please tell me the silverhair isn't who I think. You told me you killed her and the others after Juarez. I saw the giant fall from the atmosphere with my own eyes."

"George. It's been a while." David said.

The general stared at Simon and held his gaze.

"I'm gladdened to see you're as charming as when last we spoke."

The general kept staring. Simon formulated.

"Hello. My name's Simon. I'm a child of the bomb. I'm here to make an offer. I don't know if you heard us just now, but I hope you'll inherit the role of First-Citizen. Your predecessor..."

"He knows all about him." David interjected. "And this is a terrible proposition. He's a compromised man. Saving the world broke him, why not leave him be?"

The general continued to stare appraisingly at Simon. He didn't seem as broken as he had on video.

"General, sir..." Simon began, realizing he didn't know how he was meant to address him. "I've met the other surviving children. They're not th..."

"So there are others?" The general asked.

"Yes. Juarez and Hegelpitic. They're both harmless and just want..."

"I know who they are and what they want. They aren't harmless." He turned to David. "You said you killed them."

"I lied. The only direct lie I've ever told you, old friend."

The general said nothing. His face creased severely. Reading him was more difficult for Simon without overseer data, but he appeared to be thinking quickly.

"Fine. I'll accept the offer. But there are going to be conditions." The general found a desk table on which to place the two objects he held.

"Name them." Simon said. David gave him a priceless look that couldn't have expressed his distaste for the conversation being had any more clearly.

"You do nothing. Juarez does nothing. Hegelpitic does nothing. You are to live quiet, inactive lives as the tumors that you are. There's no place in the world for things like you."

Simon would have argued, but the general seemed to have lost interest in allowing him to speak.

"The country will be ruled by me, with no named successor. If I should cease living, a democratically held election will be used to determine a new leader. I shall do everything I can to prepare the country for such an election over the next decade."

"Why decade? Why not hold an election next year?" Simon asked. *I've studied you. You don't crave power. Unless I'm wrong. Please have a good reason.*

"An election immediately after a long-running autocracy of

this nature will just lead to another autocrat. People will instinctively vote into office whoever best fills the void recently left by their last despot, and people who can fill that void well usually turn out equally horrid. I'll need about a decade to re-enlighten this country. I'll teach it to once again hate men with too much power."

The general stared again at Simon. Simon had only ever observed him while alone. He was a completely different person with an audience.

"Actually...I don't entirely despise that idea." David remarked. "George, I found a delightful cubicle in Oakland thats perfect for running a country from."

"No. I'll make my own arrangements."

"Well suit yourself, asshole. I hope those arrangements aren't too royal. God knows I don't need to work under another heavy spender."

"You won't. I intend to choose one of my old secretaries to fill your role."

"Sir..." Simon said. "The deal is you inherit the First-Citizen's position. Not his unchecked power. Allowing you to demote someone you dislike seems counter to the goal we both share of ending despotism. You two hold each other to account."

The general's expression, which had just relearned neutrality, became a scowl. Simon felt he was being sized up as a soldier who had questioned a direct order.

"I don't know who you think you are, but I'm not putting up with this man, especially at your suggestion. The First-Citizen was a good friend once. David let him decay into a monster. You're probably no better."

"I don't care. David's unpleasant, and as I recently told him, his ethics astound me, but civically and logistically he knows this country better than anyone, and he helped save the world from a terrible fate just like you did. I am requiring that you work with him, if you want the job."

The general took a step towards Simon. "Or I could just get you you out of my way and choose someone I actually trust to fix this country."

"Sir."

"My title is General."

"My apologies, General. I don't think you appreciate how one-sided a fight between you and I would be."

The general 's face briefly reddened. Simon hoped this man was really the best future. His overseer instinct said he was fundamentally good, despite his obvious desire to have Simon either court martialled or killed. Perhaps it was promising that he felt that way.

The general then relaxed his posture in an impressive display of self control, and resumed his earlier neutrality.

"I'm sure David will mention you while we talk details. I'm appreciative of many things, Simon, including this proposal. Now that it's submitted, from my vantage it seems you have nothing else to offer. My old colleague is welcome to stay in my guest wing." The general turned to David and seemed unwilling to make any further contact with Simon, who took no issue. More important worries now occupied him.

"General, excuse me for just a moment," David said and walked over. The general left the room, uninterested in eavesdropping. David unraveled a sheet of paper.

"Your dad's here. Along with the others. I give you my word, for what little it's worth to you, that you won't be touched. I'm sorry for what they went through. I don't know if you can fix them. My advice: perhaps it's best you don't try too hard. The human mind can't really be untangled. Trust me, we've tried. At best, it grows around the trauma." The First-Citizen offered a hand. Simon shook it.

"You should leave before I tell the general you're sparing Maria. You won't want to be near him for that."

"Understood."

"So when are you gonna let go of the fucking cat?"

Simon chuckled despite himself. "Goodbye." David smiled, properly. Then he left. "Father" Simon uttered a few times. Months spent tracking hurricanes made him excellent at zoning in on the atmospheric coordinates David had written out.

He emerged in a bowling alley, only eight feet above the ground, and fell gracefully. His father looked up from the roll he was about to make. Beckett, Charlie, and Penelope stood around him. They all looked alive, but moved too slowly, like their blood was half frozen. There were caretakers on standby, and Simon quickly uttered "disarm" in case he was lied to again. Searchers sought out tools worth disarming and reported no clear threats. He ran to his father. To everyone. He missed his old life, and the people in it. They deserved better.

"Hello everyone..."

"I'm sorry. I didn't want this. Not any of it." Nobody responded. He didn't know what to say.

I've never tried healing others before. I don't know how. I don't even know how to learn.

He saw they were about to start a new game, but seemed to be waiting for something.

They're waiting for me.

The thought surprised him. He didn't think they would still value him, even as a mindless instinct. He wiped his eyes and found a rack from which he grabbed a ball of the appropriate size. Given his strength, he could have easily gone for the largest one, but that seemed unfair. He returned to the group with the ball he'd have chosen if he were human.

"Let's bowl."

EPILOGUE

She awoke slowly and felt it fall through her fingers. It was not contained. She would have worried, but now that it was here, it would be easy to collect again. A few minutes or days was nothing next to three and a half billion years. She hoped she hadn't decimated wherever she was. She wondered about her brother, and the strong man with the hallucinated family.

She was wearing clothing. It felt old. She felt old. And frail. She briefly considered replacing herself with the version of her who had begun the search. The act of killing the current body would be painful, and potentially inconvenient, so she discarded the idea.

She opened her eyes. She felt the desert before she could see it. Invoking the cargo had, as she feared, decimated nearly everything. Sand had fused into the glassy pitch-black rock from which those horrid crystals would sprout. Every plant in a three mile radius was almost certainly dead, along with most of the animals, the lucky ones at least.

She wasn't alone. A stone hut had been assembled around her, blocking her eyes but having no effect on her view. She felt around its recent history being built for her, by another child of the bomb, less than a day ago, next to a cave. She wondered why they were in this particular place. She knew people who had lived a couple miles east of here, but they died from pox nearly five hundred years ago.

While she tried getting up, a huge man entered the room. He froze when he saw her. She was surprised also, a rare thing. Nobody should have survived, so she hadn't bothered to look.

"What did you do?" he said in a deep, attractive voice. She instantly found herself liking what she saw, but wishing that he wasn't quite so tall. The four arms were pleasantly proportioned and held sexual promise.

"Where's David? I found something for him." She said. She wasn't sure at first if she was speaking in the local language or some dead one like Aramaic.

"He's indisposed. What did you do to the land?" The man's muscles were distracting. She found she quite liked how his third eye penetrated her with its gaze.

"The first life on earth. He asked me to fetch it for him. I had to reach quite far for it, so I was inevitably more destructive than usual..." She checked her right hand. It was still wet with the water within which Earth's last universal common ancestor was born. Someone had taken her petri dish.

"You were drugged, probably while trying to complete your task. We undrugged you a few days ago. It was potent, to take you this long to recover."

"Huh. I wonder why David did that." She decided she did know. She'd decided to kill him, after he killed Florin. The death of her brother seemed like days ago.

"I can imagine why, seeing what you just did to the surrounding desert, Last Citizen."

She had listened to many tens of thousands of people speak, throughout many ages, and was certain that English was not this man's first language. And yet, she couldn't place his accent.

"It's not so bad, silly. I didn't kill any humans. It's just, well, I can't copy something over from the past without going there first, and, well...replicating anything across time takes a lot of power. It's not my fault this universe bruises so easily."

"You are making little sense."

"I can explain later. We should fuck."

The tall muscular child of the bomb blushed.

"You've just woken up from a coma, and I'm the first person you've seen. I'm honored, but you should be less quick to action."

"No, I'm very selective in my partners. And there's no point in waiting. Undress."

The man combed his hair uncertainly with his four hands. She liked watching the arms all move together. His olympian body was surprisingly graceful.

"There's someone who will want to speak with you when he returns." he said, ignoring her command.

"Fine. What's your name?"

"Hegelpitic."

"Strange name. Doesn't come from any human culture. I'd know."

"No. It comes from mine. Our people don't live in this world."

The first man she had met from a culture she could not glimpse. The mystery of it enthralled her.

"Tell me, have your people committed any genocides? I've always wanted to undo a genocide."

"No, um, we've avoided that so far. I will go see if Simon is back. I should be the first face he sees, given what you've done here. He shouldn't be long."

Hegelpitic exited the hut, leaving her to experiment with standing. She found she could do it, with difficulty. Hegelpitic would have to apply most of the effort if they did end up having sex. Her mind drifted, and she made a list of her twenty favorite genocides.

Hegelpitic returned sometime later with a new man, a properly humanoid one. She supposed he was also attractive, although his mind did not possess the same intricacy that Hegelpitics did. There was potential in him, though. A budding capacity for limitless growth. She looked a little further into his history and saw that he'd lost someone. She found the woman, and started moving around through her history to find the important bits.

"Why did you turn the desert into a wasteland?" He shouted at her. Shouting didn't suit him.

"I wouldn't have done it if I didn't need to. I'm Maria, by the way. Or, I think that's what I'm called. I'm always bad with names. Anyways, who's Louisa?"

"How do you know that name?" Simon seemed on edge.

"She died. I'm seeing it now. Do you want her back?"

"What do you mean?"

"She's in the past. Easy enough to grab. If she were in the future, you'd be out of luck. She's recent past too, within a million years of us. Child's play."

"You can bring back the dead? That's your power?"

"I can bring back anything. Here, I'll just do it." She cast her tendrils across time, found a woman walking down a hallway, minutes from her rather amusing if grotesque death, carved out what was to be retrieved, and copy-pasted in front of the humanoid. She sensed that doing so may have damaged the physics of gravity within a several hundred yard radius. Did Simon use yards? Everything suddenly felt a third lighter. She hoped it wouldn't spread too quickly.

The woman, Louisa, appeared surprised to be in a hut. Her surprise was bemusing. Most of human history was endured in huts. How could a hut confuse someone? She had to remind herself that most people in the current timeline lived in integrated grids, so huts to them would indeed seem an oddity.

The short man, Simon, seemed even more unsettled.

"Louisa? Are you really her? Tell me you're real." Tears began gracefully flowing down his face. He was an attractive cryer.

"Simon? What are you doing here? Where is this? I'm meeting the First-Citizen."

"The First-Citizen? He killed you."

"No. No, that's not right. He loves me. He loves all of us. Where am I?"

Simon   hugged   her   desperately.   Hegelpitic,

unfortunately, did not mirror the sensual act with her. She would need to work harder to win that one over. Not that she minded.

"Louisa, I'll make you better. Your love of the First-Citizen is a sickness that I never should have infected you with. I promise I'll fix everything."

"No! We must all love the First-Citizen. I was on my way to apologize to him for your behavior recently. You've not been showing him the respect he deserves."

"I'm just glad you're alive."

"The First-Citizen is dead," Hegelpitic said bluntly.

This was news to her. She wondered if she should bring him back too. Not wishing to interrupt the reunion she created, she decided to hold back on his revival, for the moment.

Louisa collapsed onto the sandy floor. Her crying was less attractive. She needed to learn how to control her tears better, like Simon had. She was probably a better yeller.

"I shouldn't live. Not if the First-Citizen doesn't. I need to join him."

"No! Louisa, be reasonable. The First-Citizen is dead. But you can still live a wonderful life. I'll make you apathetic towards him."

"No. I don't want you to."

She decided to then interject.

"I can bring him back if you miss him. He was nice to me, the one time I met him. Just give me a sec…"

"Stop! Please, Maria. We killed him for good reasons. You cannot bring him back." Hegelpitic spoke quickly and decisively. Because it was he who spoke, she obeyed.

"Alright. A boulder rolled down a mountain a few miles east about a decade ago. I can feel its weight. I could put it on Louisa if she wants a quick death. I was considering killing myself with it a few minutes ago."

"I don't deserve a quick death," Louisa said.

"No! Not that either. Just let me fix Louisa my way."

"I can't let you do that if it isn't what she wants." The only solid backbone to the wispily capricious currents of her morality had always been consent. It had always been her opinion that anyone who fully respected consent would inevitably be a reasonably good person. And nobody should be forced to die, or to alter themselves, because of an irrefusable command issued by another, even if the alteration was perceived as good. She had a clever idea to circumvent this.

"What if I did return him? Not the one you've met. A younger one."

"How young?" Simon asked.

"Choose. Maybe you'll want to skip the early years, though. Children are annoying."

"You can return the First-Citizen to us? From death?" Louisa asked, thankfully regaining her composure. She turned out to be nearly as beautiful as Hegelpitic once the teary face hardened.

"Sure.... But I've just decided I dislike him in his later years. Have him as a child."

"But...he'll still be the First-Citizen?"

"Not by title, I suppose. But it will be precisely him as he was in his youth. You and your partner can enjoy raising him together. What age?"

"This is ridiculous," Simon said. He sounded angry. She spent another moment snooping around the four-dimensional contours of his life story. She understood his anger. His superiors had done much to him that he hadn't consented to.

"No, it isn't. You're powerful, but you're still a child. Such an entity can't be held unaccountable. That's why I was put down. I should have seen it coming, but I suppose the future has always been my greatest limitation. All the same, I can't let you force yourself on someone. This is my help. Raise a child who you've already programmed her to love. Quite the cute little solution."

"But how can I love him? He killed her. He's a monster. If

you...well, I don't know. I just don't know. You shouldn't do it."

"You're wrong. Well, not technically. The First-Citizen did kill her. But the "he" who I can give to you will be a child, who has killed nothing beyond maybe a few spiders and a moth. A child you can mold. You can help him reach the moral potential he never did in his past life."

Simon and Louisa looked at each other. They seemed to be speaking invisibly, a sort of couple-telepathy she had observed in perhaps a dozen other pairings throughout history. It was always an awkward connection to bear witness to. Louisa placed her hand on Simon's heart. Simon returned the gesture. The act clearly held some special significance to them, one she felt too lazy to decipher then.

"Can we talk about this? Alone?" Simon asked. She realized gleefully that it would give her more time with Hegelpitic.

"Sure." She walked out of the hut into the bright desert afternoon, relishing the pain of the photons pelting her eyes. Hegelpitic joined her.

The ground, which until minutes ago had been sand, was now a smooth, simmering crystalline surface extending nearly as far as she could see in every direction, refracting light into a series of soft emeralds. The color scheme would grow more deranged over the coming days. It was in no way a natural landscape, but to her, it was familiar, like staring at pre-ripened fruit. So long as the Citizenship came in and dealt with the crystals before they got too large, there was no real harm done.

"There is a place similar to this in my world," Hegelpitic said. "Gardeners tend it. Creatures of rock, diamond and amethyst grow, fracture, and blossom within our volcanic gardens. Some say these creatures are intelligent. They are among our oldest landmarks. I like to visit them whenever I have a free day to spend among my people. Those don't come by often enough."

She decided then that she would come to properly fall in

love with this man if she spent too much time with him.

"Hegelpitic, give me a name from among those of your people."

He laughed. "It's not my place to give you a name. That duty should have fallen on your creator."

"Yes, but she's dead, and I'm not reviving her. I want one of your names. A name that nobody else in the world could ever think to give me."

"Huh. You're an unusual person."

"Thanks. Now name me."

Hegelpitic considered for a moment while he enjoyed the crystalline view. She wondered if he would think they were beautiful in a day.

"Vlajishica"

"Hmm. I like it. What does it mean?"

"Nothing. Our names aren't allowed to have meanings. Meaning constrains us, and binds us by title to destinies we may not want for ourselves."

"That makes you an unusual culture."

"Perhaps. We are what we are. Your life is what will give the name meaning."

She sighed, and leaned against him, placing her head in the comfortable slot between his upper and lower right shoulder, mostly out of frailty, partially out of lust. His two right arms enveloped her comfortingly. Her legs began to feel weak.

The couple emerged from the stone hut.

"We've decided," Louisa said. "We want the First-Citizen brought back to us. As a one year old."

"Are you sure?" She asked. The decision seemed poor. Babies were a nuisance, and tended to die in winter.

"Yes. We're sure. Bring him back."

She shrugged, relishing the movement of her awakening shoulders, then traced back through the First-Citizen's life to the appropriate age.

The young First-Citizen fortunately was dressed and

diapered during his 525,601st minute. The baby appeared in Louisa's arms. She almost dropped it, then hugged it tightly in overcompensation until parental instinct showed her the right balance of force. Consequences were rarely predictable, and this action caused a slight alteration in the behavior of light in their vicinity, which made the sun appear a dark shade of purple, causing the refracting emeralds to also darken. The new desert oasis became drenched in a sickly royal hue.

"He's absolutely beautiful. Simon?" Louisa either hadn't noticed the ambient light change, or didn't care.

"Yeah, he's beautiful."

She looked at Simon again and felt more closely around his recent past. Yes, he really did have potential. He was still stuck in three dimensions, but he was using them well. Given enough centuries, he could be more powerful than she was. That could be interesting to allow.

Simon caught her looking and misinterpreted. "I think I can be happy here. This place you've created has a certain beauty to it. Combined with what I can do, I can make it a home."

"If you're staying, just make sure to keep the growths in check. My symptomatic creations tend to expand like tumors if left unchecked."

Her comment gave Simon pause, but he nodded.

"Thank you, whoever you are," Louisa said, glancing up from the baby.

"Yeah, sure." She turned to Hegelpitic.

"Now take me somewhere less hot. I need somewhere I can think. And exercise." She tugged his bottom left arm and he followed her out into the desert.

"Wait, Maria."

"Call me Vlajishica."

"If you're leaving, I won't stop you. But I can take you wherever you want to go, probably a lot faster."

"Don't worry about it. You have your methods, I have mine. And mine are more fun."

"I'll try and keep her out of trouble," Hegelpitic said. "I suppose I don't have anywhere to go either, I might as well keep her safe."

"Alright. I'll be seeing you." Simon said. He and Hegelpitic shook.

She watched the couple enter the hut with their new child, then turned to her new partner. It was adorable how he thought she was the one who would need protection.

"I've always wanted to ride a horse. You?" She asked him.

"I've ridden a horse of sorts in my world. But never an earth horse. The idea intrigues."

She found an instance of the animal from eighteenth century Europe that she'd had her eye on for a while, and reintroduced it to the universe, saddle and all. Doing so created a field of lightning discharges that shook the sky miles in every direction. "I'm weak, so I'm riding with you." She told Hegelpitic while he attempted to calm the terrified creature that had just appeared in front of him.

"I had assumed. Now, where are we riding?"

"Not sure. Somewhere North. North is cooler. And Canada has lots of large empty spaces."

"North also holds enemies." Hegelpitic lifted her onto the horse, then mounted behind her, his muscular upper arms holding her to him in a protective gesture while his lower ones took the reins. She didn't bother replying to his remark. As they rode together, her mind drifted back to genocides. She wondered if all those men and women who died in them would want to be brought back. It would be important first to find a vast enough region to decimate. She wondered if the interior of Australia still had human inhabitants while she rode past the borders of her slowly growing crystalline creation and into the sandy desert yet unreached.

Made in the USA
Columbia, SC
19 October 2024